Losing Faith

Daniel Blythe was born in Maidstone in 1969, read modern languages at St John's College, Oxford, and now teaches adult learners. He has contributed two sci-fi novels to a bestselling series, has had stories published in magazines and anthologies and has been a prize-winner at the Kent Literature Festival. His acclaimed novel *The Cut* is available in Penguin. Daniel Blythe lives in South Yorkshire.

Losing Faith **Daniel Blythe**

HAMISH HAMILTON · LONDON

HAMISH HAMILTON LTD

Published by the Penguin Group
Penguin Books Ltd, 27 Wrights Lane, London w8 5tz, England
Penguin Putnam Inc., 375 Hudson Street, New York, New York 10014, USA
Penguin Books Australia Ltd, Ringwood, Victoria, Australia
Penguin Books Canada Ltd, 10 Alcorn Avenue, Toronto, Ontario, Canada m4v 3b2
Penguin Books (NZ) Ltd, Private Bag 102902, NSMC, Auckland, New Zealand

Penguin Books Ltd, Registered Offices: Harmondsworth, Middlesex, England

First published 1999
10 9 8 7 6 5 4 3 2 1

Set in 11.5/14 pt Monotype Bembo
Typeset by Rowland Phototypesetting Ltd, Bury St Edmunds
Printed in Great Britain by Clays Ltd, St Ives plc

A CIP catalogue record for this book is available from the British Library

ISBN 0-241-14032-3

Part One Gaining

01 From Dust

We are burying her today. Old-fashioned, but it's what she wanted.

Apparently, it's all right now. The necessary has been done. History has the bits it needs, three dimensions packed into two, reality compacted into prints and swabs and slides and files. There is a report, and there is a verdict. Miss Adventure. Could be her nickname.

We can have her back. We can send her off.

We can finally lose Faith.

Does this mean they are happy with all the answers?

'Come on,' says Tanya. She is in black, but with hands gloved in ghost-white. A ravishing puppeteer. She slings a plate on the table, under my nose, under my mouth, under my brain.

The orange juice sits there. It's innocuous and I might even venture to greet it in a moment. But the breakfast sizzles and giggles to itself. A plate of traps. The bacon is pungent, alive. It crackles in my brain and fills my nostrils and mouth with hot meatiness. The egg yolk shines, a malevolent yellow eye watching me from the plate. Tanya's family call fried eggs *Spiegeleier*. Mirror eggs. I lean over it, carefully. I can see a warped face in the yellow surface.

Tanya sighs, folds her arms. 'It is not an art exhibit,' she points out. 'You are allowed to eat it.'

I dare to look at the mushrooms for the first time. I can only picture little grey slugs swimming in their own juices. I don't think I'm going to be able to do this.

'It can't be true,' I tell Tanya, my voice bleak and cracked. I look up at her, hoping she'll tell me that it's all right, I don't have to. 'About cooked breakfasts.'

She makes a face and lifts her eyebrows. Her face says: do you really expect to talk your way out of this?

'Eat,' she says, and puts her glasses on before crossing her black-stockinged legs and disappearing behind *The Times*. What a strange idea. Tanya is never behind the times.

I'm sure it is a very good English breakfast, especially for one made by someone who's not even English. She has heard somewhere that a deadly fry-up is helpful for hangovers. She probably read it in a multi-purpose fable-book. They tell of the exotic face masks made of egg-white spiced with honey, the lemon which highlights hair and shrivels spots, the wet cotton wool that sweeps up fragments of glass.

I skewer the egg with a knife and the yolk cascades out. It reminds me too much of a running sore.

I bite my lip and look up at the blank face of the newspaper, where Tanya's sharp nails are gripping a report on BSE and an airbrushed picture of Fergie. Unconnected – I expect.

'I'll . . . just have a cup of tea,' I tell her, with a tremble in my voice. It doesn't do to go against Tanya. She can be strong-willed. It could be more than a little to do with her ancestors, with their long tradition of marching in places and taking things until challenged. This is, of course, a sore and disputable point. I only ever bring it up in extreme circumstances, like after watching unbearable penalty shoot-outs, or when she tries to sort the household rubbish into five separate bins. Even then, I regret it immediately.

'You know,' she says, standing at the worktop and pouring the tea, 'I thought this country had licence laws? Like, they kick you out at eleven-twenty to count the glasses?'

'And sweep up the beer-mat crumbs. Yeah, they do. But some places have lock-ins. As long as you can pretend that it's just a private party, you're sorted.'

Tanya sniggers, swivels around and glides over, softly depositing the cup in front of me. 'Private party,' she says thoughtfully. 'For some reason that makes me think of kinky underwear and oranges.' She sits down, grabs my plate and starts to make inroads into my cooked breakfast herself. 'And you were there until . . . two-fifteen,' she says, with that precision I used to love so much.

Two-fifteen, was it? If she says so. I shrug, smile, take a sip of my tea. It tastes watery and warm. She hasn't made it too strong. She knows what I'm like in this situation, having seen it before.

'Come on,' Tanya says. 'Drink up, I'll tell you a joke.'

I take a tentative sip. Not too bad. 'Do you have to?'

'What is the quickest way out of Wembley?'

'I don't care. Sorry, I mean I don't know.'

'The *Southgate!*' she says, and goes *clap-stomp* like a music-hall comedian.

'Oh, hilarious.'

We are going to a funeral. And Tanya is telling jokes. I must remember that next time someone says what a humourless lot they are.

I hardly speak to Tanya on the M25. Her driving is smooth, punctuated by moments of crispness. She drives, in fact, like a woman who's had a good breakfast. She called it *big-fry*. She thinks it's monumentally clever, that kind of pun at one remove, boxing in the linguistic dimness.

Me? My head's hammering and my mouth's ashy.

We come off at the Guildford junction, and immediately the relative quiet hits me now that the Vectra isn't having to work so hard. Soon we're past Guildford, and we turn off the A3 near Haslemere. The countryside flashes by, and the only sounds are the gentle hum of the car and the swish of Tanya's gloves on the wheel. I can't even watch the telegraph poles jerk past the car. They're catching my eyes and pulling them in the wrong direction.

'Christ,' I mutter, and just the one syllable fills my mouth with a greasy, salty emptiness. Strange. It's like the taste of that post-pub craving when you badly need crisps, only without any vestige of hunger.

'Coping?' says Tanya amusedly.

'All right.' The syllables reverberate through me. 'Head like a pile-driver. And a throat as dry as a nun's twat.'

Tanya sniggers, as the car turns into a winding lane overshadowed by a greenish canopy of chestnuts. 'Great expression. I must work it in next time we go in a garden party.'

'I hope this isn't going to be a bloody party,' I mutter. 'People treat them like parties, don't they? Sandwiches all over the place.'

Maybe Tanya can tell that I'm just gabbling harmless stuff to hide other concerns. But it's true – the idea of chewing on ham sandwiches after having seen a body dispatched to rest is just a bit . . . too odd. Reminds me of the whole bread-of-life thing, which, as a non-Catholic, I've always found quite disturbing.

I mustn't think about food. But we are driving through the twisting streets of a village and it all looks edible. Timbered houses with humbug-stripe beams and chocolate roofs. Strawberry post boxes. Apple-green gardens swimming in a lemon-curd sunlight.

'Hatch, match, dispatch,' says Tanya, crunching the words like crisps. 'What would we do without them? Nobody would ever see more than two friends at a time.'

I realize she's right. It was frightening how quickly the old crowd fell into the pattern. You come to us for a weekend, we go to you. First of all we sleep on the cushions on your lounge floor and then, when you move up in the world, we get a bed. We, meanwhile, feel guilty that we don't have a spare room and still have to offer you the airbed, so we delay inviting you back until we move house. And so on.

Somebody said – it may have been at Mike and Nicole's wedding – that the only times we'd all meet up now would be weddings, christenings and funerals. There have been a few of the first, none of the second. And this is the first experience of that final category.

As we pull up outside the church, the sun thrums on our car. I can feel pungent pits of sweat gathering under the arms of my suit.

Tanya slips the car into neutral, and I'm aware of two dark figures under the lych-gate turning to look at us.

I smile in their direction while saying, 'Hellfire. Charlie and Jan are here first.'

Tanya's eyes are unreadable behind her mirror-shades. '*Der Teufel scheisst immer auf den grösseren Haufen,*' she informs me.

'*Bitte?*'

'An old saying of my mother. I dunno what you say. Something like, "Shit happen when you party naked", I expect.'

Tanya's already getting out. I've just opened my mouth to tell her to wait, as I have to tune my brain to sociability mode, but it's too late. I sigh, check my sunglasses are straight, and step on to the scorched pavement, slamming the door behind me.

Rubbery heat grips me. The Vectra chirps as Tanya thumbs the central locking. Jesus, we're in a car commercial with the brightness whacked up. We step forward, silhouettes in the shining landscape.

As we advance I'm conscious of the mountainous shadow of the church, the cropped heads of Charles and Jan as they turn, turn. In. Slowest. Motion.

It's hard to meet Charles's gaze. I nod briefly to him, and watch him, curved and polarized, in Tanya's sunglasses instead.

I always believe in introducing people properly – I hate the slapdash introductions which many of my generation get away with. A scatter-gun barrage of monosyllables, often across a table and through wall-shaking music. So something takes over, transcends my wobbly legs and crunchy eyes. The auto-social circuits kick in.

'Tanya, I don't think you've met Charles Devereaux, Faith's cousin. Charles is a marketing manager . . . and his wife, Jan, who works in the university library . . . This is my . . . ah, this is Tanya Behler, who works in sales for EmTrak International.'

See? It's quite painless and easy.

Charlie is scraped, grey, all vertical lines. I wonder about the word 'statuesque' and its associations with well-formed bodies. Charlie, though, is statuesque – edges eroded, features coarsened as if by bird shit and rain. He must be only just thirty – two years older than Faith – but this whole thing has stripped him of life. His hair, black but greying, is carved in a death-row buzz cut. With his hospital pallor and undertaker's eyes, he's fading from the world. I'm not surprised, really. All he's had to do, being cousin, brother, father and friend to her all at once, must have dried him up.

'Good of you both to come,' he says quietly. I shake his hand. It sticks between my palms. My skin feels clammy enough, but his is worse, clogged with moist greasiness.

Tanya murmurs something appropriate, which I don't quite hear.

Meanwhile, Jan swivels on her heels, simpers under her tight black cap of hair, clutches her prissy leather bag. 'Haven't we got a warm day for it?' she says. Her voice is, as always, a cackle. 'I said it was going to be a warm day. Charlie didn't believe me. Did you, Charlie?'

'No,' he agrees, and I think his eyes are checking her over for signs of a trick question.

Everything Jan says is a way of affirming her space. She's a hellcat pissing out the borders of her territory. She doesn't need to say anything, really. She knows looking at me is enough. I can feel her, as if her presence is branding itself with harsh telepathy. An unholy union, Jan and the sun. The acid prickling in my throat grows more intense, a pan of bile cooking on gas.

'Shall we go in?' says Tanya. She must have sensed the tension, buzzing in this sunny churchyard like an electric fence.

Charles rubs his nose awkwardly. The sun seems to redouble its force, blasting from nearby graves, turning their white marble into giant reflectors, and for a moment I think he might turn into a grey smudge and disappear from the earth.

'I don't know,' he says. 'We're . . . meant to wait here and . . . have a talk with the, er, chap.'

'Vicar,' I offer hopefully, and I immediately regret it. Every time I open my mouth, it's as if I'm inviting the vomit up to meet the world. My only hope lies in keeping everything closed.

I'm suddenly aware that the ground is moving beneath my feet. There is a firm hand – Tanya's – on my arm. She's in control again.

'We are going to get you through this,' she says determinedly. 'I'm taking you inside. You can sit and ask God to be nice to your stomach.'

I'm not going to be able to do this. There are all kinds of people here, rows and rows of hats and glasses.

I can see the back of Mike's head. He's standing two rows in front of me, next to a couple of other people who knew Faith at college. I look around for Nicole, but I don't think she's here.

When Mike turns round to face me, I meet his eyes with a momentary complicity.

His beard, trimmed to a neat spade shape, is flecked with grey (*grey*! He's twenty-eight, all of four years younger than me) and he squints from dark, creased hollows as if he cannot focus properly.

Time has been treading roughly on all of us, it would seem. If you've had an energetic youth, Time holds you to a bizarre Faustian pact. Time never forgets a face, and sends the lads round when you think you've got away with it. You didn't pay, see. You didn't pay. We're going to give you wrinkles. And rheumatism, and hernias. It might hurt. Shut the door.

Then, the hold is broken. Mike's gaze is loosened, free to fly all around the pews, his gaze diving and fluttering like a bird trapped in the vault of the church.

I suddenly realize what I have read in his face. It's panic. He wants to escape, but he can't.

I close my eyes. From the back of the church, the organ begins.

'All right?' Tanya says.

'Yeah,' I lie.

I wonder why Mike has shaped his beard like a shovel. It always looked quite stupid enough, without any need for refinements.

'Who's the bloke with a face full of bum-fluff?' I ask Faith quietly, leaning back from the pub table.

November 1987 in the Royal Oak, a pub to the north of town which we've discovered. Faith, who seems to attract fans rather than actual friends, seems to have brought quite a gaggle along with her tonight. Along the table from me, just out of hearing range (I hope), a young man with a dark pony-tail and very scrappy facial hair is expounding something at great length to two others – a pale girl in a crimson headscarf, with crimson spots to match, and a chubby, spiky-haired boy.

Faith pauses at my question, her pint of Old Peculier raised almost to her lips, and grins, displaying that odd pair of teeth which are in need of straightening. 'Michael Bradfield? He's one of ours,' she says, sticking one finger through a beer-mat and twirling it like a football rattle. She knows a wider circle of people than me, as she's got involved, already, with committee stuff, as well as doing her stint with the band. 'I suppose he does look a bit like he shaves with a cheese grater,' she concedes, in a gravely reflective voice which I find funnier than I should. 'What d'you need to know? . . . Very leftie, hard to unwind. Large plate of chips on his shoulder.'

'Ah, right. I get the picture.'

'He comes from . . .' Faith wrinkles her nose, gazes to the left of my head as she often does when she's trying to remember something. 'Lancaster? Doncaster? Somewhere in the North. God knows.'

'Right . . . It ends in Caster, though?'

'Prrrr . . .' Her black-painted lips vibrate with a sound of dismissiveness. 'Could be Chester,' she admits.

'Ah. Big difference, you know. Chester, I mean, that isn't really in the North. I mean, yeah, geographically it is – but spiritually it's somewhere near Aylesbury.'

Faith grins and leans back with her pint. I don't think she really gets what I mean, so I sneak another look at Michael Bradfield instead. He's got his hands curled around an invisible crystal ball, and he's leaning forward, eyebrows waggling earnestly as he witters on about the actual number of people who voted Labour back in June, and how it was actually the majority, and how, because we live in a fascist dictatorship (I'm sorry – we *what*?) the government can draw the constituency boundaries to its own advantage. The crimson girl is nodding eagerly, but the spiky boy is already bored, and not hiding it, either.

I smile at Faith, who I know had just squeezed into the electoral roll by June but still didn't vote. (This time I had plumped for the Alliance, who sounded trustworthy, but my folks' local Tory, predictably, kept his gargantuan majority.) 'Do you want to rescue them?' I ask her.

'Nah,' she says. 'I'll get some more in. What's yours?'

And so I'm left to listen to Mike with one ear, while one of Faith's unnaturally pale camp-followers tries to engage me in conversation.

Someone is tugging at my arm.

'What?' I'm looking blankly at Tanya.

'Stand up!' she whispers, and I am aware of people rising like an instant forest of darkness around me.

I suddenly see Luke on the other side of the aisle, looking crisp and clean as if he'd just stepped out of the past, and I suddenly feel guilty. He's looking straight ahead as the coffin advances, and I'm struck by how meaningful this must be for him, with his spiritual solidity.

I once found a metaphor for Luke's belief. I told him it was like a house which kept getting broken into, but which he still said was safe because he ignored the devastation. He frowned and said he'd think about it. Two days later, he came back and told me he didn't like my metaphor much.

Four men in suits carry the coffin. They are all tall and fleshy, thick necks bulging from their collars like soufflés from tins.

'Who are those guys?' I hiss to Tanya. She shrugs. Well, so she might. I wonder why I imagined she would know.

Luke also does a double-take as the coffin advances. It's obvious he doesn't recognize the pallbearers, either. I realize that they must be provided by the undertaker, which is quite strange, given that there are certainly enough of us to do it.

I see Luke that first time in the light of the morning sun, turning from the window with a mug of tea in his hand. Three points of light gleam from his grey-clad body. Two are his eyes, little blue laser-drills, and the third is the bright gold fish pinned to his shirt. Out and proud.

'You're very welcome,' he says in a soft, cultured voice, holding out a hand. No – both hands. An embracing, but also a restraining gesture.

He's slight, but seems to contain a suppressed, lean muscularity, as if he does regular athletics or gymnastics. He shakes my hand, with a grip that's firm but cold and I smile nervously, looking him up and down. His skull has a millimetre-thin coating of reddish-brown hair, and there's a strange, taut luminosity about his skin. It isn't the flush of health; more the pale glistening of some kind of fever, making his face jellyfish-bright. When he returns my smile, his teeth are white and even, but held in check by a glinting brace like some cybernetic attachment. He glistens all over as though he's slipped down, shining with goodness, from the intestines of heaven.

We are all silent, this unique configuration. We are all here because of the woman in a wooden box in the aisle between us. The dead summon the living to do their bidding.

The vicar is not someone I know. He's the parish priest in the village where Faith grew up. I can see an older couple next to Charlie, and I assume they are the aunt and uncle, those background guardians.

The vicar is speaking a language called English. I hear the words, and not their meaning. He calls Faith 'our sister' and says we are here to give thanks for her life.

We stand up, mumble some empty words. Strings are pulling me now. Or remote-controlled beams of light.

There is a wholehearted rendition of 'The day thou gavest, Lord, is ended'. Why? I don't remember Faith liking that especially. I think the only hymn she was ever much bothered by was 'Jerusalem', because she'd sung it at football matches. Seriously. I suppose Charlie organized the service, and he wouldn't realize she'd have preferred something more melancholy (maybe some Elgar, or 'Neverland' by the Mission).

And now Charlie's unfurling his long legs from the pew, as it seems he has been asked to speak.

Tanya is strong and safe beside me, but I almost can't see her. Strange, because it's not as if I'm blinded by memories of Faith. And I know now why I settled on Mike, why I recalled that time with Luke. I am trying to keep her body out of this. I am not thinking of anything which involves meat or blood or the melding of soft wood, peaty ground, mulchy flesh.

'– without her parents being there, we became very close, and Faith often told me –'

Think of Luke, think of what he used to say. *This body is just a shell.* That's right. All that lies in that box are some discarded clothes, a traction unit, a travel machine of intricate, fleshy tubes and water, held together with hair and nails. Something cobbled together by God (?) for us to walk in for a few score years. Or in Faith's case, a single score and eight.

'– that many of you will remember. Some of you will have enjoyed her music, a vibrant, exuberant contribution to entertainment, a line which she might have pursued professionally had she not followed up her pedagogic instincts –'

No. It doesn't work. Bodies are what brought us together, kept us going, and I cannot imagine, any more, that there is anything after this. Once, I might have done, but not now.

'– a born teacher. Some of you here today were her students, and have said that you recall her classes fondly for their mixture of lively debate, energetic iconoclasm and lavish refreshments.'

Try something else. Try to think of that wooden box as just a symbol, because that's what it is, surely? A box containing more boxes. Russian dolls. Little boxes in bigger boxes. Right down, down to the middle, to the wooden heart, where you find a tiny, doll-sized coffin with a name-plate.

'– not one to hold back if she disagreed. There will be many colleagues who remember her dramatic performance last year at the Third International Colloquium on Post-Todorovian Fantasy Criticism, where she memorably cut through the swathes of jargon beloved by many of the American scholars present, and argued her own lucid re-working –'

And inside the tiny coffin, a little cassette with all the secrets, enumerated one by one. The ultimate confessional. When I said I loved you on 25 May 1988, I was telling the truth, but on the morning of 9 June 1996, I may have been lying. And I didn't actually have trouble finding a phone box on the occasion of your twenty-seventh birthday, I just couldn't be bothered to call you because frankly, by that time, I didn't care.

'– presentation whose examples ranged through Walpole, *The Saragossa Manuscript*, the German *Schauerroman*, Jane Austen –'

It's all there, deep in the coffin. I want to run forward and grab it and take it home to listen to.

My body is weak, pummelled. I feel full, replete with food and bile right up to the neck, and yet I've not eaten for several hours.

Nothing matters but getting through this. Nothing.

Finally, the words are ended and the coffin is lifted. The four impassive strangers heft the box on to their chunky shoulders and begin to proceed down the aisle.

We walk the short distance along the road to the cemetery. The sun bites us. We are walking shadows, slices of night cut from the land. The pallbearers dominate the light in their hugeness, but they are silent as phantoms as we move through the cemetery gates.

The word *grave* echoes in my head. A small word, but massive and serious in its import. Trimly edged with green cloth, it yawns from the ground, inviting custom. I hear myself wince softly, and Tanya's hand increases its pressure on my arm.

I am watching the four hired pallbearers. They're all walking perfectly in step, like policemen. I am mesmerized by them. They form a giant spider, shuffling across the cemetery with a haul of oak balanced on its back.

And suddenly, the illusion is shattered. One of the pallbearers visibly starts to shake. I feel myself moving forward, but Luke and Charlie are there first. I watch the scene unfold in slow motion. His legs sag, as if the weight has become too much. Succumbing to the imbalance, the coffin tips back and to the side. The other three have stopped, trying to turn their heads and see what's wrong, but he's already sinking, sinking as if pierced by a spear of this angry sunlight. People are almost at his side when, without warning, he jerks up again, trying to stand. He smacks his head straight into the corner of the coffin.

If he'd been a few inches either way, he would have hit one of the sides flat on and given himself, at worst, a nasty bruise. But this is not a day of seeing things flat on, straight, simple. This is not a day of bruises to be dealt with by a simple ice-pack.

The whole party has pulled up short. The other pallbearers, unable to support the weight, have to let the wobbling coffin down on to the grass. Luke, Charlie and one or two of the aunts are clustering round the fallen pallbearer, whose forehead is a mess of wooden splinters and rivulets of blood.

'Water, any water?' someone says.

A girl in a blue dress hovers at the edge of the group. She has a young face but a bob of ice-white hair. Her eyes are masked by thick, bluish spectacles, great chunks of plastic across her face. I don't recognize her.

'– nasty knock, we'd better get –'

I exchange a look with Tanya. She's uncertain what to be thinking, I can tell, so instead I fix my gaze on Luke – and look away, quickly, before he can hold it – then let it alight on Mike, and together, unbidden, we exchange a rueful smile. Again, though, I feel that shifting inside me, a slithering of my unwanted food-cargo.

I glimpse the white-haired girl offering someone a handkerchief and it is passed forward.

Words ripple across the green. I catch fragments.

'– diabetic. Didn't have his last shot.'

'– anyone know? –'

'– mobile, I'll call –'

'– no, really –'

'– cut seen to.'

And so, with the star of the show lying patiently in her box, still and unattended, there is an interval, during which the diabetic pallbearer has his cuts washed with a handkerchief and someone's bottle of mineral water. (Shame it couldn't have been holy water from inside the church. I've always wanted to witness a miracle.)

The guests take the delay in their stride. Some drift off into groups for awkward conversation, the way people do while waiting for wedding photos to be taken. Others light cigarettes and smoke them a little guiltily. Shadows shift and meld in the golden green and grey of the cemetery. The sun still blasts down without mercy.

14

Eventually the pallbearer, his forehead now less of a battle-zone, is taken back to the church by the organist, so that he can do his insulin jab in peace.

We are ready to resume. Or, at least, I think we are. The vicar is having a very animated conversation with Charlie, Luke and Mike, all of whom, it seems, are ready to step into the breach and take the vacant fourth corner of the coffin.

'Go on,' says Tanya, 'you offer to do it.'

I look down at her, surprised – not because she has suggested this, but because I have pretty much forgotten that she is there.

'No,' I say to her, hiding behind my sunglasses. 'Not . . . up to it. You know.'

She makes a little clicking noise. 'I did not even know this woman, and I feel sorry for her already. Look at them.'

The disagreement is becoming more heated. Both Charlie and Mike have placed their hands on the corner of the coffin and the vicar, his face shiny and red, is shaking his head in an I-have-my-orders kind of way. Luke steps forward to intervene, then seems to check himself. Something is said. A look passes between Charlie and Mike, and they both withdraw. It seems to have been settled. The chief undertaker himself, a haggard man who looks well suited to his job, steps in. The coffin is lifted and the party proceeds to the graveside.

Somehow, we gather around the great hole without anyone falling in.

After that, this seems an anticlimax. But there is worse to come.

Her eyes, huge and intoxicating, mirror me. She lets her arms flop lazily round my neck. Come on, says Faith. You only live once. I can smell the cooking on her clothes, the peppers roasted in garlic and herbs.

Outside, the land sizzles as it cools, insects chirrup, night floods in, through the house.

Night bleeds through the keyhole, slips up the stairs and swamps the hall, the landing.

Her kiss tingles in my mouth, wet and electric, that combination you were always warned about before switching the kettle off at the mains. Deadly. Something small and hard slips out from behind her tongue and I feel it shooting into my own mouth.

That taste –

★

We hear more hollow words from long ago, lifting up into the sky above the hissing aspens.

And I can sense it all again, now, the pungency and the darkness and the night flooding in.

We are all silent, so silent you can hear it, buzzing in the summer sky, electrostatic. You can smell it. You can touch the unspoken tension, you can taste it like cold metal on your tongue.

I risk lifting my eyes and look at all the faces. Charlie, drained and grey. Mike, frowning intently. Luke, attempting serenity and still managing to make it look like disapproval.

The sunlight drips on them all like butter. No. Oh, hell. I can feel it coming, now. No way I can stop it.

One by one, they are lining up to cast lingering gazes over the darkness of the coffin. To stop in the liquid sunlight. To pour the earth – rich, fruit-cake earth – back down into that hole.

My head is throbbing.

Her tongue explores my mouth. She has an oddly dry, hot taste. Salty. I suddenly long to pull away from her and rinse my mouth.

Each handful thunders on the wood, echoes in my head like I'm the one down there, I'm the one being bombarded with mud and shit.

The ground comes up to meet me. There's a sudden, hard pain beneath my arms and I realize, dimly, that someone must have grabbed me there to stop me falling. I can't feel where my feet are.

And then it gushes out, pumps out, the reeking remains of dinner.

My whole body's twisted, pumped by some alien creature within me, forcing this stuff up, ripping it out of my stomach and mouth with poisoned claws.

Gasping, acid-mouthed, I crouch there in the mud. Shivering under the sun. The world shakes and rocks as if pushed by giants. There are hands on my shoulders.

I'm dimly aware of voices muttering above the buzzing noise of the sun. A giant electric lamp plugged into the sky, blasting the grass, making the people crackle, burning them up.

My eyes suddenly clear, as if sluiced free of salt, and I focus on the wooden surface of the coffin, down below me in that hole. The wood is streaked and splattered with glistening vomit.

And then I'm carried away. An avalanche of concerned faces pours past my head on molten sunlight. Their whispers echo as loud as gunshots.

Hovering in front of a mesh of green leaves is a white face masked in blue goggles, peering interestedly at me. And then someone switches off the hospital light in the sky, and there's a feeling of cool dampness and wood and stone around me, and I find myself drifting, drifting.

Come on, says Faith. *You only live once.*

Well, she did.

02 True Faith

I was grateful for one thing. She wasn't perfect. This meant she could still look just as attractive to me when she first woke up in the morning, her outlines etched with sweat and grease, rheumy-eyed. Or when she was drenched in pungent chlorine-water. Or when she was cooking, slouching in a ripped scarlet jumper, with a smear of tomato across her cheek and onion-skin hanging from her hands in eczematic fragments.

'Pass me the herbs,' says Faith, and reaches out without looking. I slip the jar into her white hand and watch her pour. Tiny fragments of herbs speckle the sauce and she stirs them in, not looking up. I watch every ripple of her body. She is graceful.

There were three sorts of girls at the university. Type A – those I fancied. These were inevitably the best looking, the coolest, but, just as inevitably, those who were most aware of their attributes and under no illusions as to how to exploit them. There was, furthermore, a more awkward problem with Type As, namely that if they were appreciated by me, then they were lusted after by any number of males, some of whom had more to offer than I did. So specimens of Type A were never short of offers. Type B comprised those I didn't really fancy, or didn't find especially interesting. A multitude of potential sinners, sheened by me with (probably) unwanted virtue. And Type C were the Christians. Some of these could be quite gloriously stunning, but it was all irrelevant. You became trained not to notice their physical appearance – to think of them not as sexual beings, but more like sisters.

After a while, I came to realize that the categories were not totally immutable. Type A often had a degree of flexibility in their morals, meaning that the Boyfriend Barrier was not insurmountable. The Type Bs often became more appealing after a pint or five. Only Type C proved difficult, but out of the hundreds who went devotedly to

Christian Union every week, I thought there had to be a wayward soul lurking somewhere.

Later, I often longed to be able to have a laddish chat about this with one of the church guys, but it just wasn't possible, not with Luke, not with any of them. They just didn't *allow* that into their lives.

Faith, luckily, was Type D. None of the above.

The time exists when she was not there, a time a different colour from the rest. A time of leaves piled like paper fragments in the streets. Of raindrops falling on books blackening the red cloth binding, and my suffering the critical stare of the librarian, who asked me sternly whether I couldn't have brought it in a plastic bag.

When did I first see her? I don't know. This may seem strange, but I have to admit it. There may have been several times when I walked past her in the street, jostled her in the pub. It's a small town, and people go to the same places.

But when I first actually *saw* her . . . she was a negative image. Literally.

It was at the mid-term bop, which they always held in the Great Hall, so that we had the incongruity of seeing the ancient oak walls, with their portraits of former Masters, blasted by light and sound from the Gallery. I'd have been impressed if I'd been less cynical and not so interested in getting my hands on some beer. The setting helped me to forget that I was in the biggest hormone tank outside the labs, although it was difficult – the place was pungent with beer, fresh sweat and sex, shot through with a drizzle of perfumes and over-musky aftershave.

This black-and-white creature stepped from the strobing crowd, like a beast from a storm, and flashed a smile of ultra-violent white. Her hair was a cloud of deep black etched in white, her fingernails glowed pitch-bright. She laughed, showed a crooked tooth.

'Bloody crush in there,' she said, and I *think* she was talking to me, although I was next to two guys from my course. 'Dropped my drink,' she added, hopping, wiping her DMs with a handkerchief, and steadying herself on my shoulder. (Curvy, I noticed, and carried it magnificently.) She thought she knew me, I suppose, but this was early in term – if we'd seen each other around, it was natural to have a word.

'I'll get you another one,' I said quickly. 'What was it?'

It turned out to be a pint of Stones, and I got myself one as well. So I found myself in a corner with an invigorating woman who was pleased to talk to me. She was called Faith Devereaux (she spelt it), she was eighteen and she was born in Chelmsford. Her parents had died when she was fifteen, so her guardian was her aunt. She had an older sister, too, but she lived in Shropshire and seldom saw them. Her favourite film of all time was *Amadeus*. Her favourite book was *The Unbearable Lightness of Being*, and yes, she would be interested in seeing the film of that when it came out, and it was soon, wasn't it?

I could still see Geoff and Simon. From time to time, they seemed to run out of their reluctant, boy's-own chat and peer sheepishly into the corner to see if I was coming back. I think they finally worked it out.

Several things came on that I would have happily danced to – Flock of Seagulls, the Housemartins, Madness – but they all made Faith groan and shake her head. At about ten minutes to eleven – yes! – a chime sounded, the opening chords of 'She Sells Sanctuary'. Faith gulped back the last of her pint and pulled me on to the dance floor, and we went wild.

And I thought: thank you, thank you, Ian Astbury, and I promise never to say your racoon hat looks stupid again.

The children seemed insubstantial. I had no hesitation about calling them children – after all, they were straight out of school, and mostly being funded by Mummy and Daddy.

I found the boys amusing and gauche, glowing with rough shaving rashes, drenched in chemically sweet aftershave, unaware of its pungency. And the girls' attempts to look casual made me smile, too. They'd wear rubbed and battered denim jackets, carry khaki satchels scrawled with the names of the bands they liked in the sixth form, and then spoil it all with a wistful, fluttering Laura Ashley skirt.

It was easy to make friends; they were all over-eager and all secretly delighted that anyone wanted to talk to them. I went to pubs, to student discos. I joined CND, where I met some pleasant, earnest types. For some reason, they never seemed to get anything done beyond sitting in a room babbling about Polaris and Trident, and saying how global thermonuclear war would basically be, like, a major downer. They were all decent enough people, though, from a broad range of backgrounds. We got round to doing some banners for a demo, but nothing ever came of it, and that was the end of my threatened brush with political activism.

For the first couple of weeks, I went largely because of a blonde girl called Nina who spoke in languorous Somerset and clasped her knees when she sat up to speak. She was pretty, slim and flat-chested, hovering just the right side of anorexia. She nodded eagerly at everything I said, and often gazed at me with emerald eyes from behind cool, wire-framed glasses.

More out of curiosity than anything, I took up an invitation that was neatly placed in my pigeon-hole one Wednesday. It said, 'Come to St Aldate's this weekend. Breakfast in Roger's first. Nina. x.' This was followed by a routine college address: quad name, staircase and room number.

St Aldate's. Right.

I was being invited on a date with a bright, attractive girl – in church.

I used to go when I lived with the folks. A lot of it left me cold, but I liked the calming atmosphere, and some well-adjusted people I knew seemed to go. Friends, who at other times had no overt objection to getting drunk with me, came to matins now and then, and in such a small village it was quite normal to see Derek, the rector, in the Black Horse. He'd sit by the door, chatting over a pint to anyone and everyone.

One time, I was leaning against the wall – agreeing with him, and a few others, that there was no earthly (or heavenly) reason why women shouldn't be ordained – when a local farmer with a rotten-apple complexion lurched towards us on his way from the toilet. Grinning and drooling, he clapped Derek on the shoulder and pointed in the vague direction of our pints.

'Now, Vicar,' he gurgled, 'I 'ope . . . I 'ope . . . you bless' that afore you dronk et!'

As was expected of him, Derek laughed politely. The farmer began to wheeze with laughter at his own outstanding wit, and reeled away, wiping his mouth, alternately chortling and choking.

Derek nodded, smiled, rubbed his dog-collar nervously. 'Yes, yes, indeed,' he murmured, more to himself than anyone else. He waited until the joker was out of earshot, and added, in the soft tones usually reserved for prayers, 'Stupid old bugger, eh?' Then he lifted his pint and took a long, deep drink from it.

Even today, I still think that ranks as one of the coolest things I've ever seen.

You didn't get any of that with the St Aldate's crowd, I soon discovered. In fact, I was often very unsure of myself with them – so many things could give offence, and you had to be so careful. Humour just didn't seem to work, unless it was of a gentle, toothless sort. Anything vaguely acerbic or satirical and you'd think I'd just farted in their faces.

That first time, I went early to the room Nina had indicated and knocked tentatively on the door. I was welcomed by Roger, who had ginger hair, curly on top and shaved up the sides, bright eyes behind big chunky glasses, and a 'Walk With Jesus' T-shirt.

'Lovely to see you,' he told me, with some unnerving eye-contact and an unnaturally firm handshake. 'Nina said you were coming. Welcome.'

That set me off feeling odd, to start with. I thought: who the hell says 'Welcome' in real life, these days? You only ever see it written on mats.

I smiled shyly, wondering whether this was such a good idea. I knew straight away that none of these people would swear casually, or get up at eleven and kick the beer can and toast crumbs off the duvet, or find *Viz* even remotely funny.

In a ceremony redolent of solemnity, I shook hands with them one by one – even Nina, who for some reason was draped over the radiator.

And then there was Luke. That scrubbed brightness, those laser-sharp eyes. When he looked at me for the first time, it was as if he saw right through my translucency. And he held out his hands. Both hands. To embrace and restrain. 'You're very welcome,' he said.

The service turned out to be so unbearably lively that it almost physically shook me. I had never before seen so many teenagers and young people swaying in harmony to 'Shine, Jesus, Shine'. After fifteen minutes, I was longing to get out, but I stuck the full hour and a half. I joined in with the ecstatic singing and amens, and smilingly pretended to have enjoyed it afterwards.

I walked home feeling rather shabby, as if I had just had a messy and unedifying sexual experience.

Back then, Faith was a Goth, or at least had taken their fashions on board: hair of a crazy, unnatural blackness combined with an artistic pallor; lipstick, usually black, or a rich enough blue or red to seem black; lashings of eye-shadow; a chain-bedecked leather jacket. She resembled the less spiky one out of Baby Amphetamine, a flash-in-the-pan band of shopgirls who'd graced the cover of the *NME* that year and whose debut 'Chernobyl Baby (Who Needs the Government?)' I'd picked up in a bargain bin somewhere.

She hung around from time to time with a crowd who liked to sit in cemeteries, and she was known to nibble at the chemical feasts they provided. She wasn't really serious enough about it, though. She looked too healthy, and only listened to *Darklands* at about seven, not eleven. (Volume, not time.) I joked that she was a demi-Goth. Or maybe a Visigoth. She found this funny, or was polite enough to pretend she did.

She made me a compilation tape, the first of many, and I still have it, somewhere. There's some obscure stuff on it, but all I can remember now is an early Sisters of Mercy track called 'Alice', and that's only because of Faith being affronted when I said it sounded a bit like the Cure.

'You're just a crinkly,' she said, slamming a tape into her twin-deck. 'Old people always say what things sound like.'

'Oh, thanks a bunch. I'm washed up at twenty-two.' Crunchy guitar-noise ripped out of the speakers, heavier and more psychobilly than her usual taste. Elephant Death Overload, or something equally dreadful.

'Yup. Val Doonican, that's your bag.' She poured me a generous amount of whisky and slumped back on her sofa.

'Awful expression. Makes me think of colostomies.'

'What do you reckon to Mike?' she asked, out of nowhere. It was the week after I had seen him holding court at the Royal Oak.

'Um . . . opinionated?'

Faith grinned, took a deep gulp of whisky from her mug. It gave her some much-needed colour. 'He's got a fucking Russian flag on his wall.'

'Has he?' I asked levelly. The flag didn't surprise me, but I found it interesting that she'd seen his wall. No – all right then – I was quite jealous that she'd seen it. 'Bit obvious,' I suggested.

She shrugged. 'He's like that,' she said. 'Ye'll see, laddie,' she added, in a cod Scottish accent. She leaned right back, drained her mug, made an exaggerated 'Aaaah!' of satisfaction.

I smiled at her, and liked her actressy exuberance. And the way that a brownish fringe stood out from her pitchy hair and fell over her forehead. And the big eyes that glistened in her white face.

It was about this time, a few weeks or so into term, that I'd seriously started going off my staple diet of fragile, insecure blondes in satin – like Nina, only with looser morals – and had realized I fancied Faith. If I was honest, I was drawn to her dangerous, edgy vibe. Maybe it was a reaction against Luke's crowd. I loved the way she seemed to have stepped from the night, monochrome, jacket slung over her shoulder and bangles jangling. And those erotic chords of dark, cadaverous rock she reactivated in my head, the songs I pretended not to like but found myself humming.

Then there was that illogical longing, opening in my stomach like a mouth of darkness, which I got when she came in the bar riding high on something. I loved a Faith adorned with saucerous eyes – sorceress eyes – and slicing up words with an alien, crisp precision. Her spooky disconnections meant I could almost be drugged-out myself, without the disadvantage of actually having to take anything.

'And what do you think of Luke, and Nina?' An unguarded question, maybe, but if I couldn't ask Faith, who could I ask?

She seemed to mull it over as she refilled our mugs. 'They're okay,' she said, shrugging as if it didn't really affect her. 'I mean – you know – okay.'

'You don't think I'm . . . odd because I sometimes go to church with them?'

She burst out laughing, almost spat whisky over both of us. 'Odd? Last Saturday, I sat around in a moonlit graveyard with fifteen strangers – with whom I share nothing, might I point out, but some aspects of my musical taste – getting stoned and talking about ways of topping yourself.' She waves a hand at me. 'Mr Kettle, my name's Ms Pot. You're black.'

She had a point.

'You like them, then?'

She laughed. 'Is it important to you?'

'Well . . . yeah.'

'Nina's . . . nice. Prissy, but nice. And Luke, well, yeah – Luke's a bit thorny, I s'pose. I don't like the way he stares right into you as if he's trying to guess what you're thinking. But he's basically good, isn't he? I mean, all that homeless stuff you said about.'

'Oh – yeah.' Luke helped to organize soup kitchens and did voluntary reception work in a hostel. The dark heart of me said it was just brownie points for the hereafter, but I was a cynical bastard even then.

'Can I give you a hint for life?' she asked, leaning forward, eyes round and bright and feline. 'Don't worry so much about what people think. You are what you are. I mean, if I didn't like people you saw, would you stop seeing them?'

'I don't know,' I told her, confused. I almost wanted to say that I'd be quite happy to commend myself into her hands, allow her to dictate exactly who I could and couldn't see, submit to the thrall of Faith. But she might have thought that was a bit weird, just now.

'Well,' she said, leaning back and lighting one of her jet-black cigarettes, 'you should be more independent. Just do what you feel.'

'All right,' I answered. 'I will do.'

When I left her company that afternoon, I was strangely unsettled. I blinked in the crisp greyness. It always seemed odd to emerge into daylight from Faith's black-draped den, rather like when you've been in the cinema. It was an autumn day of shrinking light, of mulchiness I could almost taste, of streaks of drizzle rallying together to soak me. I went for a long walk, along South Parks Road and into the University Parks themselves, which were almost deserted, and I realized then, I think, that these weeks would change my life for ever.

Luke, unsurprisingly, didn't like Faith.

He took me aside at the second Breakfast Meeting, laid a hand on my elbow in a way that emphasized the unearthly context of this grouping. What did he think he was doing, I wondered afterwards – laying on hands to heal me of my affliction?

'I think she may be . . . on drugs,' Luke murmured in what he thought to be a soft and understanding voice, like the tone you use for telling someone their mother is dying of a terminal illness. His eyes, computer-bright, searched mine as if he were waiting for my expression to betray me. He was all ready to turn me in like the shopkeeper in *1984*.

'Oh, I really don't . . .' I began, and hastily swallowed a gulp of Luke's weak Earl Grey as I wondered what I should seem to think. If I agreed, then Luke and his friends would no doubt do everything they could to steer me away from her, encouraged by my recognition of her crime. And if I denied it, I would seem naive. That's the thing about these supposedly chummy born-agains. They're always trying to catch you out. So I shrugged, grinned. 'Tea's a drug,' I offered hopefully.

Luke shook his close-cropped head, tutted quietly – but smiled, in his unnervingly beatific way – and clapped me on the arm with a heartiness I just didn't need or want. 'Trust me, mate,' he said. 'Keep from that path.'

I raised my eyebrows, drank some more tea in apparent acquiescence, and smiled inside as I had a sudden desire to go and see Faith and make passionate love to her.

I didn't think Luke had started out from a level playing-field. 'On drugs' has to be one of the most reactionary phrases in the language, and it can't be rendered into other languages with such admirable economy. 'On' implies automatic addiction (or prescription, and I know which he means here). And then we've got *drugs*, a catch-all word, like *shopping*. It doesn't even admit to the possibility of a gradation in harm. 'She's on drugs'– in terms of information, it ranks alongside 'she eats food'. (So, what is she – a vegan, a gourmet, a chocoholic? Anorexic, bulimic?) For Luke, it said all that he needed to say, and that was the frightening thing.

My life had already split off into several parts, each one seemingly irreconcilable with the others. In my attempts to be true to myself, I was indulging every facet of my being, crashing into contradictions at every turn.

It would get worse than that.

Much worse.

03 Hope Springs

At the edge of the city.

On my notice-board there is a small clipping from the local paper, fringed with yellow highlighter pen. It's just a few days old.

LECTURER IN HOLIDAY DRUG DEATH

The funeral will take place next Monday of a tutor at South East England University who died after ingesting a lethal chemical cocktail.

Oxford-educated Faith Devereaux was holidaying with several friends in the popular South of France resort of Gervizan. It is understood that she took a mixture of Ecstasy and vodka on the final night of a summer break in their £1000-a-night holiday home.

Dr Devereaux, 28, lectured in English and North American Literature at the Medway campus and was admired and respected by colleagues and students alike. The Oxford University Press was about to publish a collection of her articles on Fantasy in the Modern Novel, which have appeared in academic journals over the last few years. Her family has requested that the publication should go ahead as a memorial to her.

A verdict of misadventure was returned by the coroner's office in Chichester.

It could be worse. It's largely accurate, except for the *Hello!*-type lingering over the class stuff. Can't you smell the resentment which might waft in the fish-and-chip air over somewhere like Hope Springs? Those trigger words, which boil down to: *yuppie bitch, sex'n'drugs, too much money, serves her fucking right.* And as for the *gîte* having cost £1000 a night, forget it – half that, actually, and when you realize that was between several of us, it suddenly becomes a little more realistic. So we treated ourselves – so what? Are middle-class people with salaries meant to live like monks, for Christ's sake? I mean, what do you earn money *for*?

The whole thing was her idea, of course. It would have to be. She was the only person everyone would listen to. I think some of the arrangements had been almost political in their intricacy – it just seems so unlikely, in retrospect, to get that particular grouping of people there together at that time. Faith could do it, though. She even managed to persuade Mike and Nic to come, despite the possibility of their entire marriage falling apart for good with everyone watching. Yes, she could sweet-talk anyone.

At the edge of the city lies a wasteland.

I wonder, sometimes, what will come of all this. Three times in the week after Faith's death I was telephoned by a well-known tabloid newspaper.

Out of curiosity, I checked out my caller in one day's edition, to get the feel for the kind of thing he writes. It's not quite vicars'n'knickers stuff – I don't know, maybe they realize sex scandals don't cut as much ice any more. The big buttons he pushes these days are political sleaze, crime (preferably with a touch of injustice) and drugs. Better if they can get all three together.

Anyway, I declined to give any information, even when he started talking about money. They've somehow got hold of this and, it seems, the story won't lie down. What is there to tell? She lived (well), she died (badly), she was buried (memorably). Thank God for Charles – discretion isn't just his middle name, it's his first. He did a great job of keeping the funeral private. I don't know how, but I'm grateful to him for it.

For some reason, they think this is a story which will serve the public interest. In other words, a pleb-friendly unit shifter.

I've no desire to share my story with anyone. She died six weeks ago. I have been there, done that and bought the T-shirt. I am still coldly, quietly accepting of the fact. I have lost Faith.

And what have I gained? Hope, perhaps.

At the edge of the city lies a wasteland called Hope Springs.

Someone at the town planning office must have been having an especially good or bad day. He was either overcome with mirth and delight at his football team winning, or at getting a shag, or something that he decided it would be a great joke to play on the population. Or the world had suddenly decided to kick him hard where it hurt, and he thought the best way to kick it back was to give a local blackspot an ironic name. Either way, it makes me smile – without pleasure – every time I drive up into it.

Here, the streets are in the sky and the sky's the limit. Where dogs of debated pedigree, with creaking ribcages and teeth, sniff for edible life in puddles of urine. Where glaziers patch up the windows on the world, sheen the scene of the crime and pocket a packet. Where the children are cracked till they fall apart, smacked till they bleed, sped up to zero revolutions per century. Pseudohappy. Acidified. Glued. Ecstatic.

Welcome to Hope Springs.

Today I watch the wipers sluice the rain as I drive up to the estate. My eyes could do with a similar purging. I drive past a steel-shuttered Co-op. The car slices the muddy puddles outside 'Piercing While-U-Wait'. (I've always wondered about that sign – how could it be otherwise? 'I'll just leave this with you, then, and come back on Thursday'?)

I'm still not eating, but I could do with a camomile tea to settle my stomach. Tanya, bless her, brought me an Earl Grey before she went off to work at half past six this morning, but the scent of the bergamot was so pungent that I almost felt ill again. Tactfully, she didn't even mention the events of yesterday.

The estate has bleak, unending rows of brick council houses. Take away the satellite dishes, and you wouldn't know which decade of the late twentieth century you were in. I park in my usual place outside the old primary school. Behind me, two giant gasometers squat, like enormous buttons ready to be pressed by invisible fingers, while on the other side of the red-brick building, guilty pylons slink and slope off down into the valley of steel and smoke.

Inside, the pocked walls, once redolent of chips and plimsoll-sweat, have been cloaked in glossy green and shroud-white. I walk past the old rooms we haven't got round to equipping, with their dismembered furniture and gouged blackboards. Whoops, chalkboards. I got into trouble for that one at my very first meeting with the council –

my fixtures-and-fittings report had to be completely retyped and rephotocopied because I'd made that *faux pas*. (Sorry, I said with a grin, it's the computer. My PC isn't PC. Didn't go down well.) I gritted my teeth, had it done, and tried to forget about where the money could have gone.

In the main foyer, paint thickens the air. A sweet, smooth smell, but one that still seems to burrow into your nostrils like an eager little animal.

Tony's on his back, painting over the cracks. Like we all do, here. His radio swings from the stepladder on an elastic roof-rack tie, and it's coughing and spitting out the local station which gleefully offers the Best Music.

I gingerly pick my way through the paint pots and trays towards my office door, which is currently Apple White on the left and Turd Brown on the right.

'Morning,' says Tony.

'Morning, Tony.'

He turns on to his side, gestures with the paintbrush. 'Jenny Agutter,' he says, enunciating clearly and loosing a small drip of saliva on the double T.

'Right. Yes, I'll go along with that.'

Tony always has a Babe of the Day, and his conversation will begin by citing the latest holder of the trophy. I know, deep down, that it's a bit sexist, but the idea's harmless enough.

'What age, though?' I ask, as I unlock my office door. 'I mean, are we talking *The Railway Children* here, or were you thinking more *Logan's Run*? Or *An American Werewolf in London*?'

'Neither,' says Tony, raising his eyebrows. 'We're talking *And The Beat Goes On*.'

'I see. Current incarnation.'

'Current ink-nation. Gotcha.'

'Okay, I won't argue with that. Anyway, how's it going?' In the office, my telephone starts chirruping excitedly to itself.

'Another day or so,' he says, glancing briefly at me. 'Hey . . . how was . . . you know?'

As I realize what he's asking about – it takes a moment – I'm teetering on one foot and peeling an emulsion-crusted newspaper from my heel.

'Oh . . . not too bad,' I lie. 'Pleasant service. Tasteful. Kind of thing.' The phone continues its agitated warbling.

'Right,' says Tony, his duty done, and returns to his roller.

Kicking open the door, I throw my briefcase on to the desk. It shoots the in-tray on to the bare-boards floor and knocks the telephone flying.

There are three answerphone messages – two of them are dull stuff about funding, and the other is from Mike Bradfield, confirming that he's still on for meeting at lunchtime.

Practically makes me jump, that one. I'd totally forgotten that we'd arranged anything. It'll be odd . . . he's never seen where I work, what I do.

Years back, I'd have pictured this kind of place as his heartland, in theory at least. Perhaps I have a romanticized picture of him. I imagined he would have stamped at dawn through the skyborne labyrinths, nostrils steaming as he showered the slums of Thatcher's Britain with his visionary visitation. *What rough beast, its hour come round at last . . . ?* His footfall echoed in the walkways as he fed the tightly sprung jaws of letterboxes. He slipped past dogs with glutinous drool and rank fur. He trudged through the heaps of consumer debris – the gnarled Coke cans and the eviscerated burgers – spreading revolt on squares of sunset-red recycled paper. In my imagination I even saw him pause on the reeking stairs to smack a comrade's high-five with a denimed denizen on his way home from the night shift, and heard them exchange working men's banter in roughened voices of truth.

In reality, of course, he'd just have got his stupid head kicked in.

These days, Mike Bradfield runs a big property agency, based out in Sussex somewhere.

A squashed nose appears around my door. Below it, his beard is a dark trowel. When he slips nervously in, he's immaculately three-piece suited, with his hair immobile in a crew cut.

I see him glance at the overflowing in-trays, the blu-tacked planners and the stacks of files. I look up, lean back and smile. I'm drowning in highlighter pens and notepads, but I can look quite happy about it.

He nods in my direction, settling into the plastic chair opposite me, opens his mouth as if to speak. There is a pause, and then he finally settles on something.

'All right, are you?' he asks. His tone wavers uncertainly between laddish insouciance and genuine concern. Touching. I suppose it is an awkward point of etiquette: what *do* you say to someone you last saw being carried off after puking over his ex-lover's coffin?

I manage a weak smile. 'Yeah. Not bad . . . What do you think, then?' I ask, gesturing around.

He shrugs. 'All in a good cause, is it?' he asks gloomily, rubbing his flattened nose.

'Of course. Tea?' I ask, flicking the kettle on.

'Got herbal?'

'Naturally. We allow ourselves a bit of middle-class civilization here, you know.' I start to reel them off on my fingers. 'Camomile, mixed fruit, grapefruit – what?'

Mike is wincing, holding up fingers to his teeth. 'Don't – don't do that – *thing* with your fingers. Please.'

I've got into that habit of anyone who regularly has to speak to large groups, namely the Itemizing Finger-Bend, where you pull the fingers of one hand down with the index finger of the other. Sometimes, I've heard, the way it makes the joints go white can turn people queasy.

'Sorry,' I say to Mike with a grin.

'At least you didn't say "(a), and secondly," this time,' he mutters.

'What is this, Shortcomings Week?' The kettle quietly bubbles its assent. 'Anyway, what flavour?'

He shrugs. 'I don't know. Does it matter?'

'On the great scale of things? Probably not. But if you have one, then it means they get used up more quickly. And I buy some more from the SuperSave down the road here.' I wave towards the world outside the window. 'And so the SuperSave carries on stocking them, alongside all the sticky white bread and the gristle-burgers, and maybe that'll make a difference.'

There's a pause, during which we listen to Tony splashing his paint and singing along to the Spice Girls.

'Didn't get much of a chance to see you yesterday,' he says, glancing at the wall-planner, which he seems to find fascinating.

'No, well . . . That would be on account of my majorly embarrassing hangover, I expect.'

Tony fills the silence with clattering, sloshing and karaoke. He sounds happy. I wonder what he wants (what he really-really wants).

Mike manages a little artificial chuckle. 'Yeah . . . You missed the food. Quite a spread.'

'I can never understand how people actually eat at these things.'

'Hungry work, mourning.'

'Except we're not, are we?' I swivel on my chair and raise my eyebrows at him, surprised at my own daring.

'Eh?' He rubs at his beard and tries to look unconcerned.

'Mourning. Oh, come on, Mike. Are you trying to tell me that we never knew she'd do something like this? Faith was an accident waiting to happen.'

'Don't say that.'

His voice is sharp. I'm surprised. I feel a strange wash of emotions, a mixture of righteous pride and discomfort, and I have to get up and lean on the window-sill, staring through the slatted blinds at the slices of industrial life below. I can feel him watching me with those dark, powerful eyes, and the resentment of all the years, the hopes and fears, pounding across the room.

'Look,' he says, his voice softer now. 'I think you should take a few days off from this place.'

I recognize his tone of voice, the quiet, reasonable, stating-a-universal-truth tone he'd use in our arguments, high above the city of the screaming tyres. So there's a bit of the old Mike left. Well, it won't work any more.

'Mike, this isn't a bloody office, it doesn't run itself. If I'm not here, it falls apart.'

He chuckles. 'File under "Importance, sense of own". You think this place will make a difference? It's flea-bites, mate, flea-bites.' He's looking at me with something close to pity. 'You're wasting your energy. You could be out there earning a total fucking *stash*, you know that?'

'Yeah, I know that,' I tell him bitterly. 'Funny, isn't it?'

I turn and meet his gaze, lifting my hands to make a point. My sticky hands. I suddenly have ghost-white palms, and there are two perfect palm-prints in the fresh paint.

There is something absurd, grotesque but still strangely beautiful about my white-painted hands. But something sad as well.

I notice I am chuckling to myself. Mike raises his eyebrows. I start to laugh. And now, although he's trying not to, he laughs, too, and we go on and on laughing as if we're filling a hole with the stuff. Until my throat aches and my eyes are soft with tears.

Once, Mike Bradfield believed. He had faith. I might not have agreed with him, but he did his stuff with conviction.

Where is he now? What does he believe in? Cold, hard cash. Or rather, a kind of metacash, an atmosphere where he can inhale money without actually handling the stuff. Mike's problem: he has become a yuppie ten years too late. But earning money does seem to be coming back into fashion. You don't get so many graduates ending up filling envelopes or measuring biscuits any more. Not like in 91. Things are changing. It seems to be just me that stays the same.

'*Big Issue*, sir?'

I have stopped beside a bedraggled girl in a blue cagoule. She's standing in the doorway of a boarded-up shop. Mike, who has broken off in mid-sentence, shakes his head and stays at a distance, in the doorway of Spar, while I fumble with my change.

'Okay?' I offer a pound coin as always, to err on the side of generosity.

'Thank you, sir.'

It gets me, the way they always call you 'sir', especially the girls. 'Mate' would be better. Or 'love', even. I don't know if it's just me, but 'sir' makes me feel like a Victorian aristocrat slumming it with a back-alley slut.

I hand her the money and smile as I take the proffered magazine. 'Sold many today?'

'Only a few, actually, sir. It's the rain, innit? Keeps people in.' She gives me a crooked smile.

'Yeah. Well.' I'm suddenly uncomfortable, as I feel that before long she'll be pointing out the exact dustbins she'll be sleeping behind tonight. Stop it, stop it, I tell myself. You Do Not Need To Feel Guilty, You Are Doing The Right Thing. 'Good luck.'

'Thank you, sir, and good luck to you as well.' She sounds so bloody perky, and almost as if she's enjoying it.

I turn my collar up, shoving the paper inside my coat, as I rejoin

Mike to battle our way through the rain. Mike, it transpired, doesn't actually bother with lunch, so we stopped off just for a drink at the Anchor, on the way into town from Hope Springs. I had a bitter lemon. (That's me. Bitter and citric.) We hardly exchanged a word about yesterday. Now, I'm heading back to work and he's returning to where he parked his car – some way off the estate, I note.

'What do you drive these days?' I ask him.

'TR7,' he says proudly, and jangles the keys in my face.

'Ah. Bit eighties, isn't it?'

'Come on. It's a very affordable car, actually. And it's not eighties, it's *now*. Coming back, isn't it? All that stuff. Housing boom, stocks are up, feelgood factor. Nice one.'

I wince. Any minute now, if I don't stop him, he is going to say *sorted*. 'Errrm. No, I hadn't noticed.' Perhaps I sound a little harsh. 'Better go and sell my shares, then. Liquidize some jolly old assets.'

'Don't take the piss. You could be there too. But no, you've got your deconsecrated school and its Great Mission, I suppose . . . And what's all this, anyway?' he says irritably, tapping my copy of the *Big Issue*. 'What good does it do?'

'It's a step up from begging. It gives them something to do, a new responsibility. And they're providing something for the money. It's a sort of introduction to capitalist realism, I s'pose.'

Mike laughs. 'Yeah, right,' he says. 'You give them a millimetre, they take a bloody marathon. Anyway, half of them have got council houses.' He hurries on through the rain, clicking his tongue in disapproval. I swallow, bite my lip and hurry after him. 'Look,' he says, 'if I shoved a coin in every scummy hand I found under my nose . . .'

'I know, I know. But it's a collective responsibility. We can't leave people to die.'

'You're going to get all deep. I can tell.' He sighs, aiming a kick at a Coke can. 'Go on, then, tell me it's a sin.'

The can bounces back across our path. I pick it up and put it in the litter bin by the pedestrian crossing. 'Well, in a way it is. There are two types of sins, you know. Commission and omission.' I can tell he doesn't want to know, though, so I let it drop.

Across the ring road. Past the walls of chameleon adverts, the shifting vistas with their venetian-blind effect. Steps down to the subway.

Distantly, the pale hills beyond the town are nuzzled by fragmenting grey cloud.

I saw it coming. I *knew* all those years ago that he was a sad wanker for having a massive Soviet flag in his room while Communism collapsed like a polystyrene Berlin Wall. For telling everyone else what kind of language they should be using. For berating everyone – at least, anyone of a slightly paler red than Arthur Scargill – for being a fascist. For marching against everything that suited his cause, from poll tax and student loans and bypasses to Winston Silcott and Uncle Nelson Mandela and all. But I knew what would happen when life caught up with his champagne Communism. What he'd do when, for example, he started having a car and using the roads and realized that bypasses were actually quite useful.

Meanwhile, he just thought he was a fixed point in a changing world. Jesus. The time and energy I wasted, just for being two reality checks ahead.

It's a bit like when you tell a kid, 'Don't you dare go and play footie in the road, because a car will come round the corner and hit you.' And of course, you don't actually *know* that, but you're trying to protect them. And they keep playing in the road . . . until one day, a car comes hurtling round the corner, runs over the football and pops it, runs over the kid's head and squashes it.

And you *knew* it would happen.

You didn't know when, but you knew.

'What was happening yesterday?' I ask Mike, turning to look at him as we walk down into the subway. 'All that stuff with the pallbearers?'

He turns slightly away from me, shrugs. 'Crap. Vicar being difficult.' The artificial cave swallows us up.

'No, what do you mean, being difficult? Charlie would have had a say, surely? He was on your side, wasn't he?'

Mike glances at me. 'Thought you might come over and have a go, anyway.'

'Yeah, well.' I look away, slightly guilty. 'Didn't feel I ought to get too . . . you know. She was . . . in my life, she was . . .'

'I know. You didn't really care very much,' he says, with sudden, haunting bleakness.

I shrug. I don't contradict him. Suddenly, he stops, there in the stinking semi-darkness.

'I'm thinking of driving down in a couple of days,' he says. 'The grave, you know. Might put some . . . flowers or whatever on it.'

That's a touch sentimental for him, I think, but I wisely choose not to say so. 'Oh. Right.' I shrug. 'Well . . . I could come. If. You know.'

'Yeah.' He looks pleased for a second. Maybe he needs the company, I think to myself. I know he's currently being dragged through the bitterest and bloodiest of divorces. I wasn't surprised at Nic's absence from the funeral, as I understand they find it hard to be civil for five seconds. I don't know who to feel more sorry for – he might be a second-division tosser, but I bet *she*'s being a premier-league bitch.

We're walking on, through rancid wet patches and the piles of old chip wrappers. Piss and vinegar. Our footsteps echo. Tyres hiss on the wet road above our heads.

'What a dump,' says Mike.

'You know, someone once said to me that the true heart and lungs of the people lie on the estates.'

'Really?' He sniffs. 'Must've been a wanker.'

'Yeah, it was you, actually.'

He grins for a moment. 'I know.' He fumbles inside his coat, getting out his cigarettes and a gold lighter. 'The people's heart and lungs,' he repeats, moodily. 'Well, they're rotting with tar.'

He lights up and I watch the flare of orange illuminate the squashiness of his boxer's nose. It's a constant source of fascination for me, that broken nose. It seems to symbolize his whole transformation, changing the entire shape of his face – from the lean-and-hungry, anarchic look of those early years into a deadened lump of suffering.

'You used to say,' I remind him, 'that a revolution could start here. That you could educate people in the need for it. Into assuming control over their own destinies.'

He starts to chuckle, and for a moment the sound threatens to decay into phlegm, which he has to cough back. I glance worriedly at him, but he just waves a hand.

'Sorry,' he says. 'I was just thinking about what you'd need to start a revolution these days.'

'Well, the poll tax was –'

'Bollocks. Flash in the pan.'

'Okay . . . Europe, then.'

'Europe?' He stops dead again and looks me up and down with something approaching disgust. 'You think the *Sun*'s going to bring down Brussels by telling Hans where to stick his Wurst, or whatever they're saying this week?' He shakes his head in despair. 'Jesus,' he says, and takes a long drag on his cigarette, burning bright in the dimness. 'The only way,' he says, 'that they'd start one now is to cancel *EastEnders* without warning, and pull the Lottery. People would be out on the bloody streets. They'd be ready to take up *arms*.' He sighs, looks around the infested floor of the subway, and for a moment I wonder if he's going to spit.

I'm grinning. 'Wouldn't believe you used to be a Commie.'

He holds his cigarette carefully and jabs it into the air. 'Communism,' he says, 'it's like casual sex. It's something you grow out of.' He means it, too; this is more than just post-marital *Weltschmerz*. 'The rest of the world had to, after all.'

'Except Albania.'

'Yeah, well. Al-fucking-bania.' He waves a dismissive hand.

Back in the eighties I used to wonder what might happen, under Labour, to the likes of Mike – people who blamed all the country's ills on the Tories. It would be like using up all their Christmases at once. They wouldn't know what to do with it.

'The world tried to be more realistic,' I suggest. 'Doesn't mean we all have to abandon hope, though. I still believe in educating the workforce.'

'Yeah, yeah, your great project. Good fucking luck to you, mate, and don't say I didn't warn you.'

He's half-hearted, now. I know I might have sounded unnaturally, falsely proud. At times like this, I feel my neatly ironed jeans glowing on my body, my comfy River Island sweater brightly beaming into the streets. I almost taste my rounded accent burning holes in the air. I feel like a fraud. But I'm less of a fraud than he ever was, and I think he knows it.

We're at the steps, now, at the end of the subway. They diverge, to carry us in our separate directions. The town air gushes through, smelling of petrol and wet paper.

'You're not going to tell me about yesterday, then?'

He sighs. 'Ask Charlie, will you? I've just had enough of it.'

The rain's intensified. It hammers on the steps, sheening their grey to silver and making coins of water bounce on the concrete. Beyond, in the haze, the world is alive with rain. It crackles, like reality trying to tune itself in. The cars prowl, and their lights sweep a glittering path before them.

Mike turns up his collar. 'Anyway,' he says, 'we have to go on.'

'Yeah.' I don't know what to say, now. 'I'll see you, then.'

He nods, not looking convinced. He turns, heads up the steps into the cascading rain.

'I don't understand,' I call after him.

What made me say that? Something got into my mouth and tweaked the words from me, pulled them out.

'What?' he shouts.

'I don't understand what happened.' This is what I have been wanting to say to him all along. 'A few years ago you'd have been all for what I'm doing. You'd have been bloody *organizing* it. What the hell happened?'

He pulls the wet cigarette out of his mouth, chucks it into a puddle and shakes his head. He stands there. The rain darkens and sheens him, turns his coat into glossy pitch and his skin into dead fish. Soaked rubbish on the streets of Hope Springs. The rain hisses like static, like interference over the voices of the people.

'Reality,' he says quietly. I hear him, even over the rain. 'Reality happened.'

Then he's gone, swallowed by the curtain of water, and I'm left standing in the subway, under the world, deep under the tarred heart of the people, and listening.

Left alone with just my faith.

And, suddenly, feeling nothing.

04 I Say Nothing

It didn't take me long to work out that the university was filled not with real lives but with embryos. They were ghosts of grown-ups: kids playing at being journalists, entertainers, politicians, financiers, missionaries.

Luke, with his naive devotion to God, unshakeable because he never dared do anything that *might* shake it. Mike in that pub, the first time I saw him, setting the country's problems to lefts. And Faith herself, living out her fantasy of incursions into *NME* territory, playing at being a rock-chick, adjusting the vocal balance as if it mattered. Eighteen-year-olds, like toddlers with their Early Learning Centre toys.

Maybe it was my mature-student arrogance (mature! a full four years older than most of them), but stereotypes seemed to abound. Like a scientist with a microscope, I could see that they were developing. They, meanwhile, were convinced they were experiencing epiphanies which had evaded their forefathers.

It's easy, in retrospect, to see how this self-satisfied bunch became the nineties E-generation. Needing to believe that they could change more, in a shorter time, than their ancestors. More convinced of their worth than any angry young things before them – but finding, paradoxically, that it was harder to make a mark in a splintered and diffident world. And motivated by a desperate desire, in the days of expanding information and receding employment prospects, to *leave something behind*. So they would end up evangelizing the redemptive power of MDMA, convinced that getting off your face every Saturday night was somehow the next stage in evolution, a trip to a higher plane as – don't laugh – Phorever People. In a year or three the rave explosion, with its pseudo-intellectual baggage (Terence McKenna and all that), would turn out to be just what they needed. They could justify their play as serious experiment, claim they were expanding the collective unconscious.

That's one theory. It could just be bollocks, of course.

★

Faith and I kissed goodbye in December, and remained, for now, in the Friend Area.

Home seemed alien for the first time, and not just because of all the smashed tree-trunks, scarred roofs and new vistas. The big storm had hit the South hardest of all, but at least no one in our village had been hurt.

Christmas came and went. I had a good lot of cards, for once. Most of them were from people I didn't really like, but who had asked for my address.

At the end of Michaelmas term, the precocious Bradfield had been elected to the student committee, in the position of National Union of Students rep. It wasn't unheard of in your first year, but you needed to be a self-promoter. In our first week back after Christmas, Faith took me for tea in his room.

'He's fun,' she'd said beforehand, as we strolled across the chilly, bare-treed quad. 'You'll like him, I promise.'

Mike opened his door with a pen in his mouth, and gave an expansive wave of greeting before ushering us in. His room had an aroma of coffee and house-plants. Faith introduced me. Mike turned his chair, straddling it, hands resting on the back (danger sign), nodding, tucking back stray bits of his pony-tail (definite danger sign).

I smiled and looked politely around his room while the kettle boiled. Well, there was no mistaking it – a bright red, immaculate Soviet flag suspended above the fireplace. I tried to avert my eyes, but it was impossible – it sat up there and *brooded*, like the titanic election poster in *Citizen Kane*.

'So,' he said, lighting a cigarette and looking me up and down, 'this is your friend who's a Tory.'

I laughed. Well, you have to. I thought this was his way of breaking the ice, to be honest.

'No . . . I, ah, take very little interest in politics, as it happens.'

'How very convenient.' He didn't smile. 'And politics returns the compliment?' I couldn't recall where Faith had eventually decided he came from, but it didn't sound much like Doncaster to me. There was a slight Northern inflection, but it was buffed to a shine.

I smiled, looked at Faith for help, but she just sprawled in a Faith-like way and pushed her hair back, refusing to catch my eye. Oh, great –

thanks, you cow, I thought. It's all right being an attractive woman; you can say something thoughtless or uninformed, then you can just giggle a bit, play with your hair and flash a bit of leg, and then it just becomes part of your appeal. And no one wants to lay into you about it, because you're just too vulnerable, and anyway, they don't want to blow their chances of getting into your knickers.

'Really, though,' I told Mike, meeting his eye, thinking: come on, this is just a boy with an under-enthusiastic beard, fresh out of A levels. He can't start defining me. 'I don't know where you got that idea. I don't like Maggie much . . . I'm not a Tory, or anything in particular.'

Mike sighed. I swore he glanced up to the ceiling for a moment, like a long-suffering teacher who has seen an obtuse pupil make his usual mistake. He put his hands in front of him in that crystal-ball-caressing way. 'Everyone,' he said, with exaggerated patience, 'who doesn't stand up to the Right is, *de facto*, a Tory. If you never question, if you just accept what the government does year after year, then you're sending the message that you like it. That you're happy with the status quo. You take sides by apathy.'

Faith yawned. 'Yeah, yeah, Mike, been there. Up the fucking Revolution, and all that. Can we talk about *Neighbours*, please?'

I realized what she was trying to do, but I wasn't going to leave him unchallenged. 'That's total bollocks,' I said angrily, leaning forward in my seat.

'Well, yeah,' Faith said, 'but chill, it's only Aussie escapism.'

'No, what *he* said! It's absolute cack!'

Mike appeared very amused as he poured the hot water into the teapot. He obviously thrives on this kind of conversation, I thought bitterly, while I end up wishing we'd never come here.

On the other walls, I could see a poster for the Clash's *Combat Rock* album and some neatly spaced postcards, among them Che Guevara (of course, as this says: Hey! I'm a revolutionary), Marilyn Monroe (Hey! I'm a red-blooded male, but unthreateningly, with dead icons) and Ladysmith Black Mambazo (Hey! I respect ethnic music).

'Did you vote?' he asked. 'Or did you voluntarily disenfranchize yourself, like Faith here?'

'I didn't . . . what you said,' she snarled at him, grabbing her own cigarettes and biting the end of one. 'I was too hung over to get up.'

'No, I voted Alliance,' I told him patiently. 'To be honest, they just seemed like the best of a very bad bunch.'

Mike gave a helpless, frozen smile. He shook his head in despair, as if to say: How are we ever going to teach these people?

'Look, why's it such a big deal?' I could feel myself getting hot and flushed with anger now. I could have asked myself the same question, of course, but I didn't think it at the time. I was just affronted at his arrogance, and – thanks to my own – I thought I could break it down in the space of one afternoon. 'I mean, I'm just fed up with politics, really. I don't want anything to do with it.'

He raised his eyebrows, and as he poured the tea, he looked me directly in the eye for the very first time. 'But politics is everything, love,' he said with quiet authority.

'He called me *love*. Would you bloody believe it? I mean, could you have found a more patronizing tosser if you'd tried, Faith? Do you – do you know any *nice* people?'

'You really find him patronizing?' she asked, taking a bite of pizza.

'Hell. Can't you see it?' I folded my arms defensively.

She leaned across our table in the pizza parlour to pat my hand, gently. I suppose it was some consolation. She grinned. 'You know, I'd like to say you're beautiful when you're angry.'

'Thank you.'

'I'd *like* to say it, but it wouldn't be true. You're just ugly like the rest of us.' She started to poke around in her salad.

I sighed, leaned back with my arms folded. 'He thinks he's got all the answers, that's what annoys me. He doesn't even realize he's privileged.'

'Ooohhh, wye-ay, man, he's from a wookin-class family, y'know!' Faith exclaimed, in a mutant hybrid of accents.

'Bollocks. Look, he's privileged to be able to sit on the fence. For the next three years, he'll be a voter, but not a taxpayer – think about that. Means he can take the moral high ground. Attack the government with impunity.'

Faith grinned as she crunched on a stick of celery. 'You're not a Thatcherite, are you?'

'I'm not an anything-ite. I resent attempts to categorize me.'

'Oooh. Lovely.'

I could never tell when Faith was taking the piss, and I ranted on. 'And he had a fucking coffee percolator. Talk about the best of both worlds. Shouldn't he be drinking, y'know, Co-op instant or whatever, and giving the price difference away to the unemployed miners?'

'Now that's silly. Just because you don't like him.'

'I just hate it,' I said, 'when people think they've got acute political perception, and feel the need to show it.'

'I dunno about his perception,' she murmured, moistening her lips. 'He might have a cute bottom, though.'

I ignored the bait. 'That *love* of his, it's a trendy thing, right? Like, being confident of your masculinity or something?'

She chuckled to herself as she speared a tomato with her knife. 'Maybe.' She popped the tomato in her mouth, and added indistinctly, 'Don't let it get to you.'

I don't know if it was a coincidence, but from then on, when I wanted to see Faith, I found myself seeing Mike Bradfield as well.

'Hi,' Faith would say, as we all smiled awkwardly at each other in the corridor. 'Mike and I are just off to the shops. You want anything?'

Or in the bar, when I thought I had her to myself until, suddenly, through a haze of smoke, he'd appear, and he'd let a hand trail over her coal-black hair before sitting down. What annoyed me most of all was that she'd shift up for him so that he sat between us. Mike would usually say something derisive like, 'Make room for True Blue Boy.'

There was nothing going on between them, I knew that much, but it was often as if Mike and I were in competition for her friendship. Faith was a valuable commodity, rapidly establishing herself as one of the most popular people in our college.

He also surrounded himself with fawning acolytes. There was the crimson-spotted girl from the pub, whose name was Jacqui Potter. She was quite pleasant – shy, self-effacing, but needy. It's easy to see how she could have attached herself to someone like him. She was hopelessly in love with Mike, as it happened, and I observed this with interest.

It was the pivot of the year, the weekend when Fourth Week became Fifth and we were conscious of tilting towards lighter nights. I still sometimes went to St Aldate's, but what worried me was how *competitive* it all seemed, as if everyone was trying to say: look, look at me, I can lift my arms higher than you, and I can sing louder than you, and I can give more money than you. God was the most popular boy in the class and they were all vying to be his best friend.

I was ankle-deep in mud when they sidled up to me, flanked me.

'We're worried about you,' said Roger.

'Concerned,' said Luke, on my other side.

I looked uneasily from one to the other as we trudged, with about thirty others, through the mud of a farmyard. Only two days ago, it had been perfect walking weather – the sky and trees dripping with sun, but the ground still held fast in ice, all the mud and ripples and puddles trapped in frozen time. Since then, the thaw had arrived and the ground had come back to life, slopping up our jeans and boots, and the light had become the more oppressive kind that squats on your eyes and crinkles your brow.

'Concerned? Why?' I asked. My shirt was soaked with sweat where the rucksack had sat for the past two hours. To be honest, I could have done with stopping for a pint. But there was no chance of that.

At some point in February, I had joined the Men's Christian Rambling Association. I'd made a joke at the time, which Luke and the others must have heard too many times before: 'Christian rambling?' I'd asked nervously. 'Nothing to do with sermons, I hope?' You could have sharpened knives on the silence. I'd forgotten what a humourless lot they were.

Basically, every Saturday – when, we were led to believe, godless males were kicking heads in at football matches, or gambling on pool in smoky basement bars, or sprawled over sweat-dampened sheets with louche hussies – we took ourselves out into the hills and walked for miles in a hearty but artificial boys'-school atmosphere. And now, with Roger and Luke flanking me, a pair of unwanted guardian angels, I felt as if I might have made the wrong decision. Chastity and self-righteousness emanated from them like an overpowering aroma.

'Basically, we're worried,' said Luke, in his soft, serene way.

It was dangerous, that voice. It could always make you think it was saying something logical. Leaders of cults have such voices.

'Worried,' echoed Roger, opening the gate to let the other men through one by one. They smiled and nodded their thanks as they slipped through. It was a kissing-gate.

I smiled at each of them as we climbed the hill towards a stone wall. 'I'm not in any trouble,' I assured them.

'Trouble sneaks up on you,' said Luke, with the apparent authority of someone twice his age. 'If there's a conflict in your life, you don't often see it until it's too late.'

'I run a Men's Group,' said Roger, without a trace of shame. 'We meet at Balliol every Tuesday. I think you'd be a valuable addition.'

I concentrated on putting one foot in front of the other, allowed my eyes to wander over the Cotswold landscape as I thought how to answer. (It was a tough one: Tuesday was table-football night in the bar.)

'I'll think about it,' I promised Roger.

He clapped me on the shoulder, and must have been oblivious to the way I winced. 'You *do* that,' he said cheerfully.

Saturday night. I bellowed in Faith's ear, over the hubbub of the Lower Bar disco, and tried not to spit as I regaled her with the details of my walk and Roger's offer.

'Go along! It might be a laugh!' she yelled back at me, and giggled through a gulp of cider. A posse of her Goth friends stomped past in a cloud of hair, black denim and leather fringes. One of them tweaked her ear while another, probably by accident, sloshed half my pint over my sleeve. Faith smiled indulgently.

'Faith, it'll be bloody crap. It'll be a bunch of anally retentive guys talking about how wonderful their self-control is.'

'Their what?' She screwed her face up, leaned up to my mouth to hear.

My lips were against her ear. '*Self! Con! Troll!*'

'Oh, that.'

The dance floor was filling now. It fizzed with pheromone-steam, sparkled with light. Gawky denim jostled flirty satin. The floor throbbed under a thickening cloud of dried gel and melting mousse, of sweat-soaked Lynx and spit-choked drinks. Arms sliced the smoke in the scarlet bedlam while a hundred hopeful mouths prowled for prey, stalked a snog in the smog.

'Look,' said Faith, and the word popped in my ear. 'Don't let them tell you how to live. That's not what it's all about. Don't let *anyone* tell you. Do what you f–' and she lurched '–eeel!' she just had time to say, a slippery syllable stretched by the big-haired crowd. She flashed a grin before she was absorbed into their blackness. A second later I was shoved aside in a stampede for the dance floor as the swaggering riff of 'What Difference Does It Make' shook the speakers.

Slammed against the bar, I had no option but to order another pint. It seemed I was staying to the lager end.

I'd barely grabbed my change (forty pence from a pound) when I felt an elbow in my ribs, and looked down. Nina. Crisply waiflike in a cream shift-dress and Timotei-girl hair, with sharp lenses encircling icy eyes.

'Thought I'd come out,' she said, leaning towards me slightly.

'Really? Warm in the closet?'

She frowned, not getting the joke, then leaned even further towards me and steadied herself on my arm. There was a beer stain down the front of her dress. I realized with old-fashioned shock that Nina was drunk. This was a shock, like finding your little sister out on the pull with her mates.

'Didn't expect to see you here!' I shouted jovially into her ear. I looked frantically through the smoke for Faith, and glimpsed her right over in the corner, screaming a black-lipped laugh with the bootleg Eldritches and the brazen Husseys. She was too far away.

'Wino!' shouted Nina, and made a little gurgling noise.

'Eh?' Was she calling *me* a pisshead?

'Wino? Why – no?' Nina was on me with both hands. She took another deep slurp from her plastic pint. 'Hey,' she said, tapping me on the shoulder, and then, right up against my face, 'Hey!'

'Yes? What?' Couldn't she tell I wanted to get rid of her, for Christ's sake?

'I'm *not* drunk, y'know. Always said I wou'n' drink. Y'know. Not good.'

'Not good,' I agreed. 'Nina, would you mind –'

'Yeah, c'mon!' She dashed her beaker on to the floor. It slopped out a fan of beer under three check-shirted engineering students. It crunched under a thick-soled DM as she dragged me through the sticky pond, down into the throbbing throng. The last place I wanted to be.

Hot bodies thrashed on all sides. Nina's arms gripped me as if she knew I wanted to escape. Smoke stung my eyes. Up above us, the vast fans hung suspended like modern-art mobiles, doing nothing. The sweat had grown beyond an odour into a sentient being, lurching from body to body in a slurping, pungent mass. It licked the mirrors at the back of the room. I imagined the fluids solidifying like cheese on the walls and glass, to be scraped off in the morning in lardy slices.

Nina, dancing with the abandon of the truly pissed, gazed up at me, grinning inanely. Her glasses filled with steam, blanking out her eyes. Now 'Teenage Kicks' thumped in. The song that made John Peel weep was making Nina throb. I danced awkwardly with her, but her bony arms were tightening around my back and her groin kept seeking mine.

I just wasn't drunk enough for this, and I tried to tell her. That didn't work, because she just pulled me back to the bar and dragged fragments of her life from a battered purse in her quest for a fiver.

Over her head, Tim from my tutorial group caught my eye and grinned. He thought I was lucky. I felt like pushing her in his direction. I couldn't leave her alone in this state, but the more I stayed with her, the more responsible for her I became.

So I ordered a double whisky and Coke. Twice.

Some time after that, I had to hoist her on to a seat at the edge of the room while not letting go of my own drink. I'm not quite sure how I managed that one. Her glasses slipped off, but we retrieved them, which set her off giggling again. 'Glass, glass,' she kept saying. 'Look, not plastic. Glass.'

The dance floor, spiked with demon-light, was a vision of hell. Boiling clouds lifted to the metal struts and swathed the inactive fans as if taunting them. The sounds grew louder: first the Beastie Boys, then early house stuff, eating up all other sounds with chomping bass lines.

'Come on,' I said to Nina, not really knowing where it would take us. 'I have to get you home in one piece.'

She just gave me a slack, soppy grin and tried to kiss me, but without really opening her mouth much, so that all I got was a faceful of teeth.

'Ni– Nina.' I gripped her shoulders and tried to look her in the eye, despite the fact that two meaty rugger-lads were towering over us and pouring Guinness into each other's trousers. 'What's the matter with you tonight?'

'Dinn . . . I say?'

I sighed. 'No. You definitely didn't say. I think I'd have remembered.'

'Oh.' She looked vaguely disappointed, searched for her hands for a moment (which involved dropping her glass) and pulled my head close to her mouth so that she could spit the answer in my ear. 'Iss my sisser. She . . .' Nina waved a hand as if that explained everything.

'Your sister?'

Next to us, the rugger-buggers were wringing out their soaking underpants into their mouths.

'Yeah.' Nina waggled her fingers and hiccuped. Oh, my God, I thought, she's going to puke right here, all over me, and I'm going to have to get someone to take her to the Ladies to clean her up and then I'll have to carry her back to her room and wash her dress and sit up with her to make sure she doesn't choke on it and −

'Died.'

'Sorry, what did you say?'

'She . . . died. Yessday. Threw 'self under a . . . train.'

'Jesus.' I realized this wasn't really an appropriate thing to say, in the circumstances. 'I mean − shit, I'm sorry . . . Why?'

Nina shrugged. 'They dunno,' she said. She sounded almost indifferent, but her face was dissolving in sweat and tears. She fell into me. She smelt of beer and lavender. Now she was sobbing into my arms with great slurping sniffs. 'No . . . idea . . . whhhy . . .'

I looked around anxiously as I held her, hoping that now, at last, Faith would come to my aid. But the room echoed to the thumps of bass and the screams of the hedonists. One of the lads was now on the table, bellowing loudly in delight as his mate poured Guinness over his exposed and glistening cock. The stench of beer and hot flesh swamped the room.

'Did you . . . go to the chaplain?' I asked her gently.

'No,' she said. 'Went to the pub.'

I sighed. Faith would have to wait. Time to get out of here. 'Come on,' I said. 'I'm going to take you home, and put you to bed.'

The Lower Bar thundered beneath our feet. Somehow, I got her up the twenty-two steps (I counted every one) to the main quad and supported her, my coat round her shoulders, as we staggered towards – where the hell was I going?

'Nina, I don't know where you live.'

'Baines building.' She pointed to the President's lodgings, realized her arm was in totally the wrong place, then lurched around to point over the Gardens wall at the new buildings. 'Room . . . fifteen.'

'That's great. Great. Okay now, take it slow . . .' The thudding bass had receded behind us and the February air was biting.

'Did you say . . . you *puttin'* me . . . bed . . . or *takin'*?' she demanded suddenly, with a broad grin, her eyes still full of glutinous tears.

I sighed. 'Nina, trust me, if I wanted to shag you, I doubt either of us would get much out of it. Comatose girls do so little for me.' We tottered a few more paces. I realized how awful I might have sounded. 'I mean, don't get me wrong, you're gorgeous.' Well, she was pretty, so I exaggerated for effect. Christ, I thought, I'm sad – the only man I know who'd lie to a woman in order to *avoid* sleeping with her. 'Anyway, you don't do that sort of thing, do you?'

'Oh, right.' She stood up straight, for the first time since leaving the bar. I blinked in surprise. 'You think . . . that means I haven't got needs? You think that . . . that 'cause I believe that this world, right, this . . .' She waved vaguely around her, swayed slightly and hung on to my arm. 'This whole galaxy, right, universe, whatever, what, what, *ever* . . . wasn't jus' chance, yeah –'

'Nina – come on –'

'– an', an' I know there's someone . . . *there* making it all *mean* something, and 'cause I believe that and I . . . *love* Jeee . . . Jeeeesus Christ, right . . . you think I've got nothing . . . there?'

Before I realized it she had grabbed my hand, then she was pulling it up inside her dress, making me feel her. I brushed against damp knickers before tugging my hand away as if it had been burnt. I was more angry than aroused.

'Nina, you're pissed. Just stop it, please!' She looked as if she was about to cry again. I put my hands on her shoulders. 'No, I don't think you're somehow . . . exempt from desire, I just . . . well . . .' I shrugged. 'I tend to assume you're all into promise-keeping and things . . . you know, sex is God's wedding present, and all that – shit –'

'Everything all right?' said a smooth voice from the shadows.

I turned round, blinking. I tasted the whisky grow rough and dry in my throat. Nina lurched against me again, gripping my shirt so hard that she pulled a button off.

It was Luke, fresh-scrubbed and bright-eyed. Somehow, that subdued toughness of his had never been so frightening. He raised his eyebrows at us both as he stepped forward, gently, his body all but hidden in his loose grey tracksuit. He had stepped from Staircase Two, and now he was framed in the light of its hallway, clenching and unclenching his fists.

'I think you'd better go, mate,' he said calmly to me.

Somehow, I fought down the urge to shout at him. 'Nina's very upset,' I said in a firm voice, very unlike my usual edgy, bantering tones. 'I'm just making sure she gets home okay.'

Luke bit his lip, nodded calmly. 'Sure,' he said. 'All the same, I think Nina needs to speak to me more than you. She's obviously having some problems right now.'

'Yes, and they won't be helped by you sitting up and reading the fucking Bible to her. So why don't you just back off?'

If Luke was shocked, he absorbed it well. A brief flicker of the eyelids, another knowing nod of the head. 'I can't let you do this, mate,' he said. 'It isn't right. It's sinful.'

And he actually put his arm on my elbow – clamping his fingers there with the hot force I'd suspected he could apply – and tried to drag me away from Nina. She squealed, clung to me desperately.

I was angry now. 'Luke, will you get *off*!'

'Shuddafuckup, will you?' shouted someone from a window high above us.

Now Nina lashed out herself, flailing an arm, making Luke step back in shock.

'Nina,' he began, and he stepped forward like a luminous phantom, his hand reaching for her again.

My instinct took over – if I had stopped to consider, I don't think I'd have dared touch him. I didn't shove him that hard – just enough to show I meant business. He lost his balance and fell against the door, crying out as he thumped his head on the wood.

Nina squealed, covering her mouth with both hands in a ridiculous Penelope Pitstop gesture.

Luke, his face screwed up in pain, was rubbing at the growing bruise on his forehead as he tried to sit up.

Satisfied that he wasn't too badly hurt, I pulled Nina back into the cold darkness. 'Come on,' I said. 'We need to get you home, come on.' Unsteadily, she let herself be steered by me.

Did I expect Luke to shout admonitions after us or to follow us? I can't say. But I glanced over my shoulder as we slipped through the gate to the Baines Building, and I saw him just standing there, a grey ghost. His breath shrouded him and his hands were folded neatly in front of him.

He was still and silent, watching us as we made our escape. I shivered, turned away and pulled the gate to with a satisfying clang.

I was glad to leave Nina sleeping, fully clothed, under her skimpy duvet.

I can't pretend it never crossed my mind to take advantage of her state. There was something curiously exciting about it all: the drunken caresses, the moist and half-baked dirty nothings she spluttered in my ear as we fumbled for her keys. I did momentarily consider slipping aside that fluid dress and investigating that pale, narrow-hipped body more closely.

I would have been a total shit, though. And shagging the bereaved brings sex a bit too close to death for my liking.

So I poured her a large glass of water and left, shutting the door gently behind me.

The morning was sharp, too bright. In the kitchen, I heated up some milk for coffee. As I watched the early wanderers, the boiling milk slurped over the rim and hissed and crisped on the ring.

I swore, filled the cup with as much as I could. I was still trying to scrub the burnt milk from the pan when Faith, panda-eyed and wild-haired, nudged the door, sauntered in and planted a sisterly kiss on my cheek. She filled a glass from the sink. She was swathed in a black satin wrap and reeked deliciously of last night's sex and smoke.

'Good night, then?' I asked her sullenly.

She sipped and swivelled, then swept her hair back, releasing even more desirable odours. 'Fucking top night. Got laid.' She flashed me a ghost-white grin. 'You?'

I scrubbed furiously. The milk skin started to rip from its metal housing. 'Nothing so exciting. I got into a theological argument.'

'Oh.' Faith shrugged. Nothing seemed to surprise her. She tilted her head back, gargled proudly with the water before swallowing. 'We've got some great stuff coming up with the band,' she offered. 'You don't know any deaf dancers, do you?'

'Faith, what are you talking about?' I scrubbed at the last, most obstinate milk scar. I had charred fragments of milk under my fingernails.

'We want these two girls in black, right, doing sign-language in synch with the words of the songs. Like a dance. It's totally mind-blowing. I dunno why no one's thought of it before.' She yawned. 'You 'right?' she asked, leaning on the draining-board.

'Oh, I'm just fine,' I said, slamming the almost-clean pan down next to her. 'Don't worry about me.'

I thumped back to my room, kicked the bin hard against the wall and smashed Joy Division at the ceiling for forty-five minutes.

05 God Machine

Drip, drip, drip.

The spike of water is trying to pierce the steel bucket. It slices our life, spears our air. A line of interference on the screen of the lounge.

I stand, hands on hips, watching the water, thinking about something else entirely. When it's not raining, the hole in our roof doesn't seem to matter, so we keep putting off the job. A colleague of Tanya's knows someone whose brother is a builder, and has said he will do it for us at a fair price. We're still trying to get hold of him.

'What can we do about it?' I wonder aloud.

'Go up into the loft and mend it,' she suggests. She turns on to her side, catching streams of light in her blue satin blouse, and props herself up on one elbow. I look over at Tanya, see the edges of her mouth quiver, and realize she might be joking. 'Or you could come over here and ravish me senseless,' she suggests, folding up her glasses with a smile.

She's been reading one of those features again, I can tell. I'll go mad if I see another women's magazine article with an X-pun in the title, like 'The Sex-Files: How Do You Rate In Bed?' or 'The Ex-Files: Do You Keep Running Back To Him?' (I could do some for them: 'The Kex-Files: Twenty Top Trousers' or 'The Bex-Files: Life As A Woman Called Becky'.)

She puts her glasses on the small table, next to her half-finished tumbler of Australian wine. If it's still there in the morning, I know I'll reclaim it. The difference between the well-off and the just-nicely-enough-off: both buy quality wine from Safeway, but the latter only get it at the weekend and, faced with a half-finished glass, will decant it back into the bottle.

She smiles again, shrugs. 'Just an offer,' she says.

'Yeah, well. I ought to take another look at those costings for Hope

Springs . . . Did I tell you we need at least another twenty grand?'

'This is the new job definition of part-time, right? You want to be there every day and night. Come on, you're the boss.'

'Senior project –'

'All right –'

'– development wor–'

'Whatever –'

'–ker. Get it right.'

She stretches out. 'Have some time off.' She starts to unbutton her blouse. 'Passionate leave.'

'Tanya, this is the nineties, and moreover, this is Britain. We don't get time off.'

'You'll get . . . *einen Schlag*.' She flaps a hand, wanting the word. Her English frequencies always fade as the night draws in, like the World Service on long wave.

'A stroke? Yeah, right. And a heart attack, and cancer, and stomach ulcers. Anything else I should know?'

'Yes,' she snaps. 'I love you, stupid.'

'I know.'

Earlier today. I gawp into my mind and see rosé albino eyes behind glass of cupric blue. The sun daubs a halo on hospital-white hair.

I brood on Mike Bradfield's surliness and that weird altercation at the church. On the mobile, I've called Charlie several times and left a message, but he's not got back to me. Well, there's someone else I can ask.

I'm sitting in the car, beneath a cadaverous tower-block on the outskirts of Basildon. I have a visit to make.

'I could put some sandbags up in the loft,' I suggest half-heartedly. 'It might keep most of it out.'

Tanya looks up, as if thinking, then smiles and says, 'Is that what you call damming with faint praise?'

Clap-stomp. She's done it again.

'What did you get up to today, anyway?' she asks, turning another page.

'Just some accounts. Boring stuff.'

★

At first, I think I must have the wrong place. It can't be here. But I check the address, as two cropped and denimed boys, sitting on a spattered street name, eye me with unashamed hostility.

Inside, the lobby reeks of old plastic, wet wood and urine. I look up, up, into a great whirlpool of steps. I can imagine the teenagers gleefully wobbling atop the highest banister and unleashing hot, pungent golden jets down the great pisshole of the stairwell.

I make my way over to the lift, which is thick with graffiti, a metal palimpsest. The coloured layers overlap, shrieking their messages from hip-hop and grunge, time-tunnelling back, no doubt, to the permapaint of punk several strata below. I press the call button. The indicator lights up – as if the lift's raising its eyebrows in surprise – and the mechanism starts to clunk and churn to itself.

'No expense spared,' I mutter softly. The words curl and drift upwards, meeting the lift as it comes crashing down through its ancient shaft.

The doors roll open with a sepulchral grinding. Inside, the lift is scattered with debris – half-chewed hamburgers, abandoned bottles of Hooch. As well as smelling like a dustbin that a cat's pissed in, it's letting in chinks of light from outside.

Not a good move, this, I reflect gloomily. It begins to take me higher, creaking upwards like a machine for reaching God.

Clunk, whine, churn.

Tanya strolls in from her shower, wrapped and turbaned in soft white towel. She looks at the drips, sighs, rolls on to her back again and flips her specs on. She's having a desultory flick through the university's evening-class brochure.

She's one of those women who were just born to be bespectacled, with a look that perfectly combines the sensual and the bookish. I have a thing about beautiful women in glasses, actually, a secret fetish. We're not talking thick NHS-style beaker-bottoms here. We're talking crisp, glossy harmony. ('The Spex Files! Twenty Gorgeous Women in Glasses!') It adds to her coolness, her level-headedness, her . . . stuff that makes her different from Faith. That is important.

Tanya and I used to be just flat-mates. I moved in sometime in late 96, before . . . Well, before. She was temping for solicitors, I was on supply to a lecturing agency while getting involved in the embryo

Hope Springs project. Something seemed to happen, then, and we just went with it – shy flirtation, late-night conversations, lots of refilled glasses, especially on the general-election night. I first kissed her when she got the EmTrak job in mid-May, and we ended up in bed twenty minutes later.

By a process of osmosis, the flat became a shared one, my possessions expanding, creeping into corners and mating with hers. Our clothes nuzzled in the wardrobe, snuggled in the laundry basket. It was done. That was a few months ago now.

She turns the page, glances up.

Plumck! says the bucket.

'How about glass painting?' she asks me, her tone viscous with boredom. 'I could do that.'

I take a breath, wanting to talk to her, to tell her how my thoughts have been sloshing around – stuff about Faith's funeral and Mike and Luke and the albino girl – but she's off at a tangent. I sit beside her, stroking her reddened and pliable legs. 'Yeah, if you like.'

Loike! says the bucket.

'Or patchwork,' she says. 'I have always wanted to do patchwork.'

Woik! says the bucket.

'Support groups,' says Tanya, who seems oblivious now to the gentle pressure of my hand on her bath-softened thigh. 'Look at all of these,' she says, waving a cluttered page at me. 'Bereavement, post-natal . . .' She flips the page. 'Anorexia, bulimia . . . My God, they meet on the same night . . . Dyslexia! That is such a *cruel* word. Why couldn't they find one that was easier to spell?'

'Yeah, there was a problem with that one last year,' I tell her, recalling one of my meetings with the tutors. 'The class was on Tuesday and half of them turned up on Thursday.'

Tanya tut-tuts to herself – maybe she thinks this is a joke. Suddenly, though, she flings the brochure across the room (it cuts through the water, scattering spray for a second) and settles back on the sofa. 'I am bored, veeery bored,' she says. 'Why do you not see all your old friends much? They seem, well, a good laugh.'

She has met them all once – at a funeral – and thinks they seem a good laugh? I'm not in the mood for this. 'I don't know,' I say, sounding angrier than I intend to. 'You seem to like them so much, you go out with them.'

'Oh, I see,' she says, picking up her magazine again. 'Don't tell me, it's not the same now that *she* is not around.'

I've not really noticed before, but Tanya has never referred to Faith by name. Never. 'I'm not going to bother answering that,' I tell her crossly.

'I'm sure you're not. It might involve talking about us, after all.'

(Oh, dear.) 'Do you want to? Talk about us, I mean?'

'Not especially.'

'Well, there we are, then. Everybody's happy.' I kick my way into the kitchen and start spooning coffee into the percolator.

Tanya flips her magazine shut. 'I'm tired,' she says. 'I have an eight-a.m. meeting, so I'm going to dry my hair and go to bed, Okay?'

'Yeah, whatever.'

She leans on the worktop between the lounge and the kitchen, eyeing me from under her fluffy towel. 'Look, I'm thirty-three,' she says. 'Older than you. We don't get younger by living in the past. It just stretches us more, so we get thinner and thinner and then –' She claps her hands. 'Paf!'

'Does this have a point?' I ask.

'Just, please, get your act together. I won't be here for ever.'

I don't answer this obvious prompt. She sashays across the lounge into the bedroom, leaving me alone in the stark kitchen.

Thinking about this morning.

I get out at floor fourteen, and step tentatively on to the landing as if expecting it to shatter beneath me. Flat 144 is a flaky blue door in the corner. There's no bell, so I knock, lightly at first, and then harder. I realize that my thumps are echoing up and down the stairwell, and I step back, guiltily rubbing my tingling knuckles.

There's a rattle of chain behind me and I spin round. The flat opposite cracks open. Startled eyes stare from about five feet up. I think I can see strands of strawberry-red hair, but it's hard to make anything out in the shadows. I can't even tell what age or gender I'm looking at.

'He's not in,' says the voice. From within the flat, odours emerge: the rich, alive smell of baking, mixed with the seaweedy pungency of a nappy.

'Ah. Right.' I hold my hands up, palms outwards, as if surrendering. 'Any idea when he'll be back?'

'Nah.' I hear saliva click as something soft is passed from one side of its mouth to the other.

The door is about to close. Somewhat unwisely, I slip over and shove my foot in the crack. Spit whooshes from behind the chain – it zings off the chain and sieves itself across my cheek.

'Fuckin' leave off,' snarls my new friend. 'You fuckin' touch me an' I'm callin' the police, right?'

'Look,' I say calmly, fishing out my handkerchief to wipe my face, 'there's no need for that. I just wondered if . . .' What do I wonder? What information can I possibly glean here? 'Does he . . . own the flat?' I ask after a second or two.

Eyes flick up, then down, pointedly, at my foot in the door, and I remove it. 'What's it to you?'

Well, quite. What, indeed, is it to me? I suppose anyone's got a right to ask. 'I'm just curious.'

'Think he rents. Anyway, he's a fuckin' weirdo. You a friend of his?'

'In a way.'

'Well, do me a favour, then. Tell him to keep his nose in his own business, right?'

And the door slams shut in my face.

The terminal flashes and chugs in the corner of the lounge.

Faith used to plunge into the Internet for the pearls she knew she could find. There was a period, around 94 or 95, when her on-line time exceeded her real-life time. I knew things had got serious when she got one of those laptops with a modem attachment and started bringing it out with her. According to Charlie, they'd be sitting there, having a cream tea in Bath or somewhere, and Faith, her handbag bulging, would excuse herself to go and squat in the Ladies, frog-eyed, snorting cyberspace. Weird.

I, on the other hand, like to examine the odd nugget – George Harrison died years ago and has been replaced by a Mexican actor ever since, that sort of thing – and usually leave it there.

As Tanya brushes her teeth, I am riveted by possibly one of the saddest virtual spaces of all, the newsgroup known as `rec.music.tori-amos`. Now, I'm not exactly immune to the obvious charms of the flame-haired songstress. She has a delicious voice, especially on the more minimalist tracks of her first album, *Little Earthquakes*. The denizens of this newsgroup, though – largely male students, I'd guess – are diehard Tori voters. Back to basics. In a thread proudly entitled `Tori's philosophy`, we have this from `xraven@aol.com`, who writes:

```
yes tori is a great philosopher it seems to me. her school
is the human condition. she talks of taking control of
your destiny and finding your own center of power.
```

Fairly harmless stuff – if a little wanky (after all, if Tori had buck-teeth, lardy hair and a face like a wallful of woodchip, there might be more reluctance to interpret her *oeuvre* with such intensity). Elsewhere, among the discussions about the various remixes of 'Professional Widow' and how easily redheads burn in the sun, things get a bit worrying – for example, the message from one `doug@ixx.nettcom.com`:

```
If you were able to go back in time and save Tori from being
raped, all the while knowing that she will stay in the band
Y Kant Tori Read and never become famous or write the songs
we love, would you do it?
```

A wealth of frightening assumptions in there. And then there's the thread entitled `What if Tori died?` The latest contribution, from the esteemed `rjons1@chem.susx.ac.uk`, tells us:

```
hey ive never realy though about that before. i mean it
happens doesnt it? freddy mercurie, sid viscous and them.
i think id just give up living i mean throw myself under a
train or something because tori is the lifegiver and
without her there is no life.
```

Ah, Sid Viscous – that little-known punk who used too much hair gel. Even more disturbingly, from `03tomz@cua.edu`, comes this:

```
I would have to become a serial killer. If she were dead,
all my actions would be essentially meaningless anyway. I
would target fragile auburn beauties and allow them to die
nobly and beautifully before age withered them.
```

I shiver, and log off.

Downstairs, I can't sleep. I arm myself with toast and Irish coffee, ready for a surf through the astral channels. A bit of a song jangles in my head: something about seeing the light, and God buying you a satellite.

The rain thrums on our roof, hard as marbles. The screen paints the thread of water electric blue, like a laser cutting the bucket. There's an old *Top of the Pops*, with the Human League from 1982: Phil, Sporty Human and Posh Human doing 'Don't You Want Me?' with super-stiff haircuts.

Rain, and marbles, and the darkness of her eyes. The bone-white of her smile. And the faces of Mike and Luke.

I flick to CNN, where an American general is saying, '– a hostel mistle, and resistance is feudal –'

When I close my eyes, I see the albino again, in negative.

I think back to this morning.

I hang around on the landing for a minute or two, but I'm imagining eyes behind spy-holes, watching me and deciding how best to dispose of me. In the end, I decide to head back to the lift before I end up in a casserole.

There's no response from the call button. I press again. And again and again. Oh, brilliant. I've got to walk down fourteen flights. Here we go, then. I hold my breath and begin the descent through the stinking stairwell.

My feet clatter faster as the ground gets nearer, and at about floor 6, I encounter a frizzy-permed girl struggling upstairs. She's got a lugubrious sprog under one arm, a pushchair and, tailing behind, a sullen girl of about four in faded dungarees.

I step aside to let the woman come up, but she doesn't acknowledge me as she goes past.

'Would you like a hand with that?' I ask her.

She glances briefly behind her, doesn't even look me in the eye. The little girl trudges listlessly past me up the steps.

'Tracy, come *on*!' snarls the mother.

The girl shows no signs of acceleration. She's more interested in looking round at me.

'Tracy! Get 'ere!'

In one swift movement, the mother drops the pushchair, parks the baby on the landing and grabs the girl's hand to haul her upstairs faster than her legs can really manage. She grabs her by the shoulders and shakes her. 'I! Told! You! To get! A fuckin! *Move* on!'

And in a sudden, splintering moment, the mother swings back her arm and whacks her hand right across the little girl's face, with a sound like a ruler on paper.

I'm biting my tongue. My dry mouth fills with a meaty, salty taste. The girl's howls are tearing the building down, great banshee wails of millennial agony coiling around the stairwell as she is dragged up, up into whatever awaits her above. The last thing I see is her scrunched and scarlet face, soaked in tears, shimmering between the stairs above as if viewed through a stroboscope. There's a slam, and the sounds abruptly cease.

I'm shaking. What could I have done?

As I wander, dazed, back to the car, I'm aware of small, ridiculous details. The embossing on a cigarette packet that squashes beneath my feet. The marks on the sign saying Riverview Flats, and the crack running right through the 'a'. A bin frothing with rubbish in front of a curry house called the *Indian Star*.

Breathing heavily, I seal myself back inside the car. I slump on the steering-wheel in the shadow of that monstrosity. And I see a bruise on soft skin, first an angry red, then hard and dark, and turning as the days go by to an evil mustard yellow.

That crack. That sound of the hard hand on the soft flesh, of *marking* flesh. It always reminds me just how fragile the body is. We're like nectarines. We can be crushed underfoot. This tiny fragment of my life suddenly becomes washed up in a huge tide of sadness, a sadness as cold and as old as glaciers.

And I sit there in the car and I realize that I'm choking on a great, ugly gobbet of tears, forcing my face open, everywhere, twisting it into a cartoon of itself. I flip the visor down and blink at the car floor, hoping the ambling pensioners won't look at me. Salt water washes my face, tearing it apart. My hand is over my mouth and I'm gnawing at the skin of my fingers, tasting it.

All around us, says the voice of Luke in my head, *there is destruction, devastation and the evil of man. We have to be strong, trust in God. Never lose faith.*

★

Half sleeping now, drenched in the television's spectral light. Voices scrabble in my head. The day's leftovers refried, hissing in a pan of TV static.

'I won't be here for ever,' Tanya said.

Not you as well.

Watch out, life is saying. You could fuck up Chance no. 2 as well. You could fuck up just as easily as you did last time.

In the end, I leave a note in the mail-box to say that I came to see him. I think he will be surprised to receive it. I don't imagine Luke ever expected I, of all people, would seek him out.

To die nobly and beautifully before age withered them.

An image. Heat. Searing, sweaty heat in every pore, and dust dancing in the sunlight. Time seems to slow. Shards of glass. Unfolding, dancing in the light. And glass marbles. Cascading. Across. The floor. Faster now, they clatter, bounce from every wall, roll into every corner, twinkling as they are liberated.

The warble of the phone cuts my half-sleep. I realize I'm slumped on the sofa in front of a black-and-white film, some Ealing comedy or other.

I grab the receiver. Its slippery body wriggles out of my hands and I have to lean over to retrieve it from the floor, grunting in exertion.

'Hello?' I manage to gasp.

'Hello, are you all right?' says a man's voice. 'Sounds like you were having a bit of a fight. It's Charles here, by the way.'

'Charlie, hi. I've been trying –'

'To get in touch, I know. Sorry about that. Been awfully busy.' His voice is unnaturally perky, the aural equivalent of an argon strip light. 'So, how are things?'

'Not so bad.' I tell him about the leaky roof and he's as sympathetic as most people have been. I steer him away from it. 'Charlie, I'm really, *really* sorry about being . . . ill at the funeral. I think it must have been the heat.'

'Listen, old man, it's really not a problem. It's been a terrible time for all of us. I mean, people understand, you know, that sort of thing. They know you must be upset.'

Yeah, but that's the thing, says my wicked inner voice, *I'm not, am I?*

'I'm on some medication, actually.' Lying seems to come naturally over the phone. 'Pizotifen. For migraines. Shouldn't drink with it.'

'I see.' He says it neutrally, but I'm glad I can't see his face. Before I can ask him anything, he's saying, 'Listen, Faith had some stuff here, things from college. A whole wardrobe of rubbish. We've only just got round to clearing it out. I don't suppose you . . . well, want anything?'

The question catches me off-guard so much that I'm not sure how to answer it. 'Um . . . I . . .'

'I've been meaning to mention it to all the Oxford crowd, but to be honest, you're the only one I've really spoken to since Gervizan, and . . . you seem appropriate, somehow.' He pauses, and I can picture his long, serious face. 'You were . . . close to her,' he ventures.

'Well, thanks. I might just take you up on that.' After all, it might give me a chance to ask a question or two. 'When would you like me to come?'

Charles shakes my hand. He looks a little more bright-eyed than on the day of the funeral, but he's edged in a haze of stubble and a mohair jumper, as if a cartoonist has scribbled shading on him and gone over the edges.

'Drink?' he says.

'Uhh . . . yeah, cup of tea, please, Charlie.'

'Oh. Right.' He lifts a finger in acknowledgement, turning away from his oak drinks cabinet. 'Of course. The migraines.'

'Right.' I nod fervently, pleased to have covered myself without really intending to.

Charlie and Jan have a smart seven-bedroom Tudor stack near Chichester, just two miles from the cemetery where Faith lies buried. This was her home before she got her flat in Rochester for work. Charlie, I knew, was only too pleased to have his cousin around, but Jan the Hellcat, his wife of six years now, had made no secret of her dislike for Faith.

The lounge strikes you as you come up the drive: a glinting green jewel, embedded in the front of the house. Inside, it's a lavender-scented palace of emerald silk, jade velvet and deep carpets, drenched with light from the great bay window. Terracotta vases and an ochre rug give a warm feel. Chunky brown wood is everywhere: a mahogany long-case clock; a beechwood barometer; pine bookshelves, packed with the eclectic, multi-coloured choice of the serious reader.

'So how are you?' I ask, as he brings my tea in an earthenware mug.

He sighs, shrugs. 'You really want to know?'

'Sorry?'

'It's just that people always ask. How one is. Every day. You tend to get the idea that they don't really want to know. They want you to smile bravely and say, "Oh, fine", so that they can move on to something else.'

I take a sip of my tea. 'No, I . . . really do want to know,' I venture.

'Well . . .' He looks up briefly, smiles in gratitude. 'Good days and bad days, to be honest. Sometimes I feel I'm just getting used to the idea. I look at her picture and think of her as someone who's missed, gone, you know? I feel I'm dealing with it.' He has his hands in his lap, and I can see that he's working loose a fingernail. 'And then there's the days when this house seems so quiet without her. And I come across something of hers, or I see something in the paper that would interest her, and . . .' He gives a sort of jittery little shrug, meets my gaze for a second. 'There's no one to tell.'

'It must be hard. I suppose she's been like a sister to you.'

He nods, almost absently. I think we both have a sense of conversing in a sort of safety zone, avoiding certain areas by unspoken agreement. 'Anyway,' he says, 'that's partly why I want to get rid of some of this stuff. I was talking –' He pauses, scratches his ear and shakes his head, as if he has decided to say something else. 'Well, anyway. What I said on the phone. Hang on there.'

He's off again, leaving me in the strange soft silence of the lounge, and comes back a few minutes later carrying a large wooden box. I start to clear a space on the nearest occasional table, but he shakes his head, quickly.

'No, no. Jan'll go mad.'

'Ah. Well. We can't have that.' He can't miss the edge in my voice. 'And how is Jan?' I ask carefully.

'Out shopping,' he answers.

Deliberately evasive. That's good. We have an unspoken agreement, then, and politeness has been satisfied. That says a lot about Jan, actually – she's one of those people about whom it's safer to say what they are *doing* than how they are *behaving*.

Charlie, having placed the box on the floor, perches himself on the edge of the sofa. 'Are you okay with this?' he asks.

I shrug. 'Fine.'

The box smells musty. There are about thirty paperbacks: translations of Icelandic sagas and the Brothers Grimm, a few academic booklets and some novels, both nineteenth-century and recent. Rummaging under the books, we find some scrappy notes for academic articles: some stuff on the rise of vampire mythology, a half-page about some recent Hoffmann criticism. There's also a battered travel clock which I recognize, a dusty copy of our matriculation photo – scrubbed, innocent faces in a sea of black-and-white subfusc – and the Michaelmas 89 copy of the college scandal-sheet. As I remember, the latter had all sorts of uncomplimentary things to say about Faith (pretentious, narcissistic and shallow), Mike (loud, trendy-leftie, bad shave) and myself (vacillating, politically incorrect, crap at table-football: sins which I'd happily admit).

Underneath that, there's a Newton's Cradle, which works perfectly well once we have untangled it, a C90 tape of Northern Soul tunes cheerfully annotated in purple felt-tip, a small silver key which doesn't appear to belong to anything, and a bank-bag with a bit of Swiss currency. Shoved down the side of the box are two plain envelopes which seem to be old bank statements.

'Amazing, isn't it?' Charlie says. 'Imagine we didn't know anything about Faith and we had to deduce it all from the stuff she'd left behind. I mean . . . you'd be able to build up a sort of picture, but it would never be . . . exactly right. Anyway, take anything you want. I'm probably going to have to throw most of this out, except I might give the books to a charity shop or something.'

'I'll do that for you,' I offer, perhaps rather too quickly. 'Yeah, in fact, look, I'll take the whole lot off your hands. Let you get on with other things.' I lob him the bag of Swiss currency. 'Keep that, though, you might want it for a holiday.'

'Up to you.' He smiles sadly as he jingles the money in his hand.

I examine the silver key. 'Any idea what this is for?'

'No, it's a bit of a mystery. Actually . . .' He glances at the floor for a second, and I know straight away that there is something he needs to tell me.

'Yes?' I prompt.

'That was . . . with Faith's . . . rings and her necklace. The undertaker . . . had them stored safely for me.'

I digest the information. 'The key was on her body,' I translate.

He nods, quickly, glancing up and then looking away again.

'I see.' I'm sure this information should be important, but right now I can't see how. I put my mug down and shift my position on the disgracefully comfortable sofa. 'Was there a bit of a problem, you know, about Faith's . . . arrangements? It's just that I didn't recognize those guys carrying the coffin.'

He sighs, leans back with his hands behind his head and closes his eyes. 'It was one of those things,' he says. 'They were professional mourners.'

'So . . .'

'Faith left instructions with the church, and with me, that she didn't want any big fuss made with her friends carrying her down the aisle. Didn't think it was appropriate.'

'Instructions?' My curiosity perks up and starts panting like an eager little dog. 'You mean she had . . . a written thing?'

'Look . . .' Charlie leans forward, rubbing his fingers together in slight nervousness. 'We . . . had an understanding. With each other. We'd talked about it, you know. A while back – when was it – a year ago? Yes, about a year. Faith came to me and said it might be a good idea if we wrote out wills and funeral arrangements, just to be safe, just so as we'd know what we wanted on the day.'

'Really?' I frowned. 'Was this out of the blue?'

'I imagine it'd been preying on her mind ever since she got a job and everything. After what happened with her parents – well, it was a complete mess, to be honest. They died young, didn't leave wishes or instructions . . . Faith said she didn't want me lumbered with anything like that.' Charlie shrugged. 'That's it, basically. Luke and Mike wanted to help . . . carry her, and I had to refuse. Faith's wishes had to come first.'

'Seems a bit . . .' I shivered slightly. 'She didn't have . . . I mean . . . some idea that she was *going* to die, did she?'

White sheets of heat crash into my mind. Marbles scatter, glass shatters. A pale hand reaches up through the devastation. I close my eyes and the flash fades.

Charlie's voice is booming in a cavern. 'Believe me, if she had, she would have told me. I loved her. As you said, she was like a sister. More.' He met my gaze, opening his grey eyes wide. 'You loved her yourself, once.'

'Yeah, well.' I could feel my face scalding with shame.

'Are you all right?' he asks. 'I mean, you're . . . sure you don't mind talking about her? It's just that you seem a bit uncomfortable.'

Don't do that, don't say that, for Christ's sake! Be English, have tea and be repressed and chuckle nervously. Don't don't don't start to go all fucking emotional on me or I might end up letting it *out*, being here for hours hours hours, time ticking away in the long-case clock as the colours warm outside and darken to greyish-purple and we end up hugging . . . I shake my head to clear the rush of images.

'Faith's gone,' I say calmly. 'But we'll remember her. As long as others are here, she'll always be here.'

He seems quite pleased I've said this.

Before long, I start to make departing noises. I thank him for the box of stuff, and finish off my tea, saying I really must be going.

On the doorstep, we exchange subdued, sympathetic sounds. It's back to a typically British conversation of avoidance, thank God.

He shakes my hand again, and waves as I drive off.

For some reason, I feel the urge to stop at a country pub and look through the stuff again. I shiver slightly as I think of the molecules of her skin which must still be clinging to the objects. Sipping my half of lager at a wooden table, I try to decide what to do with it all.

I drive into Chichester and give all the books to a Help the Aged, as I've read most of them and they're a bit tatty. The travel clock and the Newton's Cradle also end up at a charity shop, as they both still seem to work. Back in the Pay and Display, I put the matriculation photo and the notes inside the magazine and shove them in the glove-box. The Northern Soul compilation goes in too, as it's got a Judy Street song on it which I like.

The key is a bit of a puzzle, as there's nothing to indicate what sort of lock it might be for. I peer at it closely. There's a number – 242 – embossed on it. I open my wallet and slip the key in with the change.

I'm about to chuck the bank statements in a bin, but curiosity gets the better of me. They're both still sealed. Surprisingly, they're not that old after all. One of them details the transactions up to about a week before Faith's death. I tear open the other one with a sigh. It carries on where the first one left off, listing credits and debits right up to the end of last month.

It's a second or two before this properly sinks in. I look again, just to be sure I haven't got the dates muddled in my own head. No. For a full two weeks when Faith was dead – *dead* – there are withdrawals listed.

I can hear my heart pounding. I look up, staring at the world outside my windscreen, cars and pedestrians coming and going in a blissful ignorance.

Some of the debits are cheques – fair enough, as they can take a while to clear, but there are others. Three debits from stores, clearly marked: a Waterstone's, a Safeway and somewhere called 'Parsons Chm PLC'. Also, there is a cashpoint withdrawal of fifty pounds – dated three days after her death – and another of a hundred pounds, from six days after that.

Very carefully, with my hands shaking, I place the bank statements in the glove-box with the other things.

I drive, on auto-pilot, out of town. The road signs, blue and white, seem written in alien hieroglyphics. On the motorway, a light drizzle begins, and by the time I reach the outskirts of town, it's turned into a great, hammering onslaught of rain.

Finally home, I park the car in the ground-level garage and get soaked running up the clanging back stairs. In the flat, Tanya is in bed, half asleep. I nuzzle a kiss to say hello, and she stirs slightly.

'Hello,' she murmurs, vague from sleep. 'You have been out all day?'

'Yeah, you know. Stuff to do.' My heart is pounding so hard I'm sure she must be able to hear it, shaking the walls of the house.

'You and your stuff,' she mutters, not unkindly, before pulling the duvet back over her head.

In the kitchen, I see that she's scrawled a note on my memo-board: *We need to talk, soon.* The plopping of the water in the bucket pulses through the house like a wet heartbeat.

I make myself some strong coffee and dim the lights in the lounge.

I put Massive Attack on the CD and plug in the headphones. Twice I start to dial Charlie's number, and twice I throw the phone aside. 'Unfinished Sympathy' swamps the sounds of the world disintegrating. Bank-balance figures jump in front of my eyes, curvy 3s and spiky 4s and bouncy 8s, all laughing at me.

Sleep creeps up on me like living darkness, chewing away at the caffeine. I'm gone. Gone.

06 She Bangs the Drums

My epiphany. It came two years after leaving school with a pair of decent A levels: the realization that I hated my life, despised the functional Social Security office where I worked, ached to leave the forgotten town where I had grown up.

I packed in the job. Some people thought this was utter madness, at that time, in the bleak midwinter of the Second Thatcher Republic. I started working evenings in a bar, just so as not to starve while I got my life together. I soon did. I dusted off my two A-level certificates, took a couple more in a windswept and creaking FE college.

Then came the crunch: I found myself, on the advice of Ed, a young college lecturer straight out of university and not much older than me, applying to read English at Oxford. I had to put it first on the form, but I honestly didn't hold out much hope, imagining that European Studies at the local poly sounded more my thing.

But stuff started to go right. I could do this. Ed talked me through the usual prejudices and convinced me that the place liked a wide variety of people. I applied, on Ed's advice, through Mode E, the old entrance-exam format which they've scrapped these days, and Ed advised me on which three colleges to choose and how to rank them. I got an interview in December 86, and heard three weeks later that I had a place, to start the following October.

It sounds simple, but I've conflated that extraordinary time in my mind. Compared with what came later, it seems like child's play now.

'Thangvery mush,' growled Faith. 'We've been deVice, you've been . . . *good*. Night.'

A crashing curtain of blackness. Whooping, applause and whistles shook the room. A tide of stamping began at the front, and gradually spread back through the sweaty audience. Within seconds, about a hundred feet were shaking the old, beer-stained floorboards and I was convinced we'd crash through to the pub below.

I looked around. Well, there was no way I'd escape before the encore, as I was rammed between a padded biker shoulder on one side and a glutinous wall on the other. We all breathed each other's stale second-hand air; heat gripped the room, tight as a rubber glove. It was easy to forget it was a cold January day outside.

Mike was somewhere behind me, leaning against the back with his Socialist Worker pals in his usual fake-detached way. Right next to me was the door to the Gents, so every few seconds I would be jostled by bodies and swamped by pungent stenches. Still, I suppose it was worth it.

It was our second year: Faith's band were quite big news in Oxford now. They had toyed with a number of names: Sunkissed, Twist, Toast, Blag, Coxuk (seriously), Batter, the Incandescents, Canned Essence, Indecency, Indie Sense (ugh), Imp, Pimp, Pump, Plump, Revel, Devil, Bevel, Swivel, and even, in one gloriously deluded moment, Auburn Party Featuring Polly Titian. (I thought that was the best one.) They even thought about Dazzle, which to me sounded like a seventies glam-rock band or a porn mag, and not a fitting moniker for purveyors of post-metallic, industrially melodic techno-goth-rock. However, they were now deVice. She insisted on the small d, which I found a bit pretentious.

They'd got themselves some dancers, which certainly caused a stir – Rosie and Carla, two sleek, ghostly girls in mini-dresses and mirror-shades, drama students from the poly who mimed every line in harmonized sign-language, but otherwise didn't move. It was unnerving to see them standing immobile, hands on hips, during Andy's string-snapping solos. Must have taken some practice.

'Sorry, mate,' said someone next to me, as he squelched through the gap and almost sloshed his pint over me. I smiled indulgently and stuck even harder against the wall.

The stamps and cheers reached a peak as the spotlights blazed and they reappeared for the expected encore. First Faith, bewitchingly wild-haired, followed by the dancers, Andy the bald guitarist, Sunil the goatee-bearded bassist, and the ash-blonde Annalise on keyboards. There was no drummer, but in true *Spinal Tap* style, they'd got through a couple. Their first suffered a nervous breakdown at the onset of his prelim exams, while the second quit after Faith, stoned and hungry, had scoffed a prawn takeaway with the aid of his drumsticks. A drum-machine – called Claude – had been brought in temporarily, and they kept it when they realized it didn't need feeding or paying, wasn't likely to roll up to rehearsals blind drunk, and actually sounded quite good.

They'd started as a Goth covers band but soon, inspired perhaps by Claude's contribution, they'd begun to slip the odd sample in, to bounce spiky breakbeats through the middle of songs and indulge Andy's more funk-orientated flights of fancy. In the space of a few weeks, they transformed. They lost a few of Faith's hangers-on – but, while they might once have made do with an audience of three pale sixth-formers and a dribbling tramp somewhere in Cowley, they now played to heaving bar-room floors in the centre of Oxford.

'S'great to see . . . so many of you,' Faith murmured. She was doing her usual pose – hands behind her back, swivelling on one heel. As always, she had the mike just above head height so she had to lean *up* to it. I didn't get this, but it was her quirk, and people remembered it. Maybe because they got a better view of her cleavage.

With a roar, several glasses were held aloft from the throng. The raucous, check-shirted guys at the front had been heckling Faith all night, but she'd given as good as she got.

'Play fuckin' "Desolation"!' yelled one of them. I shivered slightly at this – it was weird to think there were people in the city who not only paid to see Faith's band, but knew the *titles* of her songs. It was a short hop from here to stalkerdom, Hinckley and Chapman territory.

'So, ah, I'd just like to thank you . . . for coming,' she continued, undeterred, and practically licked the mike as she breathed the last word. The three hecklers punched the air in delight, and I groaned into my beer.

'Show us yer tits!' bellowed someone from the darkness, and there was a ripple of laughter.

'Later, little boy,' Faith snarled, which probably caused the already meteoric testosterone levels in the front three rows to go off the scale. 'We're gonna get off now, but, ah . . .'

They were off again, two of them singing in unison. 'Sheeeee – ain't got no kniiiii-*ckers*!'

Faith looked down at them with a mixture of pity and contempt, and pointed straight at them. 'You! Uh-huh, yeah, talking to *you*, fucking big-mouth. What's your name?'

The ringleader giggled into his pint, but, obviously enjoying the attention, shouted back, 'Terence Fotherington-Smythe!' His friends chortled, as he chose to add: 'Written on me dick, innit?'

Faith raised her eyebrows. 'Ah. That'll say "Tel", then?' she quipped.

The room exploded. Laughter, stamping, applause shook the walls.

A millisecond snapped where it could have got nasty. Then Andy slammed into the opening chords of 'Should I Stay Or Should I Go?' And you couldn't stand still if you were nailed to the floor.

If ever a crowd ate out of her hand, it was then.

And yes, she even sang the Spanish bits right.

It was always on the cards that I'd share a house with three others from my tutorial group. However, I panicked over the prospect of a grant which would barely cover the rent, and unlike the others, I couldn't fall back on parental help. Tim, Phil and Simon were sympathetic when I pulled out, saying I was going to try and live in college. Their sympathy turned to open gratitude when I got them a replacement in the Calli-pygian form of the PPE princess, Elspeth Graves (known as Flora).

And then there was Luke.

I could not understand why, but since our altercation over Nina, Luke had started to treat me with a new and somewhat disturbing respect. Almost as an equal. 'What do you think, mate?' he'd ask at the Breakfast Meetings (whenever I could be bothered to go), and I'd shrug and mutter something. What I found even more puzzling was that he was no longer on my back. He and Roger had eased off on that subtle pressure to come rambling, to come to the Men's Group – to come to church, even. They seemed to welcome me with smiles, whatever I did.

One of Luke's close friends from the church was Amanda, a scrawny, shy nineteen-year-old. Her parents, anxious to preserve her from the more challenging aspects of student life, had bought her a terraced house off the Iffley Road. Apparently, Luke and another Christian guy were sharing, and a fourth person was needed.

When Luke started to talk about the house, I was only mildly interested, until I realized he was dropping large hints about my taking a room there.

The first time he mentioned this, I was surprised. The second time, I accepted.

Faith still managed to balance me and Mike, somehow. There were still occasions when we almost came to blows. For example, I'd let my CND membership lapse (paranoia about it affecting my work prospects – spineless, I know). This caused Mike great delight, as he had always claimed I wasn't sincere.

'You're a total fucking conservative in *all* your other views,' he'd spat in my direction once. 'You're only with that bunch of lightweights to appease your conscience.'

Incredibly we still managed, somehow, to get on – largely because we knew we had to.

A few weeks after the storming gig, Faith's cousin Charlie was up for the weekend. He was a tall streak in a steel-grey jumper, with haunted eyes and a surprisingly incandescent smile. He and Faith shared that crooked tooth, I noticed, as we shook hands across a crowded bar-table.

'You're not in this . . . group of hers, then,' he said, with an attempt at joviality. He was only twenty-two, a recent graduate himself, but managed to say 'group' with the inverted commas of the fiftysome-thing, the slightly mocking tilt of the head, such that he might as well have said 'popular beat combo'.

Pool balls clicked and crashed over ribald shouts, while conversation babbled along with the Happy Mondays on the juke-box.

'No, I just . . . know Faith,' I explained, and took a quick, nervous gulp of my pint.

Faith, pushing back her tide of hair, slid on to the bench with more force than was necessary – she was a big girl, after all – and thumped her backside against mine, sloshing a puddle of beer between me and Charlie, which brought on an attack of the giggles from her.

'Charlie's a young fogey,' Faith explained to me in a stage-whisper, lolling against my shoulder.

'I see,' I said, smiling at Charlie with my eyebrows raised in apology. 'Was she always like this?'

'Oh, worse,' he told me with a wry smile.

At the pool table, Mike Bradfield let out a gritted-teeth 'Yesssss!'

as he sank another red. His new woman was there – Nicole Leonard, a narrow-hipped redhead with emerald eyes and drop dead bone-white fingers. She was ideal for him: a vegetarian, anti-blood-sports, ethnic-bejewelled Glasto-groupie who'd bludgeon the JCR into funding workshops for homeless lesbians (or whatever). An easy-option hippie with overloaded parents. I didn't like her. I wondered if it showed.

'Anyway,' Charlie was saying, 'I got you that number. Don't say I never do anything for you.' He waved a folded scrap of paper under her nose.

'Oh, brilliant!' Faith snatched it, bouncing up and down like an excited schoolgirl.

'What's that?' I asked.

'Mate of Charlie's,' Faith explained. 'Knows the Mary Chain's manager. He's been whispering sweet nothings about us, and we're holding out for a support slot.'

'Oh, I see.' I was impressed, but for some reason I didn't show it.

'Never know,' said Charlie, 'we might be seeing her on *Top of the Pops*.' He smiled, but it was rigid, forced. Something unspoken lay behind it. (And something bad, more than just my guess that Charlie hadn't watched *Top of the Pops* since Sparks were last on.)

'Are you serious about this?' I asked her. 'I mean – you want to make an actual career of it, eventually?'

She managed to shrug and light a cigarette in one movement. 'We'll see,' she said. 'We've only got two songs on the demo tape at the moment. The studio fucking rips us off – I mean, I never knew they charged so *much*.'

'You know, I bet that's why so many bands come out of America,' I suggested. 'All the college kids are so bloody rich –'

'So *goddamn* rich,' Faith corrected me with relish.

'– that they can live off Mom and Dad's money till they become more successful.'

'And they've got big garages,' said Faith. 'To rehearse in.' She gave me that wonky, monochrome grin again, the one that made me think she'd got everything sorted and I had no need to worry.

All the same, something bothered me, and I knew it had more than a little to do with Charlie. I determined to speak to him alone before the evening was out, just to see if he'd open up.

Things became more hazy. After about my fifth pint, I was aware of finding myself opposite Mike and Nicole and managing not to have an argument, which was something. We were talking about the updated *Star Trek* series, which hadn't been shown yet on terrestrial TV, although a few episodes had been doing the rounds on video.

'Have you noticed, though,' I said, 'how often Captain Picard says 'come' when he's standing right beside the replicator? Dangerous, that.'

Mike chuckled and sipped his pint. Nicole, though, smiled politely.

'What bothers me, yuh,' she said, 'is that it's meant to be a Utopian vision of the future, and yet what's missing? Mmmm?' She lifted her chin, swivelled her head round in a slightly robotic manner and opened her green eyes wide in a way I found quite irritating. Her voice was shrill, too, and her accent slightly chipped cut-glass. 'There's absolutely *no* gay presence, yuh? I think that's quite *aw*ful.'

Do you? I wondered. Or is that what Mike thinks? Wisely, I didn't say so.

'Well, you can hardly expect everyone on the *Starship Enterprise* to wear their sexuality on their sleeves,' I argued. 'Let's assume they *are* there, even though we might not have seen any yet.'

'Exactly!' shrieked Nicole, and her bangles jangled as she shook her hands in the air. '*Why* haven't we seen any? It's just reinforcing people's prejudices, yuh? Making them think that . . . well, that homosexuality has somehow been "cured" by the twenty-fourth century –'

I slammed my glass down. 'It's not that at all,' I snapped, rather more sharply than I'd intended. I caught sight of Mike glowering into his glass, obviously not happy that I had dared to challenge his mouthpiece. 'It's very interesting, actually, that *you* make the assumption everyone's straight –'

Luckily, I was saved by Faith's elbow round my neck, which cut me short at that point. 'C'mon,' she said, 'going for a kebab.'

'I hate them,' I protested. However, she physically wrested me from my seat – and my pint – and marched me out into the dark quad, where we rejoined Charlie, along with Andy and Annalise from the band. Andy's baldness reflected the college night-lights, giving him a probably unwanted halo.

'So, does Nicole annoy you as much as Mike?' Faith asked, as we walked arm-in-arm along Cornmarket.

'Give her time, she's getting there. She's the sort of person who says "girlcott", I expect.'

Faith laughed, pushing her hair back and – although she probably didn't know it – sending delicious, unbearable cascades of her scent in my direction.

The evening was something of a blur. I didn't actually have a kebab, although I must have tried Faith's at some point. I recall Charlie looking nervous when some local lads, sitting on the step of the King's Arms, started yelling comments at the girls. Annalise, though, gave them the one-finger salute, while Faith just spat a scalding stream of profanity which covered all the ground from onanism to coprophagy. That shut them up right away.

Andy had the best accommodation, an oak-beamed, two-roomed monstrosity with its own washbasin, so we ended up there, playing Pictionary. It soon degenerated after a squabble over 'clock' (whether or not one could draw numbers on the picture) so eventually Andy just threw the game out of the window and broke open his bottle of clear Manx whisky instead. We drank it in the ghost-light of a candle stuck in an old Chianti bottle.

'Wow,' Faith said, after a glass or two. 'Top stuff.'

I sniffed cautiously at it. 'You sure this isn't meths?'

'Can they call it whisky?' Charlie asked.

'There was some problem at the distillery,' Andy agreed. 'Basically they take Scotch and filter the colour out. They're not sure if they should call it whisky or spirit.'

'S'whisky in spirit,' suggested Faith. 'Cheers.' She took another gulp.

'The colour's only bloody caramel, anyway,' I suggested, recklessly inviting wrath, but no one took up the bait. All too pissed, probably.

'They're bound to be confused,' Andy said with a grin. 'It's made in a place where sodomy's still illegal, after all.'

'Yuk,' said Faith, into her drink. '*My* arse is for shitting out of, thanks.' She started to warm her glass over the candle, to a chorus of dismay.

'It'll explode,' Charlie pointed out, gently. I got the impression he was used to admonishing her, and equally used to being ignored.

'Oh, *fuckoff*.' Faith spat the retort as one word, but grinned to show she didn't mean it. She tried to focus on my face, but ended up looking past me. 'I only wanted to see what it tasted like warm,' she said with a shrug, and finished her glass with a gulp. 'Hey,' she added, 'who can do this?' She unclenched her hand, palm down, about six inches above the candle flame and started to lower it.

We watched in horrified fascination. Her hand was steady as she moved it down to four, three, two inches above the flame. Then it was right above, almost touching.

'Come on,' I said, 'enough –' and I reached out to touch her shoulder. Faith lashed out with astonishing intensity, whacking me on the arm so hard that I yelped, and Annalise, who'd been falling asleep, jumped visibly. I rubbed my arm, gawping at her as she let her hand almost touch the fire.

'Faith, stop it,' Charlie said, sounding angry now.

She was biting her lip, her face transformed almost by ecstasy, and then a second later she winced and pulled her hand away, rubbing at the redness on her palm. Charlie leaned forward and moved the candle away from her.

'You need another drink,' Andy suggested, and poured her one.

Some time after that, I found myself propped against the wall, with Charlie and the last of the whisky. Annalise was asleep on Andy's bed (a place not unfamiliar to her, I'd heard), half comatose, wrapped in harsh, smoke-roughened snores. Faith and Andy had gone off to the kitchen in search, so they said, of cheese.

'D'you . . . like my cousin? Much?' Charlie asked.

I wasn't sure where this one was leading. I knew Faith had lived with her aunt and uncle after her parents' death and I supposed Charlie must have known her like a brother. 'She's a good laugh,' I offered. 'A bit . . . well, wild, you know.'

'Yes,' he said, sucking in air from between his teeth. 'Yes.'

Obviously he wanted me to question him. I tried. 'But she's basically . . . you know, she's . . . been okay?'

He shrugged. His long grey face seemed to stretch even further. 'Don't get too attached to her,' he said. 'Faith has this . . . way of drawing people in. Before they know what they're doing . . .'

I should have pushed him for more information. I suppose I did not really want to know any more because, there and then, the last thing I wanted was someone warning me off the woman who dominated my thoughts. She had seemed unattainable for so long, and now that she was floating within reach, I wanted to grab her whatever the consequences.

So I said: 'You're probably right', and poured us another glass.

It was a sparse Sunday late in Hilary Term – with the plangent drunkards playing tin-can scallies in the thunderous rain – when Faith, bleary-eyed and gasping, rolled her curvy body on the floor, sent a full glass of plum wine slopping on to a snowy virgin rug, and laughed and did not care, as the sweat cooled on her body and I brushed her lips with mine. Her hair, waist-length now, was spread out like a great soft cape beneath her.

To my delight, she was too exhausted to speak, and I just left her there to stew in her own lemony aromas, foetal-curled, swamped by her tent of hair and the quilt I chucked on top of her. When I came back from cleaning my teeth in the bathroom, she was snoring like a pig.

So I'd finally got in the right place at the right time. They'd played pre-disco at the poly in Headington, and packed the place out. It had been a great, if unconventional performance: I'd only recognized three of their usual songs. The rest had been rough-cut new material – dicey in places – plus some inspired covers, including an Immaculate Fools song and a jittery, sparse version of Prince's 'Kiss' in which the snarl she gave to the word 'beautiful' seemed to terrify the front six rows. It seemed deVice were nothing if not eclectic.

I swelled the ranks of the Faithful by stumbling into one of her post-gig weekenders. And after six rounds of tequila and a joint or two (three?), I'd ended up joined and sweating with her on a coarse and crumb-coated carpet. 'About time,' she whispered, as we lay together.

Sometime after midnight, I stuck a tape on, a compilation she'd done for me, the tracks listed in green felt-tip with the annotation: 'Recorded live 05–02–89 at the Faithful Den. Reproduction prohibited (on the premises).' There was a flare of orange from the floor, a click of life in the sex-thickened darkness. Smoke threaded upwards.

'You all right?' I asked.

She tried to giggle, but it came out dark and dirty, a snort of lascivious delight, and she kissed a grey ghost of smoke. 'I've just been fucked into the middle of next week,' she said. 'Yeah, totally fine. You?'

'Totally fine,' I said, and allowed myself a brief grin of satisfaction.

'I am so bloody *hungry*,' said Faith, and I could see by the shifting of the shadows that she had turned on to her side to look at me. That unruly hair – real black, natural-death-dyed – obscured half her face so that she looked like a phantom forming in the dimness.

'Well, I'm not surprised. You had enough dope to bring on serious munchies all night.'

'Yeah, so arrest me. Got any crisps or anything?'

I sighed, sat up and cautiously blinked, testing my eyes for aches. 'All right, hang on.'

She gave a harsh little laugh and stroked my back. 'I'm hanging,' she murmured. 'You're lovely.'

'Nice' would have been enough for crisps, but 'lovely', that got me out in the kitchen piling a tray with Twiglets, peanuts and chocolate biscuits, and making a big pot of camomile tea as well.

I'd given the tea a last prod and was just picking up the tray when Amanda came in, all bones and spiky hair. She looked briefly startled, muttered a shy 'Hello' and went to the fridge for some mineral water. She was growing a fresh cold sore, I noticed.

'All right?' I said jovially.

'You must be hungry,' she said in her far-off voice, and wrinkled her nose as she glanced at the tray. Amanda and food were relative strangers, and when they met, they often parted company sooner than was decorous. I imagined it was her aim to shake off flesh and ascend, via starvation, into a creature of pure spirit. That made me shudder, as I hated women who dabbed at food. (Faith, naturally, ate with a zestful fuck-the-calories relish.)

'Yeah, I'm hungry.' I picked up the tray, with its two tell-tale mugs, and hurried past her into my room, motioning Faith not to speak. We munched and drank as quietly as possible, but every crunch and slurp seemed to shake the fragile body of the house. Faith had to keep putting her hand over her mouth to stop laughing.

'By the way, how's your hand?' I whispered.

She had been avoiding showing it to me. She gave me a brief flash, a hint of reddened and blistered palm, then coyly turned it back towards her body.

'Come on,' she murmured after a few minutes. Taking a mouthful of camomile tea, she pulled my lips to hers, shooting a hot jet of tea into my mouth. Giggling, she disengaged, then, without warning, rolled on top of me and grabbed my wrists.

I said: 'You're hurting me.' I tried to laugh, but ended up sounding more nervous than before.

'Good.' Her hands tightened over my wrists and her hair tickled my chest. 'Let's do it again.'

In the morning, we exchanged looks with only minimal embarrassment. Faith declined breakfast, but she had a gulp of coffee (and a quick scratch between her legs) before leaving for her nine o'clock lecture, still lusciously dishevelled, with my scarf hiding the three mottled bites on her neck. She hoisted her bag with a shy smile. Quite unlike her.

I came back from a tutorial to find the kitchen, as usual on a Monday, bright and sharp with disinfectant. There was a note pinned to the door, written on sky-blue notepaper in a childish hand:

I'm afraid it isn't really acceptable for your girlfriend to stay on a regular basis. The house simply is not big enough. It's fine to have friends over once in a while but anything more frequent causes problems. I realize Faith has only stayed once and consequently I do not know if she will be staying more often, but I just wanted to make the position clear to avoid any misunderstanding.
Yours,
Amanda.

I don't know what anyone else's reaction would have been, but I just held the note, read it, gaped at it for a full minute in silence, read it again and wondered whether this might be some bizarre example of Christian humour – had I discovered it at last? Finally, I read it again to make *quite* sure I hadn't missed any possible irony, quite apart from the idea that Faith could be called my girlfriend, which was a new one on me. I placed the note on the kitchen table as if it were a fragile piece of medieval parchment.

I crashed and jangled round the kitchen, making a cup of tea and muttering to myself, then I flopped on to the freshly-stained bed, inhaling Faith's scent on the pillow, to remind myself of the carnal world beyond the sterility of this house.

I suspected Luke's hand in this – for one thing, there was the clear indication that they had been *watching* me.

However, Amanda came home at lunchtime, and I found her in the kitchen. I caught her poking her tongue at a dry Ryvita and sniffing some grape juice. Careful, I thought, you almost inhaled. Her cold sore was glistening – Amanda wasn't a great example of the benefits of a vegan lifestyle. She had tried to cover it up, which had just resulted in a crusty yellow nodule poking from a pinkish crater.

'I didn't realize about, you know,' I began.

Amanda looked shifty and put her Ryvita down. 'Sorry? What?' It wasn't convincing.

'The note. Guests. I didn't realize. You should have said something before.'

'Yes,' she said, in a shivery voice. 'Luke just – thought – well, it didn't seem appropriate.'

'Yeah, okay.' I sat down opposite her, and I swear she flinched. I could still taste Faith on my lips, which made me smile. 'I know people whose . . . partners live in their laps . . . you know, always in the bathroom in the morning, always making pasta and leaving the pots piled in the sink, stuff like that. But I go out of my way not to cause any inconvenience when I have people round. I never even have music on loud.' I shrugged. 'I just didn't think it was a problem.'

Amanda's hand was shaking and she put down the Ryvita. She had come dangerously close to moistening it with her lips. 'I think . . . Luke . . . we just thought . . . during the day, yes, it's fine.' She risked looking me in the eye, and quickly glanced away again as if my gaze contaminated her. 'But it's a small house. You know.'

Her tongue darted to her lip, and for an instant touched against the wet tip of her cold sore. I felt my stomach twist. Maybe that was her nourishment, I thought grimly. Rather than eating real food, she would gnaw off her crispy scabs, quaff acrid sweat from her palms, chomp at her crunchy fingernails.

I tried to concentrate. 'Yes, you said in the note. The house simply isn't big enough. But you don't mind me having people round during the day?'

'Oh, n-no,' she said, and looked quite relieved.

'Right.' I frowned. 'I don't quite get the concept, you see. Does the house – shrink, at night? I mean, it could be just me. Being stupid. But I don't think it gets smaller.'

'Talk to Luke,' she mumbled, and, flushing pastel-pink, she started on some washing-up.

I was mainly annoyed with her for presuming to keep such a close eye on my affairs, but also for not being up-front. Not saying the S-word. That was the core of this, after all: she shrivelled like a sun-dried tomato at the thought of fornication under her roof. I wondered whether to let on that it happened in daylight, too. Maybe not.

Jesus had little to say about sex. Most Christian morality on the subject comes from that reliable old killjoy, Paul. Jesus liked to keep it simple: basically, he said, there's these two things. Love no other God, and love your neighbour. There you are, then. It's vague at best.

When Luke came home, he gave me only the briefest of greetings. He was more offhand with me than ever, mooching and glowering like a father whose son has let him down. He strode around the kitchen, crashing pots together. He slashed up carrots with a psychotic fervour, skinned potatoes as if stripping the world of its pestilence.

In heaven, I reflected gloomily, there might well be an abundance of Lukes and Amandas, with house rules pinned up for all to see. No parties, no guests, no loud music, no sex or drink. That's it. The afterlife is like spending the rest of eternity *living with your parents*.

Life in the house became an endless round of subterfuge. I'd smuggle Faith in and out as if under the watchful eye of a maiden aunt.

Luke's initial pent-up anger seemed to have dissipated – no doubt he had prayed it all off. Sometimes, though, he'd knock and come into my room, looking somehow . . . *pitying*. I wanted to scream at him that I was happy, for Christ's sake, so what the fuck was the problem? I didn't, of course. I sat and nodded, ummed and ahed, yeahed and yupped and s'pose-soed.

One day, I flipped, and thumped the desk, making my Tipp-Ex dance a jig over my latest essay.

'Look,' I said, half turning from the desk to where he was sitting on the bed with his mug of decaff coffee. 'I really need to get this finished right now. I don't suppose you could . . . you know, go somewhere else?'

'Oh, don't mind me,' he said, with a smile. 'I'll just sit here and be quiet.' He picked up my copy of *Private Eye* (of all things) and started to study it intently.

Yes, but it's my room it's my room get out out out! snapped the inside of my head.

'Yeah, well,' said my mouth, and I went back to scratching out my reheated critical digest. I was able to scribble down something coherent, and after about ten minutes I actually almost forgot Luke was there. Until he coughed. And came to stand behind me.

I chucked my pen down. It splattered ink. 'There is a point to this, I take it?' I asked him, not even pretending to be civil now.

He laughed. 'You're so full of energy,' he said. 'Full of life. I like that. Energy is positive, you know. It's beautiful.'

'Great. Beautiful. Whatever. Can I get my work finished, please?'

'Have you ever thought,' Luke said, squatting down so that I could feel his warm breath on my ear, 'where it all comes from? Energy isn't just *there*, you know. If a primitive man found a clock on a beach, with all the parts fully working, he wouldn't just presume it had got there by accident, would he? He'd postulate a Creator.' As he said 'Creator' his eyes lit up and his hands curled around an invisible ball, as if he were forming life out of thin air himself.

'Ah. I see. Have you read *The Blind Watchmaker*? It's really interesting, actually.'

'No,' he murmured, and touched my shoulder lightly. 'Why hold the candle of a man up to light the sun of the Lord?' It sounded like a quotation, but I suspected he had just made it up.

'Very good. Nice rhetoric. You're good at that.'

'I'm just bringing the message. Don't reject Jesus, mate. Let him in. You have to be willing to give him some slack, you know?'

I swung my chair round, jerking Luke off my shoulder. Arms folded, I glowered up at him. 'Sure. And a more cynical man might say that you have to be gullible enough.'

He frowned. 'That's not necessary.'

'Tell me something, Luke – Jesus hung out with drop-outs, lepers, the people society hated. Right? If he came back today he'd be shaking hands with Aids victims. So why, as soon as term starts, do the CU go straight round to the meek and mild and helpless? The easy touches?'

He wrinkled his nose, withdrew from me slightly. 'We only tell people Jesus is there. That he doesn't stand you up or let you down . . .'

'Yeah, lonely people. Then you make it clear that they'll be dropped if they don't keep going to church.'

'It's our duty to help people. We go where God sends us.'

'Oh, right. Funny how he never sends you down the pub. Don't you get *any* time off for good behaviour?'

He smiled benignly, as if he had heard this far too many times before. 'That's why I'm here, with you. I want you here because I *know* Jesus has a purpose for you.'

'Funny. I thought you'd want me out.' I kept my arms folded, swivelling on my chair to try and intimidate him. 'In fact, after that Nina business, I thought you'd have wanted nothing to do with me ever again.'

'That's not our way, mate, and you know it.'

'You never thought of just leaving me alone, then?' I responded, not trying to hide my irritation any more.

'I'm sure we'd all like to be left alone. That's not what being a Christian is about, though, is it? Taking the easy way.' His eyes were incandescent again, his face sheened with a light glow.

'Yeah, whatever.' I could sense this conversation slipping away as others with Luke had done. I wasn't going to get anywhere. 'Right now, though, I have the very earthly concern of an essay to finish. So if I could just have some peace?'

He sat on the bed again, smiled, picked up the magazine. 'Like I said, I'll be very quiet.'

No, I thought, that's not good enough. 'What the hell is it with you, Luke? For a Christian, you don't seem to care all that much about other people's feelings, do you?' I stood up, ripped the magazine from his hands. 'Look, just fuck right off, will you? Get *out* of here!'

He stared straight ahead for a moment, keeping his hands frozen in a ridiculous pose with an invisible magazine between them. Then he lowered his arms, sighed and slipped off the bed. 'I'll let you simmer down a bit, mate,' he said quietly, and left, glancing back just once.

I was struck by a chilling thought, namely: I could be on the wrong track about heaven and hell. Perhaps hell is a place with no pleasures, no sins, no intoxicants. Maybe those who go there are condemned to an eternity of virtue. The Christians, meanwhile, get to heaven and find that it's one big party where they can indulge all the vices they've had to abstain from all this time.

'Who's this?' I asked Faith, one Sunday.

Above the fireplace in her room, just next to her well-stocked fruit-bowl, was a gold oval frame containing a picture of a dark-haired girl of about twelve, laughing on a playground roundabout. It had that sunny, yet somehow washed-out look of the seventies instamatic.

'Angelica,' she said, briefly looking up from ripping a comb through her unruly hair. The curtains were drawn, but I could hear laughter and voices below in the afternoon spring light. Faith, unlike myself, had chosen to live in college again.

'Oh, right. Your sister. She didn't live with you when . . . ?'

'No. She moved away.'

'Right. You don't talk about her much.'

'Do I have to?' she snapped.

Tension, it seemed, crackled around Angelica's name like the static in Faith's hair, so I didn't persist with my questions. I did wonder, though, why she had a photo up of her sister if she didn't want to talk about her.

I looked again at the snapshot. The richly dark eyes, the hair so black it could be dyed, the inviting mouth slightly too large for the pale, heart-shaped face.

'She looks a lot like you.'

'Yeah, whatever,' Faith sighed. She unfolded her long legs and slipped over to me, placing her arms around my neck. 'Come on, I want some excitement.'

'She older than you?'

'You'd better be careful, love. It sounds like you're saying "Any more like you at home?" . . . Yes, she's . . .' Faith sniffed, nodded her head from side to side as she mentally added up. 'A few years older. She lives her own life. In Shropshire.'

Then her hot mouth pressed against mine, preventing any further questions.

Later, I ached with satisfaction, burned with scratches. All alone in the musty darkness, we half-slept. Candles burned. Laughter rippled through the streets.

I was realizing more and more that the way Faith made love – with a total, animal abandon, verging on demonic possession – was absolutely the best way to do it. Before her, my experience hadn't been extensive for a twenty-three-year-old. First, a desperate and best-forgotten night with Chloe Bancroft after her eighteenth birthday party, during which she'd kept the warm smile that drew me to her in the first place, but hadn't done much else. Then, eight months of secret passion with a DHSS colleague, Separated Suzannah the Supervisor. It was good, serviceable, by-the-book sex, but in the end she turned out to be not-so-separated and moved back in with her husband, describing him as 're-formed'. (To this day, I still imagine this: he is melted down, poured into a sarcophagus mould, liquid pink flesh bubbling, hardening. Eyes and mouth pop and rip open in the softness, his lumpy features smooth out, and he tears himself from the container, a whole new man.) I still managed to work with her after that, but no one's ever quite the same once you've seen them putting liners in their knickers.

It wasn't too long after the Suzannah experience that I had my great yearning to escape, and started on the bumpy road which had brought me to this room, this bed, this woman.

Yes, I supposed I loved her, but I was still doing it in a very cautious way. Giving a bit at a time, and only responding when I got something back. Unilateralist love, you might say.

Yes, unilateralist. A misunderstood concept. Despite what various people would have had us all believe in the eighties, it was never to do with giving *everything* away and hoping the other side would do the same. It was simply about making the first move spontaneously, rather than negotiating. If you didn't get a response, you had only reduced your arsenal by a tiny percentage, and you still had all your warheads trained on the opposition. It was an act of goodwill.

But you were still ready for war, should the need arise. You still had the button.

And all was fair in love and war.

★

That Sunday, 4 June, is supposedly a day of rare astronomical conjunction. The same day as the Tiananmen Square massacre, there is a gas explosion in Russia in which 600 people are killed. In college, Jason Markham, brimming with cider, crashes down the steps of the Baines Building, breaks both legs and ends up with his neck in a brace.

Also, the Ayatollah Khomeini dies. Some people are heard to comment on the phenomenon of clouds with silver linings.

In the summer, she takes me to visit Charlie and his new wife, Jan, in the big house near Chichester. For me, home is a red-brick town semi, so this is a revelation and an adventure.

I can see her now, laughing. She wears a black top and beige shorts. She is pale, free of make-up, her hair loose and shadowy as she chases me across the gardens with the sprinkler.

Reality is smooth. It gleams like OB videotape with fake colours, a drama, Paintboxed and Quantelled in post-production. The gardens glow green, while on the house, honey-gold sunlight drips over froths of scarlet creeper.

Water sparkles from the sprinkler, darkening my shirt.

'Isn't there a ban?' I splutter, dodging the cold arc of water.

'Probably.' She tosses the hosepipe aside and leaps on me, knocking me to the ground, fighting playfully until she straddles me. The discarded hose twitches as if to see what we're doing, and begins to spray across us, soaking us both. Faith shrieks in delight and descends on me, tearing off a button of my shirt with her teeth.

'Come on,' she says, pushing back her wet hair. 'Here.'

We're in full view of the house, surrounded by a vast arena of emerald lawn. 'You're joking.'

'I am not.'

A plane buzzes overhead, its contrail a line of interference on that blue video-channel sky. She grabs my hand, pushes it inside her shorts, through the dark clusters of hair and down to her secret wetness. Then, just as I am starting to lose my inhibitions, enjoying a tentative new erection, she pulls away, kicks the hosepipe aside.

'No,' she says, 'I've got a better idea. I'll make you earn it.' She nudges me with her foot. 'Come on, get up.'

I lick my fingers very pointedly, and then obey her.

Five minutes later, disorientated, damp and slightly frustrated, I watch

Faith hoist up the great door to one of the three garages. Dust, oil and darkness spill into our sunbright tableau. 'What do you think?' she says.

The car is sleek, litmus-red, impressive. It looks as if it's never been driven. Indeed, it's a G reg, firebrand-new.

'Well?' she says impatiently, sprawling cover-girl style on the bonnet. 'Is this a fit motor or what?'

I shrug. 'I'm sorry. I'm not Jeremy Clarkson. A car's a useful . . . instrument.'

'Yeah, and you're a useless tool.' She pouts, slips off the bonnet. 'Let's go for a spin.' She hops into the driver's seat.

Surprised, I slip in beside her. 'Is this yours?' It smells new, unused.

'Course. Pressie from Charlie.' She starts the engine, and we slip smoothly out of the driveway.

'Shouldn't we tell someone where we're going?' I ask nervously.

'No. That's the idea.'

The countryside flashes past. There are canopies of green trees, glittering fields of wheat. Expanses of oil-seed rape flash up, the angry yellow of a highlighter pen.

'Just feel that,' she says, as she slips into top gear. 'Fluid.'

'Yeah, I'm sorry, I find it hard to get excited about cars. I mean, they're like washing-machines as far as I'm concerned.'

She snorts in contempt.

'Really, though,' I insist. 'You don't get people going: "Hey, this baby can reeee-ally kick that dirt at forty degrees, and crease-guard is a top selling point. And look at the revs on her spin cycle, pure poetry." I'm sorry, Faith, but this is a *machine*.'

She's taking it up, the speedometer nudging sixty now, and climbing.

'All right,' I tell her. 'That'll do.'

'We're cruising,' she says. 'It's open road ahead, down to the coast. Don't you want to try this *machine* out?'

'Not really.'

She laughs, eases off on the accelerator as we climb into a bend. 'Okay, but you'll be sorry.'

We drive on. We reach the coastal road, skirting the scrappy beach car park on our right, where there are just a few midweek cars.

Faith suddenly says: 'Hold tight,' and yanks the wheel around. With a squeal of delight, she takes us at full pelt towards the dunes, screaming up the giant slope of sand between the car park and the beach.

I look round frantically, convinced that someone's going to come and tell us we can't do this.

The car groans in agony. Sand sprays around us as we climb, and I can feel the wheels struggling to get a grip on the slippery sand. Faith gives a great whoop of delight as we tear free and slowly begin to ascend, rattling and shaking like buttons in a tin. The car c-l-i-m-b-s, reaches the top of the incline, flips – overthetop and *down*. We're inscribing a path in the sand-valley now, with the sea, vast and glittering, watching from about a hundred yards away.

'Shall we?' she says.

Without waiting for my answer, she hits the accelerator. The car squeals and screams, there is a smell of burning. Sand coats the windows as if the glass is hurtling back to some primal state, and now we plunge into the ravine of sand, bumping, hurtling towards the beach.

As we level out, we pick up speed. Faith thumps the steering-wheel and gives a yelp of delight. 'Isn't this great?' she squeals.

In the distance, I can see a few figures playing on the chocolate-brown sand at the tongue of the sea.

'Slow down a bit,' I tell her nervously.

'Why? There's no one around.'

'Are you sure it can take this?' I ask, glancing at the speedometer, which is wavering around fifty. My knuckles are white from gripping the seat.

'Calm down,' she says, and takes us up to sixty, the car churning the sand behind us. We're on the wetter stuff now, and it sprays up in great, sludgy chunks, splattering the bodywork. We gouge a channel in the sand, and as the sea comes closer and closer in the windscreen I look at Faith and wonder if she's going to slow or stop.

'Ready?' she says.

The sea laps at our wheels. She twists the wheel and spins us round, round, shaking me so hard I feel I might pop out of my skin. Spray shoots right across the car – I hear it slosh on the roof – and for a second, she squeals as if she's lost control.

Then, we're back on the straight, skimming the sea, tearing up the water as we head for the peninsula.

'The tide might come in,' I tell her.

'We'll hear it,' she says.

With the front seats right down, we're lying on our backs. The car's parked a dozen yards or so from the water's edge. The afternoon sun beats on the car, but the salty air blows through the open windows. We hear the murmur of the sea, the occasional crashing boom of a hovercraft, and the laments of the gulls. Faith's smoking and has her eyes closed, while I'm propped on one elbow, watching her.

'I never know what you're going to do next,' I tell her. 'I'm not sure if I like that or not.'

She grins. 'You must like it. Or you wouldn't be here.'

'I'm worried you might get yourself killed.' I don't know why I've said it, but there it is, a sound in the seascape, like the whispering water and the keening gulls.

'Ah, shut up,' she growls. Kicking off a sandal, she manages to switch the radio on with her foot. A tune jangles out across the incoming tide: it's the Beautiful South, 'Song for Whoever'.

I nestle close to her, stroke her sweet-smelling hair, and realize that I might actually be happy for once.

I manage to persuade her to take us through the car wash on the way home, and I even pay.

Jan's at the kitchen table when we get in, swinging our sandy shoes and laughing. She looks up from her magazine, narrows her eyes. Her bob of hair shines like a beetle's carapace and her mouth tightens.

'Been to the beach, have you?' she asks, looking back down at her magazine.

'No,' says Faith, raiding the biscuit tin, 'we've been playing in the sandpit. What do you think?'

Remaining neutral, I try to smile and shrug an apology. Outside, the sunlight is becoming thick and orange, and the last listless birdsong of the day cuts through the air.

'What . . . have you done today, Jan?' I ask hopefully.

'I've had to go to work,' she says, without looking up. 'Believe it or not, that's what people do in the real world.'

Faith sighs, offers me a biscuit and pointedly slams the lid on the tin without offering one to Jan. 'Come on,' she says, taking my hand. 'I don't think we're wanted here.'

★

Upstairs, with the bedroom door bolted, we rip hungrily at our clothes.

She is soft and warm, sugared with sand. Her rich, long hair envelops her. She could be some sex-crazed mermaid come to claim a body and soul on land.

Her mouth descends to cover mine: warm, tasting of sea. She pulls me in, pushes my head down to her breasts, makes me kiss the hardening flesh of her nipples. I try to dabble my tongue across them gently at first, the way she likes it, feeling the skin pucker and tauten; but today she is moving faster. She rolls first on to her side, then on top of me, her legs straddling my face with no warning.

A pungent wetness blossoms above me, ripe and soft like the inside of a watermelon, demanding to be tasted. I press my face to her, plunge my nose and mouth right inside her so hard I can't breathe, and I inhale the delicious, lemony secretion, running my tongue across the hot, alive wetness of her sex. She shudders. Her thighs, wet and soft, press my cheeks. I feel her fingers stroke my face, then they move up and grip my hair, burning my scalp. The pain somehow kicks into me like a drug, urging me on to deeper and harder slurping. She lets out a long, needful groan as I lose myself in a deep, pink world, slippery and aromatic. Then, without warning, she pulls away from me. 'Let's play,' she whispers.

'We are,' I murmur, wiping her juice away with the back of my hand. I'm stretching out for her, but she's moved away, glistening in the half-darkness.

But she reaches for the radio-cassette, flicks some background music on. She sniggers, moves back towards me and puts my hand between her legs, making me stroke her.

'I want you, Faith.'

'Have me, then.' she whispers, affecting innocence. Then, with hot breath against my ear, 'Why not make me?'

'I . . . I don't . . .'

'Come on. Pretend to force it on me. I'll beg you not to.'

I watch her capricious mouth bloom with a mischievous smile, teeth flashing in the darkness, and I realize she is not joking. She leans back, affects a languid pose.

'Mmmm. I don't really feel like it any more,' she says, with a long, slow wink at me.

Then, there I am, slowly, stealthily crawling towards her on the bed, with a powerful, angry pounding in my head and in my cock, and I grab her arms and pin them behind her back.

And there she is, gasping, pretending to resist, pulling away, and she's so slippery with sweat that she slides from my hands and escapes to the floor, but I'm on her, grabbing her hair, pinning her down to the floor.

She laughs, then she's pleading, begging me not to hurt her, which makes me plunge into her with even more force.

It is over very, very quickly.

Faith growls as I pull my sticky cock out of her, and giggles as, with a loud slurp from between her legs, she drips a gobbet of backflow. Our mingled fluids stain the carpet and she murmurs a 'Yuk!' to herself.

For a few moments she lies beside me, pungent with sweat and sex, drawing deep breaths and unable to move. Then she sighs and turns on her side. She wipes herself languidly with a tissue and gives it a brief, interested sniff before tossing it in the bin.

'Thanks,' she says with a big grin. 'I'll remember that one.'

Over in the corner, the tape clicks to a stop.

07 Hippy Chic

'*Wankers!* You total fucking shit-brained wankers! Fucking fuck *you!*'

Mike's driving, and he's hot under the collar. He thumps the horn three times in rapid succession. The pair who have sauntered out in front of his TR7, a chunky-sideburned student and his glossy bimbo, glance at us but don't show any signs of contrition.

'I mean, would you be-fucking-lieve it?' he snarls, revving with fury. He moves off with a screech, shaking me in my seat, and takes the corner by the Methodist church alarmingly wide. 'People don't seem to *think*,' he says, slamming his hand again and again on the steering-wheel.

'All right, careful. Eyes on the road.'

'Oh, God, do you have to? . . . Okay, sorry.' He holds up a hand to forestall me. 'I forgot, you've everything to live for, with your German mistress and all that.' He sighs, shakes his head.

'Mike, is something bothering you?'

'Me? Fuck, no,' he says bitterly. 'Why should there be?'

'Want to talk about it?' I ask him.

A bit dangerous, I know. But it's the first time in years that we've been side by side in a car. Funny how it came about.

This morning, the day after my visit to Charlie. Tanya heads off to work before six. I hear the click of her briefcase and turn over just in time to see her dark-sheathed form slipping out, as the grey dawn, still tinged with orange streetlight, creeps in.

At about seven, I can't sleep any more so I get up. Armed with a huge pot of coffee and a flaking croissant, I check the bucket. It's overflowing, but the rain seems to have stopped, so I empty it down the sink and put it back in its place.

With any luck, I should be having a day off. The drive's beginning to depress me. Westpark Avenue to Hope Springs, Hope Springs to Westpark Avenue.

Things seem to be on schedule for our opening date. I make a few phone calls and check the e-mail: there's one from Geoff, my contact at the council, saying he's been able to secure a bit more money, which is good news. There's a routine one from the European Social Fund, and another from an unknown source. The address is `elektra@morning.demon.co.uk`, which doesn't ring any bells. It's entitled 'How To?' My finger hovers over delete, but I somehow find myself pressing return.

From: Elektra<elektra@morning.demon.co.uk>
Subject: How To?

```
You're not doing very well, are you? I thought you'd have
worked it all out by now, a fine mind like yours.
If you're not careful, I shall have to turn up and give you
a hand.
Bye for now.
xxxx
--
'Auch dein böser Stern war es, der dich mir folgen
ließ . . .'
```

Christ. That's the problem with putting an electronic cat-flap into your house. You never know what might get in.

I scan the message for clues. I'm sure I recognize that sig-file quote from somewhere, but I can't place it, and my German, despite Tanya's best efforts, is rusty.

I wonder whether to answer it. After a few minutes' contemplation, I settle for a one-line answer:
OK, thanks for the encouragement. So who are you?

I'm so tempted to keep it switched on to wait for a response, but I know my bills have been too big as it is. I think Tanya puts the Net in the same category as gambling and 0898 Juicy-Lucy lines. I log off, reluctantly, and have a flick through the accounts instead.

I drive to the leisure centre for a swim, but I don't enjoy it – the pool seems to be full of sweaty pre-workers disobeying the No Petting notices. I feel like Mr Sad Bastard on my lonely crawl, especially when I nearly bump into one glossy couple practising their own kind of breast-stroke. When I get back, damp and slightly pungent with chlorine, the phone's ringing. I manage to dive across the flat and grab the receiver just before the answerphone kicks in.

'Hello?'

'It's Mike.'

If I'm surprised, I don't let myself show it. 'Oh. Hi.'

'I'm going to visit the grave. I wondered whether you wanted to come with me. It's only a couple of hours' drive.'

'Right.'

All of a sudden, I'm Mr Sociable again, it would appear.

'Are you free today? You said something when I came up to your office. About coming along.'

So I did. I'm so used to people not taking me seriously that I'd forgotten all about it.

'Yeah . . . um . . . All right, then. Where are you?'

'On the ring road. By the . . .' There's a brief shuffling sound. 'The Horseshoes pub. I would have popped round,' he adds, 'but I'm not sure exactly where your flat is.'

No, you're not, and that's the way I want it to stay for the moment.

'Hang on where you are. I'll be with you in ten minutes.'

'It's Nic,' says Mike, and he grinds the gears as he slams up into fourth. 'She's fucking cleaned me out, the bitch.'

'You have such a charming turn of phrase these days.'

'It's not funny.'

'I'm not laughing. Tell me.'

There follows a potted history: a tale of blood, expensive letters and squabbling, of the guile of Nicole's solicitor, of the manipulative nature of her Gloucester stockbroker-belt parents ('It's not as if she fucking needs the cash, the spoilt little cow') and of the general plethora of knives embedded in Michael Bradfield's back.

'She said, right, get this, she said – it's easy, everything goes straight down the middle. Can you believe it? Down the *middle*? She didn't even *work* for the last three years. She just spent all *my* money on joss-sticks and . . .' Mike waves a hand to indicate an orgy of prodigality. 'You know, ethnic rugs and bangles, all that hippy-chic crap. She really hasn't got a clue.'

'There's been a recession,' I venture. These days, I seem to be cast as ACAS Man in other people's go-slows and stoppages. 'It's still hard to find the right job.'

'Yeah, but she didn't even try. I mean, Christ, she thinks she's still a fucking student half the time. She was banging on all through last year about having a party. A fucking *party*! I mean, I asked her, do we really need sixty people packed into our house tasting each other's sweat and dancing to the fucking Stone Roses? And a pile of twats in the corner, off their faces and burning holes in the carpet? And someone being sick in the oven?'

I look at him sharply. 'You went to that one?'

He ignores me. 'And so I said, right, you want everything down the middle, love, this is how it's going to be. So I chainsawed the hi-fi.'

'You did what?'

'Straight up. Sliced the fucking thing in two and posted her half. And then I started on the CDs. Those bastards were meant to be inde-fucking-structible. Well, they fucking aren't, I can tell you.'

'Mike, I don't want to sound critical, but . . . do you have to . . . swear *quite* so much?'

'Christ, what are you, Mary fucking Whitewash all of a sudden?'

'Well – it's just that it's like putting black pepper in the pasta sauce. You need a bit now and then, but if you put too much in, there's no flavour left.'

'I'm so sorry,' he snarls with exaggerated politeness. 'Where was I? Yeah, CDs. Hold them in a vice, and one fu–' He catches his breath. 'One flipping good smash with a – with a flipping solid iron mallet, and *wham*!' He breathes in deeply. 'Except for Kate Bush. Couldn't bring myself to chop Kate in half.'

'I can appreciate that.'

'Total fuc– chuffing waste of time, though. Her solicitor's insisting I sell the house, and the car, and the shares.'

'You could give her access to the car at weekends. Let her take it to the zoo and buy it an ice-cream.'

'Don't push it, son. Unless you want to walk to Chichester.'

'Sorry.' I'm quiet for a few moments, then something comes back to me. 'Did you say *shares*?'

'Yeah, Body Shop. Thought it was doing quite well recently.'

'Wow.'

'Something wrong with that?' he snaps.

'No, no. It's just that I could never have imagined you buying shares.' I'm trying hard not to laugh. 'Remember that Soviet flag you had on your wall?'

'Yes, thank you. And you had a Transvision Vamp T-shirt. So we're even.'

'Fair enough.'

About thirty minutes later, the wheels crackle and pop on the gravel by the cemetery. It's peaceful when we get out, as if ions are buzzing the air. Cawing rooks, soaring like ash, punch black rips in the sky.

Mike remote-locks his car and it chirps and flashes three times. 'Come on, then,' he says gloomily. 'Let's get it over with.'

'Are these carnations?' I ask him, hefting the big Interflora bunch. The plastic crackles in my hands as if it's alive.

'That a problem?'

'Faith hated carnations,' I inform him, as we stride along the wide paths through the ranks of the dead. The Chapel of Rest seems to watch us, resembling a giant, grim and brooding monk crouched in the corner.

'Yeah, like it's really going to bother her now,' Mike snaps.

I glower at him. 'That's not the point.'

'Anyway, come on. Respect,' says Mike, and stops, hands behind his back, at the graveside.

The headstone is a square slab of black marble, with the legend:

FAITH ROISIN DEVEREAUX

26 June 1969–14 July 1997

Beloved niece of

KATHERINE and WILLIAM

Loving cousin of CHARLES

REMEMBER

I place the flowers there and we stand beside the grave, silent. Distant traffic swishes like the sea, but otherwise we could be in the middle of nowhere.

'No mention of the parents,' says Mike, after a while.

'Or her sister.'

'Yeah, well. They weren't that close. Were they?'

'I don't know,' I say thoughtfully.

'She wasn't there, was she? Here, I mean. At the funeral.'

'No. Well, I don't recall seeing her . . . I didn't like to mention it to Charlie, really.'

A few more moments pass. I can hear our breathing, almost in harmony, over the mocking croaks of the rooks. Sunlight glints off a window near the edge of the cemetery, but there's a cold wind rushing across the silent land, shimmering in the grass and biting through my clothes.

I shiver, and wonder whether to tell Mike about things. About the bank statements and the key, and the mystery e-mail.

'Do these places spook you?' Mike asks, nervously fingering his coat buttons.

I shrug. 'Not really. I find them quite restful.'

'Oh, right. Still, I suppose you believe in all this stuff, don't you?'

'Not necessarily.' He's put me on the defensive.

'Yeah, but you hung out with those trendy born-agains. Luke Harrington and Nina Shaw, that bunch. Hey,' Mike says, suddenly remembering something, 'he was at the funeral. What the fuck did he ever have to do with Faith?'

'Oh . . . quite a lot. And don't swear on hallowed ground.'

'But I got the idea he couldn't stand her.'

'Look, just drop it, Mike. It's history.' That window flashes sunlight at me again, and I shade my eyes.

Mike shrugs. 'Yeah, if you say so.'

Yes, I think to myself, it's history if I say so. Good call. I'm going to battle the persistence of memory, freeze those melting clocks to their rocks in a permafrost. I'm looking forward.

To what, though? Blending my genes into Tanya's, our DNA writhing in passion to produce some poor bugger who'll have to grow up in suburbia and won't know who to support in the 2010 World Cup? Fighting deskbound chaos in a last-ditch education project, permanently cap-in-hand to the likes of Mike? Accepting my lot as the poor relation to society's hotter movers and cooler shakers? The future suddenly seems a bleak and desolate place when compared with the richness of the past. The past is still there. Something's still happening, and it's got me by the heart and won't let go.

I suddenly realize, glaring down at the newly-turfed grave, that Faith might have had it sussed all along. She took the easy way. And, in a sense, she might well outlive all of us.

I blink, draw in a mouthful of cold air, and notice that Mike's a few feet away, smoking hard. Waiting for me. Maybe we've had our time. That window flashes sunlight again.

No, hang on. Just a minute.

I frown, lick my lips, rummage in my pocket for my glasses. I'm not desperately short-sighted, but I need them for driving and for films with subtitles. As I put them on, I can see that there isn't a nearby house, and there isn't a window. Just a collection of graves, short and tall, black and white, like a crowd of chessmen.

And a dark patch flickers as the watcher darts behind one of the hedges.

Jesus.

I call over my shoulder to Mike, and I think he looks up, startled, but I'm already darting between the fresh graves, taking a short cut to the next path. Ahead, there's an incline with steps leading up to another level of tombstones. Something dark has just disappeared at the top.

I hit the path running and scramble up the steps. I stumble once, grazing my hand. A fountain of rooks gushes from in front of me as I reach the top. My breath's burning as I whirl around, to the left and to the right.

There's a movement at the end of the path, right down by the gates. A momentary swirl of black, like someone in a long winter coat.

I run for the gates, my breath the loudest noise in the whole cemetery. Behind me, Mike's calling my name, but I don't turn round. I get to the gates. They're shut.

I slide back the rusting catch and try to pull them open. They won't come. Rust smears my hands. Pull. Rattle and pull. *Rattle and pull.* Finally, I manage to yank the gates open and run out into the lane. Mike's TR7 is there, patiently waiting, but otherwise, the place is silent and still.

I run the twenty yards to the junction, where the lane emerges opposite the squat stone building of the Blacksmith and Anvil pub. There's nobody in either direction. The emptiness of the country road seems to mock me. Behind the pub, the wind ruffles the aspens and they hiss their soft insolence.

Mike catches up with me as I'm peering through the latticed windows at the dark interior of the pub. He wheezes like an asthmatic.

'Bloody . . . hell,' he manages, slumping on one of the benches. 'You can't . . . be that . . . fucking desperate.' He hawks up a gobbet of phlegm and projects it across the pub forecourt.

I slam the table in anger. 'There was someone watching us. I saw . . .' I open and close my hand, mimicking a heliograph. 'Sun. On lenses. Binocs.'

'Some people have weird hobbies,' says Mike. 'Christ, I need a drink . . .' He licks his lips. 'Is that place open?'

It patently isn't, so we wander half-heartedly back to the car. All the way down the strangely silent lane, I'm looking over my shoulder, as if I expect to see a dark figure standing there and beckoning me. There's nothing, of course.

Mike drives me home. He won't listen to me when I tell him we were being watched.

'Look,' he says, 'I didn't see anything. And so what if there was someone? Bloody bird-watcher or something.'

So, your average ornithologist does a guilty runner when spotted. I don't chase the point, though.

In return, I get Mike's usual invective against the pedestrians and the other drivers. It punctuates his story of how he couldn't even give work away these days: someone called Penny in his office was 'banging on' about the problem with the homeless, right, so Mike had been down to the canal and 'checked out a cardboard citizen or two'. When they started asking him for change, he'd told them where to go. 'So I said, forgive me for being a bit dense, but what does this transaction involve, exactly? I give you money, and you give me what? And get this, most of them had their noses and ears pierced about a dozen times over, and their eyebrows, for Christ's sake! Who the fuck needs to get their *eyebrows* pierced? How many meals could they have got for the price of all that fucking metalwork?' However, he announced under the bridge that he'd pay fifty quid each for anyone who'd come and clean out his garages for him and mow all his lawns. 'Could have told you what I'd get,' he says. 'Glassy-eyed stares and chewing. A few laughs and a spit. That's what I got. Surprise, sur-fucking-prise.'

Maybe it's just me, but Mike's woodchop expletives, splintering words right down the middle, sound the most irritating of all.

His car-phone chirps several times during the course of the journey, and he snaps out hands-free instructions to his minions. 'Just sell the bloody thing, all right?' . . . 'Damp? Well, get the frames painted and they won't see anything, will they?' . . . 'You get me those breakdowns by tomorrow, Sandra, or you're out, got it?'

Nice people to do business with, nice business to do people with. He drops me on the ring road. On the way home, I pick up a takeaway from the Chinese on the precinct. When I get back to the flat, I kick the modem straight into action, sipping a lager impatiently as I wait for the download.

No messages. Shit.

I get the little key out of my wallet and stare at it, watching it sparkle in the light as I turn it. It's hopeless. Faith didn't have a bike, or, according to Charlie, any convenient boxes to fit this.

Sighing, I unwrap my takeaway. The prawn crackers are delicious, even if they are polystyrene-light and shaped like bra-pads. It's like crunching on puffs of air with a light fishy tang. I'm just ploughing into my pork and ginger with fried rice when the door rattles.

'Hiya,' says Tanya, and slings her bag across the table. It whooshes on the Ikea pine and clunks to the floor, spewing a lipstick, Starburst wrappers and a brood of tampons. She sighs, flops into a chair.

'Bad day?' I ask her cautiously, and take a gulp of lager just in case.

She folds her glasses up. 'I'm going to Iceland,' she says.

'Oh, right. Get us one of those strawberry gateaux, like we had before. And that lemon chicken –'

She holds up a hand. 'I mean I have to fly to Iceland. For work. Tomorrow.'

(Oh, I see.) 'Why?'

'There is a major problem at the Reykjavik office. EmTrak want me to go and . . . shoot trouble.'

'Troubleshoot. Brilliant. I suppose they said you were the ideal person?'

'Pretty much,' she says, with an apologetic shrug. 'Sorry. It will be good for the career.'

'So . . . how long for?' I ask, leaning over to kiss her cheek. She smells of warm cologne and hot computer.

'At least six days.' She yawns, stretches, starts to massage her left shoulder. 'Perhaps it will be more. I don't know.'

'Bloody hell. Isn't this a bit short notice?'

'You want me to complain, I take it?' she asks, raising her eyebrows.

I sigh. 'No, of course not. You have to go. Just ask them for a rise when you get home.' Realizing the little key is still hot in my hand, I hold it up. 'Tanya, do you know what this might be for?'

She takes it, peers at it through her lenses, turning it back and forth. 'I dunno. Could be for a suitcase. Or a – *wie heisst das auf Englisch, Schliessfach?*'

'A locker?'

'Yeah. A locker. Like, at a train station or something.' She tosses it back to me and I catch it. 'Where you get it from, anyway?' she asks, getting up and buttering a slice of wholemeal bread.

'Oh, it was . . . in some junk I was clearing out.'

Tanya doesn't seem too interested, and doesn't pursue it. At the same time, though, I ask myself why I should worry about telling her. This is the woman I live with. I think I love her. So why can't I share it?

Because it belongs to that past, that scarlet darkness we don't mention, the name which has never been uttered between these walls. Even the funeral could have been any friend as far as Tanya was concerned. I watch her making a pot of tea, admire her angular body and her slender neck, and realize that she is loved without being adored, sexy without being passionate. That, perhaps, is where Faith had the edge.

It's so true, so obvious. I would not steal, lie or kill for Tanya. But there was a time. (Remember.) There was a time when. (Remember.) There was a time when I would have done. (No, don't.) For Faith, I would have done.

Later, I'm lying on the bed, watching patterns in the ceiling. I'm thinking, and I can't think properly standing up. I'm happier horizontal.

I often lie down in the evenings, as my legs seem to ache more than is good for me. So I need to lie. I'm a compulsive lier.

It would not make sense, the key being for a station locker, as those things have a time limit, don't they? After seventy-two hours or whatever, left luggage gets impounded. No. I'm thinking along the wrong lines.

Tanya's taxi, bridal-white, scoops her up at sunrise. I watch at the window with the computer booting up behind me.

The cab zings away, slicing puddles to shreds, as the glittery city awakens in the land below the Avenue. A milk-float whines, clinks, rattles. I watch it flirt with the cab when they nuzzle at the end of the street. Somewhere, a cat mewls. Clouds daub the sky as the dawnlight tunes itself in, and the streetlamps blush crimson, embarrassed by the day. Deep below, in that urban crucible, life begins its stutter and gabble and I imagine the pulsing lines of power embracing the city. Particles zoom in the urban web, forming its pattern, sizzling along the Nobody's Fault, the crack that runs from Hope Springs to Westpark Avenue.

The mail downloads. I take a large hit of coffee. There's a message.

From: Elektra<elektra@morning.demon.co.uk>
Subject: Honestly

You know, you're doing so badly I really will have to come and help you.

The message jitters in my brain.

It rolls like a loose marble, all the hooting, choking way from Westpark Avenue to Hope Springs. And then from the scabbed car park to the painted corridors.

In the half-painted lobby, it's pounding with Elastica. Tony sees me coming and nudges the volume down. He waves, yelps a hello.

'Patsy Kensit,' he offers.

'Yeah. Whatever you say, Tony.' I kick open the office door.

There's a rustle of newspaper, a thud of boots as Tony hops off his ladder and trots over to my office. He pokes his head round the door, grins.

'Wassup? Not playing today?'

'Sorry. Um.' I look up from the pile of mail. 'Patsy, yes. Top totty. Post-*Luna*, I hope?'

'Post-*Luna*. Pre-Liam. Say no more.' Tony nudges his nose.

'Nice one. Sorted.'

'Sorted.'

'By the way,' I tell him, 'you've got paint on your nose.'

At ten-thirty, I have a talk with Jocasta, the secretary and general dogsbody for the project, and Wes, our placement trainee. They're both bright and eager: Jocasta, a pale thirtysomething, wide-eyed and bushy-permed, sleek in a grey suit; Wes, burly and bomber-jacketed, with an expanse of teeth set in an ebony face, usually with Mark Morrison or R–Kelly cackling in a low-slung Walkman round his neck. Jocasta once asked him to turn the Walkman off, but he just grinned and said he'd do her for racial harassment. Ever since then, they've been a bit frosty with each other. They're both pretty handy, actually. Wes has been helping the technicians get the computer suite up and running, while Jocasta's been fielding the numerous requests for updates from the Local Education Authority, the European Social Fund and the Further Education Funding Council, plus the odd sponsor or three.

Lunch is a droopy sandwich from Mr Mahoud on the corner, then I have a meeting with Geoff and the council people. I tell them our projected opening date is in two months' time, and they seem happy.

Not a bad day, all in all. It's just getting dark as I head home. I say good night to Jocasta and then to Dave, our ex-army security guard.

I sling my briefcase in the back of the car and escape from Hope Springs intact once more. A light rain sparkles in the street lights. I hope the bucket's on standby.

On the clogged roads of the town, buses glide in convoy, great boxes of light packed with palefaced white-collars. Headlights jiggle around the endless roundabouts, tyres swish in the thickening rain. We dance through junctions, under spotlights of red, amber and green, twirling in the dry-ice of our exhaust fumes.

About a mile from home, I realize I forgot to ask Jocasta for a file I needed. I pull in to try and call her before she leaves, but my mobile's packing up again. Brilliant. I drive on through the rain, tapping the steering-wheel in agitation, looking for a telephone. Luckily, the phone-booth by Texas Homecare on the main ring road is unoccupied, so I pull in, hop into the putrid box and call the Hope Springs office.

Headlights nestle in behind my car, further down the lay-by. Just my luck if someone else wants to use the phone.

It's ringing, but there's no answer. I let it ring about twenty times. The headlights in the lay-by are dimmed, then a second later shut off completely. Rain swamps the glass of the phone box, and I can't clearly see if anyone is waiting.

I let the phone ring about thirty times before I decide to abandon the idea. The rain is much worse now, and I shiver and button my coat right up before making a dash for the car.

I start up the engine and the wipers swing enthusiastically into action. I check the rear-view and I notice that no one seems to have got out of the car behind. I can't see the driver clearly at all.

I feel a sudden, involuntary shudder as I remember the flash of darkness in the sunlit cemetery yesterday.

A gap opens in the sizzling traffic and I slide in. I can't be sure, but I think the car behind gets stuck back in the lay-by.

When I get to the garage, I look up and down Westpark Avenue, but I can't see any headlights.

Must be getting paranoid. I shake my head, lock the garage and head up to the flat.

There are two messages on the answerphone. One is from Tanya, very brief and businesslike, to say she's arrived safely and she'll call me tomorrow. She gives me the name of her hotel in Reykjavik, but a crackle eats it up, so it could be anything.

The other is from Luke.

'I heard you were here the other day,' says that soft, precise voice. 'Please don't come round again. It's not . . . appropriate. I'm not trying to say I don't like you any more, I'm just trying to keep things separate now, trying to make a new, positive life. I came to that funeral for you. Because you asked me to. But I don't want any more of it. All right?'

I'm astonished. I didn't know he felt so strongly about it. The thought occurs to me that I didn't know he had a phone, either. I dial 1471, but all I get is 'The caller withheld their number.' Interesting.

I play the message again. And then a third time. Something's not quite right with it, but I can't quite place what it is.

Trying to shake off my worries, I do myself a meal: microwaved haddock in a tomato-and-herb sauce. Normally I'm handy in the kitchen – Tanya's been impressed with my chicken casseroles – but I can't really be bothered when it's just me. I rest a tray on my lap and have a flick through the TV channels, as the pinging bucket monitors the rain. A gormless advert assaults me, trying to persuade me to visit Ireland: apparently it's full of rolling hills, wild horses, jaunty fiddlers, jovial types quaffing ale as they share old stories in front of roaring pub fires, and bewitching emerald-eyed colleens in virginal white, dipping their delicate toes in sparkling mountain springs as their auburn tresses ripple in the breeze. Fuck *off*.

I go to the window to watch the rain falling. Down in the city-hollow, the orange lights smear as if seen through a haze of drink. I think of the torrents cascading on those graves, drenching the headstones, soaking the ground, bubbling in froths of mud. Sinking in.

Suddenly I'm cold, so I get a glass of brandy and stand at the window with it, contemplating the rain. Across the street, the railings of West Park glisten.

I frown. There's a dark patch against the railings. Trying not to take my eyes off it, I fumble for my glasses.

It's an umbrella. Motionless. Held by a tall figure in a dark coat.

My mouth is dry and my heart's hammering as if it wants to get out. I press my face hard up against the cold glass. The umbrella twirls, scattering raindrops. I can't see the figure's face.

I grab my shoes, lock the flat and run down both flights of internal stairs to the lobby. I fling open the main door. The rain and wind snarl, unleashed like demons. I double-check I've got my keys before hurrying down the steps, scanning the other side of the road for the watcher. I'm about to cross, but there's a roar –

A hiss of airbrakes –

A bus hurtles past, a shimmering monster reeking of fuel.

I make it to the other side, pushing my wet fringe out of my eyes. I can smell and taste the rain, like musty, recycled water, creeping into my nose and mouth. I'm soaked, but I don't want to go back in until I have made absolutely certain. There's no sign of anyone on this side of the road.

Up in the three-storey building, I can see various lights on, and I locate my own lounge. Clearly visible. Someone knows what they are doing. I'm seized with panic.

This isn't helping. I check for traffic and hurry back up the slippery steps to the main door. I'm back in. The door clicks firmly shut behind me. The lobby, with its thick carpet, larger-than-life plants and chunky wooden letterboxes, is warm and reassuring, and I catch my breath again, try to tell myself I'm being stupid. Tanya would say so, surely.

Sighing, I trudge back along the hall, pushing my wet hair back. Humanity reminds me that I'm not alone here: an Oasis song is playing in the ground-floor flat, where Sarah the trainee surveyor lives, and there's a woman's laugh from inside as I pass the door. It's a life-affirming sound, and I grin as I feel some warmth coursing back into my cheeks.

I climb the stairs to the next landing and drag my keys out of my back pocket. There's a warm, peppery smell of cooking wafting from under the door of the first-floor flat, which is shared by Isla and Val, two young primary-school teachers.

I pause, sorting my keys out, beside the framed map of Britain at the foot of the stairs to the next floor. Rain pelts the landing window like an angry crowd.

From above, there is a strong scent of perfume and the air shifts slightly.

The back of my neck prickles. There's a kind of electricity in my body, an alien presence hollowing out my stomach and thumping my heart. Fear.

I turn around.

I look up.

Ten steps above me, there is a fluid column of darkness. I stare and stare, feeling the life draining from my body.

It is a tall, slim woman. I see black-stockinged legs, shapely and long, beneath a shimmering wet macintosh. Pale hands, their fingernails painted night-black, clasp the handle of an umbrella. Up, up to a white-buttoned black silk blouse, a choker on a slender neck. Her face is outlined in shoulder-length hair of the richest, darkest black. The face now seems to draw my eyes to it, ordering me to look. It's a beautiful, sleek mask of white, adorned with a luscious mouth, smiling as if in welcome. And those huge, dark, crashingly Celtic eyes are open wide as if to lure me into an eternal darkness.

'I've been waiting,' she says softly. 'Waiting for you. Now, at last, we can play the game again.'

Part Two The Persistence of Memory

08 Getting Away With It

'I know it's what everyone says,' Mike Bradfield announced with a politician's smile, 'but this really is the happiest day of my life.'

There was wild, drunken applause. Some of the twenty-odd tables resounded to appreciative thumps. Glasses of champagne were unsteadily lifted.

I leaned back and clapped gently. Faith, next to me, was a voluptuous, vampiric anti-bride: she wore a low-cut black dress of liquid-smooth satin, with a neck-scarf, black stockings and crimson slingbacks. These days she went easier on the Goth trappings – even had colour in her cheeks – but her nails were painted tar-black and she sported a silver and ebony crucifix over the scarf.

High above us, chandeliers glittered on the vaulted ceiling of the Cargill Hotel, Gloucestershire. It was obvious that Nicole Bradfield, *née* Leonard, had parents who weren't short of a few quid. Her father had delivered an eloquent and self-satisfied speech, and now it was the turn of the man himself.

'Well,' Faith muttered to me over the applause, 'it's the bride's day. The groom has to remember that he's only slightly less important. Than the cake.'

I grinned, took a deep, fizzy gulp of champagne. Nicole, seated beside her husband at the high table, wore a traditional ivory dress and a jade tiara which, I had to admit, set off her red ringlets beautifully. With one hand poised beneath her chin, she listened intently to Mike's heavy-handed speech.

'We had a decision to make,' he was saying, 'about whether Nic would wear her glasses during the ceremony. In the end, she decided against it. She said we weren't going to have any specs before marriage.'

This produced groans from some quarters, and belly-laughs from others. Faith and I exchanged knowing, ironic looks. She made a slight adjustment to the chiffon scarf and I suddenly felt my body prickling with heat. I glanced away.

Jacqui Potter – unkindly dubbed Jacqui Spotter during our second year – was seated the other side of me, looking wistful. She had on a soft velvet hat with a matching top. She had made a decent effort to cover her blazing acne, but it was 11 August 1990, one of the hottest days of the year, and her mask was already melting beneath a fresh layer of sweat.

'When I first met Nicole,' Mike went on, shuffling his cards, 'I reckon she thought, who's this annoying socialist with the poncy pony-tail?' There was a titter, but only a small one: the key to self-ironizing is to get there before other people. 'Anyway, we've moved on a bit since then.' Mike tilted his head, pouted in a shampoo-commercial style, showing off his new short-back-and-sides and trimmed beard. 'But I like to think I'm still an annoying socialist from time to time.'

I cheered and clapped – alone in my irony tower – but I felt myself turning red when everyone looked at me. I relaxed when Mike gave me a thumbs-up and said: 'See, I've brought my fan club,' which prompted the first truly relaxed laughter of the afternoon. Faith gave me a playful thump on the elbow. I met her eye for a second. We knew what we were saying.

Mike ploughed on with his thanks, and finished off to an appreciative round of applause, during which I caught Jacqui Potter's eye. She smelt of a cheap scent and powdery make-up, permeated by a tang of perspiration. (All right – sweat.)

'You'll be next, then,' she said, with the grim determination of the pessimist.

I laughed. 'Don't be so sure.'

'Why not?' she asked, biting savagely into her wedding-cake. The crumbs avalanched into her lap and she ignored them. 'Iff the deftiny, ifn't it?' she attempted through a mouthful of cake. 'The ulfimate middle-claff aim.'

I watched the best man, one of Mike's school-friends, being fetched from the bar to do his speech. 'Mmm, well. I might not be the type,' I said with a rueful grin.

Jacqui looked over at Faith, who was helpless with laughter at something one of Nic's fellow Greens had said. 'Does she know that?'

'Oh, yeah. I don't think she's the type, either.' I wasn't going to say any more, certainly not to a big-mouth like Jacqui. Luckily, I'd decided tonight that I felt quite well disposed towards the world. 'So, Jacqui,' I asked, venturing on to thin ice in the interests of keeping a conversation going, 'what kind of guy would you say *you're* looking for?'

Jacqui made a noise which might have been a derisive laugh or a snort. She folded her arms, set her mouth in that expression we all knew, the one that said: I'm Preston Northend, and the rest of the world is Sheffield Wednesday.

'Me?' she said through gritted teeth.

'Yeah.'

'Unattached and straight,' she snapped. 'If you bloody find any, will you be so good as to let me know?' She grabbed her clutch-bag and, glowering at her feet, threaded through the tables in the direction of the Ladies.

Faith slipped into the warm seat, eyebrows raised at the departing figure. She leaned towards me. 'Have you been upsetting Jacqui again? Someone really needs to find her a man.'

'She needs to find herself first,' I muttered.

'And what about you, darling? Have you found yourself?'

I looked hard at her, gently reached out a finger to stroke the silky scarf at her neck. 'Oh, yes, I think so.'

She smiled. Her laughter-lines were deeper these days, and she'd acquired the beginnings of crow's-feet around her eyes, pencilled in by late nights and substance abuse, but I didn't find that a problem. If anything, it made her sexier.

Wild applause slammed into our conversation. The best man was on his feet, nervously checking his prompt-cards.

'Well, ladies and gentlemen, and others. What can I tell you about Michael which hasn't already been quoted in numerous lawsuits . . . ?'

It does not surprise anyone when they announce the engagement. Nicole tempers Mike's extremism to some extent, but basically she worships him. I enjoy watching her green eyes harden defensively if anyone brings up the subject of the vanishing Soviet flag. I never do find out what happened to Mike's proud symbol: some time during the winter of 1989/90, it must go from left-wing to left-over in the space of a night. Perhaps it turns into tattered rags like Cinderella's ball gown.

Nicole, to my mind, has already allowed her own personality to become a basic extension of Mike's. She goes in one term from an active Green to a loudmouth leftie with the occasional token opinion on the environment. And I come to dislike her even more. You can say what you like about someone who puts on wellies to drag aniseed-flavoured rags for miles and divert fox hounds, but they are *doing* something, and you can usually tell what they will and won't support. Nicole, though, shifts from doer to talker. She starts to rehash Mike's opinions and claim them for her own.

She collars me after a revision seminar, bashes my ear all the way down St Giles with New Nicole propaganda:

'I mean, I used to tell people there was no such thing as a wasted vote, yuh, that they had to vote Green if that was what they believed in, right? But that was before I really realized, yuh? We *have* to act together, we have to vote Labour to have any hope of getting the Tories out.' (Et bloody cetera, ad sodding infinitum.)

She hasn't, though, totally lost her idealism. As she prattles on, I recall her spell of notoriety.

'I don't believe this. How could this happen?' Nicole kicks savagely at the wooden door of her room, and it squeals in protest. Mike puts a hand on her shoulder, but she just leans against a wall and whimpers.

'Just sit down,' says Faith calmly. She's made some tea, and is pouring it into mugs for everyone.

'Yeah, come on. They might be back,' I add.

We've been out on the town. We've had a good time. The usual format: an early I-Really-Fancy-Some-Poppadums moment, followed by a predictable Who-Remembers-*Ivor-the-Engine*? excursus, and an inevitable Not-Pernod-and-Black-Oh-What-The-Hell? incident. However, this is an unexpected end to the evening.

Of the five girls who share the house, Nic is the only one to stay up after Ninth Week, as she has an extra tutorial to fit in. The others, whose parental contributions aren't quite as extensive, disperse to their summer jobs.

This term is where Nicole dips her toe in the subculture and acquires a club of clingers-on. They aren't so much drop-outs as were-never-ins:

a ragtag bunch of acid-casuals, Goa-heads and E-adders. It appears that one of these new friends, a trust-funded eco-terrorist who delights in the name of Tarquin, has cajoled her into lending him a key, spinning a yarn about an evil landlord who's kicked him out. Nic goes away for a few days, during which time Tarquin proceeds to let the entire crusty population of the city squat in the house.

Nicole, drenched in tears, seeks out Mike, Faith and myself, hoping we'll go and deal with it. I point out that they'll have squatters' rights, but Mike, exhuming his A-level Law, remembers that if they want to assert them, they must be on the premises. So we go round, and when we find they're not in, Nicole opens up and we step into Hippy Hell.

It isn't the debris so much as the obvious neglect that has Nicole shivering and whimpering, holding a handkerchief to her mouth in disgust. There is an all-pervading stench of decay, as if a giant has belched through the front door, farted down the chimney and sealed the house up. The bedrooms are bad enough: mattresses on the floor, covered in rubbish, overflowing ashtrays and some stains that nobody really wants to investigate. However, the kitchen surpasses the lot. The sink is piled high with saucepans in a wedding-cake sculpture, decorated with lentil-coloured stalactites. Fag-ends, cans and bottles fester under tables and behind doors. Glutinous blobs of a tomato concoction decorate the floor, and they've spawned their own little colonies of bacterial and insect life.

'Oh, look,' I say, pointing at the floor. 'Alternative culture.'

'I thought these people were meant to care about the bloody environment,' mutters Faith, looking round in disgust.

'Hey, peace 'n' love,' I say, fingers aloft in a V. 'Back to nature, man. Makes you wonder why we don't all do it.'

Faith returns my Winston Churchill salute and flips it into a Harvey Smith.

Nic's slumped, head in hands, in the hallway. Mike, wearing his hair loose and tucked behind a studded ear, talks to her in a low, urgent voice. He manages to cajole her to go round with a notepad and write down what's missing or damaged, a sensible idea that I wouldn't have thought of. Faith eventually gets us sitting at the kitchen table with our mugs of tea, after moving aside some congealed spaghetti and molten candles.

Nic's trying hard to control her breathing.

'Come on,' Mike is saying. 'Your exercises. Do your exercises.'

She sits back, closes her eyes, starts to clench and unclench her hands, making soft, moaning sounds.

'I suppose that helps?' says Faith, sounding sceptical.

'Have you seen *When Harry Met Sally*?' I whisper.

'Shut up, you two,' snaps Mike. Nicole's breathing calms down and her moans abate slightly.

I lean back, arms folded, and exchange glances with Faith. 'Look,' I say in Nicole's general direction, 'what are we going to do when they come back?'

'Will you not raise your voice at her like that?' Mike growls. 'She's upset enough as it is.'

'Yeah, well. If she'd not given the key to a bunch of scuzzy lentil-eaters in the first place —'

'Just shut it, son!' Mike's finger is two centimetres from my face, but I am not going to let on that I'm wary of him.

'Oh, go on,' I tell him in a tired voice. 'Make something of it, please. I could do with a laugh.'

To be honest, I am tired and pissed-off, and I've been looking for a chance to goad Mike all year. He loves to make me feel guilty for being a middle-class Southerner from a non-dysfunctional family. I recall I put it to Faith that he gets on better with her because I'm not PC enough, and anyway she can 'revel in proletarian orphan angst' with him around. She was moody for a few days after I said that.

'Just calm down, the pair of you,' Faith says, and gently nudges Mike's finger to one side.

Mike glowers at me. It's lucky that he's capable of taking care of himself, or I'd have been tempted to deck him before now. It could have happened during some of our post-bar sessions, when he goes on about being born in a poor area of Manchester, endlessly quoting unemployment and crime statistics and telling everyone what a rough time the kids had on the council estate — leaving out the fact that his upwardly-mobile parents moved to the suburbs when he was eleven. If there's one thing I never could stand, it's someone notching up the working-class-hero points.

'Come on,' says Faith briskly. 'Why don't we make a start on cleaning the place up, mm? And then we can —'

A high-pitched warble interrupts her, and everyone jumps. Mike goes into the hall, lifts the telephone receiver, looks puzzled when the ringing continues.

Faith says, 'It's coming from . . .' She brushes aside a pile of crumpled newspaper. Sitting on the table, incongruous among the wreckage, is a mobile phone.

We stare at the thing as if it's a giant insect which has crawled on to the table. I pick it up, then realize I've never held one before. Faith shows me the button to press.

'Yeah, hello?'

There's a crackling sound, then a young male voice drawls: 'Crispin? Is that you?'

'I'm afraid not.' I look desperately at Faith, who gestures at me to keep going. 'Who's this speaking, please?'

'. . . You're not Crispin . . . Who' you?'

'Smart lad, aren't you? Quick on the uptake. Let me guess, Crispin would be a friend of, er, Tarquin's?'

'Yeah, 'sright,' says the voice, sounding relieved. 'You know Tarq? He there?'

'He not here. Terribly sorry. This is, ah, Detective Sergeant –' I glimpse the newspaper '– Gascoigne of the Thames Valley Police. Can I help at all?' I grin at Faith, who's stuffed her knuckles in her mouth and is turning pink.

There is a sound very like a squawk from the other end of the line, and then a click.

'Gone,' I say, switching the phone off with a shrug and a smile.

Faith lets loose a burst of giggles which threatens to have her under the table, and I'm chuckling too.

'Come on,' Mike says with a weary smile, getting to his feet. 'Let's tidy the place up. Nic,' he adds, throwing her the mobile phone, 'get on to the others, tell them what's happened.'

She looks up, her green eyes sluiced in tears. 'Do I have to?'

'Yes,' says Faith, holding down a giggle, 'you do if you want to live. And I'll find you a locksmith from Yellow Pages. You'll have to get those locks changed.'

I go down to the corner shop and buy some bleach, rubber gloves, cleaning fluid and sponges. By about three in the morning, we have managed to get the house looking vaguely habitable again, and there is no sign of Nic's hippy friends.

In fact, they don't surface again. Eventually I assume that my brief bit of scaremongering on the mobile has done the trick, or that they've moved on to their next squat. We never do find out.

'You know that graffiti in Queen's Lane?' Faith was saying at the hotel bar. 'I was so bloody stupid, right? I was convinced for years that it said *Fuck That Cher*. I thought, what have they got against a top Sixties musical icon? Till you pointed out to me that it said *Fuck Thatcher*. Amazing what you can miss.'

I was aware, as she babbled on, of the surface triviality with which we spoke these days, as if this whole business of being among other people was just a piece of theatre. Weddings were more theatrical than most occasions, of course. What I'd said to Jacqui was true: I couldn't see myself ever going through the whole palaver. I turned my mind back to the present.

'Yeah, I always thought that was a bit obvious,' I said, repositioning my carnation. 'It's like writing Hitler Was a Bastard . . . Bloody students, I ask you. Think of something more original.'

'Too right,' Faith muttered. 'This JCR . . . *condemns* everything which is not Pee bloody See.' She slurped from her glass, wobbling a little on her feet, just as the groom himself slipped past on his way from the bar. 'Michael-angelo, daah–ling,' she cried, thumping him on the back and making him spill drops of Guinness over his shoes. 'You used to *condemn* everything. Such an orator.'

He smiled, like a man who was genuinely enjoying himself. 'Yeah, well. You're only young once.'

'Good speech, mate,' I offered. 'I liked the jokes.' I hoped he would realize I was being sincere, while I tried to ignore the fact that he had a red Aids Awareness ribbon pinned next to his carnation. (I mean, honestly, at his *wedding* . . . you can take these things too far.)

'Yeah, nice one,' Faith agreed. She prodded his chest. 'Oi, I hear they've got a massive fuck-off four-poster in the honeymoon suite.'

'Nah. Five-poster,' said Mike with a wink.

Faith and I exchanged looks of mock outrage. 'He used to be such a well-brought-up young man,' I said.

'Did he?' said Faith. 'When?'

'Since tomorrow,' Mike offered.

'Now, talking of conjugal things – re-mem-ber,' and she prodded him in the chest with each syllable, 'don't go sprogging all over the place just 'cause you've got a headstart.'

He grinned. 'Why not?'

'For one thing,' said Faith sternly, 'think how big a baby's head is. No matter how well-off you are in the trouser department, big-boy, there's no competing with *that* kind of girth.'

'In fact,' I added, 'I would go one further, and discourage Michael from reproducing at all. It's safer for the world as a whole.'

'I'll remember that,' he said, and gave a sigh.

'When do you start your PGCE?' Faith asked him. Mike and Nicole had sorted out a rented flat in Greenwich, and were both off to South Bank Polytechnic to do a year's teacher training.

'Straight after the honeymoon, pretty much. Have you heard about your funding yet?'

'Nah. Should be any day now.' Faith held up crossed fingers.

Faith, despite spending so much time with the band, had got a First. Her college had been happy to keep her for a Ph.D. (Supernaturalism in the Modern Novel) but only on the usual understanding that the British Academy was forthcoming with funds.

'If not, you can always sell your body,' Mike suggested with a grin.

'Right,' she said, 'that's a book paid for. What about my living costs?'

'Obviously, this is Wit City,' Mike sighed. 'I can't take too much more. If you'll excuse me, I have to go and talk to some coffin-dodgers.'

He threaded his way back through the guests, which I could see was going to take a while, as they all wanted a word with him. I watched him go, unable to stop the usual pang of jealousy at his easy, cool-headed banter with Faith. I'd always try to join in, but I'd still feel as if I was the child being allowed some amusement.

'That ribbon,' I muttered, shaking my head.

Faith smiled. 'Interesting choice of buttonhole.'

'Bloody showy if you ask me. People wear them to say: Look! I'm getting some.'

'Christ, you sound like Luke,' she said, faintly disgusted.

Maybe I did. I remembered Luke last term, his face glistening with horror when he was offered a ribbon by Nicole. He gave her a short lecture about how they were 'the wrong kind of education' and how Aids awareness taught people 'not how to do right, but how to do wrong and not get caught'. Nicole, naturally, took issue with 'caught', saying that Luke was coming dangerously close to calling the syndrome a punishment.

As I bought our drinks, I spotted Nic having an animated conversation with two of her brothers and their girlfriends on the far side of the bar.

Faith nudged me. 'I give them three years. What d'you say?'

'I say don't be such a cynical cow.'

She laughed. 'Can't help it. Sorry.'

'Well, it should see off a few rumours,' I suggested, looking across the room from groom to bride and back again.

'Don't you believe it,' Faith murmured.

Mike had not done much to dispel gossip about his sexuality: in fact, he revelled in it, enjoyed toying with people's image of him. He loved being seen with gay people and would call them 'my queer friends', as if staking his claim to their vocabulary. This struck me as the worst kind of point-scoring. I knew how 'queer' was being reclaimed from homophobes and used as a term of affection in the LGB community, and I was all for it – but I knew the word could only sound insulting coming from me, as a straight man, so I never used it. Mike, though, had to show he was one better than us, a member of their club. It was the plumage of a PC peacock, and it made me want to smash his face in.

'Come outside,' Faith whispered in my ear.

The house lights had dimmed, and the massive sound system was shaking to the Fine Young Cannibals, but lights skated over an empty dance floor. People were still clustered round their tables, letting the meal settle.

I frowned. 'I don't want to.'

'You don't have a choice. Remember?'

I remembered, of course.

There had been last summer. The beach, the car. The bedroom. Her face, gleeful and satisfied.

After that, she had seduced me in a variety of places. Upstairs at parties (too easy). In the toilet of the Paddington to Oxford Inter-City (made up in brutal excitement for what it lacked in comfort and hygiene). Across a violet Mazda in the car park of Oxford Poly (strangely satisfying). And, of course, in the garden of the Turf on a beer-drenched night after our last finals paper (largely unsuccessful, as there were too many people around).

Then, when we came up for the day to get our results – she got a First, I got an Upper Second, and we were both happy – she had the idea of hiring a guest room in college. I wasn't really happy with that, now that I'd left for the real world, so we stayed in a guest-house up on the Woodstock Road. It was there that she stuck her Walkman headphones over my ears and played me the music of our making love.

It was, more specifically, that gorgeous, animal fuck from the day of the beach. Thudding through my head, making my body tingle – the sound of Faith gently murmuring, Mmmm, and Don't, and then No . . . please, no. Then came the shriek as I entered her, so loud it rattled my eardrums and I ripped the headphones off.

Christ, I muttered, rubbing my ears and leaning against the head-board. Was I loud? she murmured innocently. Her squealing and pleading continued in the abandoned headphones, like a mouse trapped in the corner. Just a bit, I told her. I met her eye, saying, look, that . . . was only a game. Sure, she answered with a shrug, and tucked her hair behind one ear. It's just, I ventured, that it . . . sounds quite real. Mmmmm, said Faith, it does. Makes it more exciting.

'Is this wise?' I asked.

'Shut up and hold that.'

She gave me her glass of champagne, spat on her hands and rubbed them together. Then she swung her foot back and kicked hard against the door of the toilet cubicle.

The door vibrated. From within, the hideous sound of sobbing continued.

On our way to the gardens, we had been intercepted by a harassed-looking woman from the hotel staff, who asked us if we knew 'the girl in the velvet hat'. Unfortunately, Faith admitted that we did – and so found herself being sent on a quest into the Ladies to see if she could 'talk to her'. She forgot to let go of my hand before undertaking her mercy mission, which was why I found myself sheepishly hovering by the Tampax dispenser and offering useless advice.

Faith kicked again.

'Can't we do something else?' I muttered, taking a quick gulp from her glass. This was the first time I'd ever been in a Ladies, and I was beginning to worry that an aged relative would come in, gasp in horror and swoon on to the tiles. Still, you had to say one thing: it wasn't as pungent as your average Gents.

'Just shut up,' said Faith, 'and keep watch.' She hammered on the door with both hands. 'Jacqui? Will you open up, love? It's Faith. Come on, now, don't be silly.' Cisterns trickled, the disco pounded outside, and the sounds of misery from the cubicle's occupant did not abate. Faith sighed, placed her hands on her hips. 'Look,' she said to the toilet door, 'as long as you stay there being bloody miserable, there's nothing anyone can do for you. But if you open up, I might be able to help you.'

There was a sudden silence from the cubicle. From the ballroom, I could hear the chiming and swirling guitar of the Charlatans, 'The Only One I Know', together with assorted squeals and cheers. Jacqui's silence continued.

'Nice one,' I muttered. 'You should be in the diplomatic service.'

'No,' Faith said. She kicked off her shoes. 'It's when they go quiet that you have to start worrying. Leg-up,' she added, stretching up to reach the top of the cubicle partition.

'Beg pardon?'

'Fucking *leg-up*, come on!'

I shrugged, put the champagne glass on top of the tampon machine. I bent my knees and interlocked my fingers, then hoisted Faith up so that she was looking over the top of the partition. The crying suddenly turned into a yelp.

'Hmmm,' said Faith from above me. She leant right over the partition, and the satin dress tautened smoothly against her bottom. 'Well, I can confidently report that she's neither slashed her wrists nor choked on her own puke. She is, however, swigging from a very unhip flask which I imagine she secreted in her handbag. Woah, noooot good.'

My arms were aching. 'I can't hold you much longer, big girl.'

'Put me down, then, you poof,' she snapped. I lowered her gently. 'Christ, I'm only a fourteen.' She wobbled, steadied herself on my shoulder, just as the cubicle door snicked open. 'Aha,' said Faith. 'Open sesame-seed. Come on, then, what's the toil and trouble?'

'Sexual frustration,' I muttered.

'And you,' Faith added, pointing at me with enough force to put my eye out, 'stay out of this. I know what your bogside manner's like.'

'You do?' This was news to me. I sneaked a look: Jacqui was slumped morosely on the floor of the toilet, with her back against the bowl and a green glass flask clutched tightly in her lap. Her hat was placed on the floor beside her, and a fringe hung, limp as seaweed, over storm-battered eyes.

Faith perched herself on the seat. 'Gimme that,' she said, dabbling her fingers in the air over Jacqui's bottle. The girl looked up, surprised, as if she hadn't even heard us come in, then handed the bottle meekly to Faith. 'Obliged,' said Faith, and she lifted the lid of the cistern and poured the whisky in. 'Now,' she said, taking a huge roll-up from her handbag, 'tell Auntie Faith what the prob is, eh? Stop *looking*!' she added for my benefit, as she fired up and inhaled with relish.

'Is that a good idea?' I asked, nodding at the spliff.

'It's *always* a good idea. Just Say Ta.' She scattered ash as she flipped the narrow end towards me.

'Thanks, but no thanks. My shit's together enough. And I'm permanently paranoid anyway.'

'No, they're just all out to get you. Didn't I say?'

'Probably.'

This whole exchange seemed to pass Jacqui by. She tilted her head, staring at me as if noticing me for the first time, then slowly turned to look up at Faith.

'He did it,' she said in a soft, faraway voice. 'He actually married the bitch.'

'Ahhh.' Faith nodded understandingly. Her joint glowed as she sucked hard on it. She seemed to think deeply, eyes closed, as she held the smoke in her mouth. 'Well,' she said eventually, 'speaking as a bit of a bitch myself, I can sympathize with both sides, y'know? But if I were you, I'd look at the things you can change, rather than the things you can't.'

'Iss so bloo'y unfair,' moaned Jacqui. 'He's s'pose be into equality and fairness, stuff like that. And yet he won' even gimme a *chance*. He's *prej*diss. He *discriminates* 'gainst me. 'Cause I'm ugly. If I was black, I could do him, couldn' I? Have 'm up for it.'

I secretly admired this tragic logic, although I didn't let on. I held up Faith's glass. 'Do you want this, or are you on the hard stuff now?'

She flapped a hand at me, which could have meant anything. 'Jacqui, love,' she said, patting the girl's head, 'let's have you looking respectable again and get you out there dancing, eh? And beauty's in the eye of the beer-holder, remember that.'

Jacqui managed a weak smile.

'Anyway,' Faith muttered, dragging hard on her joint, 'the way they both are, I reckon they'll be divorced in three years.'

I was shocked. It was one thing saying it to me as a half-joke, but . . . 'Faith! For Christ's sake, you can't say that sort of shit at someone's wedding.'

She chuckled. 'Sure I can.' She wafted the joint in front of Jacqui's mouth. 'C'mon, love, bang-bang and forget him.'

Just then, the door swung open with a squeak. I was so startled that I dropped Faith's champagne-flute. It smashed on the floor, right in front of an unmistakable cascade of tulle and ruched silk, with a pair of smaller versions in tow.

'Hi,' I said awkwardly, 'I was just . . .'

Nicole raised her eyebrows, and the junior bridesmaids started to giggle.

'My fault!' Faith sang, popping out from the cubicle, draping an arm around my neck. 'I brought him in here for, ah . . . well, maybe we should go somewhere else.'

'Yes,' agreed Nic rather coldly. 'Maybe you should.' And she swept past, the two girls tottering behind to lift her dress off the tiles. I wondered briefly how much she'd heard from outside.

'Let's go,' said Faith. 'And you,' she added to Jacqui. 'Off that floor, now.' Sheepishly, Jacqui obeyed, staggering slightly and taking deep breaths.

I gestured over my shoulder. 'You know, I've always wondered how they – you know – in a wedding dress?'

Faith sighed. 'I'll tell you outside,' she said, shoving the joint between my teeth, 'if you're good. Come on.'

We sat on the terrace, dangling our feet over the sunken garden. The night smelt of lavender, beer and herbs. Behind us, the reception blazed and throbbed through the elegant bay windows of the hotel. The grounds were picked out in mustard-yellow spotlights, leading down the path to the great darkness of the lake.

I'd moved on to whisky and soda, while Faith was becoming overindulgent with her usual narcotics. She stubbed her second roach out on the flagstones and let her head rest against my shoulder.

'So, how are things between you and Big God?' she murmured.

I was surprised at the question. 'Oh . . . about the same. Not really speaking much these days.'

'Ah. These lovers' tiffs.'

'No, more like a trial separation, actually,' I admitted.

She laughed quietly. 'You're both seeing other people, I take it. What brought this on? The Housemates from Heaven?'

'Nah, they aren't the problem.' I sighed, and swallowed a deep, harsh gulp of whisky. 'I'm the problem. Shall we take a walk?'

We strolled hand in hand down the gardens, following the yellow-light road. We passed under a horse chestnut and I grinned at the hot, bedroom smell of its flowers.

'So is this likely to become permanent, then? You move out, he gets the Teasmade, that kind of crap?'

'Don't be flippant. I started having these weird conversations with myself, you know? All that stuff Luke used to say —'

'What's Luke doing now?'

'Last I heard, he was in Essex, training for the priesthood.'

'Ah. Sorry, go on.'

'Well, you know, he used to say about how human consciousness couldn't have evolved randomly. Started me off thinking . . . yeah, and by that argument, what are the odds that something capable of *creating* human consciousness could have come about? Vastly more unlikely.'

'Good call. Nice one. I refer the dishonourable gentleman, and all that.'

'But then . . .' I sighed. 'You aren't supposed to start that, working it out. After all, you don't pull a computer apart to see how you work the utilities. You just click, click, click.' I mimed the action of a computer-mouse on a pad. 'You assume it'll work. It's faith.'

'What?' She frowned.

'No, I mean . . . Y'know. The thing. *La foi.*'

'Ah, I see. And you're having what zee French zey call a *crise de foi?*'

'That's good, I must remember that.'

'Yeah, well, call it what you want. I reckon you just think too much,' she said, stifling a yawn.

'And you act too much without thinking,' I told her recklessly.

'You like it, though. All the thrills you ever wanted.' We stopped, faced each other. The hotel glowed distantly, the beats of an indecipherable song bouncing out through the dark gardens.

'Well, just maybe I'm growing out of that.' I sounded angry.

'No,' she said softly, with a little laugh. She came right up close, gave me the full effect of those haunted eyes. 'You and me, baby, we go all the way.'

The warm summer air seemed to gather itself up and slip away from me, leaving a hollow of chill in my body. 'I sometimes wonder how serious you are,' I said.

'Deadly,' she answered. I looked at her. She was beautiful, ghostly, feral. Against her moonlit skin, her lips were black and full, promising an ultimate, beautiful absorption. 'When I first spoke to you, I had the idea that your death and mine would be linked in some way. Just one of those things.'

'I don't want to talk about this.'

'No. I know. But just think what we could talk about instead.'

Those eyes. Hard and polished.

'You're right,' I told her with a grin. 'You really are a bitch.'

'Takes years of practice. Nic, she's still in the nursery.' Faith angled her head slightly, as if listening to something beyond my hearing. 'Learning, though, bless her.' She slipped an arm around my shoulders, nuzzled my neck. 'Look,' she whispered, and moved her mouth up so that her lips were moist against my ear. 'I love doing what we do. It's our thing. But we keep getting better. Bigger and better. And we'll reach a stage – some day, some month, some year – where we can't go any further.'

'I don't think I want to get that far,' I told her, turning abruptly. 'Are you coming in?'

She moved slightly away from me, looking sulky. 'Not till you promise yourself to me.'

What new game was this? 'Look, people will be wondering –'

'Yeah, they will. And I could tell them an awful lot. I mean, really, all the things you've been forcing me to do . . . it's quite outrageous. Got it all on tape, haven't I?'

I laughed, not sure whether to take her seriously. 'You think you could tell people that we . . . Say that I . . . You think people would *believe* you?'

'Woah, yup. Noooo problem.' She slipped her arms around my waist, moved her mouth so close to mine that I could feel her breath on my lips as she spoke. I felt slightly queasy. 'Take Mike, for example . . . Always very protective of me, our Mike. Charming, in a way. As if I need protecting. God, the things he'd love to find out about you.'

'But you wouldn't deliberately cause trouble.' I was beginning to wonder, now. Just beginning.

'Darling, I wouldn't need to. You know as well as I do that your friendship with Mike hangs on a feeeeeeble thread.'

'That's not true. He likes me.' I knew as soon as I'd said it that she'd have an answer for that one.

'Yeah? He could turn round like *that*' – she snaps her fingers – 'and lay into you like you were his worst enemy. You know he's only friends with you 'cause I asked him to ease off.'

'That's crap. We're just getting on better.'

'Phhhww! Boll-*ocks*. I mean, look at all your cardinal sins. You said it yourself once. He's itching to have a go. Remember when we found those hippies had been camping out in Nic's house? He could have punched you that night.'

I sighed. 'I'm not scared of Mike.'

'Well,' she said, 'just stick with me, and you can't go wrong.'

'I don't like it,' I told her.

'Oh, you will,' she murmured, and slipped her arms around my neck. 'And who knows?' she added. 'Maybe soon, you'll get to say hi to your friend God after all.'

She kissed me, tasting of dope and wine. I held her, stroking her rich hair and knowing, just knowing that she had me exactly where she wanted me. 'You,' I said, 'are mad. Barking.'

'Oh, beyond. Out towards Romford and Upminster, I am. Shall we go back inside?'

★

'You gotta listen,' Jacqui Potter was saying. 'You know . . . you making . . . a mistake, yeah?' She was hanging on to Mike in the hotel lobby, gripping his lapels so hard that her fingers turned white. Clusters of guests had gathered to see Mike and Nicole off, but their conversation had suddenly become very subdued.

Mike was smiling, trying to extricate himself. 'Look,' he said. 'I'm sorry. I really have to go. The taxi's waiting.'

I glanced nervously at the doors. Nicole, resplendent now in an emerald green velvet dress, was hovering there, fiddling with her bouquet and glowering at the little scene. Her mother, auburn and glossily face-lifted, tut-tutted disapprovingly.

'Jacqui,' I murmured, touching her shoulder gently. 'Don't cause a scene. Remember what Faith said.'

Jacqui hiccuped and took a step backwards. 'Yeah,' she said, and I heard liquid slurp in her throat. 'Yeah, I know what she said.' Jacqui wiped her mouth, nodded, smiled. 'Three years! Three years, she gives you. Me too. An' I'll be waiting.'

Mike overheard this. 'What do you mean?' he snapped.

His wife was tugging at his sleeve now. 'Michael. Come on. We have to go *now*.'

Mike had reddened with anger as he realized what Jacqui meant, and he was looking around angrily for Faith. Nicole pulled him away and he was forced to smile and wave like her, but I saw his eyes narrowing as he scanned the crowd.

Jacqui slumped against a pillar, sniffling. Applause and cheers shattered the air around her, as if for her performance.

Nicole smiled, blew kisses, thanked her adoring public like a film star. They kissed the two mothers goodbye, and gave a final wave. Mike was still glaring into the crowd, wearing a fixed grin beneath evil eyes. They alighted at last on me. I looked away.

As they hurried down the steps towards their waiting taxi, Nicole turned, remembering something. She lifted the bouquet, laughed, and, giving it top-spin, sent it hurtling through the doors, high above the crowd in the lobby.

I see it now, cartoon-bright in the camera of my mind.

I look up, applauding with everyone else. The flowers spin in the half-light, as if in slow motion, and Time seems to stop. The bouquet arcs, reaching its zenith. I hear the clattering of the can–bedecked car as the flowers descend, pirouetting towards a dozen hungry hands.

For one awful moment, I am convinced the flowers are heading to smack Jacqui Potter in the face. Then, something comes adrift and the trajectory of the bouquet shifts. There are two of them. Three. A dozen. The ribbons have somehow come loose and flowers are raining, white and yellow against the dark mahogany of the lobby. People gasp, then start to laugh. Flowers float down, buffeted by air, some fragmenting into petals and fluttering, gentle as snow, on to the burgundy carpet. Some settle on shoulders and hats. Aunts and uncles are chuckling softly.

A broad sweep of headlights slices through the window as the car accelerates down the drive.

I stand at the doorway, see the car rounding the bend into the road, and I shiver slightly as I watch the tail-lights dip out of sight.

09 Comfort and Joy

The shower hisses. In the pale Saturday morning sun, I sit at the table, drinking strong and sugary tea. Normally I hate sugar, but today I crave it, feel empty without it.

In the corner of the lounge, the rumpled futon is evidence of my visitor. I leaf through my newspaper, but the headlines are just fresh-smelling patterns.

The noise of the water stops. After a few minutes, the door opens, and she emerges in a soft cloud of steam. She's wearing Tanya's white bathrobe and is vigorously towelling her tousled, wet hair. She smiles at me.

I can see now that they don't look *exactly* the same. My visitor is just as beautiful, but in a more classical, restrained way. Her hair is worn shorter, just under shoulder-length, and as she rubs at it I can see the greying roots. Her nose is more pointed and bony, and her lips are fuller, more generously expressive. Although she is tall – almost six feet, I'd guess – there is an air of gawkiness about her, as though she feels trapped in a long-limbed body and she can't decide which leg to use first.

'Hi,' she says, perching beside me on the table. 'You recovered?' She is scented lightly with peach shower gel. I look up, into a familiarly impish expression. God, this is *weird*.

'You'll have to forgive me,' I tell her. 'I'd started to be convinced you didn't actually exist.'

She smiles, and starts to run a comb through her hair. 'Well, she was always the imaginative one.'

Her neck, I notice, is still that of a young woman, as is her face, despite the gentle laughter-lines and crow's-feet.

'Coffee?'

'I never touch the stuff. Do you have any herbal tea?'

'A frighteningly wide selection.' I wander into the kitchen-area, switch the kettle on and lean on the worktop so that I can still see her. 'Sleep well?'

'Lovely, thanks. I adore futons.'

'Good. Is Orange Cinnamon Zinger all right?' I hold up the sachet.

'Great, yes.'

I take a deep breath. 'So, in return for my hospitality, are you going to tell me why the hell you've been following me ?'

She laughs, showing a perfect set of white teeth. 'I thought you'd have worked that one out for yourself.'

'You gave me quite a shock last night.'

'I'm sorry. That was rather cruel. I used to work in the theatre, you know. I suppose I've maintained a flair for the, ah, dramatic.' She twirls her hand in a jester's mime.

'Melodramatic,' I correct her sternly.

She shrugs, gracefully conceding me the point. 'As I say, I do apologize.'

Her voice is clear and precise, with a rich, dark Home Counties accent. Faith used to veer off at tangents from a husky, almost Sloanish drawl, and tried out so many different accents that her true one became swamped in mutated vowels. I also get the idea that my visitor is quite proper by comparison: she doesn't seem to swear, smoke or even let herself be ruffled.

'I want to know what you're doing here.'

'Ah, well. I rather think we ought to help one another. You see, I have an idea that something's troubling you, and it might just be what's troubling me.'

'Have you been sending me e-mails?' I surprise myself with the direct accusation.

'Me?' She affects innocence, places a hand over her heart. 'Well, what do you think?'

'I think,' I tell her sternly, folding my arms, 'that we're not going to get anywhere unless we're straight with each other.'

'Let me get dressed first,' she says. 'May I use your bedroom?'

I open up my newspaper again. 'Be my guest, Angelica.'

Five minutes later, she wears a smart pair of black suede jeans and a white cotton blouse with a paisley scarf knotted at the neck. Her earrings are big gold hoops and her left wrist is adorned with a slim, black bangle with an inlaid diamond. She wears no nail varnish or make-up as far as I can tell, and she looks even less like her sister now.

Angelica smiles, settling on the sofa with her tea. I have had today's first hit of coffee, but I feel no better for it.

'You can ask me five questions,' she says languidly. 'Yes–no answers.'

This annoys me. 'You think you can just dictate terms to me?'

She sips her tea. 'Yes,' she says with a smile. 'Four questions left.'

'That wasn't a question!' I snap at her, feeling incongruously like the hapless customer in the 'argument' sketch from *Monty Python*.

She shrugs, smiles, continues to sip her tea with maddening calmness.

I sigh, slumping back in my chair. 'All right. Have you been sending me e-mails under the name of Elektra?'

She looks amused. 'Yes.'

'Okay . . . Did you spy on me and Mike in the cemetery?'

'Yes,' she says, with a sideways smile. 'Two questions left.'

'Have you been in touch with Charlie?'

She wrinkles her nose, as if I'd mentioned something she would rather not talk about. 'No.'

'Ah-ha.'

'One left, sugar-pie, so make it good, won't you?'

It comes out before I can stop myself. 'Do you think there's more to Faith's death than you've been told?'

Angelica lifts her chin, looks me directly in the eye. 'Yes,' she says.

'Right. So now we're getting somewhere.'

'Don't you think the same?' she asks.

'I don't know.' I look away.

'Ah, but you don't like to talk about it. I see.'

'It's not that,' I tell her angrily, and move away from her.

I find myself over by the window again, watching the cars rushing by in the morning light. It's beginning again. Today, hundreds of football games will be played, twenty million lottery tickets sold, six billion lives altered by some small event or other. The traffic-lights shift in their unending dance, the Belisha beacons flash like alien machines. Over in the park, a man throws a ball for his dog. Life goes on. I trace beautiful, smooth lines in the creamy condensation.

'So what is it?' she asks. 'I mean, you were there, you . . . saw what happened.'

'That's just it. I didn't see anything. Nobody did.' I have my back turned to her. I am gripping the window-sill hard, watching the Belisha beacons flash a bright Kia-Ora orange. Clouds snuggle the sun, casting slabs of grey across the town like the shadows of gigantic spaceships. Come to destroy us all. Calling my name.

Angelica says my name again, softly.

'Sorry, what?'

'You . . . started to say something. About Faith.'

'Did I? Maybe I did. I often say things these days and forget I've said them. Maybe I'm getting old.'

She laughs. It's a clear, silvery sound. 'Come on, I'm not far off forty. Although I do sometimes feel younger.' She pauses. I hear her taking a small sip of her orange tea. 'Look,' she says, 'if you don't want to talk about what happened . . .'

'No, it's not that. It's just that I . . . don't really remember.'

'You don't remember?'

'It's . . . a problem I have. With it. I try, and I can't. I think I've got something, and then . . . I hit a wall. I get these fragments, images.' I turn to face Angelica again, suppressing a shiver at the way those dark eyes draw me in. 'I mean, I know . . . *how* she died, the technical details, if you like. But I sometimes think that's only because I heard it all at the inquest and read it in the papers, right? Like it all happened to someone else. And I remember about the stuff . . . afterwards, sure. Mike on the phone. Loads of French. On and on. I didn't have a clue what he was saying. What any of it meant. We all just sat there in the lounge. Stunned. And drank . . . We drank, can you believe it?'

'Go on,' she says.

I draw a deep, shuddering breath, closing my eyes, trying to summon up the ghost of that intensely hot night. I close my eyes.

— *the room is filled with the aching, claustrophobic heat of the French summer night, with the sting of midges and the ceaseless, electronic-sounding chirp of cicadas* —

'There was a helicopter outside. To take her to the hospital. It landed in the plaza and it . . . blew the newspaper around, and . . . it . . .' I swallow, hard. Reality crashes back in. 'I'm sorry. I can't do this.'

'That's fine. Don't worry.' Angelica smiles reassuringly, and it's like a huge daub of red, a clown's smile stretching across her face. 'You don't recall who found her?'

'It was Charlie.' I'm clear on that point. I surprise myself. 'Yeah, Charlie. He still looks the way he did that night. Empty.'

'Hollow,' suggests Angelica.

I look at her in surprise, as that's exactly the word I was looking for. 'Yes. Hollow. As if her death just sucked the spirit out of him.'

'He was closer to her than I ever could have been,' she says softly. 'But you don't have any clearer memories?'

'Look, the police took statements from everyone. I mean, I said something, God knows what. There was . . . a room, a small, hot room. Stank of smoke. An interpreter babbling away. I must have been lucid at the time, I mean, Christ, they must have been happy with me, or I'd be in Gervizan jail now, wouldn't I?' My voice, I realize, has been getting higher, and it ends as a slightly hysterical squawk.

'All right,' says Angelica softly. 'So you can't remember.'

'That's just the problem. I remember. All the sodding time. I do nothing but remember.' (I know I only have to close my eyes and it all begins, Time starts to creak like an old wooden ship in a storm.) 'I just don't remember anything useful.'

'Go on,' she says thoughtfully.

'These past few days, I've not been able to stop remembering. Like I've plugged myself into the past. It's all playing out in front of me, like a film, and I can't leave till it's over.' I take a big, hasty gulp of my coffee and it scalds my mouth, makes my eyes water. I swallow it down, gasping. 'I remember when I first met her, exactly what she was wearing, what make-up she had on, what she said, what we drank. And the gigs she played, who was there, which heckler said what.' I start to pace up and down, taking ruminative sips of coffee. 'I remember stuff about Luke, and the house I used to live in with this Christian girl called Amanda who had cold sores and got all uppity about Faith staying overnight. And Mike Bradfield and all his pseudo-liberal crap, and Nicole, and their wedding . . . I mean – why? It's futile.' I take a deep breath. 'Why? Why am I remembering all this shit? It won't bring her back, will it?'

'All right. So if you can't remember . . . tell me what you *feel*. When you think to yourself, she's dead. Faith is *dead*. What does that do?'

I lift my head, stare into the eyes of the past, the eyes of the future.

I think. I physically try to force myself to feel. Feel. What does it mean, feel? What is an emotion? Isn't it just a biochemical reaction?

'Nothing,' I tell her.

She sighs in relief, leans back and curls up on the sofa. 'Now we're getting somewhere,' she says, with a flash of teeth.

'The other day,' I say tentatively, 'I saw this little girl, right. In a tower-block, some god-awful council flats. I went there looking for Luke. He . . . I dunno, he's got some crazy idea that he can best do God's work in the worst places, I think. Anyway, I saw this little girl, about three, four years old. She was dawdling along and her mother told her to hurry up. When she wouldn't, the mother slapped her. Hard, across the face. And Christ, I wanted to kill that woman. I stood there on the stairs and I thought, you bloody bitch, I could knock you down these stairs right now without a second thought. You know?' I grip my coffee-cup so hard it starts to burn my hands. 'And I went back to my car and I cried and cried.'

'Well, that's understandable.'

'I cried because I told myself I'd never seen anything so desperately horrible and sad. And yet I *have* . . . Well, you must know. You and your bloody Miss Marple tactics.'

'Actually, I think of myself more as a mixture of Jemima Shore and Dana Scully. But do go on.'

'I've worked with kids, boys and girls of fifteen, who couldn't see further than, you know, their next bag of glue.' I pause. It's been a long time since I've actually stood back from it like this. 'You used to think, Christ, that mouthful of crusty sores is going to be round some seedy bloke's cock tonight, no matter what I say to her. And then just last year, a boy came in with "4 Real" slashed into his arm. Course, he'd done it just because Richey from the Manic Street Preachers had done it. You know. That kind of thing. You think you've seen some life. And then an everyday, greasy-faced kid-slapper brings on an attack of total existential despair.'

'It's not that uncommon. Believe me.'

'And *then* I start seeing you. Weird. Only I don't know it's you. And I want to drink, and I want to taste a cigarette again. Just one, would be nice.'

She laughs. 'Now that's just stress. We've all been there.'

'Yeah, well. I've been stressed a lot. I made a bit of a dick of myself at the funeral, actually. I was . . . rather ill. In fact, I chundered. Right in front of everyone. They've all been very tactful about it since, but I'm not going to forget that in a hurry.' My fingers cover my face and I pull d-o-w-n, stretching my eyelids. 'I puked in her *grave*. Christ.'

'I know,' she murmurs. 'I was there.'

'You?' I look up, startled. My hands fall into my lap. 'But –'

'You didn't see me, no. Actually, that was the idea.' Her smile flashes across her face again. 'Mistress of disguise, I am. I don't suppose you remember. Blonde hair, big specs?'

A pale face bounces in front of my tired eyes, peers from behind copper-blue glass.

I've said it before I realize. 'The albino.'

'As I said. Mistress of disguise.' She bobs the teabag in and out of her cup, and winks at me. 'Now, then. Shall we start with that key?'

I'm suddenly aware that the little silver key is sitting on the coffee-table next to the sofa. I must have forgotten to put it back in my wallet after showing it to Tanya. I look up at her again, and she's smiling benignly. She must somehow know the key belongs to Faith, which is odd, because I have not said so. How much does she really know?

'Well, you can if you like,' I tell her guardedly. 'I've . . . got no idea what it's for.'

She sighs, holds the key up to the light. '242,' she says thoughtfully. 'Just a thought, but Faith went to a gym, didn't she?'

'It was attached to the university,' I say in slow realization. 'Topley Road, or something? Topliss Street?' I grab the Medway A–Z from the shelf and start leafing through it. 'You think it's important?' I ask her, still a little wary.

'You obviously think it is, my dear,' she answers with a teasing smile.

I wonder if she knows what I know about the key. Where it was found. 'Here,' I say, finding the road on the street map. 'Toplands Court.'

'Well, then,' she says, putting her mug down on the table. 'Let's go and have a look, shall we?'

★

In Angelica's metallic-green Escort, we ruffle the pages of Saturday suburbia. In the margins, kids kick the sunlight on swings, sponges dribble soapy water on cars, lines of washing ghost-dance in the breeze.

Her eyes are polarized, painted over by tiny circles of colour. She drives smoothly, sensibly. The sun drips over us between the branches of the beeches.

Another thought has occurred to me. 'And . . . the bank account? That was you as well, right?'

She raises her eyebrows. 'You really have been busy.'

'No, I just sort of . . . stumbled into a couple of her bank statements. So how did you get away with that one?'

'We shared a lot more than people knew,' she says abstractedly.

'I see. Her cards and PIN numbers, you mean? What did you do, steal them?'

'Mmmmm, no. It was more what you might call a kind of mutual arrangement.'

'I see. You could get arrested for that sort of thing. I take it the bank hasn't been informed of her death, then.' Just then, to my annoyance, my mobile trills. 'This'll be work. Yup?'

It's Jocasta. The news isn't good.

Angelica drives on into the great grey motorway-land with its sharp blue squares of reassuring information, and I listen to Jocasta's agitated squeaking. Things are not good at Hope Springs. Apparently Dave the security man found two windows smashed and a massive lump of concrete lying right in the lobby, and graffiti on the walls, dreadful obscenities, can't possibly repeat them –

'Ca–' I begin.

And they might have done something else through the hole as well, an awful stench on the walls, and they've been trying to clean it with bleach and they've bought some air-freshener, but –

'Calm –'

And Dave says he's pretty sure there were two of them, teenage boys, he thinks, but they'd made off by the time he got there, it's only to be expected, with them being out at all hours, and the parents don't care, you try talking to them with their awful dogs and their lager –

'*Calmdownjocastanlisten.*'

There is a pause, some desperate breathing. Angelica sniggers.

'Shut up,' I snap at her. 'No – not you, Jo . . . Now listen, do your

139

best to clean up. Then write down exactly what's been damaged and ring the police station, tell them exactly how it was found. Ask for Sergeant Greenaway, if he's available. And get Tony to block the hole with some hardboard . . . What? No, *hard*board, Jo, not cardboard . . . Then ring, ah, just a minute – the glaziers on Pennhirst Row? You know? . . . Right, good . . . And don't *worry*. We're not going to let a bit of petty vandalism stop everything, are we? Mmm? . . . Good girl. All right, I'll be in later. See you then.'

'Trouble at mill?' says Angelica softly.

'Our secretary. Slightly overwrought. I think it'll be okay, though.'

'So what do you do exactly?'

'Community education. We're building a multimedia training centre in an old primary school. We had to fight, but we got a council grant, and some money from Europe, plus industry sponsorship.'

'And do you often get vandalized?'

'Now and then. The estate's got a bit of a reputation. You know the kind of things people say – you can spot the visitors, they're the ones with full sets of teeth, and all that. But then, that's the point, isn't it? We have to take the rough with the dog-rough.'

'How on earth did you get into that? Bit different from the city of the spiring dreams, isn't it?' She flashes a grin at me.

'Oh, a few reasons. I had it hard when I was younger. I mean, it was nothing like as bad as Hope Springs, and I didn't ever go hungry or anything, but I was always aware that my parents struggled.'

'Uh-huh,' she says, concentrating on the road.

'And, yeah, I suppose I was fed up with people going on about *issues* and never actually *doing* anything. Universities are prime places for that.'

'I don't think our Faith ever really got into politics,' says Angelica with a wry smile. 'She could just about tell you who the Prime Minister was, and that would be it.'

Further on, I say to her, 'You didn't tell me why you were spying on us at the cemetery.'

'I was intrigued,' she says. 'Besides, I had no idea where you lived.'

'So you followed us all the way down to Sussex and back? How?'

'I knew where *he* worked. Your friend Mr Bradfield. It was just a question of watching him until he led me to you.' She glances at me, giving nothing away. 'I couldn't have known you were off to the cemetery, of course. That was an unexpected little detour.'

'How did you find the time? I mean – do you work?'

She checks her mirrors as we enter a roundabout, and until we come off at the exit, she doesn't answer me. 'I earn money,' she says.

'That's not what I asked.'

'Sorry. You'll find out.'

'I will?'

'Mmm,' she says, and refuses to be drawn.

We park at the sports centre, which is a large, white building, fronted with blue glass and set among expanses of well-tended football and cricket pitches.

I'm worried about the balding porter, sitting behind his desk with the *Mirror*, but she just smiles and breezes past him. He doesn't seem to want to stop us, and Angelica heads through a pair of swing doors as if she knows exactly where she's going. We find the locker-rooms at the end of the corridor.

'Ah.' I stop, looking up at the big LADIES CHANGING sign on the door. 'Do you think . . . I mean –'

She sighs, opens the door a crack and pokes her head inside. 'No one here. Come on.'

With a disturbing sense of déjà-vu, I follow her uncertainly across the tiled floor, not even wanting to breathe the air in case that makes me some sort of pervert.

'Look,' she says, pointing to a locker. '242.'

'Right, then.' I offer the key to her. 'You do the honours,' I say, stepping back so that I'm closer to the exit.

'Honestly.' She takes the key in her left hand, tries it in the lock. 'Did you have your spine removed at birth or something?'

'You've got a way with words.'

'That's not all I've got away with,' she answers, tugging at the door. It seems to be sticking, and I step back instinctively. Angelica thumps the door a couple of times.

Biting my lip, tasting saltiness, I glance over my shoulder, convinced that someone's going to come in. She steps back, pushes her fringe out of her eyes, reaches for the locker door and yanks it.

The door flies open. I brace myself.

'Well?' I ask her.

She shrugs. 'Nothing,' she says.

'What?' *Nothing will come of nothing* is the phrase that bounces through my head. I step forward, peer into the locker. It's empty. 'But there must be something. Faith was – she had –'

'Yes?' Her eyes are narrow, questioning.

'She had that key on her when she died. It was in a box of stuff Charlie let me have.'

'Charlie gave *you* a box of her stuff? Why?' She emphasizes the last question by slamming the locker door shut, and the sound booms in the confined space. For the first time, her cheeks are flushed with what could be anger.

'Well, no one else wanted it,' I say defensively. 'It was just books, and a music tape, and some old notes, and . . .' I nod at the key. 'That.'

Angelica, hand on hip, sighs as she tosses the key up and down in her hand. 'How very like my sister,' she murmurs, 'to leave us with a Chinese puzzle.' She frowns. 'I wasn't expecting it to be empty.'

'Have a look again. Just to check.'

She peers into the locker again. 'Nope. Absolutely nothing.'

'Just a minute.' I swing the door right back. 'What's this?'

Stuck to the inside of the locker door, almost invisible, is a metallic grey envelope. It's fixed there with steel-grey insulation tape. Angelica and I look at each other.

'I think you should do the honours,' she says.

'I don't like this.' I suddenly feel dizzy, disorientated. 'It's as if someone meant us to find it. I don't like this at all.'

'Oh, for God's sake.' She rips the envelope off the door and tears it open. It contains a standard high-density computer disk, and a colour photograph.

Angelica is obviously as puzzled as me. 'Hold that,' she says, giving me the disk, and peers at the photo.

I move round to look over her shoulder. 'It's Faith.'

'Evidently,' she says.

The photograph is small, square, ultra-bright, and appears to have been taken in a busy city street. It must be a recent shot, as it shows Faith with her hair medium-long and reddish-black. She's wearing mirror-shades, smiling, and standing next to a brown-haired girl I don't recognize.

'Who's that?' I ask Angelica.

'I've absolutely no idea, darling. I was just about to ask you.'

I shiver slightly in the cold changing-room. 'I really feel odd about this.'

'What's up?' says Angelica briskly, as she pockets the photo. 'Someone walk over your grave?'

'No. Vice-versa.'

'I see. Well.' She opens her eyes wide, comes over to stand right next to me. 'I've had an idea,' she murmurs.

Thirty minutes later, we are sitting in an office in the university computing department, Venetian blinds shutting off the outside world and a feeble Anglepoise lamp providing the only light. A huge *Deep Space Nine* poster covers the inside of the door.

Angelica used my mobile to call a computer technician called Serge, who apparently helped Faith with her file formatting and other problems. As soon as he found out who he was talking to, it was open house. Serge turns out to be a small, nervous Frenchman with a big grey moustache, a glistening bald head and a Metallica T-shirt. He jitters as if he's got an internal motor, and drinks mineral water constantly. His office is fragranced with a lemony air-freshener.

'It is good for the system,' he explains, taking a gulp of water as he sits us down in front of his impressive-looking bank of PCs. 'To purify, you know.'

'It's good of you to take the time for this, Serge,' says Angelica softly, moving aside a pile of manuals to perch herself on his desk.

Serge puts down his mineral water for a second or two, strokes his moustache nervously. 'It's no problem. I was fond of your sister. She brightened the place up, you know?'

'So what have we got here, then?' I ask him. I'm more agitated than either of them, perhaps because I don't want to be here at all. Serge narrows his eyes at me. I don't think he likes me much.

'This,' he says, holding up the diskette, 'is file-protected. I don't know who did it, but it is a bloody good job.' He shrugs. 'I think it will take maybe three, four days at least to penetrate the files, and that is if I am doing nothing else.' He adds a very Gallic '*Pfouilh*,' to indicate that the chances of his having nothing else to do are pretty remote.

'But what *is* it?' I ask agitatedly, taking a sip from the flat orangeade I got from the machine in the lobby.

Serge widens his eyes, coughs nervously and crosses and uncrosses his legs, glancing nervously at Angelica. Very slowly, as if I am an imbecile, he says, 'You see, I cannot tell until I have read the files, okay?'

I sigh. 'And you think you can?'

He gulps down another quarter-bottle of mineral water before answering. 'Give me time,' he says, addressing himself to Angelica rather than me.

She hops off the table to pat him on the shoulder. 'Serge, you're wonderful. I know you'll do your best. Now – what about that?'

She points to the big hi-res screen on the wall, on which Serge has scanned in the picture of Faith and the other girl. Pixelled for posterity.

'Yes,' he says, grabbing the mouse, 'here I think we can help. What exactly do you want to know?'

Angelica and I exchange glances.

'Well,' she ventures, 'I'd like some clue as to who the other girl is, I suppose.'

'For what it's worth,' I mutter.

Serge, though, is already at work. He does something with the mouse, presses a couple of keys and slices out a square of the picture, one which contains the brown-haired girl's collar. There's a small circle of white on it, like a badge or a brooch.

Angelica leans forward, a glistening reflection of the screen in her irises. 'What's that?' she murmurs.

'I can flip it out for you,' says Serge. 'It'll be quite blurred. Hang on . . . I load up the image-intensifier software, okay?' He looks up at us, shrugging again. 'It will take a minute or so.'

A minute? I realize this man lives in an accelerated, hypertextual world, a wonderland of instant file-grabbing.

The disk churns and chugs. Serge audibly gulps his water, leaning back, the striplights shining on the dome of his head. He wipes his mouth, clicks the mouse again, and then the screen flickers, blossoming into a perfect, hi-res replica of the badge the girl was wearing.

It's a black, stylized sword against a white background, surrounded by a circle of red dots. At the bottom, there are some letters: MADS. I blink. Mads. *Mads?* The possibilities run through my head. It's a band I've not heard of. Or a night club. Or her name's Madeleine.

Serge shrugs. 'And there it is.'

'Can we have a print-out of that?' I ask him.

As the printer whirrs to itself, Serge shrinks the window and flips back to the original image. 'You know, you have not mentioned what I think is the most important thing about this picture,' he says.

'What do you mean?' I ask, and Angelica overlaps me with, 'There's something else?'

Serge shrugs. 'Well, sure. I think maybe it's obvious, so I didn't say, yeah?'

'What's obvious?' I snap impatiently.

He clicks and homes in on the left-hand edge of the photo, magnifying ten, twenty times. The edge looms on the screen. Before, it seemed straight, but at this magnification we can see it's unevenly serrated.

Serge gestures at the image. 'It's not a photo,' he says, 'it is half a photo. Someone, you see, has cut something off.'

'Listen,' she says, driving back, 'you know what you were saying, about your memory? I think that might be the key here.'

'The key?'

'Absolutely. I mean, there must be a reason for your block, right? There's a space you can't go to, like a blank square in the middle of a map. I think if we can find out what it is that you're frightened of – well, we might be getting somewhere.'

'I think I'd know if I had amnesia.'

'You haven't forgotten it, you just don't want to go there. It's like people who get freaked out by snakes, say, and don't let themselves think about them. I was reading this article on it.'

'Yes. I'm sure you were.' I sigh. 'You know, I'm beginning to feel like my half of the script's missing.'

She laughs. 'Good. I must be doing something right. Now listen. Tomorrow morning, we need –'

'A lie-in,' I snap. I don't mean to sound so sharp, but I've decided I would like some control back over my life, rather than being at the mercy of female caprice every time I have a day off.

'I see. You think this is easy? You think we're going to solve this from our beds?'

'Solve *what*? Angelica, this isn't Murder She fucking Wrote. Your sister took an overdose and died. I'm sorry, but there it is.'

'Says you.'

'Says everyone! Says the police, the coroner, her family. As for the rest of the gubbins from today, well . . . she's got her own reasons for being devious. Knowing Faith, she's probably having a laugh from beyond the grave. At our expense.'

'In the morning,' she goes on relentlessly, 'we need to plan. Meanwhile, you – oh, yes, one other thing. Who was actually there? At that place you hired over the summer?'

'The *gîte*?' I frown. 'Me, Faith, Charlie, Jan . . . Mike and Nic.'

'A happy little band,' she says with a smile.

'Yeah, I don't think. We were trying to be jolly and friendly about it all . . .'

'If you don't mind my saying so,' she offers, 'it was a little bizarre for you all to end up together like that. Hell might be other people, but absolute hell, my dear, is going on holiday with them. But, well, I'd imagine you didn't have much say in it, though.'

'Faith could be very persuasive. If she got it into her head that something was a good idea . . .'

'Ahhh,' says Angelica, nodding sagely. 'Sorry, you were saying? About being jolly and friendly?'

'Err . . . well, you know. Outings, games, acting up for the camcorder, that sort of thing . . .'

'Uhh-huh. Interesting. Whose camcorder?' she asks.

'Mike's, I think. Yeah, Mike's. I hate the bloody things myself. More of a holiday-snaps man. I doubt anyone's going to feel much like watching it now.'

'Mmm. Now, listen,' says Angelica, and her voice takes on a fresh tone of urgency, 'if anyone tries to call you – especially any of that lot – you be very wary, okay?'

'Angelica, trust me. If Faith starts making phone calls to me, I'll be more than bloody wary.'

'You know what I mean. The rest. Don't arrange to meet any of them on your own,' she says firmly, turning to look at me for a second. Her expression is deadly serious. 'Don't trust *anyone*.'

I can't believe this. 'Now you're sounding more Mulder than Scully. What are you, paranoid?'

'No. Just sensible. Now, then – tonight. When you're drifting into sleep, call up your past and ask it a few more questions. Oh, and make sure you have some dreams. They're cheap-rate calls to history. Think yourself back.'

'I see. And how exactly do I induce dreams?'

'Welllll . . . There are several possibilities.'

'Such as?'

'Do any hallucinogens at all?' she asks, with a quick glance at me.

'Not especially.'

'Hmm, makes it more difficult. Try having cheese before you go to bed.'

'Cheese. Right.' This is becoming surreal. 'Anything else?'

'We have to find that no-go zone,' she says. 'It's in there somewhere. Your X marks the spot.' She points to my forehead. 'There's the answer.'

I sink back in the seat, watch the road hurtling past. It's going so fast it seems to chafe against my eyes, and I imagine the flimsy corneas peeling like grapes.

She drops me at home, and drives off before I have a chance to ask her in. I wonder, very briefly, where she is staying.

It's all too confusing. The picture and the badge. Mads. MADS? And the cut-off edge. And that disk. Serge has promised to get back to us. I am just a little uneasy now, worried about what it might contain. Somehow, that little square of plastic, metal and silicon is more chilling than a leather-bound diary of secrets.

My X marks the spot? Is that what she said? I pull down my eyelids in the bathroom and horrify myself with my pallor, red rims, grey hollows. Why *my* X? Why say it that way? I push back my tangle of hair, decide to have a shower. As the jets of water pummel me, I suddenly realize what she must have meant. Faith is *my ex*.

Not that I ever call her that. It would be pretty stupid, these days. She's *dead*, for God's sake. She was my ex before she was dead, so what is she now that she's an ex-Faith, like the ex-parrot? (An ex-ex? Ex-squared? More like ex-squared plus why-squared.)

I'm towelling my hair so hard it hurts, and I think to myself that I never use the expression. People who say 'my ex' still think the person is part of their life. 'My' is the tie, the possessive adjective. Ex becomes the X. It marks the file on the unknown. It's the mysterious, the unattainable, so nebulous it might one day be a revenant.

In there somewhere, she says. It's got the answer, she says.
   What, though, is the question?

10 Please Be Cruel

'The sixties,' says Faith, tipping her last cigarette out on to my dining-room table, 'were so *shite*.'

'Oh, right,' I answer with a grin. 'Like you remember the sixties all of a sudden.' On the black-and-white portable, in the corner of the screen, *Telly Addicts* dips into the recent past, sending blue ghosts flickering against the wall.

'I mean they're *boring*. I'm sick of it. People banging on about Carnaby fucking Street and Mary bloody Quant and the Beatles and that sad, sad – wossname – you know. Naked people with horrible moustaches, loads of mud?' She lights up, sinks back into her chair.

'Woodstock?'

'Yeah, Woodstock. On and on about it. As if nothing else important ever happened, before or since. Like if you didn't grow up back then, you missed out on one great big party and you – have – no – life. Christ on a unicycle.' She takes a deep drag on her cigarette, sucking the bright orange tip until ash cascades to the carpet, exhaling with relish. 'I liked the eighties,' she adds wistfully.

'Oh, sure, brilliant decade. Aids, unemployment, famine . . . Jive Bunny . . .'

'So what's your favourite?'

'Must I have one?' I ask her, pained.

'Yup, it's compulsory. I just decided.'

'Okay, the nineties. I'm giving it a chance.'

'Christ,' mutters Faith. 'I'm sleeping with an optimist.' She holds up the wine bottle to the light. 'You *are* half full. Nope, doesn't work. Can't do it.'

'You're not trying.'

She grins lopsidedly at me. 'Some people say I'm very trying, angel. Anyway, it's time.' She puts the fish-knife on the table between us, twirls it hard. It spins, slicing the light from the cheap bulb above us.

Ninety-one, when the Mirror group floated and Maxwell didn't. The year we found out what Scuds and Patriots were, and Terry Waite came home to embrace the rain, and Freddie Mercury sang his swansong. I first saw Mike and Nicole's new house in this year. I'd heard about it: new, detached, in an up-market suburb of Guildford.

'Just remember,' said Faith in the taxi, 'avoid politics, and we'll be fine. And don't mention that flag he used to have.'

I sniggered. 'As if I would.'

'Yeah, well. You would.'

'He bloody asks for it, though. Always going on about tolerance of this, that and the other.'

Faith had heard this before. The thing about Mike's alleged broadmindedness was that it was never *challenged*. As he was continually telling me that what people called 'political correctness' was no more than 'good manners', it would be interesting to see how well-mannered he could remain in a one-to-one with, say, a committed Tory.

'True tolerance,' I went on, 'okay, even Christian tolerance, if you like, that's putting up with views you dislike. It's nothing to do with playing up to the disenfranchised, so you can feel all superior and martyred when they gratefully accept your help.'

'Yeah, yeah,' muttered Faith, in that just-leave-it-boys way she used to have in college. 'Got it out of your system, lovey? Good, 'cause here we are.'

Even my cynicism hadn't prepared us for the house. As Nic whirled through the rooms, delightedly flinging open door after stripped-pine door, I felt we had stepped into an Ideal Home. It was washed in waves of aquamarine carpet, softened by clouds of blue velvet curtain with gold trim, and it smelt of polish and new paint. A wooden tribal mask hanging in the bedroom was the only trace I could see of Nicole's former persona. The kitchen, brooding under wood and chunky terracotta tiles, was designer-rustic, a farmhouse pantry snapped between the inverted commas of suburban chic. Even the bathroom was a showpiece: bright ceramic shells, seahorses and starfish (somehow, I'd expected those) and bales of towels in harmonizing blues.

I didn't suppose two new teachers' salaries could buy all this: Mike's brand of socialism allowed the odd backhander from the in-laws, I imagined. But for what? The house rang hollow with sadness. Even the books and records, those barometers of individuality, were tucked away behind latticed glass cases. I might have theorized about the catalogue-perfection of the place. I might have seen its coldness as a cry for help, a need to be filled by the cries of children, their blotchy artwork and their tiny shoes. There was one undecorated room upstairs, a small, musty bedroom with bare boards and green paint. 'We haven't got round to doing that one,' Nicole said, and quickly closed the door as if she could not bear to face the emptiness.

She did not know, back then. It was to take her another two years to be sure that she was barren.

We had spinach roulade, followed by coq au vin (Nic was, as I'd guessed, a fair-weather vegetarian) accompanied by a Spanish red in heavy crystal glasses.

'So how's the teaching going?' I asked when we came to the main course.

Mike glanced at Nic. She looked up, then quickly back down again, as if hoping not to be drawn.

'Sorry,' I said hastily, 'shouldn't I have asked?' I began slicing my chicken with an unnecessary fervour.

'I'm . . . changing schools,' Nicole said, with a brief look at Mike.

'Oh, right. You've only just started there, haven't you?'

'I'm sure Nic's got a good reason,' said Faith, raising her eyebrows at me.

All right, I thought, I'll shut up. I shrugged and took a long, careful sip of wine instead.

'One of the kids took a dislike to Nic,' said Mike. 'She's looking around. To apply to somewhere else. You know.'

'It was a bit more than a *dislike*,' Nicole muttered.

There was an awkward silence. It was clear that Nic didn't really want to discuss this, but that she didn't want us to be left hanging on Mike's half-explanation, either.

'Do you want to share this, darling?' asked Faith gently.

She shrugged, looking down and poking at her food. 'One of the Year 10 boys. A troublemaker. I was giving him a lecture about calling these girls slags, and he . . . attacked me. Hit me.' She paused, laid down her knife and fork and folded her hands under her chin before continuing. 'Hit me there,' she said, tapping her left breast. 'Really hard. Hurt like hell. I've still got a bruise.'

Please don't show us, I thought grimly.

'Nic, that's terrible,' murmured Faith. 'Was he excluded?'

'No. He . . . they took . . . stuff into account. About his home life. The family. Always in trouble and they're being rehoused.' She shrugged, flapped her hands as if shaking off a minor worry, and picked up her fork again before looking at each of us in turn. 'Mother's off somewhere, older sister's a heroin addict. Great role models.'

'And he's back in school?' I said.

'Will be.'

'But it's just one little sod,' said Faith, waggling her fork. 'Presumably you can ask not to teach him?'

'It's *not* just him,' she sighed, pouring more wine. 'The place is full of evil little bastards. I'm giving up. Looking for a school in a nicer area, and I don't even mind if it means travelling an hour each way. Anything's better than teaching that scum.'

'That's not really fair.' Mike's comment was so unusually soft that I looked up in surprise, almost not realizing it was his voice. 'They're disadvantaged kids, that's all. Left on the scrap-heap by the system. If they had decent opportunities –'

Nicole laughed derisively. 'Oh, yeah. You give them nice new textbooks and they'll transform into human beings overnight. You're too bloody *understanding* of these people, Michael.'

He slumped back in his chair, took a moody slurp of his wine. 'Perhaps I want to be. Perhaps it comes of having grown up in that sort of deprivation.'

'You poor, deprived grammar-school boy,' I murmured. Faith shot me a warning glance. 'Sorry, sorry,' I added quickly. 'I know, mum and dad worked hard for their money. So did mine.' *But I don't go on about it*, added that more daring voice inside my head.

Faith smiled, leaned back, stretching her arms. 'Darlings, that was a *love*-ly meal, so let's not spoil it by setting the world to rights.'

'The dessert needs to defrost,' Nic admitted. 'Sorry.' At least that was something we could all have a wry, complicit smile about.

'I'm going for a fag,' Mike announced. 'See you outside,' he added to Faith.

I grinned. 'Nicole, love, I'd no idea he kept little boys to polish his shoes. Where does he hide them?'

'Silly,' said Faith, snapping her gold lighter on and off. 'He means he's got a secret supply of homosexuals, didn't he tell you?'

'I'll help you with the plates,' I offered to Nic.

The candle flickers. The room smells of hot wax. The knife wobbles, comes to a halt with the sharp end nearest to me. I sigh in resignation. Faith giggles and claps her hands.

'My dare,' she says. 'Right.'

The TV's off now. She's put on a CD of crashing club anthems. I used to hate all this house and dance stuff until I realized what it was *for*. I started to see it, or rather feel it. The sound painted deep, broad strokes and you scribbled in the details. This music wasn't trapped in verses and choruses: it didn't want to know if oooh, your baby had left you, oooh in the *rain* and aaah in the, er, *pain*. They were about experience, depth, impression. They were submarines of sound crashing through cold oceans with their radar pinging and whalesong bouncing off the hull. The more you listened, the more you heard echoes, too: of Celtic folksong, of the white noise at the edge of your radio, of the roaring chants of football terraces.

I could get all this without the aid of drugs, so I couldn't understand the attraction of whacking up your serotonin levels, getting slack-jawed and sparkly-eyed and hugging pheromone-soaked strangers. But each to her own.

'I've got one for you,' she whispers.

Nicole stashed the plates in the sink with enough fervour to break them, and ran a token amount of hot water over them to sluice away the stains. 'I want a Woman Who Does for all this,' she muttered. 'I'm useless at it. Housework, all that shit. Mike won't have anyone, though. Says it's unsound.'

'It's unsound to create a job for someone? Mmm.'

Nic shrugged, pouring me some more wine. 'He says paying someone three pounds an hour to scrape up our dust is degrading. Especially as dust is mainly human skin.'

Skin, she said, and it bounced through my mind. *Skin is the tough, pliable, waterproof coating of the body. It is the largest organ in the body and is sensitive to touch, pressure and painful stimuli.*

'If he feels that bad about it,' I suggested, 'he could always offer to pay more.'

'Quite,' she said, as we moved back into the lounge. 'But he's happy to have me skivvy for nothing. I sometimes wonder quite what his principles cover.'

Out on the patio, Faith and Mike were swapping jokes and cigarettes in the setting sun.

'She almost caused hell at the wedding, you know,' Nic murmured.

'Really?' I took a gulp of wine to cover my surprise.

'Making remarks to Jacqui Spotter like that. Very nearly ruined our honeymoon.' I looked her in the eye, but she didn't smile. She rarely smiled, these days.

'I'm . . . sorry. On Faith's behalf.'

'Doesn't matter,' said Nicole briskly, refilling her glass, and mine. 'They never fight for long.' She nodded out at the patio. 'After all, when she's got her claws in him . . .' Then she blushed, as if suddenly remembering who she was talking to. 'Sorry,' she muttered, glowing.

'You think . . .' I pointed towards the patio. 'Ohhh, no, look, I mean . . . They're close friends, certainly, but —'

'Close friends who *fuck*,' Nicole spat.

She hardly ever used the word, so I was as taken aback by the zestful fricative as I was by the accusation itself. 'You can't be serious, surely?' My mind was racing, now, trying to add up all the instances when Faith and Mike had been alone together, in college and beyond.

'Oh, yeah. They keep in touch, you see. Send each other dirty little messages on e-mail.'

'On what?'

'Electronic mail. You know, computers. One of Mike's work-mates says everyone'll have it soon, although I can't see it myself.' She sighed, took a ruminative drink. 'Yeah, they flirt by microchip. That's the technological revolution for you.' She shrugged. 'Sorry, I thought everybody knew about them.'

I blinked, wobbling slightly, and tried to analyse how I felt.

My relationship with Faith had touched on love and was now speeding out of the other side into something darker and stranger.

The thought that she probably entertained herself with other men had already occurred to me, and in a way I had accepted it. But this was Mike. This was the precocious Bradfield, the one who smugly left exams an hour early. Who always got her to shift up so he could sit beside her. Who had to win every argument. The self-appointed expert on politics, tolerance and the great leap forward. This was different.

'Have you . . . I mean, can you be sure?' I asked Nicole, watching them carefully.

She shrugged, took a deep gulp of the wine. She'd been drinking a lot, tonight, especially after going on about those kids. 'I don't need to. He's said enough.'

'God, has he?' I finished my glass, wondering whether I wanted to laugh or shout.

'But you two . . . I mean, you had a thing, didn't you? But you're . . . I mean, you're not any more?' Nicole was looking at me earnestly. She had obviously gathered this from somewhere, so I nodded, shrugged.

'Yeah, you're right,' I said. 'Not any more.' It was what she wanted to hear, after all.

Out on the terrace, Faith stroked Mike's cheek with one pointed fingernail.

Sensitive to touch, pressure and painful stimuli.

They both laughed, leaning towards each other. Then she said something to him and turned to come back into the house. As she strolled in, I was affecting the middle of a conversation with Nicole.

'. . . So I said, yeah, nothing wrong with teaching EFL for a while, thinking it'd be a couple of months, you know. Ends up being the best part of a year . . . You okay out there?'

'Fine,' said Faith with a brief smile. 'Just going to admire the gorgeous bathroom again.' She staggered upstairs, la-la-ing the chorus to 'Kinky Afro'. Nicole sank into her drink.

I glanced briefly back out at the terrace, and I almost jumped. Mike's expression, for an unguarded moment, was dark, terrifying, before he caught my eye and sheened his face with blankness.

Christ, I thought, *what a politician.*

I didn't know what Faith had said to him as she turned to come in, but there was no mistaking that look. He'd been staring after her with something very close to hatred.

I hurry through a dark and silent street. A Medway town, chilled and stinking of drains, washed in rainwater and orange light. The rain sparkles in the air, a light veil of static on the off-tuned land. Street lights shimmer in puddles, fizzing like dissolving aspirins. Somewhere, a dog barks and a door is slammed shut.

I turn my collar up and hurry on. Cars squat at the side of the road, their carapaces sleek and purple in the lights. Some glow with the adornments of security: yellow wheel-locks, tangerine gear-clamps. The air is harsh, lung-burningly cold as I hurry along, and my squashy footsteps are the only sound I can hear as I turn into the arcade. The shops are silent, still, gagged and blinded by grey shutters. Some, though, are merely dimmed or darkened, left to whisper enticements out into the concrete land.

It is three-thirty in the morning.

I stop, shivering, and draw the video camera out of my bag like a weapon. I frame the world. The red heartbeat of the machine pulses in the corner as I zoom in on the window-display. Sleek, featureless women draped in animal furs of black, brown and white.

My heart is pounding. I keep thinking one of those shaven plastic heads will open its eyes, swivel towards me, raise its hand to strike me down.

I turn, and the camera jiggles with me, the lights painting follow-streaks on the tape as I scan all round the deserted arcade. There are no immediately obvious security cameras.

I turn back to the fur shop and reach into my hand for the little bomb she gave me. An impact device of plastic so brittle I've been convinced it would shatter in my pocket. It sits in my free palm, the size of a cricket-ball, the dark contents sloshing.

For a moment, I hesitate. I almost walk away. Then I think of her deep, commanding eyes.

The plastic ball sits in my hand, sticky and hard.

I throw it. The trajectory is good, the distance only a few metres. The ball shatters against the window, and the pig's blood sloshes in a gigantic exclamation-mark across the glass.

I duck behind a rubbish-bin, sure that someone will have heard, but when I realize that the world has not even breathed, I lift myself up and do a final scan with the camera, making sure to get in all the details of the dripping blood.

Then, I switch the camera off, shove it in my bag and duck into the underpass, not looking back.

After the meal, we took a taxi home and I didn't speak.

Back at Charles and Jan's, she could tell there was something bothering me. She slid up behind me in the kitchen, wrapped her arms round my waist as she gave me a glass of water. 'Staying here tonight?'

'Don't know,' I murmured, stroking her hands.

'Suit yourself.'

'Nicole thinks,' I said, not looking at her, 'that you're having an affair with Mike.'

She laughed, pulled away from me. I studied her as I turned round. To be honest, I thought she looked genuinely amused more than anything.

'That's very flattering – I suppose.' Faith laughed, kicked off her shoes and sat down at the kitchen table. 'What do *you* think?'

I shrugged. 'I've learnt not to prejudge things.'

'Look,' she said, 'Mike's a darling, but . . . well, you know he's always fancied me. I just don't fancy him back. Nothing I can do about it.'

'You still play with him, though. Tease him.'

'Perhaps.' Her eyes were wide, glistening. 'Anyway, does it matter?'

I sighed, shrugged. 'Maybe not.' I lifted my head, met her gaze as I felt a smile stealing across my face. 'I'd do the same myself.'

'Mmm.' She wrinkled her nose. 'Nah, wouldn't work. You're not his type.'

'Very funny. Nic sounded pretty convinced, you know.'

Faith perched on the table, making a dismissive 'phhwww' sound. 'Oh, yeah. Come on, we're talking about the girl who used to be *convinced* the Green party were going to save the world. And a bunch of mummy's-boy hippies were her best mates, remember? Then she was a socialist for a while, and now I don't know what the hell she is.' She lit a cigarette. 'Give her two months, she'll be accusing the Pope of shagging him.'

Knowing I could melt her guard, I smiled, leaned on the table and brought my face up close to hers. 'You do see other people, though.'

Her eyes glistened in surprise. 'Darling, haven't we discussed this? You know the position. There's no one quite like you.' She shook her head as she blew a jet of smoke, and her barrage of teeth glinted in the dimness. 'Can you imagine us being like Mike and Nic? So tied to each other that we watch every little move?' She narrowed her eyes, impersonating a predator scanning the kitchen shadows. 'Where've you been, who've you seen, all that crap?'

The kitchen door opened. It was Charles, in jeans and an untucked green denim shirt, his hair in late-night spikes. 'You two back already?' he asked, heading for the fridge. 'I'd expected you to be chatting away till the small hours.'

I shrugged, smiled. 'Funny expression, that. Why are they small? . . . Anyway, what are you doing?'

He took out a beer, offering us one, which we both declined, and snicked the top off with a bottle opener. 'A report on our market rationalization project,' he said apologetically. 'Well, you did ask.'

Faith smiled adoringly at her cousin. 'Devotion to duty.'

'Not quite.' He took a long, moody swig of his beer. 'Evasion of other duties, more like.' For a second, his grey eyes looked guilty, hunted, and he rubbed his already-tousled hair into an even more tangled mess. 'Jan, as she wants the world to know, is ovulating. She's started mapping it on the computer.'

I suddenly felt like an intruder. 'I get the idea I should . . . leave you guys to chat,' I said awkwardly, heading for the door.

'No, no, it's all right,' he said. 'No great secret, after all. She's been going on about having kids since the age of seventeen.'

'A lifetime's ambition,' Faith added, with a fervent nod. 'Doesn't she do graphs of her cellulite levels as well?'

Charles grinned, took a deep gulp of beer. 'You're not supposed to know she's got any.'

'It always sounds like a product to me,' I put in. 'You know, some sort of miracle lotion. New Cell-U-Lite! Available now!'

Faith covered my mouth with her hand. 'I must apologize for my friend's very existence on this planet. He is an unfortunate accident of DNA. Do go on, Charlie.'

I kissed her palm.

He shrugged, downing what was obviously a much-needed beer. 'We've not even talked about it,' he said gloomily. 'She just assumes that now's the time, and can't understand why I'm not leaping on her in every moment of fecundity.'

Faith sighed. 'Look,' she said, making a brief, chopping motion with her hand. 'You've just got to be firm with her.' It evidently wasn't the first time they'd been through this conversation. 'Tell her that kids are foul creatures whose orifices compete to see how much they can produce. They're drooling, babbling and incontinent. Like old people, only with energy.'

Charlie slumped at the table. 'Christ,' he said, and he meant it. 'Marriage, mortgage, maturity, and now maternity. I sometimes wish I could be more like you two.'

Faith glanced at me, and quickly looked away again.

The aftermath. She smiles, leans up to envelop my mouth with a warm, wet kiss. In the background, the splattered shop front gleams from the video screen, held in thrall by a pause button, the picture rippling slightly at the edges.

'Very good,' she mutters in my ear. 'You see how easy it can be?'

'I felt very stupid,' I tell her crossly. 'Supposing I'd been caught? I wasn't even doing it for a cause, was I? Animal rights or anything. It wouldn't have been worth it.'

'That's the point,' she whispers. 'They'll round up the usual suspects. Smelly crusties in plastic shoes, I expect.' She pulls back from me slightly and her grin is ghost-bright in the darkness. 'Tell me what you want.'

I don't need to tell her.

I embrace her naked body and bend my knees, slowly descending into a kneeling position, so that I am against her breasts, then her waist, then her buttocks, her thighs and finally her booted calves. I feel her hands stealing towards my hair and the crackling thrill of it impales me from head to foot. I curl up. I slowly unfurl my arms from her hot, sticky body. I lean back, close my eyes. Without seeing, I know what happens. She lifts her hand. Opens her palm.

When the blow comes, it seems to strip the skin from my face. It knocks me right off-balance, crashes my body against the floor. A bright, clamping mask of hot red pain fixes on the right-hand side of my face.

I lift myself up on one elbow. She is walking towards me, her heavy lace-ups thumping the floor. A taloned hand grabs me by the hair and jerks my head back. She bends her legs slightly.

I lean forward, begin to lick the smoothness of her left thigh. She allows the grip on my hair to become relaxed, almost affectionate. Then she swings her leg back, aims her foot and kicks me in the stomach.

Pain is the stimulation of nerve endings, for example by tissue damage. Pain receptors initiate responses in the spinal cord and convey information to the brain. However, the body contains natural painkillers – endorphins and enkephalins – which are released into the brain and spinal cord, and the level of these is determined by psychological factors.

In other words, mind over matter.

I drift in and out of wakefulness, aching beautifully, soft and sore. She straddles my back, rubs the coldness of an antiseptic cream into my scratches.

'I've heard from Mike and Nic,' she says. 'They want us to go to dinner. At their new house.'

'Mm-hmmm,' I manage to say, and let her hands stroke me into a disorientated sleep.

Stimulation of one body region can reduce pain in another. The opposite can also happen: recurrent pain in certain areas can sensitize others so that they become trigger zones, affected by even the lightest touch.

Her face – the memory of her face – is a trigger zone.

11 Fire and Water

The sunlight's blasting the land with heat. Those squat buildings glow, white on lemon-yellow, beyond an expanse of rippling green. The church bells clang out across the vineyards and I glimpse them in their toffee-brown tower, kicking the light as they swing.

At the open shutters, the air smells of hay, heat and lavender. I spy her, a silhouette two hundred yards from the house. Now. Turning. Glancing back at the house, a coal-black ghost in her wraparound skirt and sparkling shades. She stares through me across that expanse, seems to look up at my window, yet continues. She gives a half-smile into the light, almost raises a hand, and then she's over the crest, dragging a torpid shadow.

I wonder why she's heading for the town, but I don't call out. That turn, that look over the shoulder, is a time-lapse photo leaving traces on the sky.

It is four-thirty in the afternoon and the bells crash on through the valley. The light throbs. She has gone.

I awake, sweat-soaked, feeling I have seen a gash in the fabric of eternity. As sleep pulls me back, I wonder why that slice of the time continuum is the one to burn with heat and light, to call me with its sonorous clang.

'Are you all right?' says Angelica in my mobile. 'Shall I come over?'

I listen to the wind hurtling through the old church, and I tell her no, I'll be fine, and I flick the mobile off, let it fall from my hand on to a split hassock. I break the seal on the bottle of Jameson's, and remember how I ended up here.

Two hours before. The rain is a barrage, unceasing. Every drop thunders on the roof of the flat as if it intends to be the one to breach the human world, to reclaim the flat for Nature. The place already smells damp, putrid like a wet Labrador.

Tanya, crackly and distant, has told me on the answerphone that the problems are sorting themselves out, the bleak mountains are depressing her and there is nothing to do in the evenings but drink over-priced lager. She thinks she will be there for another few days.

'Mads,' I mutter absently to myself, as I stride up and down the lounge. The windows wobble with rain, rippling the grey evening light so that I feel as if I'm living inside a giant swimming pool. 'Mads, mads . . .' I'm drinking from a carton of orange juice. On the stereo, Inspiral Carpets: moody stuff about feeling lonely and small, and your world meaning nothing. Tell me about it, Tom.

Out on the edge of town, where Hope Springs rises like a carbuncle, the clouds are dustbin-grey, solid. There's a band of red sky, too, painted on the rain as if someone's brushed the sky with blood.

Now that can't be right, surely? I wipe the window, the cold glass biting my hand. The world, soft and wet, shimmers.

Just then, the telephone starts to ring.

Shadows gather in the stone.

They are hyper-black, crawling from the walls like waking demons. High above me, the flutter of pigeons tears through Time, or it could be the shuffle of ghosts as they clamour to peer at the solitary human slumped in his wooden pew.

I taste the cold bottle, and then the warm comfort of its contents.

Blue chunks of light shatter across the floor of my mind and marbles cascade to the four corners of a room. A spectre stretches its hand from the darkness. I know I have to pull the creature back, but that if I do, I will surely perish myself, dragged into the soft earth.

I close my eyes. The vision flashes up in negative ultracolour, like computerized stained-glass on my retina, then starts to fade.

'No good,' I mutter to myself. 'Can't fix it.'

Anyway, not important now. It's ending. Life is ending.

Or perhaps just beginning.

So, after the phone call I drive, drive, heading for Hope Springs.

The traffic is directed by lunatics, flashing under orange and blue strobes. Rainwater soaks us all. Wipers squeak, dancing madly in the darkening city. The traffic is trying to kill me. This is the only conclusion I can reach as I weave my way through it, gripping the wheel. I am stuck, absurdly, behind a scaffolding van sporting the legend 'Satisfaction With Every Erection'.

Across the city, a storm rages. A tempest of hatred and fury, written in red and orange against the sky.

The world feels warm, soft at the edges. I'm not sure if I can quite find the church floor. How long have I been here?

The demons whisper in the darkness.

Think back.

I can see three fire-engines on the Mills Road, sleek and glowing red. Great jets of water are sluicing from the firemen's hose-pipes, making no appreciable difference.

A ghost looms. A policeman in a fluorescent jerkin. He's young, pale and tense. 'I'm sorry, sir. We're having to ask people to take an alternative route through the estate.'

I tell him why I'm here and show him my documentation. He radios to someone while I wait, then he lets me stop my car and get out.

As soon as I step out I'm knocked back by the roar and the heat, a blistering blast which fizzes the rain, squashes it into steam. The brightness of the fire wrenches life from the sky, a great, incandescent pyre crashing up into the angry night. In the midst of the inferno is a crumbling frame, an effigy in blackening brick and collapsing wood. It seems to eat up the jets from the hoses as easily as the rain.

As I watch, a beam splinters, falls in a fountain of sparks, and then a wall follows it, dissolving like paper as the flames gnaw away at life.

Silently, I mouth the name of Jesus. Useless against this devastation.

Two more police cars are appearing over the hill, scattering blue light across the redness. The young policeman's taken my arm and is pulling me back behind my car. 'Best not to get too close, sir. We'll let the fire boys deal with it.'

'Do they know . . .' I begin, and realize my voice is too hoarse to be heard. 'Do they know how it began?'

He shrugs, as his radio starts to crackle questions again. 'Sorry, it's just too soon – Four Zero receiving?'

All around is red, aching with heat. The sky roars. Devil-flames dance, laughing at me and at the hopes which sprung here. It's over. Hope Springs is dead.

'Holy fucking shit,' I mutter, slumping against my car. I'm mesmerized by the sparks as they ride high in the sky, borne on wave after wave of pitchy smoke. My back is sloppy with rain, while my front crisps and shrinks, drying off at the edge of the heat-barrier.

There's a shadow at my side. I look down.

There's a shadow behind me. I look up.

It's her. Standing in the nave, hands on hips.

'How did you know where to find me?'

'Intuition.' Her footsteps click smartly, punching holes in my head. I try to sit up, realize I can't. 'Ah,' she says, leaning over me. 'Let me guess. Father, son and unholy spirit. For sharing?' She nods at the bottle.

I thrust it at her. At least I'm not quite drunk enough to clutch it protectively.

'Is it a disaster?' Angelica murmurs after a while.

I shrug, and I'm sure the Virgin Mary winks at me. 'For the moment,' I manage to slur. 'Yyyeah.'

'You'll get it back on the insurance, though?'

'Phhwwwww . . . Things were at a delicate stage. Problem. Might have to . . . cough some up. Selves.'

'Please do it quietly. Look . . . I might be able to help.'

'You?' I intend to turn to her and fix her with steely contempt, but I'm still sober enough to guess I end up looking manic.

'Why not? I'll see what I can do,' she says, and takes a long gulp from the bottle. 'You've not got anything catching, have you?' she asks, wiping her mouth with her hand.

'Just nostalgia.'

'Ah. That's terminal. Luckily, though, I've had the jab.'

'You' right then.'

Bright eyes in a dark face, hovering at shoulder height. It's Wes, for once devoid of his totemic Walkman.

'Wes! What are you doing here?'

'Saw it, didn't I?' he mutters. 'Knew they'd rung you.'

'Wes – do you know something about this? Do you have any idea who was responsible?'

'Don't matter, does it? The police'll round up the usual suspects. Bound to have been one of 'em.' He shrugs. 'Could've been an accident, I s'pose.'

I shake my head and take a deep, harsh breath, staring into the hellish heart of the inferno. 'No,' I murmur. 'Nothing burns down by itself.'

I point up at forty-five degrees, indicating the stained-glass window. 'I reckon *she* mus' had more history than she let on. Virgin Mary. My arse. Good PR, I call that.'

'You might have a point.' (Is she just placating me?) 'You know there's a statue of her in Bordeaux that's supposed to menstruate? Rather more impressive than the weeping ones, I'd have thought.'

'Blimey. Never thought. Mary on the rag. Imagine the museums fighting over a Turin Sanitary Towel.'

If she finds this tasteless, she doesn't let on. 'Apparently,' she says, 'the local Catholic girls wipe the blood between their legs. They say if they do that, they'll never get pregnant.'

'You' making this up.'

'Swear. Guides' honour.'

'I use' believe in miracles,' I tell her gloomily, and lift the bottle once more.

In the end, there is nothing to do. Given the choice of watching the devastation or driving away, I choose the latter. The smoke is visible right across town.

From destruction, she said to me once, comes creation. It's a cycle. They're the same thing. In technical terms, matter can be neither created nor destroyed, did you know that? It's a scientific principle.

I said that went against what I was supposed to believe in, but I could see the sense of it more and more.

Everything broken is reborn in a new form, she told me. You have to shatter the bonds. As I did.

I drive to the abandoned church and park outside. I sit there, breathing hard, for several minutes. Then I get out, and walk to the off-licence. And I head back to the church and go inside.

★

Angelica lets her hand fall on my shoulder. 'Look, don't take this hard. Maybe it's a sort of sign. That this isn't what you're meant to be doing.'

My derisive laugh echoes through the church. 'Oh, don't tell me, my true destiny lies in pig-farming. Why'd I never think of that?' I gulp down another numbing mouthful of whisky. I've reached that stage where it's not quite sure if it wants to stay down. Remember in *Tom and Jerry*, where Tom's eyes flash up saying *full*? That's me. 'This is what I *do*. It's me, Faith. It's what I fucking do, I can't be anything else.'

There is a strong, deep silence, as if a curtain has fallen between us. Something is not quite right. I rewind in my head, but the tape gets tangled. Heads need cleaning. Joke there, somewhere. Yeah, *Head Cleaner*. My tape. Great album, that. Minimalist.

She says: 'You called me Faith.'

Shocked, I sit up, a shot of adrenalin punching me a little further back into sobriety. 'I did not.'

'You did.' She risks a glance at me. She can't seem to decide between annoyance and amusement. 'It's all right. I'll take it as a compliment. You can think of me as the Faith in the future. The Faith yet to come. What's a few years between friends, after all?'

'Look, I'm sorry.'

'Why? I can be Faith if it makes you happy. Like Time's jumped a groove. She's got older and you stayed the same age.'

'Please don't.'

'It's just a name. They're powerful things, names, aren't they? Someone has your name, uses their name, they've got a kind of hold over you. In fact,' she goes on, 'there's that theory, isn't there? When you start to let your own *name* slip away, stop using it so much, you lose your grip on the world. On what makes you human.' She pauses. 'Have you ever thought about that?'

'No,' I answer moodily, not looking at her.

She breathes hard, and I listen to her, and I don't speak. After a moment, she says:

'Look . . . something good might come out of all this.'

Matter can be neither created nor destroyed.

'Sorry?' she says.

'I . . . Did I say anything? Didn't realize.'

She sighs. 'I found out what Mads means. If you still want me to help you, I'll be outside.'

She found out what Mads means.

I ought to try and lever myself out of this pew, then.

There's a splintering, tinkling sound, which has me looking around, twisting my neck to try and see which window the demons have punched open. I realize it's my bottle, lying in pieces in the nave. I lean forward, trying to steady myself. Stained glass isn't the best thing to look at when you're pissed. It's the jangling colours, the piecemeal reality. Maybe that's why Christians abstain.

I have to concentrate on something, so I look at the broken bottle in its damp patch of whisky. The shards slice the dim lights of the church into harsh little blades of purity.

Blue. The shards are blue. There is a hand reaching from them.

I blink. The vision scuttles deep. I heave myself out of the pew and begin the long, wobbly trek to the door.

12 Be My Downfall

'Look at this,' said Mike in a voice of cracked desolation. 'Just look. We spent six weeks putting this exhibition together. And now look at it.'

I shrugged, nodded. There wasn't really much I could say. Every window in the classroom had been smashed – from the inside, judging by the glass and splintered chairs lying in the playground. The walls screamed FUCK and WANKERS in menstrual brownish-red, the letters dribbling on to the floor. *A Century of Writing* had been destroyed. Every poster and collage was slashed, every display shattered, every desk overturned. A broad stripe of white paint crossed the room from door to window, curving as it sloshed across floors, desks and chairs, and there was an all-pervading stench of piss.

Mike sat on the single intact chair, his feet tucked under him, staring at the wasteland through a haze of smoke.

'You can't give up,' I told him. 'You can't let these people win.'

He shook his head. 'Christ, you know what? I don't want to be the loser who picks through it all, sluices it all down.' He took a long drag on his cigarette and stared hard into the heart of the burning tip. 'I want to purge it all. Burn it. Just say, fuck you, then, if that's what you want. Fucking burn it all to the ground and start again.'

'Look, don't do anything silly. Mike, it's not the kids, I mean, not all of them. It's a minority. Some stupid vandals. You have to find out who they are and . . .' I waved a hand. 'Expel them, or whatever.'

'Exclude,' he said gloomily. 'It's called exclusion these days. Permanent exclusion. Great name, isn't it?'

I tried to console him. 'Look, you owe it to the other kids, Mike, for God's sake –'

'Oh, it's for God's sake, is it? Might have known. Where was he when all this was going on, then? You know what I think about God? I think God's a sod. He's a fucking screwed-up *bastard*.' Mike was practically spitting with anger. 'He thinks the same about the world as I think about this exhibition. We tried, we failed, so let them all burn. I've had enough.'

Although I'd not been renewing my own faith much recently, I was still quite shocked by this outburst. It went beyond atheism and out the other side, into pure hatred.

'Look, Mike –' I began, but there was Nicole at the door, rushing forward to hug him.

'Oh, Christ,' she muttered, taking in the full extent of the devastation, 'this is terrible.'

'Mike doesn't want to clear it up,' I told her, 'he wants to consume it all in a pagan pyre. What do you think?'

Nicole prodded the paint with a well-manicured finger, sniffed it cautiously. 'Can we salvage anything at all?'

Mike jumped to his feet, shaking his head. 'The caretaker says he'll clean up the worst of it. I'll come in tomorrow, if I can face it. Right now, I need a drink.'

In the pub, we found a corner table. There was a loud, vocal crowd around the giant screen for the European Championship match – it wasn't England, so I wasn't especially interested, but Faith would no doubt be keeping an eye on it. I wondered, momentarily, where she was, and who she was watching with.

Mike's big hands embraced three pints of London Pride, and he set them down without a wobble or a splash. He seemed to have calmed down a little. I think he was embarrassed about his pyromaniac outburst, and it didn't take him long to move on to familiar territory.

'Michael,' Nicole said, 'do you have *any* idea who would have done it?'

'I could make a shortlist,' he answered. 'Dunno if you know,' he added, addressing himself to me, 'but thanks to the government's wonderful system, we've got everyone else around us going grant-maintained. Like the lovely dainty girls' school where my darling wife teaches.' Nicole glowered at him. 'So basically, we get the kids no one else wants. Great idea, from an admin point of view. All the bad eggs in one basket.' He took a long, indulgent drink from his pint, setting it down with an I-needed-that sigh. 'Look where it's got us. Bloody Tory shits. Five more fucking years. Jesus.'

It definitely wasn't the best time to mention how I had voted back in April. I cleared my throat and looked for something to say, but Nicole got there first.

'Someone's got to make the bad eggs, though,' she murmured. 'If the kids were well brought-up, it wouldn't matter whether you were grant-maintained or not, would it?'

'She's got a point, Michael,' I said admiringly.

He snorted and hid in his beer, but Nic wasn't stopping there. 'Come on, you've seen them,' she said. 'Parents let them play video-games all day, never read them a book, let them dress like little thugs with earrings. And they're always slapping them and saying – you know – effing this and that, shut the eff up.' (I smiled at her prudery.) 'It's no wonder they don't have any respect. They'd hardly be better-behaved under your precious Labour, my darling.'

This was weird: it took me right back to that dinner-party of theirs, eight months ago.

'*If* we had a government that cared,' Mike began, his hands caressing his invisible crystal ball again, 'then –'

'There's never been any such thing,' I snapped. 'They do whatever they need to stay in power. And don't pretend your lot have some precious moral high-ground, because they don't.' Someone had to cut Mike off before he got into full flow, gripping the air, stating opinions as facts all over the place. I'd had enough of that over the years.

'He's right. Face it, Mike,' Nicole said, her eyes glinting (I'd have sworn she was enjoying this). 'The problem is not the government. The problem is that the kids who trashed your exhibition are scum. The world would be better off without them.'

Mike gave a kind of two-directional sneer, aimed across his pint at both of us. 'Oh, great. I come out for a drink with my wife and my mate, and I get a fascist diatribe from the pair of you. I bet you'd like them all to be sterilized.'

'Might be good for some of them,' I said, and Nic giggled. Mike knew I was baiting him, though. Five years ago, a comment like that would have got me flattened in a pile of glass and beer. Now? He just made a snorting noise and took another gulp of his pint.

'Bloody Tory bastards,' he muttered again, but the insult was laughably limp. It was like being stabbed with old celery.

I knew it, then: his great revolution had come as far as it ever would. He had arrived in the station he should have been dreading. He had reached that echoing Euro-terminus called Apathy.

I went home, promising to see them soon. Back then, I was renting a small flat on the fourth floor of a converted rest-home. It wasn't much, but it was mine, it was near the language school, and I certainly had no intention of running back to Mum.

As I unlocked the door on the creaking landing, I saw a Post-it stuck to my door. It said:

'Luke rang.'

A memory. It is dark and still in the room. Frames of light surround pictures of darkness on the walls. She breathes. I hear her. I step slowly towards her on the soft carpet.

'Well?' Her voice licks a word-sized hole from the air.

I bend down. I can perceive her only as a shape in the darkness, a rustle of breath and an aromatic, feral scent of arousal. I move my mouth close to hers, feel the heat of her breath on my lips, hear the click as her tongue reaches out for mine.

'No,' I tell her. 'Not yet.'

I know exactly where to find her belt on the floor. It is smooth and comforting in my hand. She does not resist as I pin her arms behind her back and tie the belt tightly so that she cannot use her hands. She gives a small murmur of pleasure, but no other sound.

Now, I lean down to kiss her. I allow myself only the lightest of touches on her lips before skimming down to her warm neck, pausing briefly on her breasts and then licking a trail down to her navel. I feel her shifting in pleasure, trying to move her body closer to my mouth.

'Please . . .' she mutters.

'You want to say something?' I whisper, kneeling next to her.

Her mouth, as it always does, nuzzles my ear, her breath hot and animal in the opening. The words come from deep within that breath and that warmth, pushed up by lust from deep within her body.

'*Hit me.*'

'Here,' Luke said in the car park, 'carry this', and he piled three large cardboard boxes into my arms. They were astonishingly heavy.

'What's in here?' I gasped as we staggered into the church hall.

'Soup,' he said, 'and beans, stew, vegetables . . . anything else we can get our hands on. People come to rely on us, now.'

He seemed taller and thinner, I noticed, and he'd let his hair grow a little longer. He wore his dog-collar with its purple shirt under a faded denim jacket, and studs glinted in both his earlobes. In the London parish where he worked as a curate, they didn't mind the unconventional approach.

'I didn't . . . get a message, or anything,' I ventured, as I helped him unpack the boxes on to trestle-tables in the hall. 'Only that you called.'

'Yeah, I know. Just wanted to see how you were.' He gave me a brief, genuine smile. 'You seem to be well. My curiosity is satisfied.'

'Mine isn't,' I said, hefting a tin of beans thoughtfully.

He sighed. 'Well . . . actually, I did wonder if everything was all right. That girl you were seeing at college – Faith?'

'The one you warned me off, because she was the evil junkie spawn of Satan, I seem to recall?'

His laugh was clear, genuine. 'Yeah . . . I was a bit of a fundamentalist back then, wasn't I? Not so good on the old, ah, tolerance stuff.'

'That's all right,' I said, amused. 'So what about her?'

He frowned, leaned on the table for a second. 'It's just that she phoned me a couple of weeks ago.'

'She phoned *you*? . . . But she hardly exchanged two . . . I mean, all the time we . . .'

'Yes, I did think it was strange. But then, in my vocation, one gets all kinds of people suddenly coming to one for advice. You know, as if I'm qualified to dish out anything more than common sense . . .' He shrugged, smiled. 'She left a message on my machine. I have to have one, these days. Goes with the job.'

'Mmm. I suggest your boss gets one.' I glanced skywards for a second.

'An interesting theological point, which I shall have to go away and think about. If it comes to an insult I shall follow it up,' he said with a smile. 'But, well, she left a message saying there was something she had to talk through. No number to ring her back on, though.'

'So Faith rang you for moral guidance? Bizarre.'

'Yeah, and then there was another message, a week or so later, saying that she was fine now, and she was sorry to have bothered me.'

He shrugged. 'You can't cast any light, then?' His eyes, bright as always, fixed firmly on me, searching for an answer in my face and not in my words.

'No,' I said, my mind flashing full of images like a disjointed film-trailer. 'Not at all. Weird.'

'Have you seen much of her?'

'To be honest . . . not much at all. Not recently.' I didn't know why I lied. Misguided loyalty, perhaps.

'Oh, well.' Luke smiled. His bright blue eyes stared hard at me for a few moments longer than was comfortable. 'If you do happen to run into her, then do say I was asking after her, won't you?'

'Yeah. Sure.' I wondered if he caught my shiftiness. Probably. I imagined he was trained to notice that sort of thing.

'Right,' he said. As he passed me on the way to the door, he put a hand on my forearm for a second, almost too quickly for me to notice. I didn't know whether it was meant in sympathy, or affection, or in recognition of something else entirely.

The blow is firm and sharp. She recoils, doesn't quite lose her balance, and then smiles up at me, creasing the bruised skin.

A bruise is an injury to the skin and subcutaneous tissue. The skin is not broken, but the underlying local blood-vessels are damaged, and this causes the inevitable swelling and discoloration.

A bruise is not something new. It is formed from the genetic material already present in the body. Nothing is created, nothing is destroyed. But it is both creation and destruction. It is a transformation.

'Thank you,' she murmurs. 'Now do it.'

As before, in the roles we have defined, I will rub my hardness on her face in the hot, smooth circle where her bruise is growing. She will whisper the darkest obscenities to me, let her strands of hair stroke me lightly, until I come, the sticky fluid gushing on the reddened flesh of the bruise as she moans, and then she tilts her glistening head back and smiles. As before. As always.

I am bound to her, the fragments of our skin flaking as one into dust. We will be dust together. We will come together. And I think she is right in that dark prediction of hers: our deaths will be linked, as our lives are. Somehow, we will die together.

13 Chemical Sister

An angry wind stalks in from the north.

It kicks up litter in the dark urban valleys, rips the squealing ghosts from their dustbins before hurtling into suburbia. It pauses to shake the tiles and kick the clothes on the washing lines into bloated jigs. And then the rain begins. Together, the wind and rain batter the grass and the brickwork and the tiles until the land moans in pain.

'What do you want?' asks Angelica.

The police think it was arson. That's the latest.

Earlier, Angelica hustles me into her Escort outside the police station. I look at the clock; I have been in there for three hours. I realize, as I sink back into the seat and take a grateful gulp from the hip-flask she offers me, that I have been undergoing questioning.

I just thought they wanted as much information as possible about Hope Springs in order to catch whoever did it. But no. They were subtly eliminating me from their enquiries. I suppose it crossed their minds that I might have done it for the insurance.

We go once round the town square. The statue of Queen Victoria is proud against the greying sky. Kids kick a ball outside the churchyard.

'It was deliberate,' I tell Angelica.

'I thought we knew that,' she mutters, as we drive into suburbia.

'Not officially.'

She drives on.

Back at the flat, she makes me a strong Irish coffee, and I smile gratefully up at her.

'You poor dear,' she says. 'Have you any idea what's going to happen about your Hope Springs now?'

'I've got an emergency meeting with the backers and the council reps. Just as soon as the police have finished going over it.'

'How do you feel?' she asks, leaning forward. I can't help noticing her blouse tautening over her breasts, but I'm not even in the mood to react.

'Numb,' I answer. 'Perhaps you're right. It was an Act of God. Kicking something out of my life that was never meant to be there.'

'At least no one was hurt,' Angelica says, settling herself back in the chair. She tucks her hair behind her ear again. 'It's only things. You can always replace things.'

'Maybe.'

'So,' she says, 'you want to know about Mads?' She holds up the grey print-out of the badge, which has been sitting on my coffee-table.

'Go on.'

'It's Medway Area Dangerous Sports. Found them in the clubs and societies listings in Chatham library.' She raises her eyebrows, looking slightly smug for a second or two.

'And does this help us? Faith's friend was a member, right?'

'Right. So it's obviously important. The key was in the box, the key opened the locker, the photo and the disk were in the locker.' Angelica slumps back in the chair, sighs.

'Christ,' I mutter with a rueful grin, 'I feel like Anneka Rice.'

'I bet you do, but you can't have her, darling.'

It's obviously important.

She is making us work.

I can see her laughing, now, that big red mouth open wide and those beautiful teeth glowing in the dark like a Hallowe'en monster. She's shot in negative, dancing on the sand under the moonlight. Flashes of blue slice across her.

(We turn, as one, our eyes on the approaching vehicles . . .)

She's making us work. And I just don't get it.

'Any news from Serge?' I ask.

'*Rien de rien*, I'm afraid.'

'Yeah, and that's what it'll be, I bet. It'll be a bunch of old computer games she kept and didn't want anyone to know about. Or some song lyrics, or something.'

'Or porn,' says Angelica, with a twitch of her eyebrows. 'Off the Internet.'

'Or it'll be nothing.'

'Perhaps.' She sips her tea. Her face is unreadable.

Minutes pass.

'What do you want?' asks Angelica, pouring another shot of whisky into my coffee.

'I . . . want to remember.'

The rain hisses in my ears like static. Our breath paints the windows a soft, friable grey. One layer beyond, the off-tuned world flickers in its rainstorm, shimmers in a faulty vertical-hold.

'Then remember,' she says, and she leans forward, placing her lips very gently on my forehead.

'I can't.'

She sighs, draws back from me. 'Tanya called earlier. She left a message. She's missing you, and wants to know why you're not returning her calls.'

Tanya wants to know why I'm not returning her calls. She belongs to another world, that's why.

Angelica says: 'Tanya's the future, you know that? But before you can go forward, you have to get the past sorted out. Do you understand that?'

I understand that. I nod.

'There's nothing you're holding back from me, is there? Nothing you've remembered and you won't share with me?'

There is nothing I am holding back from her. There is nothing I will not share with her.

(*Shattering, like ice.*)

'Nothing. I promise.'

(*Slowly, the shadow turns. She must see me at the window. Is that half-lifted hand acknowledging me? The black dress deactivates light, cutting a hole in the sunlit landscape. And then she slips behind the crest of the hill to go down, down . . .*)

'Come on,' she says. 'I want you to go back. Sit cross-legged and close your eyes.'

I do as she says. I am warm and drowsy from the whisky. 'I'm going to regret this.'

'Just try and picture the *gîte*,' Angelica is saying. 'Think of the details, think of the furniture and everything. Try and see if there's somewhere you can't get to in your mind.'

'I want to be out looking for that girl.'

'Trust me, we will. Do as I say.'

The rain is just a background noise, now. The scent of her orange tea has filled the flat, and I inhale, hoping it will give me a kind of heady clarity.

I start to do what she suggests, picturing each part of the main living-room, and funnily enough, it seems to work. Half-forgotten details spring out at me, things I have never had any reason particularly to forget or to remember.

'I can see stuff.'

'Good. Tell me.'

'The carved lion's head on the banister. The yucca plant next to the stairs. Moving across . . . there's the big Georges de la Tour picture on the wall, next to that. *Le Tricheur*.' The symbolic light and shade of that painting is clearly in front of me now, the observing eyes of the maid and the concealed card of the cheat.

'I know it. Go on.'

'The light's coming in from the big glass doors. They lead out to the terrace and down to the gardens and the beach.'

'What do you picture everyone doing?'

My mind-picture is tracking, now, moving unsteadily across the sunwashed scene. I have a hand-held camera in my head.

'We're all sitting there on the sofas. They're big, blue leather sofas around a glass coffee-table. We're playing a game . . . yeah, it's the last afternoon. Before it . . .'

My eyes flicker. The picture is unsteady.

'*Don't lose it*,' she orders.

'No. Right. We're playing Articulate. That game where you describe words, you know? But we've banned the use of foreign translations. The rules don't allow for that. We're sitting round the table playing the game . . . I can't be sure if I'm playing. No, I'm not.'

'Describe everyone.'

I concentrate. I go deeper, summoning details in context, and it works. One at a time, the ghosts appear.

'Mike's reading out. He's wearing shades, a white V-neck shirt and black shorts. Nic's leaning forward to listen to him. Her hair's really long and wild. She ought to get it cut. Her mouth's red. She's painted lipstick over the edges to make it look bigger.' I smile at the memory. 'She's laughing with him, touching his knee. She knows, though. Knows all about it. She's thinking of a divorce . . .'

'Move round. Come on. I need to see more.'

'I can't . . . quite . . .'

'Can you see Charlie? And Jan?'

'Yes, they're both there. Listening, as Mike reads out. Charlie's wearing a blue shirt. He's got his hand on Jan's shoulder. She's holding his hand. Almost clamping it down on her shoulder.'

'And Faith?'

The camera bounces across the room, scanning. Mike punches the air in delight as Nicole gets a sixth answer right within her time. Outside, the sky burns blue.

'I can't see her.'

'You're sure?'

The scene is as clear as if it had happened yesterday. I hover across the back of the sofa. Is someone hiding there? No, it's just the light. Crash-zoom on to the terrace. Deserted. Pull back, as the sunlight is burning too brightly. No sign of her.

'I can't see her. She isn't there.'

'Open your eyes.'

The picture snaps off.

I emerge, blinking, into the greyness of reality. Rain spatters the windows and the trees sway in the wind. Angelica is watching me.

'She wasn't there,' I say firmly.

'She was still alive, then. That was the last afternoon in the *gîte*.'

'Yes.'

'Was it normal for her to go off on her own like that?'

I frown. 'No. Not really.'

'Then I wonder where she was,' says Angelica softly.

Almost to herself. As if I'm not here.

She wasn't there.

Something very obvious is missing. It's like that picture where some people see an old woman, and some see a young woman.

Missing.

If a thing is missing, it is missed. People notice it has gone. And if someone removes it, they do so for a reason.

Christ . . . I almost had something then.

★

'Oh, hell, I forgot,' she says over her shoulder as she rinses the mugs out. 'You know while you were at the police? There was another message. A chap called Luke.'

'Luke?' I feel the back of my neck prickling. 'Did he say what he wanted?'

'Not really,' she says, stacking the cups. 'Something about you having been to see him?'

'Did he . . . sound okay?'

She shrugs. 'Fine.' She starts to dry the cups. 'Is he a mate?'

'Yeah. Kind of.'

She sleeps on the futon again, wearing a denim shirt of mine beneath the heavy continental quilt.

I pour myself a double whisky and I watch her sleep. As I watched over her sister, that time.

Angelica is a peaceful sleeper. She does not shudder with great stentorian breaths, nor does she mutter secret messages while wrapping herself tightly in the quilt. In this respect, she is unlike any other woman I have seen sleeping.

We had a conversation in the pub about snoring once: Faith and Mike were there, and Jacqui Spotter, and Andy. D'you snore? Faith had asked Andy, in all innocence, and he grinned and said he thought he did, quite loudly actually. Mike admitted that he sometimes did. I had seen the way the conversation was going so I tried to steer it on to something else, but it was inevitable: Jacqui Spotter got very cross indeed and stomped off to the bar. D'you realize the sub-text of your conversation? I asked the others. You're asking people to say if they've been *heard* snoring. That's the important bit. How strangely British and euphemistic.

I watch her. I pour another whisky, without coffee this time, and I watch her sleep.

The world is starting to blur at the edges. Rain crinkles the windows, covers the ground outside in a sparkling coating. I think of it washing the embers of Hope Springs. Not dead, just transformed. Ashes. Returning to the ground.

14 You're in a Bad Way

The timer-light snicked off when we were halfway along the landing, and at first we couldn't find the keyhole. I could hear our breathing, soft but heavy, in the confined corridor. At last, I felt the key slide in, and I kicked the door open so hard it thumped the wall behind it, squeaking as it juddered back towards us. We supported her through the hall, and I kicked the door to the lounge, reaching for the light switch. Four yellow globes lit the room, one in each corner.

'Thanks,' I said, 'let's put her down.'

Luke and I lowered the insensible Faith on to her sofa. She lolled there like a corpse. Her face was fish-pale, streaked with spidery mascara, and her skin glistened like shrinkwrapped chicken.

We stood there for a second or two, getting our breath back. I shook my head, not sure whether to laugh or cry. 'You wouldn't think she was that heavy, would you?' I muttered.

He smiled, straightening his shirt and dog-collar. 'Does she have any other cushions?' he asked, looking around. 'It's best to support her head. In case she vomits again.'

'Christ. Sorry – I mean, yes.' Obviously used to dealing with drunkards, I thought gloomily. We grabbed a couple of cushions from the other chairs. Faith lolled, moaning something, and her face disappeared behind a cloud of hair as I made the best job I could of propping up her head.

Luke went to the kitchen and filled a glass with mineral water. 'She'll need lots of this,' he said. 'Look . . . I can stay, if you want?'

'No, it's all right. Thanks, Luke.' I sighed. 'No doubt you'll have a few words for her about putting a thief in your mouth to steal away your brains?'

He smiled. 'I don't judge any more, mate. No point. She'll feel guilty enough.'

I doubted whether she would, but I nodded anyway. 'Yeah, well. You've . . . done a lot. Thanks.'

'How's the hand?' he asked quietly.

'Oh, er . . .' I'd almost forgotten about my smarting knuckles. 'No lasting damage, as you can see. On my side, at least,' I added, wincing slightly.

Luke perched on the arm of the sofa, folding his hands under his chin. 'So, did you want to tell me what that was all about?' he asked.

'I'll save it for another time, if it's all the same to you.'

He spread his hands. 'Sure. Whatever.'

There was a bubbling noise, like boiling soup, and I noticed too late that Faith, her hair still shaggy in front of her eyes, was trying to sit up on the sofa with a half-whispered moan.

'Whoops,' I said, 'I think –'

A second later, her groan became a retch. Her body jerked and a yellowish-green liquid spurted from her mouth, festooning her hair, splashing on to the carpet and a couple of abandoned pizza boxes.

I stood, frozen in horror, but Luke was already saying, 'I'll get a cloth, don't worry', as a sour, vinegary odour filled the room.

We all sat in that living-room, eating pizza out of the cardboard boxes and watching *Blind Date*. Two awful girls were there, and I can't even remember their names. They smoked, giggled and swore, usually all at once. I had no objection to these pastimes, if they were accompanied by cerebral activity.

I still felt uneasy in her company. This past year, I had stolen a radio Walkman for her in return for unashamed exploration of bicycle-chain bondage. I'd walked up and down the Charing Cross Road in a pink sandwich-board proclaiming 'Only Drinkers Survive', for which she had rewarded me with her own brand of special attention. I still bore the bruises.

She had not dared me for months now, not since the incident where I stole her a car for the night. But it was like having a chemical inside you, a poison that could be activated by a trigger word. So, whenever our lives brushed together, as they still did, I kept a very close eye on her indeed.

One of the slappers – I designated her Girl A – sneered at the contestant on the screen. 'She is so fucking *dog*,' she said.

The usual volume of Thoughts Best Unspoken buzzed through my head – such as the fragility of the average greenhouse roof under the impact of projectiles – and I hid behind my glass.

'Gold lycra. *Big* mistake,' opined Girl B.

'I think she looks quite fit,' I murmured. 'Statuesque.'

'They ought to just make the questions more explicit,' Faith said, licking together one of her expert double-walled joints. 'They should have it on after midnight and call it *Blind Fuck*. It'd be a winner. You could have the cameras on them all the time they were doing it.' She teased a flame from her lighter and winked at me.

'I bet the moral guardians of our nation would love that,' I offered.

'Moral guardians. Christ.' Faith reached behind her and plucked her old school hymn-book off the shelf. 'Look,' she said, 'it's all sex-substitute stuff. Where are weeee . . . ah, hell-oh. The Lord's my shepherd – yeah, *right*. The Lord's my boyfriend, more like.' There were sniggers from the two girls. 'He makes me down to lie, mmmmm, I bet he does, the dirty git.' She inhaled deeply from the joint before going on. 'In pastures green he leadeth me, *uh-huh*, the quiet waters by. Phwoarrrgh!' She scrunched her face up in a mockery of lust.

'You're obsessed with sex,' I told her. Girl A snorted and nudged Girl B, and the two of them squeaked at a private joke.

'Just comfortable with my body, precious,' Faith retorted. 'Shows that a girls' school didn't totally screw me up.' She slammed the hymn-book shut and gazed into the distance. 'God, showers after games were total hell. Miss Tomlinson used to stand by the door and *watch* us. I wouldn't have minded so much, only she was our music teacher.'

I smiled. 'So you spent your school years spotting the Finbarr Saunders bits in the hymns, then?'

'Well, come *on*, love. The quiet waters?' She tossed the book over her shoulder. 'If that's not a pussy-metaphor, I'm a Dutchwoman.'

'Double-dutchwoman,' sniggered Girl A, and they all joined in, their laughter rubbing the air, harsh as steel wool.

'Double-dutch Woman speaks with forked tongue!' screeched Girl B, pointing at Faith with a wobbling finger as if casting out a demon. 'She's the devil, innit?'

Faith snorted with laughter and collapsed into the sofa, laughing madly and cupping her nose. 'Oh, fuckity-fah. Snot alert.'

Girl B took the joint from her quivering fingers. 'You mucky bitch,' she said. She inhaled, then waggled her eyebrows at Girl A. I swallowed hard as Girl A willingly circled the burning end with her mouth, giving Girl B a power-hit by blowing air right through. Effective, I knew – and intimate – but it still made me wince at the thought of potential mouth-burn . . .

'It's a three-mile walk to this beach, you know,' I said as I poured a glass of Frascati. I seemed to have the wine to myself tonight.

'You're bloody joking,' Faith exclaimed from behind her hand-kerchief.

'No, I am not.' I sounded sharper than I intended, but the two tarts were irritating me. God alone knew where she'd dug them up – I had the vague idea they were shop-girls from one of her temporary jobs, and that she'd invited them along as amusement. 'I'm sure I told you,' I said.

'Shit.' Faith sounded more ruminative than angry. She took a long gulp from the litre bottle of Pepsi beside her. 'He expects me to remember everything,' she confided to the girls in a stage-whisper, and that set them off giggling once more. It seemed to be their main form of expression. Still, at least you knew where you were with them.

There might have been a hundred people there on the sand, maybe even two hundred. Fires licked the night, stroked the sharp lights from the turntable-stack. The beach was pungent with smoke, sweat and a dozen different perfumes and aftershaves. The speakers pounded the sand like pile-drivers, thumping out music that eclipsed mere sound: melody and harmony were pulped into beats and loops, the ripples shuddering through the grains, up into our bodies, filling our flesh. Distantly, the town sparkled, but this far along, only the odd isolated light glowed. The sea murmured, wobbled greyish-blue in the dark-ness, occasionally grabbing the alien colours of the party, flipping them around or fragmenting them.

I remember she leaned against the stacks for about an hour. She was wearing a tight white top and a wraparound satin skirt, red roses on black. She laughed, joked, fended off her admirers and swigged from a bottle of a suspiciously clear liquid.

I imagined the vibrations rippling into her body, whacking cells for six. The body is made up of cells, which consist of a nucleus and cytoplasm surrounded by a membrane. The body contains millions of cells. Or trillions. I don't know. The body is a prison.

'What's that?' I asked, nodding at the bottle as I sidled on to the rock next to her.

She just laughed and pulled my head down close to her mouth. 'Dunno,' she growled. 'The proof of the bottle's in the drinking, know what I mean?' The blonde girl next to Faith screeched with laughter, as if the comment were the most wildly funny thing she'd ever heard.

I took the bottle, sniffed it. Odourless.

'It's water, you stupid bastard,' said Faith, as if she was fed up with me and wished I'd go away. She snatched the bottle back, and took a deep, hard gulp.

She was still stoned, I realized, and I watched her eyes trying to tune themselves in to me as I sipped from a can of Guinness.

'Anyway, 'scuse me,' she said, 'vitamin time.' She had a small pill between her thumb and forefinger, embossed with the symbol of a dove. 'You're not interested, I take it?' She flickered in the firelight, her smile lasting only a spectral second.

'Thanks, but no thanks. It may have escaped your attention, but this isn't 1988 any more.'

She shrugged, knocked back the tab with a mouthful of water, scrunching her face up at the taste. 'Y'know, someone could make a killing flavouring these with strawberry . . .' She flipped her gaze back to me. 'I tell you, E ain't what it used to be. Cut with speed, mostly. But I take what I can get.'

I shook my head. 'I've not come here to listen to you being a drug snob.'

'I am *not* a drug snob. I just know good shit from bad, precious.'

'You're pathetic. Like those tossers who get addled in Thailand every year, then have palpitations at raiding Daddy's whisky cabinet.'

She laughed, leaned forward, stroked my face. 'Daaaah–ling, you're sooooo *negative*. And I thought you were in touch with your spiritual side.'

'Oh, sod off,' I growled, and took another much-needed gulp of Guinness.

'Come on, then, talk to me like a grown-up. Got maybe an hour before it kicks in.' She snuggled me, wrapping her hair round my head. 'I'll give you my Sensible Time, how's that? Can't say fairer. Then when I'm whirling round later, telling everyone I fucking *lurrve* them, you can maintain a discreet distance.'

I pushed her away. 'You're annoying.'

Something made me want to grab her, shake her, tell her she was totally sad and she had to get her life together. But at the same time, I didn't *want* her to. She was my pet wild-child. And anyhow, there was still something bewitching about her, a darkness that seemed to drag you in. Her face had the power to pull Time out of synch so that the shimmering beach and the laughing people became no more than shadows of the fire, echoes of the whispering sea.

'You're staring at me again,' she murmured.

'I can't help it. You're beautiful.'

'Yeah, well.' She shrugged, smiled, her eyes down for a second. Modesty? I found it hard to believe. 'And I can't help *that*. Sometimes I wish I wasn't, y'know?' Just for a second, her eyes betrayed her, and I saw her glance beyond the stacks to the familiar face of Mike Bradfield. He was red and demonic in the firelight, surrounded by fawning acolytes as usual.

'You told me there was nothing there,' I said anxiously. 'You said he wanted more than you could give.' The words pulsed out like the industrial beats beneath us, staining the air with their intensity.

'Yeah, well. He did. Like I said, he's a nice plaything.' She shrugged. 'Sorry,' she added.

It's a magical elixir, this Sorry. A top drug. (Got any Sorry? Nice one.) It washes your conscience smooth like a stone in a mountain spring. No need to worry about *doing* anything to make it up, just say Sorry and you're away. Off to do it again and again.

A green-haired girl slipped out of the throng, placed a hand on her shoulder. 'Hi, I'm Keela. You must be Faith.'

She winked. 'Do I have to, darling? I was Faith last week.'

It was Nicole's sister, I realized, one of the engineers behind the whole thing. I left them to it, and made my way through the thunderous music and the bodies to where Nic herself was mixing cocktails at a makeshift bench, assisted by Charles. He was in the middle of explaining a philosophical concept.

'So, until you open the box,' he was saying, waggling the corkscrew unsteadily at her, 'you dunno if the cat's alive or dead, right? Two possibilities.'

Nic frowned, tipped her head one way then the other. 'Right,' she said uncertainly, smiling up at me. 'Here, do something,' she added, thrusting a bottle of tequila into my hand. 'Do *you* understand this . . . Schopenhauer's cat thing?' she asked me.

'I'm more of a dog man,' I admitted.

'Schroedinger's,' Charlie said, with a hint of exasperation. I wondered how long he had been going on about this. 'But when you open the box – at that point, that quantum leap from closed to open – the possibilities dissolve and you're left with one certainty. Whichever way it turns out. Yeah?'

'Yyyyyeah,' Nicole said, holding her sample cocktail up to the firelight. 'It sounds quite . . . cruel to me.'

'You don't *actually* stick the cat in a box,' Charlie snapped. 'It's a *concept*.'

'If I was the cat,' I said, 'I'd have buggered off long before. Great party,' I added, scanning the crowd for Mike.

'Thanks.' She glanced up, pushed her newly braided hair back and grimaced. 'Hey, sound like you mean it.'

'Sorry. Just been talking to Faith. She's on another planet.'

'Don't look at me.' Charlie was halfway into his beer. 'I'm not the one who buys the stuff for her.'

Nic seemed to wander away mentally. 'I think this kind of thing's really *important*, you know?' she said. 'Really close to nature. That's the problem with society, we're too boxed-off from our environment. Oh, thanks, Jas,' she said, as a tall black boy brought her a veggie-burger from the barbecue.

'Mmmm. I see what you mean,' Charlie answered cautiously, raising his eyebrows at me.

I nodded, holding an involuntary thought: the cigarette boxes, crisp packets and bottles currently being crushed at a hundred b.p.m. by booted feet. Oh, well. On such contradictions is this generation built. 'Is your darling husband around?' I asked.

She wrinkled her nose as she yanked the top off a bottle of red Martini. 'Please,' she said, 'don't.' And she smiled awkwardly at me, as if to acknowledge that it was not my fault, and to forgive me.

I gave her a smile back, and we each extended an arm, encircling our waists in an unpractised half-hug, one of those where you're both aiming to avoid groin contact.

'Sorry,' I said. And winced.

Just say Sorry and you're away.

After the vandal attack on his exhibition, Mike's attitude to the pupils slowly shifted. Phrases he had previously spurned would slip out: 'thickies' rather than 'less motivated students', or 'little bastards' instead of 'those with behavioural problems'. He gave less and less of his time willingly, and became impatient and resentful at the hours he was expected to spend outside the classroom. He started drinking more heavily, too.

There had always been an anger in him before, but it was sharp and lucid. Now, it was a pernicious thing, a disease gnawing away at him. Nic could not talk it through with him. No one could. Nic knew she no longer loved him, but she worried about him, as a friend, perhaps. But her own teaching was going through a good patch; she was fired with enthusiasm for the girls' drama projects and had little time for negativity.

From what I've been told, I think it went like this.

It is a Monday morning, in the dawning days of the year. Breath freezes in the air and the road is sluiced with a cold, hard winter sleet.

The alarm chirps, punching into the darkness. A few minutes pass and it sounds again, faster and more insistent this time. Mike shivers as he gets out of bed and begins the search for his dressing-gown. Nicole murmurs, turns over, wrapped in her pre-Raphaelite hair. She always walks to her school. She has another fifteen minutes in bed now that the alarm has gone off, and she intends, as ever, to make the most of it. In the semi-darkness, Mike tries to make his way to the door, but somehow he manages to bang his shin against the bookcase, and he hobbles to the bathroom, swearing loudly. The bright light cuts into his eyes as he splashes warm water on his face and peers gloomily beyond the mirror at the cold world outside.

Downstairs, the aching in his shin begins to wear off, and he opens the cupboard to find some coffee. He stares in disbelief through the horribly transparent jar. No coffee. He slams the door shut, gets himself a glass of fruit juice. He thumps back upstairs and drinks his fruit juice while trying to do up his tie one-handed. He asks Nicole, irritably, why she didn't buy any coffee. She rolls over, pulls the duvet up around her neck and murmurs that it's not just her bloody job to do the shopping, she's not a bloody housewife, and if he wants to drink coffee he should think about buying it himself for once.

As Mike is unlocking the front door, he remembers that the garage is full of boxes of stuff they are intending to take to a boot-fair soon. For that reason, the Golf is sitting outside in the road, and this morning it is encased in a crisp shell of ice. He swears again, throws his briefcase down. He rummages in the kitchen cupboard, eventually finds the de-icer and the scraper, and sets to work.

The street is cold and deserted. A slow, reluctant winter sun is crawling up across the land, but it has yet to reach their road. Bleary-eyed, he sprays, scrapes and sprays again. Before long his hands are numb and aching, but the de-icer is effective, and soon he has cleared some space on the windscreen. Encouraged, he sets to work on the other windows of the car until they are clear. Breathing heavily, he stands back, nodding, glances at his watch. He has lost only about five minutes. Not too bad. He gets his keys out, then does a double take, stands back, staring. He realizes what he has done. He has quickly and efficiently cleared the ice from every window of next door's Volkswagen Polo.

Ten more minutes have elapsed by the time Mike has de-iced his own car and persuaded the reluctant engine to start. His head is beginning to throb. He curses to himself as he recognizes the symptoms of caffeine deprivation. There are, predictably, roadworks in the town centre, exacerbated this morning by the weather. The traffic moves slowly and cautiously through the glistening streets, and he begins to lose time.

Increasingly agitated, he tries again and again to pass the pick-up truck which has been in front of him for about three miles. It won't let him past. The driver is being cautious. On the radio, the local travel news jabbers of exceptional delays and adverse weather conditions. The sleet begins to descend more thickly, sloshing across Mike's windscreen. Eventually, about two miles from the school and fifteen minutes late, the pick-up truck takes a left. Mike steps on the accelerator and almost immediately feels the car begin to slip from his control, spinning across the road. With his heart hammering, he eases off on the accelerator and gets the car back on a steady course. He's late, but he's still not going to try that again.

He continues, exhaling deeply, gripping the wheel, not letting the speedometer get above thirty. He is now going to be at least half an hour late, but he is not going to risk anything. He finally turns into the school drive at five past nine, about forty minutes after his usual arrival time. He has missed registration. He feels disorientated, hassled and resentful. The school is in chaos. It smells of damp, the corridors are slicked with mud and there are jostling kids everywhere. One or two of them call out to him, making some comment on his lateness, and he tells them angrily to get to their first lesson.

It's cold, even inside – Mike can see his breath as he hurries up to the staff room. There is no heating today. In brief exchanges with colleagues at the pigeon-holes, he manages to gather that the head is determined not to close the school, but that no decision has been taken. He slams his briefcase down on the staff-room table and begins rummaging for his papers. His headache is worse. He is shaking with fury and frustration.

Just then, the phone begins to ring. Insistently. Mike is nearest, so he has to answer it. The caller is Tessa, the biology lab technician. There is an 'incident' happening in the corridor and Mrs Hill has yet to appear. A member of staff is needed urgently. Mike shouldn't really go. He has a class waiting, but it's A-level, and he knows they will be sensible, so he snaps his briefcase shut and heads on down to the science block. He has nothing to lose. In fact, he is simmering, and if someone is spoiling for a fight, Mike wants to know about it. *Now.*

Paths, slicing the ice like tyre-tracks, converge on that point in space-time, on that corridor, smelling of sweat and mud and paper, humming with the energy of a hundred recalcitrant adolescents.

One of them, an earringed chunk of meat called Kevin Watson, is laughing as he swings a fellow playmate by the collar from the door of his locker and spits chewing-gum into his face. He gives the poor unfortunate one last swing. Then he turns round and sees Mr Bradfield, his English teacher, striding towards him, his face burning with hell-fury.

I was not there, but it is easy to picture Mike trying to argue the case with a Year 11 boy who's easily his equal in height. His briefcase lies against a half-open door, the clasp not quite done up. He's still in his long coat, spattered with rain; his dark shoes are streaked with the mud of the car park. He's breathing heavily, dripping. His hands are clasping that invisible ball again. He is saying: listen. He is saying: be reasonable. He is saying: if only you see everything as I do, the world will be a better place and we can all live in socialist harmony.

And Kevin Watson stands there: tie askew, arms folded, slack-jawed mouth working away at a rubbery piece of gum. His head is tilted at that 'So fucking what?' angle so beloved of the brain-dead teenage thug.

Mike is rapidly losing patience. He is frustrated, and there is a nagging pain behind his eyes, reminding him that this hooligan is preventing him from getting his caffeine fix.

And then Kevin glances at the growing crowd, and makes a comment – something which might have gone unremarked on any other day, perhaps, or in any other corridor, or even to any other teacher. But this is today. It is this corridor. It is Michael Bradfield.

It happens.

The moment crystallizes: it is over-determined.

It happened because the roadworks and the morning ice had delayed Mike Bradfield by forty minutes. Because he'd not eaten breakfast or had coffee. Because his wife was no longer having sex with him. Because he was eaten up by a gnawing, monstrous misanthropy. Because so many of his schemes for these kids got chucked back in his face. Because he subconsciously remembered, perhaps, the times when people had got the better of him in arguments and he had seen it as part of the Great Conspiracy, and he had now, finally, had enough. I suppose there are only so many times you can tell a man to go fuck himself.

Alternatively: because Kevin was a thug. Or because Kevin was so misunderstood. And because Kevin's stepdad told him to go fuck himself so often that the phrase had become common currency in the home, and so he thought nothing of saying it to a mere teacher.

For these reasons and more, Michael Kenton Bradfield, aged twenty-five, teacher of English at St Wilfred's Secondary School, Guildford, dealt Kevin Watson, a pupil aged fifteen, a single blow to the face at 9.13 a.m. on Monday 11 January 1993, causing mild bruising to the cheekbone. Michael Kenton Bradfield was immediately suspended.

At the subsequent inquiry into the incident, he was dismissed from his teaching post at St Wilfred's. Although there was, apparently, some discussion of criminal proceedings being instigated, the matter was taken no further.

At first, Nicole had worked on in a kind of shell-shock, knowing that she could not stop, could not think. At home, she barely touched him or even looked at him. Whatever happened, she had to keep working. Earning money, while he sorted himself out. She said she was giving him space, but as she admitted to me later, she knew she was avoiding the issues.

He, meanwhile, mooched around and measured out his days in newspapers and coffee and cigarette smoke and video games. Old activist friends rang, tried to get him to come down to Hampshire to protest about a bypass. He didn't return their calls. The only person to get through to him – literally and metaphorically – was Faith Devereaux.

On the beach, I watched Charles, thinking how exhausted he seemed in the firelight. 'Any news?'

'Put it this way,' he said with a drunken grin, pulling open a beer can, 'I'm definitely not firing blanks. So, it must be her.' He gave a brief, satisfied smile and lifted the can. 'Here's to infertility.'

I didn't look at Nic. 'Whatever,' I said awkwardly, and my eyes strayed to the shimmering sea in the momentary hope of being carried away from all this.

'Fuck, I need a drink,' muttered Nic, breaking the awkward silence, and she swigged straight from the Martini bottle.

From Faith, I had managed to piece together that all was not well in the Devereaux household, although I knew I was being spared many of the details.

At Christmas, faced with Charlie's continued reluctance to inseminate her, Jan had offered him an ultimatum: a marriage with children, or no marriage at all. I knew that, since then, they had been trying – Jan had it all planned like a military operation. She wasn't ruling anything out, not even adoption, but they were going to try everything possible first. I think she was doubly keen once news of Mike and Nic's situation leaked through on the grapevine.

It all seemed bizarrely out of control. 'I don't understand it,' I confessed in one of my rare phone calls to my mother. 'My friends have decided that they're going to take the "human race" literally. They think there's a gold medal for the quickest to sprog.' Drowning, I thought to myself, in glasses of urine, ovulation charts and jars of sperm.

The vibrations stopped.

Everyone looked up at the stacks. The music had twisted, screeched to a halt. A hundred breaths were held in the salty night air.

I glanced over Nic's shoulder and saw the dunes dancing with electric-blue light, like a displaced aurora borealis.

'Pretty,' I murmured, a second before I realized.

There were two cars, thundering like tanks over the dunes, wreathed in ghosts of sand and exhaust fumes. Their lights, two beacons of harsh, bright blue, flashed like strobes across the murmuring crowd.

I heard Nic draw breath, right beside me, and felt the gentle pressure of her hand on my forearm.

And then the Górecki crashed in.

I recall the unearthly, minimalist song echoing across the beach as the two police cars rumbled to a halt. The Third Symphony: latest big popular success from the classical world. It seemed Nic's brother had an emergency copy tucked away for just this eventuality. It didn't change the nature of the party, but it changed its appearance, and that was all-important.

Couples were laughing, now, dancing like ghosts on the sand. Keela and her friends were smiling and joking with the two policemen, who both looked quite young. She gave one of them a sausage roll. The taller of the two said something, pointing to the speaker stacks, and made a small twiddling motion with his fingers, like someone adjusting a volume control; I saw Keela nod and smile, pushing back her tangle of green curls and jutting her breasts forward.

Nic looked up at me, gave me a relieved grin. 'I don't think anyone's going to be arrested,' she whispered.

'I should think not,' I said. 'We're not doing anything wrong.'

'Most of us,' she muttered.

Surrounded by all the phantom fecundity, a gigantic dress rehearsal for family life, I was grateful for the laid-back arrangement with Faith, who showed no desire to get into the whole baby thing. When I asked her, once, if she would want to be a mother one day, she wrinkled her nose. 'Not sure,' she said. 'I mean, they smell, don't they, kids? And I like being the size I am. *And* I'd have to give up my lifestyle. Still,' she added, shrugging, 'I might do. Don't wanna get married, though.' She gave me a wicked grin. 'I'd just find myself a good fertilizer.'

'Any man would do, then,' I said, smiling sadly. 'We're all shits.'

We'd meet up every two or three months – in haunted country pubs, or bustling cathedral towns, or seaports echoing with gulls and the crashing boom of hovercraft – and we'd talk, and we'd drink, and we'd laugh. Sometimes we'd get very drunk and we'd go somewhere to fall on each other with starving lust. Anywhere. A hotel, a park, a back alley. It was tawdry, dislocated from life, thrilling.

There was the tacit agreement that our encounters did not have to lead to sex. In this way we avoided the traps of the clammy office workers with their photocopier-room affairs. I imagined them, hot and sweaty, loosening ties and chucking off high-heels, slurping away those few desperate minutes until the 6.30 to Orpington and Sevenoaks. Just extensions of work pressure. ('Have that fuck on my desk by five tonight, Ms Jones: it's vital for the TQM assessment.')

'You know you can see me whenever you want,' she'd say with a cool, wonky-toothed smile, and she'd fire up a cigarette, sheening her face with a demon-glow. And she'd look smug in the knowledge that it wasn't true. We met on her terms. Always.

She'd lost the appetite for her dares – pure illegality was just too safe for her, I reckon. Instead, the bedroom became her battleground. And if I hesitated at any of her suggestions, she only needed to remind me. Like the time she slid up to me, draped her arms around my neck and opened her eyes wide in mock innocence. 'Oh, no,' she said. 'Please. *Don't*. Oh.' She moistened her carmine lips, just once. 'Ring any bells, sound any buzzers?' she asked, tapping my forehead lightly. 'Lights on? Anyone home? Goooood boy.'

We carried on, as before. Meeting and drinking and shagging. Every so often, she'd give me an update on the Charlie and Jan thing.

Whether by accident or by design, Jan was to fall pregnant that summer, just a few weeks after Nicole and Keela's beach party.

★

It seemed to have gathered momentum. People floated in, like ghosts from the sea. I was adrift. I didn't recognize anyone. The music had become ragged, primal again, and it would touch for a few minutes on something I recognized – Bomb the Bass, Secret Knowledge – before veering off into a patchwork of sirens, drums and screaming whistles. Someone was having fun on the decks.

It happened at about midnight.

First, Faith cannoned into me. I caught her. She grunted, gasped. The satin was slippery against her body and she smelt of shampoo and woodsmoke. She was pointing vaguely behind her and trying to say something.

The largest fire roared just metres from us, and people I didn't know were laughing, joking, toasting crumpets on spears of driftwood.

She twisted her head round, pushed back her wild hair and stared hard, right through me. 'Tell him,' she slurred. 'Just tell him to fuck off.'

Her mouth, I noticed, sent warm, pungent air across me. 'Oh, you haven't,' I muttered, holding her up. 'You *stupid* cow.' A bottle of Gordon's sloshed in the pocket of her skirt. It was open, and the gin described a wet arrow on the satin, down one leg to her feet.

Suddenly, Mike was there, his shirt loose, his beer can dangling from his fingers. 'It's all right,' he snapped. 'We were just having a chat.'

Charlie was behind me. 'What's the matter? What's going on?'

There was a pulse, a ghost beat inside my head, as if the music had crawled inside my skull and was breeding rampantly. 'I'm not sure,' I said, trying to hold Faith up. She was clawing at my shirt while humming fragments of tunes, like some demented cross between Ophelia and Mrs Rochester.

'I just . . . want to talk to her,' Mike said, wiping his mouth with the back of his hand. He was shuddering with suppressed energy. He looked dangerous. 'Have a drink. Siddown. Come on.'

The heat from the fire was growing uncomfortable. I felt wet, pungent, prickly with sweat. Faith's gin bottle was hard and cool against my thigh.

'A drink.' I looked up at Mike as it dawned on me. '*You* gave her a drink?'

'Christ, what the hell . . . What does it fucking matter?' He stepped forward, so that only a foot or two of sand separated us. 'You've always tried to stop me from being friends with her. Haven't you?' His face looked like a scrunched-up cartoon. 'You think you're so fucking great, don't you? Her *special* friend. So special, she doesn't even *like* you.'

Faith moaned, shaking her head, and slipped, almost elegantly, from me to Charlie. He held her by the shoulders, looked into her eyes. I had stepped forward to meet Mike Bradfield's gaze.

'You don't know the half of it,' I murmured. I felt strangely calm, controlled. I was in the dominant position here. I was on top. No reason to let him get to me.

'The bottle,' Nic was saying. 'She shouldn't be drinking.'

'She can drink if she wants,' Mike snarled.

'Watch that temper,' I told him softly. 'Gets you into trouble, *Mister* Bradfield. Remember?'

'You *shit*,' he said quietly, and pushed me hard, once, in the chest.

I spread my hands, backed off. I'd begun to experience that weak, aching feeling, half guilt and half fear. 'Hey, all right. Look, I didn't say that. Let's just calm down.' He pushed me again, shaking his head, a word forming on his lips. 'Look,' I went on, 'I'm just concerned.' I still kept my tone level, determined to ride this one out.

'Oh, yeah, I bet you are.' He shoved me once more, and my back was right against the fire. People were scattering behind me, making worried noises. 'So what's it to you? She your fucking property, or what?'

'Well, I care about Faith.' I glanced nervously over at Charlie, my eyes saying *help me*. 'I think you're . . . you're . . . asking her for something she can't give you. And I don't think that's very nice. Especially as your wife's here,' I added under my breath.

He ignored the last comment, or didn't hear it. 'You really think she values you? You're nothing to her.' He was sneering, now, palpably enjoying himself.

'Well, if you like to think that.'

'Believe me. She didn't ask *you* about the fucking abortion, did she? No, not you.'

The fire was furiously hot against my back. The beats were thundering over the roar of the flames, and the sea, distant and powerful, washed it all like static. My breath was ragged and furiously loud. Everything was red.

The word he had said still hung like a dagger in the air.

I looked from Mike to Faith. She tried to stand on her own, and Charlie was uncertain whether to let her go. She couldn't focus on me. My field of vision wobbled back to Mike again.

He raised his eyebrows. 'You didn't know,' he said in slow realization. He licked his lips. 'Jesus, you didn't know.' He shook his head slightly. Then he turned, as if to move away from me. And tossed a contemptuous little smile away into the night.

That was when I broke his nose.

It must have happened quickly, because at first I didn't feel my fist contact with his face at all. Then my knuckles throbbed, and Mike was kneeling, whining obscenities through a pinched nose, and Keela and Nic were bending over him, concerned, as the blood gushed down the sleeve of his shirt. Every few seconds, he let out a huge, terrifying bellow of pain.

Faith's arm was round my shoulders again. She was murmuring something incoherent, but managing to stand unaided. I could tell her eyes were desperately trying to interpret the colours and shapes in front of her, to make them into events. She was hot and heavy against me.

'Come on,' I said to her, making an instant decision. 'I'm taking you home.'

I used her mobile to call a taxi to the coastal road. She got worse, and I realized, while we waited, shivering, on the dunes, that I couldn't do this on my own.

Well, there was someone who would be willing to help a soul in distress. He lived in East London, didn't he? That was near enough.

I started to dial the number, hoping I'd remember it.

'Thanks again,' I said to Luke in the hallway.

'Least I could do,' he answered. 'Just make sure she gets plenty of fluids when she wakes up. Let me know she's all right, won't you?'

I sat beside her in the lounge. The room's pungency was softened now with pot-pourri and air freshener, and the town slumbered on the other side of the curtains. A goods train rattled distantly across the

Medway bridge. I stroked her fringe. She slept on, her face puffy and pale in the dim light.

It crashed in my brain, what Mike had said. It rattled like loose pots and pans in a ship's galley, and it crashed against another memory, too. That she had phoned Luke last year.

I was suddenly aware of her fragility, her humanity. I had always assumed Faith would be here for ever, outliving us all. I'd once pictured her becoming a cantankerous old biddy cackling from her wheelchair. While we all slipped into early graves despite eating low-fat kippers and doing yoga, she smoked dope and drank whisky every day and remained healthy and happy until she was about a hundred and twenty. I realized, now, that she walked on a knife-edge.

But she was a certain kind of woman. Men would flock to her room to see her if she was ill, bringing her fruit, medicaments, flowers. They would be lining up to hold her hair back if she threw up, jostling to clean her mouth.

I was one who would, perhaps, be inclined to leave her and see what happened. In that sense, I was dangerous.

Hard to believe that this was the same woman who held me in thrall. I stroked her white face, listened to her clogged breathing, thought how much power I held, right now. What I could do, and why.

It frightened me.

Three years on, I fought my memories.
 As I had fought the desperate urge to kill her.
 And almost won.

Part Three *Art and Detection*

15 Ghostdancing

Angelica is still sleeping.

She is leading us a merry dance. This is madness. We are playing right into her milk-white hands. We are puppets on strings and *she wants us to find something out.*

I can see her hair, glossy and black, falling in tangled curls to her white shoulders. I can see that black dress, clinging to every curve of her body, and the crucifix swinging between her breasts. I can see the whirling, gnashing dragon tattoo which glistens under a thin layer of sweat on her forearm as she moves up and down above me. I hear her gasps, her sighs.

All this I can recall. And I can describe her, perfectly, fitting in each part as if for a police photofit. But she has receded, a ghost fading in Time, a retinal image slowly shifting its light until it blends with the reddish darkness and is nothing.

I cannot picture her face.

16 Do You Remember the First Time?

Date: Fri 01 July 1994 14:20:01 +0000 (BST)
From: Faith Devereaux<f.r.devereaux@mku.ac.uk>
To: 101103.3734@compuserve.com, chad@gb-harp.com,
             mkb@bradfield.demon.co.uk, zelda@st-matt.ox.
             ac.uk, cath.barnes@lmh.ox.ac.uk, d.g.tomlin
             @mku.ac.uk
Subject: I've been doctored ! ! ! (fwd)

Well, you can kindly bow down and abase yourselves,
mortals. At lunchtime today, my fabulous external, Prof
Perkins from Leeds, said he would, pending minor
alterations, recommend my PhD. Yesssss! :-) :-) :-) I'm
off to get rat-arsed. Hope 2CU there – the Black Cat first,
then Kimi's from 10-ish.
Lurve, Rioja and ciabatta,
The One International Faith.
--
+
'There's a theory that if you give enough monkeys enough
typewriters, they'll eventually produce the works of
Shakespeare. The Internet disproves it.'
Visit Faith's top cool homepage at http://www.mku.ac.uk/
comms.engl/fdev and check out the **deVice** homepage for
the history of a great lost band! http://www.mku.ac.uk/
comms.engl/device/index.html
+

Date: Sat 09 July 1994 12:40:34 +0000 (BST)
From: Faith Devereaux<f.r.devereaux@mku.ac.uk>
To: 101103.3734@compuserve.com
Subject: How's it hanging, big boy???

Thought you'd like another few lines from your fave Net
Goddess. I'm supposed to be teaching what the Merkins
refer to as a 'Creadive Riding' class this afternoon, so
I'd better get my pretentious thinking-cap on. If it's
anything like last summer's, it'll be full of arty girls
in big skirts writing wistful stuff about their cats, and
speccy sci-fi boys churning out testosterone-driven
cyberpunk-shit. Never mind, if I do this for long enough,
I might even get a Real Job (TM), eh? :-)

Fucking nightmare last week: had my hard-disk eaten by a
virus. Do you know anything about them at all? I was so
naive: I just downloaded this file from New Zealand which
was supposedly about post-feminism, and it turns out to be
a fucking electronic rapist. Someone's idea of a sick
joke, I imagine. ROTFL, I don't think. :-(:-(:-(

Hope you are still having fun bashing the present
continuous into the heads of foreigners. Lots of 'I going
at cinema' to put up with, I expect. Rather you than me.

Things are a bit strained between Charlie and me. We had
a day trip to York together – he and Jan and I – and she was
so fucking miserable all the time. What Mike would call a
right mardy cow. Didn't want to do any of the things I
suggested, like the City walls or the cathedral or the
ghost walk. Anyway, we ended up in this little
coffee-house, which was nice for a sit down, and I thought
we would work out what we wanted to do, but it seemed she
just wanted to go and look round fucking clothes-shops. I
mean, Christ, you can do that in Chichester. What had we
come away for? I ended up getting really annoyed with her.
You know what she's like – such a smug bitch, and she
always turns everything back on you. She snapped some

comment at me, something to do with not understanding what she's been through, and having to make allowances.

Charlie was trying to placate us both – but, well, I was ready for a row by now, wasn't I? It had been brewing all day, after all, and someone's got to tell her. She ended up saying how stressful I was to be around, and – get this – she pretty much implied that I'd caused her miscarriage. I mean, can you believe it?

Also, I'm fed up with having to cover for Charlie over this creative accounting stuff, and it almost came out. Majorly bad vibes. So, needless to say, things are not at their best. We shall see.

--

*+
'Revolutionaries only change the world: the thing however is to explain it.'
Visit Faith's top cool homepage at http://www.mku.ac.uk/comms.engl/fdev and check out the **deVice** homepage for the history of a great lost band! http://www.mku.ac.uk/comms.engl/device/index.html
*+

Date: Mon 18 July 1994 11:14:09 +0000 (BST)
From: Charles Devereaux<chad@gb-harp.com>
To: 101103.3734@compuserve.com
Subject: Some stuff

Thanks for your kind invitation to come and stay for the weekend. I really would love to see you again, but it's a bit awkward. Don't know if you know, but things are rather unfortunate between Faith and myself at the moment. Basically, Jan and I had a day out with her in York, and it didn't go at all well. Jan was doing her best to get on with Faith, although they do both find it difficult. I realize Jan is partly to blame for this, with those unnecessary asides about perpetual students and that kind of thing, but I have had a word with her about it.

Faith, on the other hand, never misses an opportunity to have a little dig about how keen Jan was to get married, and makes more comments than necessary about interior design. Let me make this clear, there was only one occasion, only *one*, on which Jan decided that we would not go on holiday, when we needed to save up for the pelmets and the wooden curtain-rings. Every other time, she has been perfectly amenable to my suggestions.

Anyway, there was a minor altercation over the bill, which got blown up out of all proportion. Jan, in the end, just wanted to settle it as quickly as possible because, as you well know, and I'm sure Faith knows as well, she can't have stress interfering with the regulation of her biorhythms, especially not when we're trying for a child. Faith, for some reason, took this to be a pointed comment about her.

I'm sure this will sort itself out. I'll write again when things are clearer.
Best wishes, Charlie.
--

DISCLAIMER

The views expressed in this message are those of the individual correspondent and do not reflect those of the Harper-Remington Corporation. Unauthorized distribution or reproduction by any means of this message is not permitted. If you have received this message in error, please destroy it and report the error to your system administrator.

```
Date:     Mon 05 Sep 1994 17:45:07 +0000 (BST)
From:     101103.3734@compuserve.com
To:       Faith Devereaux<f.r.devereaux@mku.ac.uk>
Subject:  Just hello
```

Hi. Hope you're enjoying life as a Post-Doctoral Fellow.
Write if you have time.
:-) love from me. xxxx

```
Date:     Mon 12 Sep 1994 09:09:56 +0000 (BST)
From:     101103.3734@compuserve.com
To:       Faith Devereaux<f.r.devereaux@mku.ac.uk>
Subject:  This
```

> Also, I'm fed up with having to cover for Charlie over
this creative accounting
> stuff, and it almost came out. Majorly bad vibes. So,
needless to say, things
> are not at their best. We shall see.

Hey, I just found the above in one of your old messages.
What did you mean?

```
Date:     Wed 21 Sep 1994 18:43:17 +0000 (BST)
From:     101103.3734@compuserve.com
To:       Faith Devereaux<f.r.devereaux@mku.ac.uk>
Subject:  Earth calling Faith
```

Anyone there?
Why are you ignoring my messages???

17 Catastrophe Theory

She rides the sunlight, black dress fluttering in the breeze. Her eyes, polarized, flash as she turns her head back, for an instant, towards the house. She lifts her left hand very slightly. Perhaps it is not sunlight in her lenses but the intensity of fire, a flash of a future-shock, a blast into the past.

But then, the grasses ripple, the cloud passes over and she is gone.

Why do I keep seeing that scene?

And why does the poncy little director of *My Memories* (PG) decide to shoot it like a French art-house movie every time?

I wonder about it now, as I shade my eyes from the sun, and watch a giant, dark bird circling around, some distance from the cliff top. I am waiting for the bird. It's bringing me news.

It's been a hell of a day, and it started with Angelica's hangover.

'Oooph,' she says, sitting up very slowly. Her hair is knotted into an unwashed tangle and her eyes are crumpled, but she still looks intriguing. Runs in the family.

'You all right?' I ask from the kitchen.

'I'm not sure. I think there's a family of woodpeckers living in my head. Did we drink a lot last night?'

'A fair bit.'

'And you're fine, I suppose. You total git.'

I grin, pleased to have got the better of her just this once. 'Yeah, well, I'm used to senseless alcoholism. My brain cells carry Exit pamphlets. Here, have this.' I pass her a mug of camomile tea and some toast.

'Thanks.' She takes it, unsteadily. 'There's . . . some paracetamol in my bag . . .' she says, gesturing vaguely around the flat. 'Wherever you've put it.'

'Yeah, hang on.'

Her holdall is shoved out of the way under the hall table. I unzip a pocket at random to look for the tablets, but I just find various clothes, obviously stuffed in the bag in something of a hurry. There is a paisley sponge-bag, and I look inside it. Various toiletries from Body Shop, a toothbrush, a powder-compact, a make-up brush. A bottle of something that looks like hair dye. Funny, I'd never have thought of her as that vain.

I try the front pocket. I don't find them in there. I do, however, find three sleek, neatly-tied clear plastic bags. One is filled with crumbly, greenish-brown dried leaves, and two are packed with a fine white powder.

Just then, the phone rings on the hall table.

I freeze for a moment, wondering if Angelica will come out to get it. After about four rings, I answer it. From the dining-room, I can hear Angelica cautiously crunching on her toast.

'Hello?'

'It's Mike.'

'Oh. Right.'

'Look, I'm sorry to bother you at home again. Hey, I saw on the news about that . . . place of yours. The fire.'

'Oh, that. Yeah, well, the police are working on it. We have to live with these things.' At least Mike hasn't accused me of torching it myself for the insurance. (I wonder if he's ever considered doing that to one of his houses? It's the kind of thing I wouldn't put past him these days.)

'Mmm. Well, look, d'you fancy going for a drink at some point? That is, if you promise not to take me for any breakneck runs round graveyards, or to ask me anything whatso-fucking-ever about that demon-spawned hellbitch who used to be my wife. Is that clear?'

'Clear as mineral water, Michael.' From the kitchen, I hear the chomping suddenly stop, and a chair scraping quietly. 'And if you promise not to swear too much, and not to go on about how the unemployed don't really want to work, I'd be only too glad to meet up.'

He laughs. 'Yeah, right. I can't promise anything, but I'll try. Listen, there is something else, actually . . .'

'Yes?' I ask cautiously, sensing that this might be the actual reason for the call.

'Well, I know it's weird, but . . . I was wondering about the video. From the . . . Well, from France.'

'What about it?'

'Charlie was asking me if I had it. I think he'd quite like it, y'know, as a sort of last memento of Faith. I mean, if you think about it, the thing's a record of her last few days of life, isn't it?'

'Yyy-eeessss . . .'

'Yeah, I know, a bit fucking creepy, seeing the place where it happened, and all that, but I can kind of understand it, can't you? Thing is, I'd sort of forgotten about it, after . . . it happened. And what with all this shit hitting the fan with Nic, I can't remember what happened to the tape.'

'Uh-huh.' I glance at the door. I wonder if Angelica is listening.

'I was pretty sure it was left in the camera, but obviously there was no way I was going to get it out after what happened. Anyway, it's not there now. I didn't even think about it until Charlie asked. But I just thought it was worth asking if you might have got it?'

'Me? The tape? No. Sorry, no.'

I'm remembering what Angelica said to me in the car a couple of days ago. About not trusting any of them for now. And I wonder whether talking to Mike is such a good idea, after all.

'Oh,' he says, 'right. I can't think where it is, then. Can you give Charlie a ring? He sounds quite keen to have it back.'

'Yes. Okay. Look, Mike, about that drink . . . I'm really busy with the insurance and all that, so, um, I'll call you in a week or two when I've got a bit more time.'

'Fine. Whatever.'

When I ring off, I realize my heart is pounding. Almost as if I've nearly been caught doing something I shouldn't be doing.

Why?

I look in her bag again, stroke the plastic bags cautiously. I think of zipping it back up, saying nothing. But no. I take the bags out and go back into the dining-room with them.

Angelica is hunched over the table. She has nibbled at her toast, but the tea is silently steaming, untouched, at her elbow. I'm distantly aware of a song on the radio, about God being a stranger on your bus, and whether you'd talk to him if that meant you had to believe in him. It brings back a flash of a conversation I had with Faith, but

Angelica is looking at me, now, raising her eyebrows. 'Who was that on the phone?' she croaks, trying to sound nonchalant.

I chuck the plastic bags on the table in front of her.

'Never mind the phone. I think I've found out where you get your money.'

She groans, moves the toast aside and slumps slowly down so that her chin rests on the table. 'I could really do without this now,' she croaks.

I sit down opposite her, fixing her with an unrelenting, hard gaze. 'Drink your tea.'

'I really . . . don't feel like it.'

'Look, I'm fed up with this. You won't tell me *anything* about yourself, you won't give me any insight into your motivations, and I think you know far more than you're prepared to let on. And now I find out you're a sodding drug dealer. Drink your tea.'

She sighs, closes her eyes once as if in intense pain. 'It really isn't what you think,' she says.

'I don't know what I think.' I prod the bag of dried leaves. 'That looks like skunk, so I imagine you've got your own little hydroponics centre somewhere. They're a fire hazard, by the way. And infra-red cameras can pick them up. As for the other stuff, well . . .' I sigh. 'You must be doing some pretty sharp moving to play with the big boys, that's all I can say. What do you do?'

'Look, I provide a service. I meet consumer demand.'

'Oh, right. Don't tell me, you hang around the school gates every Friday? Give them the first one free, that kind of thing?'

She sits up, her eyes widening, and slumps back in the chair. She looks stunned, as if I have just physically slapped her. 'I do *not*. What kind of person do you think I am? I sell to responsible adults.'

'Like who?'

'Friends, mostly. And media people.' She mentions some names: a well-known novelist; a fresh-faced children's satellite TV presenter.

I am genuinely shocked. 'Not her! Surely?'

'What, you think she's naturally full of boundless energy at seven in the morning? Get real.'

I sense that we're losing the point a bit. 'Angelica, I'm supposed to trust you.'

'And so you can,' she says with a weak smile, leaning back and scratching under her arm. 'Look, if you can't find the paracetamol, fruit juice would be nice.'

'The Medway Area Dangerous Sports club is meeting today,' I inform her as I pour her some Britvic. 'Hang-gliding and bungee-jumping on Pedriell Cliffs. I think I might go down and have a look.'

'I . . . have to be somewhere,' she says, taking a cautious sip. 'I'll have a shower, see how I feel.'

I sigh. 'You do that. I'm going for a walk. I need to . . .' I wave a hand at her, the table, the drugs, all of it. 'Get away from you.'

After buying myself a newspaper from my usual stand, I wander for a bit, then go to the wooden bridge in the park and lean on the rail, watching the willows caress the water. A few early morning dog-walkers and joggers are out.

I am trying not to think too hard about Hope Springs, or about Angelica's vocation. For some reason, the call from Mike is uppermost in my mind.

Certainly, the videotape is not something I've given any great thought to up until now. We were all taking it in turns with the camcorder, I remember that much. We must have pretty much filled a tape. I know that the machine was a bit dodgy, though. Mike had bought it cheaply from a mate, and the record button was inclined to be temperamental. I try to think why the tape would not still be in the camera. Surely he would have left it there?

The other possibility, of course, is that Mike Bradfield knows perfectly well where the tape is. And he's just looking for a pretext to see me. About something else entirely.

The wind rustles the aspen leaves on the ground. The ducks skim the water of the lake. The year is getting colder and greyer, and it tastes of damp.

I'm beginning to get a shadowy, creeping sense that Angelica might be right to mistrust the others.

But I try to forget about it, and drive out to Pedriell Cliffs instead.

Some young men walk past me on the cliff-path, and they are able to identify the girl in the photo straight away. In fact, one of them points straight up into the air. Lucy, apparently, is their star hang-glider. I decline their invitation to come and watch the bungee-jumping, and

I head, on their advice, for Landrangers, the café by the car park.

I find that the café is reached through an outdoor pursuits shop, an Aladdin's cave of maps, guides, pamphlets, cagoules in a range of water-resistant, snow-resistant and no doubt shit-resistant fabrics, and an equally wide selection of tents, some of which are suspended from the ceiling like gigantic lampshades to demonstrate their volume.

The café is full of people in boots and waterproofs, looking earnestly at Ordnance Survey maps and eating hearty sandwiches. It's easy to spot her when she comes in and leans on the bar, smiling as she orders a mug of tea. She's trim and tall, attired in a crimson and black jumpsuit. Mid-thirties, quite attractive, with pale eyes and high cheekbones, but looks as if she can't be bothered doing anything with her unkempt brown hair, which is going grey.

I sidle up next to her, feeling faintly seedy. 'Excuse me. Lucy?'

She turns to look at me. 'Yes?' she says, in a rounded voice. She looks me up and down and I feel myself redden slightly. It's as if, somehow, she knows I shouldn't be here, and that the most dangerous sport I have ever willingly undertaken was an unwise experiment with vodka and crème de menthe.

I flip out the photograph and show it to her. 'I was just wondering,' I said, 'if you recalled having this taken. I'm . . . doing some research.'

She takes the picture and stares at it in wonderment. 'Where on earth did you get this?'

'I'm . . . well, I was . . . a friend of Faith Devereaux.'

She narrows her eyes slightly, looking hard at me as if I have said the wrong thing. Her tea arrives on the bar in front of her. 'You want one?' she asks.

When she pays, she peers at the blackboard behind the bar. I realize the apparent hostility in the way she narrowed her eyes was actually down to simple myopia.

We find a table near the window, looking out across the cliffs. It takes me five minutes to explain the edited highlights of who I am, what happened to Faith, and what has happened since, including where I found the photo and how I tracked her down. Lucy nods occasionally, and when I have finished, she takes a sip of her tea.

'I saw about Faith,' she says. 'In the papers.' She doesn't seem overly concerned.

'Yes. Well, don't believe everything you read.'

'I don't,' she answers impatiently. 'What do you want to know?'

'I imagined that this picture might be important, somehow. Faith must have thought so, after all, if she had it taped to the inside of her locker . . .'

'Mmmm.' Lucy peers at the photo again. 'Excuse me,' she says, and gets a pair of fashionable wire-framed glasses out of her inside pocket. 'This is about six or seven years old,' she says. 'I was going out with a friend of Charlie's. I think it was when we went up to Scotland for a power-boat contest.' She nods, takes her glasses off and suspends them casually from one hand. 'That would be about right.'

'Oh. And that's all?'

She shrugs. 'What else do you want to know?'

I explain about Serge and his computer wizardry.

'You see, he magnified the picture, and it's very clear, on this edge, here.' I indicate the sliced edge. 'It's been cut. Quite roughly, in fact, with a pair of scissors or something. It isn't even a straight line. You can see, if you look closely.' (Well, you probably can't, I thought, given that you can hardly see your hand in front of your face. I see now why letting you go hang-gliding would be classed as dangerous.)

'Maybe she thought it wasn't a very good picture,' says Lucy with a shrug. 'You must have done that? Got your holiday snaps back and thought, Christ, I look like a lobster on day release, but that's a pretty good shot of the Eiger? . . . We've all done it.'

'Cut ourselves off pictures, yeah. Cutting someone else off is a bit more interesting, though, surely?'

Lucy frowns, taking a long, deep gulp of her tea, and then puts her mug down carefully on the table. 'I think we're talking at cross-purposes,' she says, tucking a greying strand of hair behind one ear.

'Really?'

Some climbers in the corner burst into uproarious laughter at some ribald comment or other, and I'm startled for a moment.

Lucy taps the picture with her fingernail. 'Faith cut herself off this picture,' she says, 'or someone else did.'

I stare at the pale face next to Lucy on the photo. 'Then –'

'That's not Faith,' she says, shaking her head. 'That's Angelica.'

18 Independent Love Song

There were times, that year, when I wondered if I could love her better in death.

An icon. Unchanging and still. And unable to infuriate me, to repel and excite me at the same time. No longer able to make me demented.

There were days when I knew I could not see her in person, and so I looked at her photograph for hours. I would lie on my bed, not moving, dimly conscious of approaching hunger and thirst but unable to do anything about it.

I did this several times. The final time, I took the picture down from my notice-board, touched its corner with a cigarette lighter and watched her burn.

Mike had not been inactive for long after losing his job. 'Human beings,' I remember him saying, 'are unreliable. I could never do another job based around so much potential for human error. But land, bricks, mortar – they're solid and stable. Prices may change, but you can deal with that. It's economics. You know where you are.'

I didn't offer any of the obvious arguments against this view, as I could see it made him happy at the time. Mike spent the year doing a class, two evenings a week, for an NVQ in Property Management. Before long, he had a grounding in the skills he had previously despised.

He was good at it, too. Luck, loans and sound share investment all helped him along. As the country clawed its way out of a recession, he set up in business with two others from the course, and before long he was buying semis, terraces and flats to 'tart them up', as he put it. He was no fool: he went for spacious but none-too-new properties in the suburbs of Southampton, Portsmouth and Brighton, places with a steady stream of students and nurses. He'd also reckoned, correctly, on some of them having affluent parents to help out with his monthly rents, which weren't exactly at the cheaper end of the market. In the first year, they broke even – the other partners were happy with this, but Mike wanted profit. He was talking seriously of expanding into Reading and Oxford.

His newly flattened nose suited him. He wore it with pride. He never seemed to acknowledge the fact that I had actually decked him. In fact, it was as if neither of us could quite believe it, because we only referred to the event in the most oblique of terms. On one occasion, he even called it 'the accident'.

I couldn't quite understand his attitude. He would still call me from time to time, and he still seemed happy for us both to be there if a group of us were going out. It was as if he somehow needed me. I thought I might get Faith's insight, but it was something I needed to do face to face, and she was elusive these days.

She and I also had our boundaries. We knew there was something we had not talked about, a ghost which chilled the rooms of our intermittent sexual encounters. We never referred to it. This made our conversations strangely abstracted, stilted. It made our sex impersonally lustful and desperate, as if we had forgotten the people within and made ourselves into bodies, just hot and wet flesh seeking satisfaction.

Her lecturing duties ate up her time. She would e-mail me occasionally at the EFL Centre, but as for actually talking, her answerphone was permanently switched on. Its message – quirky the first time, but increasingly annoying thereafter – went: 'Hi there. This is the Machine. But then, aren't we all?'

There were other developments. Mike, for one. I didn't 'officially' know until the craft fair at Nicole's school, which I think we both attended out of a strange sense of duty.

'You just used the word *love-nest* without a licence, do you realize?' I told Mike. 'Either you've been reading too many tabloids or you're trying to be funny again.'

It was a day which boiled and baked the flesh of red faces, steamed bodies in pungent sweat, smeared sticky fingerprints on wooden bowls and hand-painted mobiles. Enterprise had produced a handful of oniony burger-vans and sickly pink candyfloss dispensers, as well as the odd funfair stall, bright orange and plasticky. They didn't even have the decency to look apologetic.

Michael would affect a total disgust for anything 'proleish' (as he called it) while enjoying some of it from behind the safe barrier of irony. Therefore he could read the *Mirror* as long as he tutted his way through every sex scandal and soap exclusive. He could eat in cheap curry houses, provided he looked with paternalistic indulgence on the Formica tables and plain crockery. And it was fine to enjoy football, provided one occasionally nodded and smiled in appreciation of a goal, rather than whooping and clapping like a demented primate. All this I had observed before, and it showed again now in the supercilious, amused way he lined up his light-gun at the gallery of tin ducks on the shooting-range booth. As he was enjoying himself, it had seemed a good time to ask.

'Sarah? Yeah, she's totally sorted.' He sounded casual. 'Brilliant woman. And she fucks like a bitch on heat, too.' He fired. *Ka-chang.* A duck fell.

'Ah,' I said, munching uncertainly on a veggie-burger. 'More information than I needed to know, really.' To my dismay, he seemed to *enjoy* talking about the whole sordid business, as if it were a matter for gossip, something which had happened to someone else.

There were few surprises. I'd seen him with her: she was slim, dark-haired, in her twenties, with eyes carefully outlined to look big and sultry. She had a husband of five years' standing, who didn't yet know. Mike had met Sarah through his business, and I had thought his official admission of her existence meant his marriage was finally limping to an end. However, he seemed happy to let the marriage continue, on the grounds that ending it would be a costly and inconvenient business. He and Sarah, as far as I could gather, went out together quite overtly, and if they wanted to spend the night together, they had the services of a bungalow owned by a mysterious friend of hers.

'Yeah. She *goes*,' he growled, as he picked off another duck. His tone had a spirit of laddishness which I was unwilling to share. 'We usually manage it twice a week. What you might call a standing order.'

Laying order, I thought. I had yet to work out exactly how much Nic knew of all this. 'What about Nicole?' I asked. I glanced over to the bookstall, where Nic, her auburn ringlets almost waist-length these days, was smiling and laughing with some parents and sixth-formers.

Mike ignored me. With a triumphant grin, he fired, and – *Ka-channng!* – felled his third duck in rapid succession. 'Yesss!' he cried, and bared his white teeth in triumph. The stallholder, a lardy-faced woman with a surly expression, wobbled over to the shelf of prizes and handed Mike a bottle of bubble-bath in the shape of a naked woman. He took it, smiling in thanks, but remembered quickly to temper his gratitude with a hint of postmodern distaste. He waggled the plastic totem in my face with a mock growl of earthiness.

'What about Nicole?' I persisted, as we shouldered our way through the crowds.

He shrugged. His eyes were unreadable behind Ray-Bans, and he did not even look in her direction. 'She's a stupid cow,' he said. 'Only fun when she's drunk.'

In touch with the caveman within, I thought to myself. 'Now, that's not necessary,' I said, trying to sound dignified and shocked. This was quite difficult, as I was wearing a T-shirt saying, in deliberately blurred letters, IF YOU CAN READ THIS YOU'RE MORE PISHED THAN I AM. 'You're still married to her,' I said carefully. 'And you show little sign, if any, of wanting to leave her. Wouldn't you say that was true?'

He shrugged. He wasn't interested.

I watched the sunlight blazing in Nicole's hair, painting her pale face honey-gold, and I was shocked to find her truly beautiful for probably the first time. I couldn't understand how Mike could turn his back on her. It didn't make me angry. It just made me sad.

We had paused at a booth selling trinkets – floating candles, crescent earrings and the like – and Mike prodded interestedly at one or two of them. I noticed it was the kind of stuff Nic loved, and which he thought was a waste of money.

For a second, he turned briefly in my direction, and his mouth flickered in something that could have passed for a smile. 'Well,' he said, 'she's drunk quite often these days.' He held up a yewstone relaxation pebble. 'How much is this, please?'

One day in July, I was soaking in a warm but still strangely uncomfortable bath. Eight hours of assessing student coursework, plus other exertions, had left me drained. When my mobile rang, I cursed, thinking I had switched it off. I was so tempted to ignore it, but I decided it had to be important. I pulled a dressing-gown on with one hand and tried not to drip too much on the landing. 'Hello?'

'Cockatoo!' crackled Mike's voice. 'Spare's gonna breed a dozen!'

'What?' I answered irritably. 'Say that again.' I dripped my way into the bedroom.

'Sorry, is this a bad time?'

'Look – just – what did you say? Before?'

'I said I don't know what to do. Sarah's going to leave her husband.'

'Aaah . . . Right.' I sighed, sat down on the edge of the bed and tried to towel my hair while talking to him. 'Well, that's. Mmm. Her, um. Decision, obviously.' I was trying to use neutral language wherever possible, as I felt a pang for this nameless, faceless husband of Sarah's, the victim who would doubtless not get the sympathy he deserved. After all, there was no reason for me to take Mike's side over his. He might be a nice guy – probably was – while Mike could often be a total shit. 'It's . . . what you want, isn't it?' I asked.

'No, it bloody isn't! This is going to mess up everything. Totally. Jesus, what the fuck am I going to *say* to her?'

I sighed, moved the dripping receiver to my other ear. 'All right. Listen.' With some effort, I attempted to put my mind into a Mike-space, to tune in to his current wavelength. The husband is the enemy, all you want to do is be with Sarah. Think like that. If you can. (This is a *horrible* place to be. I'm glad I don't have to stay here.) 'Michael, surely if she's not with her husband then at least it's all out in the open? You two can see each other when you want, without all this skulking around. You can have a proper relationship at last.'

'That's just the bloody point, isn't it? That's what she wants. To make me proper. Make me *property*.' I could almost feel him spitting down the line.

'Well, if that's how you see it –'

'He owns their house. Do you understand that? It's not theirs. It's his!' Mike's voice had switched into a gabbling, desperate tone – he just wanted to speak, not listen. I felt quite affronted. He'd obviously chosen me as the friend most likely to hum and hah and generally sympathize with him, and not offer an opinion – which was why he'd not called Faith. Well, he wasn't getting away with it.

'And?' I prompted. 'Your point being?'

'If she leaves him, where the hell is she going to go? I don't want her deciding it's all cosy-wosy and she can move in now! She can't live here, for fuck's sake!'

I allowed myself a smirk. There was something quite satisfying about feeling Bradfield squirm for once. 'You really are a bastard. You'd actually prefer it to stay as an affair, wouldn't you?'

'Look, it isn't . . . What the fuck do you know, anyway?'

'Michael, you rang for my advice. I'm giving it.'

'That isn't advice, it's judgement. All I'm saying is, I'm not going to clear the place of one load of knickers and lipstick just to replace it with another.'

'I didn't think Nicole wore lipstick. She claims they all test on animals, even when they say they don't.' I was quite enjoying this, I had to admit.

'Look – Jeeesus, I didn't call you to talk about the bloody morals of the cos-fucking-metics industry, all right? How do I stop her *doing* this?'

'You should have thought of that before you started dipping your bread in another man's fondue, shouldn't you?' I was trying hard not to laugh.

'Don't patronize me. You're just jealous.'

'Sure. If you like. Actually, Michael, I'm glad you've forced me to confront the issue. I've been after your body for years. These women, they're just no good for you –'

'Look, are you going to be serious for a minute?'

I sighed. 'No, Mike. Sort it out. It's not my problem.' I flicked the mobile phone off and chucked it on to the bed, where it snuggled in a fold of quilt. 'Well, it isn't,' I added petulantly, in the direction of the curvy bump under the duvet.

She turned over, her hair a dark fan on her pillow. 'I worry about that young man,' said Faith, lying back and languidly stretching her arms above her head. 'Nice bath?'

I rolled over to her and kissed her. She tasted of sex. 'I said you should have joined me.'

She pulled her moist mouth away from mine for a second, trailed a wet finger over my lower lip. 'Dipping his *bread*,' she repeated, her eyes wide and mocking, 'in another man's *fondue*?'

'Phhww . . . sounded good at the time.'

Her tongue became more eager in my mouth, just as the telephone beside her bed started to ring. We ignored it. Later, we would play Mike's agonized message back, and exchange a complicit smile.

*

I sometimes felt, perversely, that Mike was being more honest with himself than I was.

He knew what he was doing. He had to get things sorted out with Nicole, that much was obvious, but no one was going to be terribly surprised at a divorce. His lust was blatant, almost sanctioned by convention. He was a man who would leave his wife for his mistress – end of very boring story.

I, on the other hand, lived in perpetual fear of a love that could easily destroy me. A blinding, angry passion which could control me, which should have satisfied me and yet left me feeling hollow and unloved.

There should have been one thing. One thing I could do, to show I was not commanded by her. To show that I was *me*.

There was nothing.

September, in a small tearoom, where the rain sparkled on a square beneath the sharp spires of a cathedral. I don't even recall which town, but I think the location appealed to her sense of irony. The radio behind the bar was playing Portishead, who had just won the Mercury Music Prize. People came and went, shaking water off their cagoules and umbrellas. The windows acquired their etch-a-sketch surface of condensation, and dampness pervaded the aromas of coffee and fresh cakes. She was late. When she arrived, she was soaking, her wet hair tangled across her face.

She tapped her index finger on the table as she sat down. 'Before you ask,' she said, 'I am *not* talking about Charlie and that wife of his. Clear?'

'You said it.' Again, she was in command. I felt myself unable to challenge her. 'Shall we order?'

After the coffee arrived, she seemed to lighten up a bit, and gave a sigh of satisfaction as she leaned back, her hair drying out rapidly.

'What about Michael, then? He ought to hate me,' I said, as I uneasily scooped foam from my cup with a fragile vanilla biscuit. 'Don't you think so?'

She shrugged. She'd put on some weight, I noticed, but she carried it well. 'He probably does,' she said, giving me her favourite teasing glance. 'Don't worry. He never really liked you much anyway.'

'Oh, great. Thanks a lot.'

'Well, darling, you're too complex sometimes. I mean, it's easy for me to know if I like someone. I just throw my knickers at the wall and see if they stick. You're more discerning.' She caught the look I was giving her, half indulgence and half impatience. 'All right, look . . . Mike probably doesn't give you much thought, to be honest. He has a lot happening in his life right now.'

'Like Sarah, I suppose.'

'Mmmmm. Weeeell . . .' Faith sipped her coffee and pushed her hair back, securing a handful of wayward blackberry-coloured strands behind her ear. 'Mike thought he was really into the trappings of wedded bliss, y'know? After all that rejection of capitalism bollocks . . . I dunno, he decided he rather liked the idea of all that shit, didn't he? Owning a nice house, nice car, nice wife and all that.'

'Beautifully bracketed together. Do go on.'

She raised her eyebrows, stroked a sharp fingernail down the bridge of my nose. 'Don't mock me. It just happens, doesn't it? You get married. You earn a decent salary. You get the wine rack, the coffee grinder, the garlic press. Beep-beep, didn't he do well?' She splayed her fingers out, still balancing the index finger on my nose. 'Bang, you're middle class, and you never saw it coming.'

'But who gets the wine rack when . . . ?'

'Pree-cisely. I'm glad to see you're paying attention, darling, as there will be a short test at the end. No, ever since it – all –' She waved her hand in the air to indicate the complex rituals of being suspended from a teaching post. 'You know.'

'Went a bit pear-shaped?'

'Mmm.' She tilted her head to one side, as if listening to the sound of the words. 'Odd expression. Some people think pear-shaped is good. Pear farmers, I imagine, positively rhapsodize over the prospect. Yeah, well. Whatever.'

'Get to the point.'

'The point will get to me, precious. Have some patience. Now, come on, surely you're good at seeing the gaps grow between people? Ever since it happened, Mike . . . well, he isn't exactly on the same wavelength as Nic any more.' She tapped my wrist and shook her head, as I had begun to indulge in one of my habits, folding a sugar sachet over until it was taut and ready to burst.

'Yes,' I said irritably, 'I'd noticed.' I pushed the sachet aside and played with my spoon instead.

'Well, I was always wondering who the other woman would be.'

It wasn't you, then, I thought. 'Were you sure there would be one?' I asked.

'Darling, trust me. Men never jump ship till they see land. Giving up on a shit relationship *because* it's shit is a female preserve.'

'Oh, right, and you're not, ah, generalizing hugely or anything.' Quite apart from the confusion as to whether the marriage actually is over, I thought to myself.

She shrugged, smiled. 'Not for us to apportion blame. Sure, in an ideal world, all marriages would be rock-solid, but, y'know, these things happen.'

These things happen. The great human capacity for making events into something which *happened*, thus removing the need for blame. A relationship just 'ends', as if the participants were knitting a scarf and ran out of wool. A smack on the nose is the same thing as the loose paving stone which trips up a pensioner. A dead child is a dead child, whether hit by a car or scooped half-formed and bleeding from a womb. Accidents, unfortunate incidents, tragedies. I shivered.

I wondered how often Mike Bradfield penetrated Faith, and how much of an accident that was. My jealousy had stabbed me again, an automatic reflex which made me realize I still loved and hated her in equal measures.

'No,' I said, 'I don't buy that. Someone has to make it happen.'

'Oh, lighten up.' She folded her arms, made a tutting noise, then finished her coffee in one gulp.

Signs of irritability – I quite liked that. I could still cause her to feel unwanted emotion. It hurt, though, at the same time, as this was a parody of the easy coolness we used to have.

'Look,' she said, leaning forward and leaning on her elbows. The tearoom was quiet – most of the other customers had gone, and the only background noise was the gentle gurgle of a percolator, mixed with the soft pattering of the rain. 'At the end of the day, the Monogamous Relationship, with its painted skirting-boards and cute little fruit-shaped fridge magnets, and Le Creuset saucepans – it's just *one thing*. It's a possible path, an experience. And breaking it up, that's another. It's a positive thing. Don't knock it.'

'A marriage breaking up is a *positive* thing?'

'Of course.' She opened her palms, stared at me fixedly with her big, dark eyes. 'Two people who used to feel one thing are starting to feel another. Two forces, interacting. They come together.' She slapped her palms together just in front of my nose. 'They fight.' She squashed her hands tightly together. 'The things they don't need from each other any more – love, sex, companionship – they're shattered.' She bunched her fists, tapped her knuckles together. 'And they turn into something new, right? Matter can't be created or destroyed – only transformed. It's brilliant. Fighting, fragmenting into chaos – it's how we move on, it's what makes us *strong*.'

I was a bit taken aback by this sudden foray into philosophy. Objections ran through my mind: what about abandonment, what about unrequited love, what about confusion? But I said: 'You've been doing a lot of thinking about this, I can see.' I sounded disapproving, even to myself.

She shrugged, lounged back in her seat. 'It's how I live my life, darling,' she said, and then she laughed. It sounded shrill, almost surreal in the empty tearoom. She laughed and laughed.

I did not join in. I was thinking about what she had said, and wondering if I would ever fight so hard I would shatter, and if I would ever transform into . . . what?

I was suddenly cold, and frightened of the rain.

The bill arrived. It sat between us for a few seconds while we watched the rain shimmering in the cathedral square. We did not look directly at one another.

We had been here before. This was different, though: *she* was different. I had not really connected with her today. Each time I met her, I felt more distant – as if she were a faint, crackly radio station, the frequency slipping as she tuned herself out of my life.

I glanced at the bill, pretended to wince. We shared a familiar smile. I flipped it over to her and we put exactly half each in, plus a small tip, just as we always did. A gold clasp, embossed with DKNY, glinted on her handbag. Then she fluffed her hair up and stretched her arms out, and I watched her firm breasts tautening against her black lambswool jumper. 'Right, then,' she said briskly, and caught my eye. We put our coats on, paid at the counter, and smiled our goodbyes to the primly aproned waitress before stepping out into the chilly rain of the real world.

We stood on the wet stone, as we had stood on a hundred pavements before. The great cathedral soared above us, pointing to a heaven she had never believed in, and which I had long since left behind. The world smelt damp, but fresh and alive, as if waiting for something.

She smiled, as if seeing something interesting in the distance. She turned to me with the smile still on, so that it brushed across me for a second, then flicked it away into the greying sky, as if she was not really bothered.

'My . . . car's . . .' I waved towards the cathedral. 'Behind there, somewhere.'

She nodded, swivelling on one heel, and shivered slightly, doing up a couple more buttons on her black moufflon coat, fiddling with the clasp on her handbag. 'I'm getting the train,' she offered. 'That way.' She nodded in the opposite direction, towards the main street.

'Good to see you again,' I said.

'Yeah. Good.' She nodded, giving the kind of tight, closed-mouth smile I had seen from others before, but never from her. It was ordinary. It was human. I wanted to hug her.

'I'll . . . see you, then,' I said. Normally, this was where it could go either way. All it needed was for one of us to say, 'Or . . .' The word, the opening of the option. It was a gateway.

'Mmm-hmm,' she said, nodding again.

There was a stark silence between us. I could hear the thudding of my own heart above the murmur of the town. The rain was dripping from my hair. It tripped and twirled around us, as if daring us to making a move. I blinked. It suddenly seemed ridiculous: in an impersonal room decorated with a Teasmade and a vase of dried flowers, I would tug at this woman's blouse, freeing it from her smooth, firm waist, while she pulled at my hair with her long, bony fingers, drawing my mouth down into hers as she fumbled to undo my belt. Yet here, in the open air, I was afraid to touch her. Afraid to let her have the kind of hug I would readily give to Nicole, say, or my mother.

She smiled, shrugged. She hoisted the designer handbag further up her shoulder again. She said, 'Maybe we –' and I began, 'I think –' cutting across her. We laughed. 'You first,' I told her.

'Okay. I was only going to say we should have some sort of reunion. You know, in Oxford, maybe. Hire a boat or something.'

'Mmm. Yeah. Good idea.'

'I'll call you,' she said.

'Yes, call me,' I agreed, nodding rather more energetically than was good for me.

She turned a wobble into a lunge, went for the wrong cheek and chuckled as she kissed me on both, in Gallic fashion. I tried to place her perfume: something subtle and peachy. Then she skipped away with a wave and hurried across the square in the autumn gloom. I watched as she passed under the blue and white Boots logo, under the swinging sign of the Four Mariners, and was absorbed into the darkness of the alleyway. A shape, a shadow, then nothing. The only woman I ever needed to love had slipped away from me once again.

Her signal was weak, drowning in static, eaten by the alien burble of short wave.

Perhaps it was there and then, in that cold September rain, that I realized it was almost over. Maybe I already knew that I was losing Faith.

19 Electronic Female

It is dusk. I'm driving, my mind attacked by numerous horrible possibilities.

I stop at the garage on the edge of town. The street lights are starting to nuzzle the greying sky. The air smells of evening: fossil-fuel pungency mixed with curries, tobacco and . . . roses?

My petrol slowly clocks up on the pump. It is half past six, and I'm not sure whether to head straight back to the flat. I replace the nozzle in the pump, then head across the forecourt to pay for my petrol. As I push open the door to the garage shop, the rack of newspapers catches my eye. One of the slightly classier tabloids, in particular.

I pick it up. It is fresh, soft and smooth. The main headline, which almost passes me by, is something to do with Scottish devolution, but it's the multi-coloured sidebar at the bottom of the page which I'm staring at.

It bears a picture of Angelica.

I pay for my petrol and the paper in a daze. I sit there in the forecourt, oblivious to the other drivers, staring at the full-page article on page five. The massive headline is DAILY GRIEF OF DRUG DEATH LECTURER'S SISTER. Next to a poised, serene-looking photo of Angelica, there is a faded shot of the two of them as sisters, side by side in school blazers, in a garden.

The hack has laid it on thick. The majority of the article is given over to recounting stuff which is already known – the circumstances of Faith's death, her education and family background, all neatly poised for maximum emotive effect. He's still managed to get bits wrong, of course. There are occasional, interspersed quotes from Angelica, to make it look like a 'personal' piece. If they are genuine, they must have been given in a hurry, perhaps over the telephone. I stare at the words with mounting anger.

'Faith and I were more than sisters,' murmurs Angelica, an attractive 37-year-old brunette who works in Public Relations. 'We had a special bond, something almost telepathic. I felt physical pain when she went.'

Her brow furrows and her eyes become distant, as she recalls the terrible day when her 28-year-old Oxford-educated sister died from the notorious killer rave drug. 'I can't imagine that she would have wanted to take her life. She had so much to live for. It was obviously a very unfortunate, stupid accident. I'd give anything to be able to go back in time and tell her not to do it.'

Faith Devereaux was the outstanding English Literature student of her year at Oxford, but she was certainly no shy blue-stocking. Her raunchy rock group 'Devices' regularly played the pubs and clubs of the town and, as her sister readily admits, drugs and men figured prominently in Faith's life . . .

It doesn't mention me by name anywhere, but the sub-text is clear: Faith as man-eater, Faith as self-destructive intellectual tart, Faith as high-class junkie slut.

I start the engine and drive home in a daze.

The flat is quiet, but the holdall is still there, shoved under the hall table where I left it. I imagine she is out doing what she calls work. Making deliveries. I sit in my armchair in the lounge and try to think. I am strangely calm.

I get myself a coffee before checking the e-mail.

There is one from the university. The address is s.desmoines @mku.ac.uk, and I realize, with a jolt of excitement, that it has to be Serge. Fumbling, I click on the message, and get an information-box telling me it's in two parts, a standard text message and an attachment called decoded.wav, which I know must be a sound file. The text of the message reads:

This was the content of your disk, a single .wav file. I thought you might like to have it mailed to you as soon as possible. Sorry it took so long. I have to say, whoever encoded this knew what they were doing! Say hi to Angelica.
Amitiés, Serge Desmoines.

228

I extract the sound file on to disk. However, I can't do any more than that. My PC, for all its merits, does not possess speakers.

After about half an hour, just as dusk is shifting into darkness, the buzzer rings. It's her. I let her in.

She sweeps into the flat, her long coat trailing behind her, and she settles herself on my sofa once more, hands deep in her pockets.

'So,' she says, with an impish smile, 'what news?'

'Nothing,' I tell her. 'The girl couldn't tell me anything useful.'

(I think to myself: two can play at this game.)

'Really?' She seems surprised.

'I want to wait and see what Serge turns up.'

'Fair enough.' Her eyes are steady and her tone gives away nothing.

'You seem to have been busy,' I say calmly.

'Really? God, I could do with a drink.'

She starts to get up from the chair, but I have slammed the newspaper down on the table between us. She jumps.

For a second, she meets my gaze, her eyes full of deep and crashing guilt. She is momentarily tipped off-balance. Then the Angelica veneer is restored – the wide smile, the air of confidence which hangs around her like an expensive perfume – and she settles back in the chair again, pressing her fingertips together.

'Ah,' she says, nodding to herself as if she expected this. 'You've seen it, then.'

'How much did you get for this?' I ask her, holding the paper up in disgust. My voice is still calm and quiet.

'Oh, look, the money –'

'*How much*, Angelica?'

'About twenty thousand,' she admits, scratching her ear and looking away.

I stare at her for three seconds, then throw the paper down and slump back in my chair. 'Well, congratulations, Angelica. You can go on your cruise of a lifetime. I'm sure Faith would have been delighted. Or, don't tell me, you've put a deposit on a little place in Kensington you've had your eye on? Christ.' I shake my head. 'I get it now. I see where you're coming from. You just want some juicy details from me, don't you? Then, in a week or so, you can tell them another story.'

'It's not like that,' she says, keeping her voice level.

'Isn't it?' I've got her on the run, I can tell. I've got her pinned down.

'No, actually,' she replies, giving me a superior smile. 'I'm giving the money to charity.'

'Oh, please.' Now my contempt is complete. 'You can do better than that.'

She raises her eyebrows. 'To my favourite charity, actually. A little-known local project.' She reaches into her pocket, unfolds a small oblong of yellow paper and places it on the table in front of me. 'I hope this will help with the restoration.'

It is a cheque for £20,000, and it is made payable to 'The Hope Springs Foundation'.

I stare down at it. Then I look back at her, unsure whether to laugh or cry.

'It's all right,' she says. 'You don't have to thank me.'

We get takeaway pizzas from Antonio's, just opposite the church on the edge of the ring road. The darkness is deepening, and street lamps blaze above us, their thick orange light making the drizzle sparkle like pixels.

'Look, what was Faith doing with that key on her in the first place?' I am thinking aloud. 'And why leave the disk where someone could find it? Just doesn't make sense, if you ask me.'

'So where would you have put it?' she asks, looking up, her eyes glossy and dark.

'I . . . haven't really thought.'

'Haven't you?' she says, biting into her pizza. 'You mean you've never considered what you would do if you had to get rid of something in a hurry, but you wanted to pick it up again later without any problems?'

'No. Is this leading somewhere?'

'Just tell me what you'd do. Think for once.' She licks her fingers. 'Mmm, wonderful anchovies . . .'

'Well, I could always stick it in the second-class mail,' I offer, shaking my head. 'What? What's the matter?'

'Congratulations,' she says, and she pulls a small, padded envelope from her left pocket and throws it on top of my pizza box.

It has a label on it, with my name and address, in my handwriting.

'What the hell is this, now?'

'That, my dear, is the videotape of your holiday in France, which you posted to yourself shortly after Faith died.'

'What?' I'm confused. Again.

'As is normal post office procedure, they would have tried to get it through your letter-box, and, if you weren't in, they'd have left a card saying to pick it up from the delivery office. It was buried under the documents in your bureau – you do have quite a lot, don't you, dear? – but it was there. And luckily, when I took the card along to the delivery office this morning, they were still holding your parcel for you. Oh, I had to forge your signature. Sorry.'

I look down at the neat capitals of the name and address. I stare at Angelica in the glow of the street lamps. Time seems to fracture between us.

She smiles that uncanny, red smile again and the ghost of her sister dances on her lips. One step ahead. As always.

'I don't understand.'

'No, I genuinely believe you don't.' She sighs contentedly. 'We've always known there was something in your memories that you didn't dare excavate. Something so . . . *dangerous* that you can't go there. What you did with the tape is part of that. As for why you did it, well . . .' She shrugs. 'That's something I'm hoping we'll discover.'

We're back at the flats, now, and I fumble for the keys. 'You mean I posted this to myself and I can't even remember doing it?'

'Well, evidently,' she says with a smile as I let her in.

Inside my flat, I put the pizza down and I open the envelope. I have the tape in my hands and I'm staring at its black plastic surface. The small cassette from the machine has been slotted into a larger VHS tape so that it's ready for playing.

'That's right.' She smiles, as if that explains everything. 'Go on, then,' she says. 'Put it on.' She nods at the video recorder.

'I'm . . . not ready for this.'

She shrugs. 'But would you ever be?'

And she holds the remote control out to me, like Eve offering the apple.

★

231

Blue light crashes against the walls of the flat.

On the screen, clear and bright, we can see the rear terrace of the *gîte*, white and sun-bleached. The shot is focused on the terrace from somewhere in the garden.

Bobbing slightly, the camera pans across the sunlit terrace. It is following Faith as she carries a drink outside. She looks like part of the summer in her long, silky dress and shades, and I shiver as I see her push her hair back in that classic gesture.

Angelica's hand touches my shoulder gently. 'There she is,' she murmurs. 'Beautiful as ever.'

On the screen, Faith sets a glass of lime juice down on the table and exchanges a smile with Nic, who's there trying to decipher a French newspaper. Yes, I remember. She would buy one every day and work her way through it with a dictionary, sometimes accosting me to ask words in a hideous accent.

Moving back across, we encounter Mike strolling out of the lounge and on to the terrace. He looks vaguely worried about something. He scratches his beard, looks up into the sky and retreats back into the house again. Despite the poor focus, we can still just about make him out, a silhouette rummaging in the magazines on the lounge table.

The camera pulls back slightly. There are Charlie and Jan, sharing a brief moment of relaxation on the sunbeds, both still and shaded and slowly browning. As we watch, Charlie turns on to his side, checks his watch and nods, before turning over on to his back, which looks paler than his reddish-brown chest. I smile in sympathy, aware of my own patchy attempts at a tan.

'Pause a sec,' says Angelica, and she flicks the button, holding the picture on Charlie and Jan on their sunbeds. She goes to the kitchen, puts the kettle on and starts buttering scones.

I watch her in the flickering blue light from the video screen, and smile at her uncertainly. My ally? My enemy?

She smiles briefly back. Her big, red mouth dominates her face. I think she looks younger in this ghost-light, and she seems to have done something with her hair. It looks fuller, longer, the ends curling at her shoulders.

'What is it?' she says, unscrewing the jam.

'Nothing.'

'You're staring at me. Enraptured by my charm, no doubt.'

'Sorry.' I continue to watch her intently. I remember the chill, the shock I had the first time I saw her on those stairs outside. I knew what she knew. It could so easily have been another. A flair for melodrama.

(Lucy from the Dangerous Sports club frowns at me, puzzled. 'That's not Faith,' she says. The name crashes in my head like a disintegrating iceberg. 'That's Angelica.')

I look back at the screen. The paused picture is vibrating, as it only has a limited time before it collapses and continues.

'Back in a moment,' I tell her, heading for the bathroom.

'Don't be long,' she says through a mouthful of scone, waggling a finger at me. 'The pause won't hold.'

In the bathroom, I am shocked at how tired and thin I look. In my mind, the last few days have existed out of time, an unreal interlude in my life, but my body hasn't seen it that way and is demanding sleep and sustenance. I am suddenly tired. I ache in every limb. My breath mists over my face in the bathroom mirror.

The hair dye is sitting here on the shelf in front of me. I pick up the bottle and stare at the label.

She is standing in the blue-lit lounge as I return, holding the remote control in her left hand. Her body, against the juddering picture, is tall and dark and lithe.

'You do it,' I tell her.

She presses the button. The picture continues to pan across the terrace. The shot gets back to the glass doors just as a familiar figure in a white T-shirt and green shorts emerges, with a plate of rolls and Brie in one hand and a can of beer in the other.

It's me.

I stare at myself, with a strange sense of dislocation.

'Just a minute,' I say. 'I want to see that again.'

I sense Angelica tense beside me, and then I flick the rewind button and run back over what we have just seen.

I can scent her and feel her, now. I can realize for the first time just how dangerous she might be. She looks up at me, and for a second her eyes are glistening with tears.

I press play to run the few seconds of tape again. Faith strolls across the terrace and plonks herself down next to Nic, who is poring over her newspaper. Pan back across to Mike, who looks up at the sky and then goes back inside. Pan across to Charlie and Jan, watch Charlie deciding it's time to turn over. And then back to the terrace, just two seconds later, and I come out.

'Jesus,' I mutter to myself.

'Something wrong?' she says, but the catch in her voice gives her away.

'What have we just seen?' I ask her.

'You lot,' she says, 'relaxing.'

'Yes. All of us. Which begs one very obvious question.'

'Namely?' she says, arching her eyebrows, but the wicked smile tells me that she is already there before me, as usual.

'Namely – who the hell was filming us?'

She laughs, and suddenly swivels round in the chair, hands behind her head. In the spectral light of the video, her eyes glow blue and her mouth is a deep, rich purple. Her skin gleams, as if she is some electronic ghost despatched from cyberspace to kill me.

'Who do you think, darling?' she says, and her voice is deep, cool and resonant.

And then, with a memory-flash like a sudden incision, time shifts, and another piece falls into place.

A dark, living shadow against the summer-yellow, her eyes shaded with sunglasses, she is hurrying down to the town. Why is she in such a hurry to get there? Because she is not.

Looking at the picture from a predetermined angle, I had seen what I wanted to see, Faith hurrying down towards the valley path for some reason, briefly lifting a hand to acknowledge me.

Pause, rewind. See it another way, look without prejudice. Then, it all makes sense. A woman in a hurry is not necessarily going somewhere. She could just as easily be running *away*. As fast as possible. Before anyone sees her. And why? *Because she is not supposed to be there.* Just as she heads over the rise at the end of the garden, she cannot resist one last glance over her shoulder. And she sees a flash of sunlight on a window, she sees me, looking out across the lawn, and what does she do? Her reaction is immediate and instinctive. Look perfectly natural. From a distance, who will know?

She raises a hand, briefly and without ceremony. A left hand.

That vision deceived me. What I saw from the window was a brief, unplanned glimpse of the darkness which haunted the edges of our days in Gervizan. Of the watcher. Of the ghost. Of Angelica.

20 Walk Away

I suppose I remember the easy stuff first. The things I could deal with. But the other memories permeate it, sharp as the smell of cooking.

Meat sizzles on the barbecue. It always smells pungent and alive when you haven't had any for a while. I went through a vegetarian stage last year, more out of curiosity than from any great moral conviction. (Verdict: I like bacon too much, and popping the B12s is a pain in the arse and can't be called natural.) Nic and Keela have volunteered to be on barbecue duty. They are not unduly bothered about reinforcing gender stereotypes – for one thing, I am out here too, and for another, Faith will be there with the others in front of the portable TV as soon as the teams line up.

The evening's light and warm: the sun won't set for another couple of hours yet. It is late June. The canal laps at the side of the moored barge, and a flickering blue light can be glimpsed within the boat itself.

I watch in amusement as Faith totters along the roof of the barge, holding a bottled beer in one hand and the TV aerial in the other. She's slimmer these days, sinuous beneath a strawberry cotton shift dress. Her black hair is shoulder-length with just a hint of curl, and her only make-up is a pale cyan eyeliner.

She fixes the aerial's plastic suckers right on the window of the main living-area, and holds it steady. 'Better?' she calls down.

'Yeah, stay like that!' answers Charlie's voice, to a chorus of laughter.

'Fuck off,' she says, leaning precariously over the edge, and very slowly lets go of the aerial. It does not fall. 'Yesssss!' She punches the evening air and rolls over. 'Coming in?' she calls to me. I'm leaning against the bow rail, by the rudder. 'Oi!' she yells when I don't answer immediately, and she waves her bottle, singing: '*You com-ing in! You com-ing in! Are – you – com-ing in?*'

'Yeah. Won't be a minute.'

'C'mon, you'll miss the kick-off. We're gonna bash those Krauts.'

I watch the sun, swollen and orange, hovering over the distant fields. 'Sure. Course we are,' I say with a gentle smile.

She sits on the roof, swings her legs round and slips through the hatchway with a shimmer of black and red.

We hide so much, these days.

I remember.

By the end of 1995, everyone I knew seemed dislocated, disjointed, drifting through life.

I was frozen, like the ground. Held fast in a job which had been exactly the same for three years. Mike and Nicole continued to live under the same roof, but could not stand the sight of each other. Luke, I knew, had been moved from his urban parish to a Hertfordshire village – no doubt nearer to heaven for some, but not for him.

Faith, it seemed, still thought she was a rebel, based on the way she drew attention to herself with her sarcastic comments, gave her students off-the-wall exercises like building walls out of bricks with different words on them to test their powers of association and – the clinching one, this – filled in magazine quizzes back-to-front, working upwards to Question 1. Couldn't you just hear the sound of empires toppling?

Anyway . . .

As I descend the steps into the barge, I come into the middle of a conversation. It seems that Charlie's friend Martin – who sports a mid-eighties mullet haircut, brown with blond highlights – is, in between slurps from his beer, recounting his experiences of being an Alternative Action protester.

'We got beaten by the police,' he says. I am aware that everyone – Mike, Nic, Charlie, Faith – is listening intently. The portable black-and-white television flickers with the last of the pre-match tension.

'Are you . . . going to *tell* anyone?' Faith asks, horrified.

'God, no.' Martin wrinkles his nose. 'It's quite embarrassing . . . I mean, would you?' he appeals to me, as I sit down.

'I – um – well . . .' I'm aware everyone is looking at me. 'Yes,' I say eventually. 'Actually, it sounds as if you should.'

'How many of them were there?' asks Faith.

Martin stares at her as if she is stupid. 'Eleven. Well, actually, there were only ten by the end, but . . .' He shrugs and sips his beer. 'They still totally overwhelmed us.'

I lean forward, concerned. This sounds serious. 'How . . . bad was it?'

Martin sighs. He lifts his beer can to his mouth, puts it down again and stares into the distance, obviously recalling some especially painful memory.

'Seven–nil,' he says. 'Still . . . no shame really. It was just a charity match, after all.'

She had remained incommunicado for several weeks at the end of the year. Then, suddenly – and typically – she threw out a casual invitation to me by post to spend a couple of days between Boxing Day and New Year at the house, which I accepted.

The company turned out to be Faith, Charlie and Jan, along with Jan's sister Paula and an ageing aunt of theirs who was convinced – quite reassuringly, as it happened – that she was in Blackpool. Faith had the bright idea of giving her a cup of tea, pointing out the distant glow of the television transmitter and saying 'If you look over there, Auntie Beatrice, you can see the tower.' After that, Auntie Beatrice kept asking when we were going to go and see the illuminations.

Faith, Charlie and I went for a meal in a windswept, hilltop pub. I couldn't help but wonder, as the three of us walked against the icy wind, how much Charlie knew about me and Faith. About where we had been, and where we were today. When we all talked, it seemed insubstantial somehow, as if there were subjects we were avoiding, and Charlie seemed to get irritated with Faith a couple of times.

Faith and I were, diplomatically I thought, put up in the same room but in separate beds, thus keeping all our options open. As it happened, I watched *Silent Running* with Charlie on the first night, and we polished off a great deal of whisky together – although even when gently inebriated, his reserve and propriety did not seem to drop. I hit the bed without even bothering to get undressed, and I was vaguely aware of Faith snoring contentedly on the other side of the room.

When I awoke, I saw the dim glow of the round night-light, and I could hear the television still on downstairs. The clock read 03.34.

I winced, turning over on to my back. Charlie had either fallen asleep with it on, or he had acquired a sudden and inexplicable interest in *Late Zone*, or whatever it was called.

Why was the night-light on? I sat up, shivering slightly as the duvet fell from me, and I squinted over to Faith's bed. She wasn't in it.

I went out to the landing and listened. I was now aware that it was not the television I could hear at all – it was the sound of raised voices, filtered through curtain and pine and carpet. There was some music playing in the lounge – Palestrina, I think. It wasn't very loud, but it did occasionally block out what they were saying.

'– supposed to do about it?' That was Faith's voice, for certain.

'Just . . . think it through.' Charlie. Quiet but urging. 'Look, everyone's doing what they can to screw the system. I thought you were supposed to be the rebel in the family?'

'Oh, right. Non-declaration is really fucking subversive, isn't it? Anyway, rebels play it cautiously, Charlie. They don't get caught. Otherwise it defeats the object.'

'No one's going to get caught.'

'Oh, right. You know that, do you?' I imagined Faith folding her arms, glowering at him, her eyes as dark and intense as they were back in the days when she circled them thickly in mascara.

'I know Andy, all right? He was a friend long before he joined the tax-spotters . . . Anyway, listen to how you're going on about it. You'd think we were importing drugs or something.'

There was a silence, punctuated by the sound of someone walking across the stripped-pine floor of the lounge, pouring a drink, clinking ice. Faith, I imagined. Charlie had already had more than enough.

'It just disappoints me,' she said. 'That's all.'

'It disappoints you that you didn't think of it first.' I imagined Charlie lifting a long, bony finger, pointing unsteadily at her. 'That's what you don't like, isn't it?'

There was no answer. I heard Faith's deep, angry sigh, and then her feet crossing the floor again, heading for the door.

I hurried back to bed, but then I heard her go to the kitchen.

She didn't come back to the room that night.

'Want one?' Nicole offers her dry-roasted peanuts around. Mike takes one, without really looking. Their eyes meet for a second.

There is a ghost between Nicole and Mike, the sense of something left uncompleted. They talk, but each sentence, each word, is taut with the unspoken. Still, at least they are making an effort.

'They're so *grey!*' complains Mullet Martin, peering at the screen. 'You can hardly see them.'

'John Major's influence,' says Faith, sprawling on the top bunk. 'Should have got the red shirts out, guys. Spirit of 66 and all that.'

'The reception doesn't help,' says Mike drily, munching his peanut.

'Well, I'm *soooo* sorry.' Faith sticks her tongue out at him. 'I did my best, so if you –'

'Oh, yes!' Charlie is leaning forward, pointing at a darting, fuzzy figure which might be Paul Ince. 'Yes, come on!'

We have all frozen. The grey figure shoots, a hell of a long way from the goal. For a wonderful moment, with the game barely underway, we all hold our breath.

Then, as the German goalkeeper, Köpke, knocks it clear over the crossbar, we all exhale together.

Charlie leans back, flushed. 'Oh, well,' he says. 'He tried. Good show.'

February the fourteenth is a day when people are seized with an inexplicable urge to buy one another heart-shaped balloons, boxes of chocolates tied with pink ribbon and other hack-work fakes of Love. Flowers are different; I can cope with them. They are, in fact, a fine thing, and one should be encouraged to buy them for a special person, but preferably on a day of one's own choosing. I bought some flowers the following day, 15 February 1996, for a very good reason. They were for a woman I hardly knew, but they were important.

At ten past eight on the evening of Valentine's Day, a graphic designer called Stuart Birchwood left his house in Richmond, South London. He had shared the house with his wife, up until the previous year, when she had left him for another man.

His movements on that night have been very precisely documented. He bought a newspaper and a packet of Extra Strong Mints at a newsagent's, then made his way to the station and caught a District Line train at twenty past eight. During the journey, which took approximately twenty minutes, Stuart Birchwood put his glasses on, ate half of his peppermints and read his copy of the *Evening Standard*.

When his train arrived at Earl's Court, Stuart alighted, with his newspaper folded under one arm. He crossed the platform for the Upminster service. He then proceeded to sit down on the platform, much to the annoyance of those who were hurrying home late from work, and the amusement of those who were on their way out for the evening. He removed his glasses, folded them up, put them inside his newspaper, folded the newspaper in half and placed it carefully in front of him, right on the painted safety-line.

Above, an electronic board announced that the Upminster train was due to arrive in one minute. Stuart spent that minute sitting with his hands around his knees and silently crying. One or two people watched him and wondered what to do. Someone, at some point, alerted a railway official, by which time the train was thundering in the tunnel as it approached Earl's Court. It was fourteen minutes to nine as the train emerged from the tunnel. At this point, Stuart stood up. He blinked once, twice. Then he stepped forward, to the edge of the platform and beyond.

The roar and squeal of the train almost drowned the screams of the passengers on the eastbound platform.

The resulting hysteria was expertly controlled by the four police officers who appeared on the scene in seconds, and who were soon joined by reinforcements. The station was cleared and closed off, and announcements appeared on boards all along the District Line announcing that there would be considerable delays due to an 'incident' at Earl's Court. It made a paragraph in the morning papers, no more.

About an hour later that Wednesday evening, the police located Stuart's estranged wife, to inform her of the tragedy. When the WPC reached out to ring the doorbell of the maisonette, Sarah was upstairs, screaming, her mouth hanging open, eyes tightly shut and her entire body shivering. For the doorbell rang as Sarah was rocking her body to her first ever multiple orgasm, impaled upon the penis of her lover, Sussex-based property developer Michael Bradfield.

We rejoice at an early goal. For a while, it really looks as if England are going to do it for once, but it doesn't take long for the inevitable equalizer.

'Kuntz, *Kuntz*,' mutters Faith, as she cracks open her third beer and throws one over to me, which I catch. 'They're all a bunch of Kuntz!' she adds with relish. 'Cheers.'

'Why can't Seaman catch like you?' Martin says to me with a grin.

'Oh, come on, he's excellent. Not his bloody fault, is it?' I put in, my eyes fixed gloomily on the ominous 1–1 in the corner of the screen. 'We should just never underestimate Germany. They *always* come from behind.'

Faith sniggers.

'She's off,' mutters Mike under his breath.

On a cold March day, we sat in my car above a glittering valley, listening to the rain on the roof. An old church, its roof a mass of crumbling tiles, squatted on the hillside behind us.

Time was falling fast, never to be recovered. The light was beginning to fade. Trees etched themselves against the reddening sky. They were hangman's trees, black and stark, with strong, gnarled branches. An icy wind was gathering. A wind of change, blowing through the winter of contempt, cleaning out the world in readiness for a new spring.

'Do you still think about it?' she asked me.

'What?'

'You know. Dying.'

'Oh. That. No, I try not to, if I can possibly help it.'

'Uh-huh,' she said.

'Christ, Faith. Are you trying to depress me?' She didn't answer. 'I hate this time of year,' I went on. 'It always reminds me of the things I've not finished.'

'I'm not trying to depress you. I just . . . wish I could have seen it coming.'

I sighed, thumped the steering-wheel. 'There was nothing you could have done,' I pointed out.

'I could have talked to him. That night, last year, when he rang you on your mobile, then rang me afterwards. I always felt guilty about that one.'

'Yeah, well, don't,' I advised her. 'You'd have only ended up advising him to do what felt right, wouldn't you? Which was exactly what he did.'

I surprised myself, to be honest, with my lack of guilt. I refused to take any responsibility for Mike Bradfield's actions. Maybe it would have been different if I'd liked him more, but I just could not see that blaming ourselves made any sense. We had not left Sarah's husband to die through our omission. We had not even known him. It was a sad, terrible thing, but . . .

She shook her head. She was biting the material of her glove, now, making it stretch. 'It's all such a mess,' she murmured. 'Isn't it?'

'These things just "happen", maybe,' I said, with a wry smile.

'Right,' I say. 'Time to pray?'

We are in the brief lull before extra time.

Faith is making a pot of tea. 'How many?' she asks.

'Everyone,' says Charlie gloomily. 'Tea is compulsory at times like this. Tea may yet save us. Tea, you are our only hope.'

'Sign up tea for England,' I offer. What a stupid conversation. We are all jittery, now, and why? Because we face the prospect of eleven men failing to put a ball in a net. It's ridiculous, really, when you think about it.

'So, let me check I've got this right,' says Nicole, raising a hand like one of her own schoolgirls. 'When someone scores, they just *stop*? Just like that?'

'Yup,' says Faith, with a wicked grin. 'Good, innit?'

'Wouldn't it be great,' Nicole mutters to me, 'if all matches were played like that? The first team to score wins. Some of them would only last a minute or two.'

But then it begins again, and even Nic's face lights up with excitement. The players begin to distribute themselves, the cups of tea somehow find their way to their owners, and we're off.

The church door creaked. I could smell damp wood and freezing stone. I stood there blinking in the darkness, watching my breath curl into the black air like tired ghosts.

'Well?' Faith demanded impatiently.

I heard a skittering, fluttering noise, and I was sure black shapes flitted across the arches of bluish-black which marked the windows.

'It doesn't look popular,' I whispered. My voice, amplified with a kind of terrible beauty, resounded in the stone vault. 'Unless you count a few pigeons.'

Faith swished in behind me and clicked her cigarette lighter on, casting an orange glow for about a metre around us. 'Hmmm,' she said. 'The living Christian church.' She strode further in, using her lighter as a torch to examine the font. 'I wonder what Luke would have thought.'

I was surprised she had mentioned him. 'Well, he'd never have come anywhere like this, for a start.'

'Do you have time for all this?' she asked, looking up at me, suddenly, urgently, as if it really did matter. As if she wanted to know, there and then, what I thought of God and life and death. As if it mattered more than I could imagine.

I shivered. 'I'm . . .' I shrugged. 'I know the church does a lot of good. It makes people feel unnecessarily guilty, too. But I like to think that's our fault. Not God's.'

She smiled sadly. Her teeth glowed, whitish-orange in the darkness. 'I'm glad to know you have an opinion.'

'Is this because of Sarah's husband?' I asked.

'Not especially.' She stood up, holding her lighter up and casting around as if looking for something in particular. 'No, it's all just part of the same . . . Aha. Knew they'd be here somewhere.' She had found a couple of tall, white candles in brass holders, and she lit them with her lighter. 'No, I'm just interested in all concepts of post-mortality,' she murmured. 'It fits in with my research. You see, the Fantastic is obsessed with death, but not as an ending. Rather,' she continued, passing me a candle, 'as a point of entry. A threshold.'

'Well,' I said, holding the candle up somewhat awkwardly, 'Luke might have agreed with you about that. Life's just a rehearsal as far as your average born-again is concerned.'

'Well . . . we're not talking the beginning of a new life, not in a Christian sense. We're talking about death as a boundary, a line that can be blurred.' She swung round suddenly, her face blazing orange. 'Think about that. Blurred. Do you ever think about that?'

'I try not to.' I shivered.

'Don't you ever wonder,' she murmured, 'when you're standing in the bright sunlight on a summer's day and all the colours are so bright it's like . . . like someone's turned up the contrast on the world, yeah? And you think – what's in that shadow in the bushes?' She came right up close to me, holding the candle up as if to ward off the watchers gathering in the gloom. 'Don't you ever think what it might be like to go *beyond* the shadow?'

'Have you been drinking?'

'Certainly not.'

'Then it's time you started. Come on. I don't like it here.'

'Fine,' she said, and with one brief puff she blew the candle out, switched herself off. For a second, she had gone, almost as if she really had blinked away into the darkness. Faded to black.

That night, she came to me again. I remember it still.

I am standing in a pew, but it is returning to Nature all around me, sprouting tendrils and leaves, growing roots which skewer the hassocks and plough up the floor of the church. Suddenly, now, the aisle is full of water, clouded by thick, yellowish steam which obscures my vision. I am dressed in a black morning suit and there is a black flower in my buttonhole. There are people all around me, almost recognizable, but all the women are wearing enormous hats, the size of dustbin lids, in garish hues of magenta and lilac.

I turn, sweating in my black suit, and I see Faith beginning to move up the aisle in a long, sleek barge of black glass. She is standing upright, silent and still. Her eyes are shut. Her dress is a shift of black silk, her face is pale and bright, and she carries a bouquet of black and white roses.

Closer, closer she comes. There is a jarring chord of music, like a loop of guitar noise being fed through the organ, and then she smiles, still with her eyes closed.

She is standing beside me. I understand now that this is to be our wedding. I am panicking, realizing I am unrehearsed. The sound of the chord is twanging again and again, sounding more like the bawling of a terrified infant now. I look to Faith, not knowing what to do. The yellow steam gathers around us.

Her eyes open.

She has no eyes. Just two empty black holes.

I cry out. There is a ring on my finger, a thick band of jet. She holds her hand up, showing me her matching ring of alabaster. And then her smile becomes a drool, and I realize the yellow steam is dissolving her face. Her jaw drops. It splatters in chunks on the glass boat. A deep, glutinous sore opens in her forehead and begins to eat the flesh. Softening like an overripe nectarine, her skull folds in on itself, gobbets of creamed flesh splashing outwards.

I woke then, which was just as well. I had a sneaking feeling that my dream had just blown its special effects budget.

'I can't bear this,' says Faith.

She is perched on the edge of the bunk, clasping her warm and near-empty bottle between her thighs.

I shake my head, unable to watch. My hands are slippery and pungent, and I know I will be unable to hold a bottle, so I just exchange a desperate look with Nicole. Next to us, Mike, Charlie, Martin and Keela are like a single being, a spring coiled around the television.

We watch, hardly breathing, the evening birdsong astonishingly loud, the lapping of the water on the barge like a slow, inexorable pendulum, as Stuart Pearce places the ball on the penalty spot.

Seconds later, the ball hits home and the silence snaps. Nobody dares cheer. We just exhale. The next German player steps up. The wash of static is now drowning out the commentary.

'Who's that now ?' I ask.

Martin peers forward to read the number on the shirt. 'Reuter,' he says confidently.

'Come on, now,' says Faith, and her eyes are glinting with blood-lust. 'Miss it, you fucking sausage-eater. *Miss it.*'

Late in May, I went to see Luke, at home.

His Hertfordshire rectory was small, but beautifully furnished. There were oak bookshelves, soft carpets and an assortment of attractive trinkets: a gold pen-holder, marble ornaments.

I smiled wryly. 'Nice place,' I said, as I sat down.

'Comes with the job.' He shrugged as he poured me a glass of sherry. 'If it was up to me, it would be a lot more austere, but there are . . . you know. Expectations.'

'Oh, I know all about expectations,' I said softly.

'People tend to give one *presents*,' said Luke awkwardly, standing at his bay window and looking out over the countryside. 'Bottles of whisky, baskets of fruit, that kind of thing. Even cufflinks. I can't really refuse the edible stuff, as they often ask how it was and I can't actually *lie*, you know.' He gave me a complicit smile. 'But, well . . . some of it goes to good causes.'

We sat at the window together, chatting away for an hour and a half or so. Two men, not exactly friends, but by no means enemies. He asked about my family, and about Mike and Nicole – he had heard the news, of course, and made all the right noises – and my other friends. When he inquired about Faith, I was able to give a suitably noncommittal answer.

He spoke, now and then, of his work in the parish, his numerous charities, and I saw his eyes light up when he told me of a project for young homeless drug addicts he had visited in Manchester. There was something about this man, I thought, which ought to give me complete confidence in the sanctuary of heaven. Something implacable, trustworthy, sound. Luke was *genuine*. Since those zealous days at university, he had calmed, had found inner peace, no longer felt the need to proselytize or judge. His faith was evident just from his presence, and to deny the afterlife would hurt him immensely, cause terrible offence to a friend. And yet I could not find it in my heart to go back to those beliefs. Not now. My freedom had been gained at a price, a price too high to let it go.

As the shadows began to lengthen, I realized I had to begin my journey home, as I still had some revision sessions to prepare for my students.

When I got up, though, the copious sherries made me say something like: 'I'm very dissatisfied with life, you know.'

'Who isn't, mate?' That 'mate' sounded funny, now, in his newly rounded rector's accent. I noticed he had even lost the earrings, although one small stud still glinted in his right earlobe. 'It's lovely here, in its own way. But I want to be somewhere I can . . . *work*. Somewhere it's more *difficult*.'

'Like Bosnia, you mean? Or Rwanda?'

'You don't have to go so far afield. God should be *seen* in the tower blocks of our cities. It's my great ambition.' He nodded, staring into space as if he could see his tenement of potential converts waiting for him out there. 'One day.'

From anyone else, it would have sounded hollow, but I knew that he meant it. I felt obliged to say something, all the same. 'It must be tempting to stay here, though? Surely?'

'Weeeellll . . . Some days . . . You know, everyone who comes to see me is unhappy about something.' He sighed. 'It's the nature of the job. No one ever seeks you out to tell you it's a beautiful day, and that they're happy.'

'What about weddings and christenings?'

'Ah, well, they're ritual, aren't they? That's not the same as waking up and feeling joy at a beautiful sunrise, or the snow on the ground. No, it's just . . . getting yourself "done", as they say. People aren't happy from *within* on those ritual days.' He presses his hand against his chest. 'They think they need to be happy, so they are.'

'I never thought I'd hear a Christian being so cynical. Congratulations, Luke. I didn't think you had it in you.' I was only partly being sardonic, as well.

He smiled sadly. 'A couple I married last year have just had an annulment, you know?' He sighs. 'Never had anyone want one before. I mean, divorce, sure, that's happening all the time. I hate it, I think it's sad and terrible, but at least a divorce is some sort of admission that life moves on, that a Christian marriage wasn't right for you, or that you weren't suited to a Christian marriage.' He sighed. 'But an annulment, that's sort of saying the last two years aren't real, trying to wipe them from the record. Bit of a cop-out. People are allowed to be *wrong*, you know.' He smiled, and I looked into his sharp, blue eyes again, seeing warmth and trust there. 'God doesn't expect people not to make mistakes. But he likes it if they admit them. Know what I mean?'

'Sure, sure.' I wondered if this was leading anywhere. 'So you'd say,' I ventured, 'that there are sometimes occasions where the heart knows better than the church?'

He smiled again. 'Who knows?' he said, and his face was just a few centimetres away from mine. 'You've not . . . married?' he asked tentatively.

I smiled, shrugged, feeling a little awkward. I felt sure he didn't want to hear about my sexual adventures, and in any case, there had been little happening for quite a while. 'Things . . . got in the way,' I said cagily. 'It never seemed right.'

'*He has never married*,' said Luke. 'You know that phrase? I think it's shorthand. For something. Don't know what, do you?'

'Errrrm . . . Never found the right woman?'

He nodded, then tipped his head to one side and back again. Close up to me. 'Yeah. The right person,' he said. 'Maybe some people do, though, and the right person doesn't want to know. Doesn't see them that way.'

I thought of that girl and her obsession with Mike. What was her name? . . . Jacqui. Yes, Jacqui Potter. I know about her: she got a dose of antibiotics, cropped her hair and ended up quite a babe, actually. Married a South African stockbroker.

'You're absolutely right,' I said, although I felt anxious to get off the subject. 'Look, I'd better . . . you know . . . make a move.'

'You can't stay for dinner?' he offered. 'For once, you know, I'm not required at any meeting, and it seems a shame . . .' He spread his hands, making the offer.

I smiled, shrugged. 'Really sorry. Things to do.'

'Sure, sure.' He had seemed to be on the point of saying something, but he had decided against it. 'Well, look, it's been good to see you. And take care.'

'Yeah. Sure.' I held out a hand to shake. He took it, and then moved forward, placing his other hand on my elbow, drawing me to him in something which was almost a hug. I was quite touched, and surprised. As we drew out of the chummy embrace, I thought I felt his fingers brushing my cheek, but I wasn't quick enough to see. Perhaps I imagined it.

He stood at his porch and waved me off, with a dignified hand, like the queen. I could swear he seemed genuinely sad to see me go.

'Who's taking it?' Nicole asks.

Nobody answers. With the score at a perfect five penalties all, the screen is now awash with interference, making it nearly impossible to see which player is stepping up for the sudden-death kick.

'Jesus, fucking reception,' mutters Faith.

'It's –' Martin leans forward. 'Can anyone see?'

'The radio,' says Mike, galvanized by panic. 'Get the radio!'

On our screen, we watch the ball placed on the penalty spot. And then we strain our eyes to see the grey and ghostly figure who is stepping back to take the kick.

'I think,' says Martin, 'it's Southgate.'

'Where's the radio?' Mike yells, and he thumps the bunk-beds in frustration.

The window vibrates and in a slow-motion second, I see it — the suckers which hold the aerial on to the window slowly unpeel themselves.

The aerial tips. Faith sees it just in time and lunges out of the hatchway for it. The aerial hits her fingers and swings wildly on its flex across the side of the boat.

As Gareth Southgate's foot contacts with the ball, the picture dissolves into a million swirling dots.

I lie in the darkness. But I do not tell the truth in the light.

There has already been a death between us, a tiny soul lost. I try, though, not to think of it in those terms. I am trying to be adult and nineties and intelligent and realistic. No one *did* anything bad. No one was to blame. It was something that happened.

The problem is, I am no longer sure I believe in the soul, or heaven, or any afterlife. I cannot see death as an ascent. A gateway. Faith, on the other hand, seems convinced that it can be this. I think she is half in love with death.

I watch her slumbering form. Just for a moment I shudder, as I think of her smooth curves rolling on top of me, her hair wrapping itself around me, and that smooth white face with its crimson lips descending upon mine, ready to suck the life from me, to draw me into an unwanted *Liebestod*.

Half in love with death.

Some of the others are down below, but Faith and I lie on the roof of the boat. The radio blasts the canal. It's Stuart Maconie on the late-evening show, and he's playing 'Everything Must Go' by the Manics. It reverberates through the roof. Through the boat, like an engine, rippling the canal.

We lie and watch the stars burning in history, thousands of light-years away. Scorching themselves into the universe, burning through to their cores on their way to death. We turn that bittersweet, angry, valedictory song up shatteringly loud, and we sing. And we do not care.

We are alive, and we want the world to know.

21 And Then She Said . . .

'You were there,' I whisper. 'You were in Gervizan. You must have come to the house, the day Faith died.'

'And?' She gestures, beckoning more memories from me.

'And the afternoon before she died, Faith wasn't there. I thought that was strange at the time. We were all sitting around playing games, and I don't remember her being there.'

'Yes,' says Angelica softly. 'She came to see me. I was staying in a hotel in the town.' She slips her arms around my neck, moves her mouth so close that I can feel her breath on my face. 'She came to tell me something.'

The videotape fizzes and creaks. It seems to have come to the end of the sequence, as the picture is starting to distort.

'To tell you what?'

'That she was ready for the ultimate experience,' murmurs Angelica.

A flash of memory: I cannot recall if it actually happened or if I dreamed it. Faith straddling me, her body hot and pungent, taunting me with the fear of death without salvation . . .

All I can do is ask: 'Why?'

Angelica shakes her head. 'I'm still not sure I entirely know,' she says. 'All I know is, she knew there was only one way to get *you* to understand.' She strokes a fingernail across my lips. 'She believed that she could never actually *die*. That the destruction of her body would mean nothing . . . it would only be one more stage.' She opens her eyes wide, and I see myself, pale and unkempt, in her irises. 'Perhaps she thought there would be a little bit of her . . . living on.' Her mouth is so close to mine that I can almost taste her. 'Living on inside me,' she murmurs.

The video picture has broken up, leaving a bright square of blue filling the screen. 'And do you believe that?' I ask her.

She smiles. 'We used to play, you know? Play these games. We would pretend to be one another. We weren't so far apart in our ages, after all.'

'What games?' I ask, watching her carefully.

'Oh, you know. She would be me. I would be her. We'd tell people the wrong names, just for the fun of it. Pretend to be each other, to see how far we could go. If we could get away with it.'

'And did you?'

She lets her fingers stroke my neck. 'What do you think?' she murmurs.

She knows, of course – or she can guess – how my conversation with Lucy from MADS must have gone. She knows what I know. I can't help smiling. She smiles back, her mouth opens slightly and then she leans up, her breath mingling into mine.

Angelica does not kiss like her sister. Her tongue feels cool and gentle, where Faith's was always hot and eager. She moves it slowly, interestedly around my own tongue, as if she is more inquisitive than aroused. Then, without warning, she plunges it deep into my mouth and her lips are crushing mine as if trying to suck the life from me.

I break from her. She raises her eyebrows impishly, tries to pull my mouth down to hers again, but I draw back.

'What's the matter?' She clasps her hands behind her back and lifts her chin slightly, as if reaching up to speak. Or to sing into an invisible microphone. She swivels on her heel, from side to side. A familiar pose. 'Look, I thought we could just have a bit of fun. That's all . . .'

The street light falls from outside, illuminating one side of her face, turning her into a kind of demented harlequin. I am dimly aware that the blue square on the screen is starting to crackle with whiteness at the edges, as if there is something still left to show.

'Darling?' she says. 'What's wrong?'

I sit down heavily on the arm of the sofa, gnawing at a fingernail. What is wrong? Some feeling that none of this has been quite real, that it has all had a staged, constructed feel. As if I am being siphoned, poured into a mould, without having any influence at all on my own destiny. Just like when she was alive.

'All I know,' I tell her, looking up, 'is that I no longer trust you.' I stand up and face her, and she backs away from me slightly.

She is backing up. She is moving towards the worktop, between the living-area and the kitchen.

'All this time,' I murmur, 'you have known far more than you've told. You knew where the video was, and you didn't tell me. You knew where she was the afternoon before she died – she was with you, measuring out the final hours of her life – *and you didn't tell me.*'

She glances over her shoulder. Her foot nudges the coffee-table as she backs off. She has lost something of her poise. Because I am advancing on her. Because she knows I have it in my power to hurt her.

'And,' I go on, 'I think you knew who was in that photograph, and you also knew it wasn't really important, didn't you? Oh, yes, I've found out a lot of things I've not told *you.*'

Angelica takes another step back and is up against the worktop.

She can't go any further. She looks me in the eye and still doesn't speak.

'The only reason you sent me to find out about that photograph,' I tell her softly, 'was to make me *realize*. To make me see how the two of you had chopped and changed in the past, so that I could think of you as a substitute. The Faith of the future – that's what you called yourself, isn't it?' She does not answer. 'You were jealous of your sister's achievements,' I tell her, pointing at her face, and my finger is just inches from her eyes. 'Her death was the perfect opportunity for you to step from her shadow. You think you've got a chance to shine.'

I take another step forward. She swallows hard. She knows she is trapped. She knows she cannot get out of this one.

'It's not like that,' she whispers.

I come closer. 'So what is it like?' I grab her arms. I force them back against the tiled worktop, aware now that her tall, lissom frame is quite fragile. 'What is it like, Angelica? What is this *really* all about?'

'I . . . just . . . wanted you to see the truth . . .' she is saying. 'The truth of what she really thought about you . . .' She swallows, closes her eyes for a second. 'But you – you had to discover it yourself, you see? You had to be convinced we were doing detective work. Finding things out. I had to make you think we were in this together.'

'Keep talking.'

'You're hurting me. You'll bruise my arms.'

'A bruise is neither creation nor destruction. It's a transformation. Think of it as a reminder of where we are. So talk.'

'You had to think it came from her.'

I frown, and tighten my grip on her arm. 'What do you mean?'

'You had to get the idea that she was – that she'd – left some puzzle for you to work out. You needed to get hold of the locker key. It was thanks to me that Charlie got in touch with you about that.' She licks her lips nervously. 'You needed to have the photograph and the diskette. That's important, you see, it tells you what she –'

A hissing, stretching noise comes from the video recorder.

I glance over towards it. In that split second, Angelica kicks my shin.

As a sharp pain cuts into my leg, she darts to one side and I make a grab for her arm. She squeals, the sleeve of her blouse rips and I am left staring at a useless scrap of material. She regains her balance, glances over her shoulder, then trips over the coffee-table and sprawls inelegantly on the carpet.

I stand over her. She tries to scramble to her feet.

'You gave her the drugs,' I say, and I've only just realized it myself. 'You killed her.'

On the screen, something is happening. A new, distorted picture begins to appear.

'No,' she says, her hands over her mouth, and she shakes her head from side to side, furiously, dementedly. 'We both killed her.'

I stare at the image which is slowly being grabbed from the tape and played on to the screen in my flat.

The memories burst open, like old stained-glass lit by the light of a megaton blast, seconds before shattering inwards and melting in droplets.

It is all there. I know.

I have always known.

22 Nothing Lasts For Ever

'Faith, there never was a Seaman Staines,' says Charles with an indulgent smile. 'It was Seaman *Baines*. You're talking rubbish.'

'No, honestly! That's why they had to ban it,' Faith insists, pushing back her hair. 'And Roger the cabin-boy.'

'And Master Bates,' I add with a knowing smile. 'It's an urban myth. I thought that was laid to rest years ago.'

We are shaking and sweating inside a rickety white taxi: our driver is one of those grim, shoulders-down types in a donkey-jacket. We're following another, similar vehicle up a steep and pitted track beside acres of sloping vineyards. The seats smell of chewing-gum and cigarettes. Above us, the sky is a hard, polished blue, punched through with a bright hole of sun, gushing liquid metal. Below us in the valley, the town shines, salt-white and terracotta. And Faith, naturally, is talking about *Captain Pugwash*.

'Surely not,' she says in astonishment, lowering her sunglasses. 'Charlie? Is that really true?'

'It was Tom the cabin-boy,' says Charlie languidly, 'and Pugwash had a Master Mate.'

'But he did speak with adenoids,' I point out. 'So it could have *sounded* a bit like Master Bates.'

We roll up into the forecourt, hot gravel crunching. The taxi in front stops: Mike, Nicole and Jan start to unload their bags.

'Well, shit,' says Faith, slumping back in the seat, arms folded. 'Next you'll be telling me Johnny Morris wasn't really a zoo-keeper.'

On 2 May, I had woken up with two realizations. One: I had, by now, voted for all three of the main parties in three separate elections. Two: the new government was, again, one I had voted for. I hoped they'd repay my confidence better than the last lot.

I'd been working for the best part of a year with the community education project, basically a lot of fund-raising, a lot of arse-licking, and a great deal of running around like a demented chicken. Now, it really looked as if it would all come to fruition. We'd found a venue for a new training centre for adults, and we were already discussing the possibility of accrediting courses at the London colleges.

I was immersed in my work: however, even now, Faith still held a fascination for me. I realized I was attracted to Tanya – and that something might well happen if we continued to share a flat – but at the same time I was well aware of the influence Faith still exerted over my thoughts.

Initially, I was very polite to Tanya, and we gave each other space. She had her shelf in the fridge (for yoghurt, a wide range of cheeses, soya milk, white wine and tubs of coleslaw and salad) and I had mine (for beer, chocolate mousse, bacon, eggs, real milk and chicken Kievs). We both kept our music down, cleaned the bathroom in turns, cleaned up crumbs with the DustBuster and assiduously booked the video recorder in advance. However, the politeness gave way to friendliness, along with a more relaxed attitude to housework.

I remember when we sat opening bottle after bottle and watching the Conservative Party getting slowly, inexorably thrashed like never before. Tanya's interest was academic at first, as she hadn't had a vote, but she ended up enjoying it. 'Who is he?' she would ask periodically. 'And his majority was *how* much?'

I felt something between us that evening, and I was quite cheerful at the prospect that things could well happen with this woman. She finally went to bed just before four, brushing my cheek with her lips, and I was happy. In fact I was relieved that nothing took place that particular night. I don't imagine I could have performed very well if I'd suddenly looked up and seen Sir James Goldsmith or Michael Howard leering down at me.

Tanya knew of my ties to my college friends, and didn't find it strange that I would not introduce any of them to her, although I thought an opportunity might arise before long.

I could almost have told myself I'd seen the last of Faith. But no.

In the frame: cool marble floor and oak walls of the entrance-hall. Fresh plants hover at discreet intervals, the fronds brushing the lens as the camera bounces past. *Charlie gestures up the carved wooden staircase which twists up to the bedrooms and bathroom, and the camcorder obligingly pans up for a second ('Look at that,' says Mike's voice from behind the lens) before returning to Charlie, who leads the shot through the oak door to the kitchen.*

Faith is there, with shoulder-length curls, metallic spiral earrings and a shimmering orange satin top. 'Now this is a real kitchen,' she says, thumping the brass pots on the wall, clang clang dong!, *then running her hand along the wind-chime arrangement of spoons and ladles,* twinklydoink. *She turns to see the lens nuzzling her shoulder. 'Oh, bollocks. Is that bloody thing on already?'*

'You want to make it eighteen-certificate?' quips Mike's voice. 'We might have to edit this, if Nic's mum and dad want to see it.' Zoom in on Faith, sudden blurred focus, then clear resolution again.

'In that case,' she says, and her face bulges in the lens as her huge mouth kisses the words out, 'Espèce de con, putain de merde! *Piss, wank, arse!' The picture zooms out, and she's giggling against the worktop, holding up a finger,* swivel on that. *For a second, she yanks open her satin blouse and reveals an enticing flash of white breast. 'There. You can't keep it now.'*

Cut to: Jan, flaring her nostrils in disapproval, pretending to ignore Faith. She's caught rubbing a finger on the table, nodding knowingly as she holds it up, dust-smeared, for Charlie to see.

He frowns at her. Linger on Charlie, reddening. Hold.

That night, we play cards on the square of polished mahogany in the dining-room. The table is firm and smooth, adorned only with golden fleur-de-lis coasters. At its centre is a blue sphere – a vase, about the size of a beach-ball, made of translucent, ice-smooth glass, and filled to the brim with marbles of different colours.

Heat grips the house, tight as PVC, and no air moves despite the flung-open windows. I find it difficult to breathe.

Charlie gets the ice bucket from the fridge, sticks his hands in it and trails them over everyone's forehead in turn, each of us pleading with him to be next.

The lens is filled with blackness. It recedes, forming itself into the distorted shape of my hand, then my arm and the rest of me.

'Is it on?' I ask cautiously. The camera sits motionless on the kitchen table.

'Get on with it!' calls Nicole, from somewhere out of shot.

'Oh. Right. Okay. Um – Hi, Tanya. As you can see, we're having a great time here. Here's, um, the kitchen, where we, um – cook – Oh, look, this is crap. Can I start again?'

My hand reaches forward, and the screen erupts in static.

We go into Gervizan the next day. It seems sliced from salt blocks, cut by a white-hot knife. Every edge is a right-angle, every surface flat and warm to the touch. Or, I imagine with a touch of delusion, perhaps the sea recedes, leaving these geometric stalagmites of salt behind, a place grown rather than made.

Rearing above us is the great, smooth lighthouse, which Charles and Jan have chosen to explore. Clusters of café umbrellas and souvenir shops splash colour on the ultra-white promenade. At the harbour wall, Faith and Mike are taking turns with a battered two-franc telescope. Out beyond them, the Mediterranean slices the sunlight into white shards. The sea breeze is hot and thick, tasting of dust, fish and salt as it licks across the bay. I push my hair back and it feels sticky and salty.

'*Votch-rer glace, mon-sewer,*' says Nicole, in French as dribbly as the white ice-cream down the cone.

'Murky buckets,' I answer.

'Eh?'

'It's thanks, in French. Sort of.'

Her dress and my hair flutter in the wind. We stroll towards Faith and Mike, trying to get our mouths round the ice-creams as delicately as we can.

'Still chummy, aren't they?' Nic mutters through a mouthful of ice-cream cone.

I glance at her, grateful for the way sunglasses relieve the need for eye-contact. 'Yeah, well, there's nothing going on, all right? I mean it.'

She shrugs. 'If you say so. Now Sarah's off the scene, I can only wonder, can't I? . . . Anyway, what's the phrase? *Let he who is without sin cast the first stone.* Isn't that what your mate Jesus says?'

'Mmm-hmm. And a stone zings past his ear, and Jesus turns round and goes: You know, there are times, Mother, when you don't half get on my nerves.'

She laughs. 'Can you say stuff like that?'

'Sure, why not? If God exists, he *must* have a sense of humour.' I wince. 'He created men's genitals, after all.'

Nicole giggles again, then stops, swivelling on her heel like a little girl as she licks a deep channel from her cone. 'You're not sure, then? That there's a God?'

I smiled. 'Serious?'

'Serious. Please.'

I shrugged. 'Certainly not a vengeful Old Testament one, no . . . But the caring, sharing, hug-a-minute version's hardly any more convincing, is he?' I pause, look at the white trickle of molten ice-cream which is stealing its way into my sleeve. 'Quite apart from anything else,' I say, pausing to lick the trail, 'you'd think he'd invent a better design of ice-cream. I suppose that's free will for you.'

We are at the telescope, now. Faith turns, catches my eye. She slips over to me, slow-motion in the shimmering heat, and slides an arm round my waist. 'What are you wittering about?' she murmurs.

'Theology.'

'Which ology? Oh, *the* ology. The one and only. Might have guessed . . . You mean I've not converted you to total amorality yet?'

'Don't listen to her,' says Mike, who's still squinting into the telescope. 'Morals are cultural conditioning, no more, no less.'

Faith, having said she didn't want an ice-cream, has borrowed mine and is nibbling round the edge. 'Scollops,' (or something) she mumbles.

I lean on the harbour wall, beside Mike. The white stone is searingly hot. A water-skier cuts a gash in the satiny sea, like a gigantic cigarette-ad. 'But there must be *some* absolutes, though,' I say. 'I mean . . . people need to know that some things just aren't done. Like murder.'

'Murder's too obvious,' snaps Mike. 'People don't murder because they don't want to go to prison, that's all.' He runs a finger against his squashed boxer's nose and I feel a sudden twinge of guilt.

'Or because they don't want to *be* murdered,' suggests Faith, slipping an arm round each of us. 'Do as you would be done by. Hmmm?'

I reclaim my ice-cream. 'Nic, help me out,' I say, 'what's that, you know, thing the Wiccans have?'

'*Do what thou wilt, an it harm none,*' she chants, bobbing her head from side to side. She wrinkles her nose. 'Never quite got it, myself.'

'It's hippie pagan bollocks,' mutters Mike, scanning the path of the water-skier. 'What's harm, anyway? You tell someone you won't go out with them, that could be classed as harming.'

'Passive smoking,' says Faith, lighting up with her chin on my shoulder, and blowing an eye-watering jet of smoke across my face. 'Having a fag's what I wilt. Will. Whatever. But it's bound to offend someone.' She places a warm kiss on my cheek. 'Don't worry, I'll take it away,' she says, and tweaks Mike's ear before wiggling off to examine some postcards.

'Fucking flirt,' Nicole mutters, staring after her with narrowed eyes.

It takes great courage, I've always felt, to end a relationship. Actually to bring it to an end, rather than just to accept it has ended – there's a big difference. We're not talking about moving on to someone new (serial monogamy). Or deciding it's best to part because you've got that dream job in Hong Kong (get-real geography).

No, to actually end it because things aren't working out. You need to be brave to cut loose, cast yourself adrift. How long can you survive, with the rations and the rocket-flares? How long, until you see that boat on the horizon? You might be waving in vain, like those doomed but strangely muscular survivors in the Géricault painting. You might starve. You might drown. You might go mad.

And when it is not even a relationship – just a terrible, addictive situation over which you have no control?

Then, you need to find control. You need to repaint yourself on the canvas of the world.

If there could be a way to end things.

The days slip by in a haze of white wine, joints and paprika crisps.

I discover the quirks of the house. The cupboard door which you have to lift as you close it, otherwise it refuses to shut. The bathroom with its roaring, cavernous pipes. The one step, halfway up the staircase, which always creaks when you are going downstairs and, for some reason, never when you are coming up.

I also find a shop at the edge of the town which sells some wonderful two-layered chocolate called *Nuit Blanche*: I carry it back on a string, so as not to melt it, and store it in the fridge.

In the evenings, the sky above the coast is striped with red. Ultra-blue thickens to velvet as the midges swarm and the pungent scents of herbs fill the air. Heat rises from skin, making arms and legs painful to touch with cooler hands.

'Hi, Tanya. Now, this is weird, because as I'm saying all this, you'll be stuck in a boardroom somewhere with a strategy chart, but we'll be watching this together, so – Um . Yes. Well, er, Mike caught this lizard. He called it – can I say? – well, he was up for calling it Mandelson, but the rest of us chose Portillo, so he was out-voted there. Haha.

'He was trying to persuade it to run through the croquet-hoops, and then he was looking for another one so that they could have races. Nic got angry about it, though – she said it was cruel – so Mike had to let it go.

'Charlie and I found this great bar in town – typical sort of place, just these old guys sitting round playing cards and drinking, ah, whassit called? Absinthe, yeah. Absinthe makes the heart – all right, I won't do that one. Anyway, we won some money off them, but then we realized the patron *had been topping us up with whisky as we went along – thought he'd just accepted us as one of them, but it turned out we had to pay for it all. Oops. Luckily, we just about had enough from our winnings. Jan was seriously pissed-off when she found out what we'd been up to. So, not entirely wasted.*

'What else? Oh, yeah. Wish you were here.'

The afternoon of the fourth day.

We have just finished a half-hearted game of Articulate: the cards and board are still strewn on the floor by the sofa. Sunlight passes through the blue globe-vase and paints a picture of light on the wall: a circular, haloed head and wings lifting up on either side. It could be an angel, or a ghostly woman, or a drowning man.

Mike is peering down the lens of the camcorder. 'What the fuck's up with this?' he says irritably.

'What's the matter?' I ask, looking up from stirring the cock-tails.

He slaps the side of the camera with his palm. 'I think it's buggered,' he says. 'It won't record when you want it to, and then you put it down and come back to find it's been filming the bloody wall for the past twenty minutes.'

'Have we wasted much tape?' Jan asks, tight-lipped.

'Nah. I can record over it. *If* it stops playing up.'

Jan crosses her legs, blinks once. 'I suppose,' she says, to no one in particular, 'that one can only expect that kind of thing from an old-fashioned model.'

Faith comes in from the terrace, beer dangling from her fingers, and trails her other hand in the cooling globe of marbles, letting them slip through her fingers with a little shudder of pleasure. 'They're great, these,' she says with a smile. 'Look good enough to eat.'

'Yeah, well, don't,' I tell her. 'You'll choke.'

Charlie looks up from the sofa, where he's watching a Patricia Kaas video on M6. 'You sound like her mother,' he says quietly.

The comment surprises me. I pause in mid-shake. Faith slinks past me, peeling a banana and biting into it with unnecessary aggression.

'Is that good or bad?' I ask.

'Leave it,' she says, just loud enough for me to hear, as she drifts past me on her way to the kitchen. 'Michael, darling,' she adds to Mike, who is still peering into the camcorder lens, 'even you can't be that vain. Put it down.'

I stare after her, tapping the cocktail-shaker absently. She glances over her shoulder as she leaves the lounge. Her eyes beckon me.

Upstairs. Heat slurps at the bedroom like a giant mouth. It smells of sleep and old, unpolished wood. I can hear voices from the terrace – Mike and Charlie, I think. Thin slices of light slip through the slats of the shutters: I go over to open them.

I release the catch. A second later, I'm jerked back, pulled into the room as the shutter swings open.

I'm struggling, but my arms are pinned behind my back, and I feel something tight restraining my wrists in the same moment as my legs buckle in sudden fear. There's a hot hand over my mouth. I struggle, and for a second I consider biting, but then I find myself twisting round, looking into Faith's big, laughing eyes.

Some starve. Some drown. Some go mad.

I pin her down in the darkness. The murmur of life recedes, and there is nothing but her welcoming wetness, her hot mouth probing mine.

★

'Are you happy?' I ask her afterwards.

'I don't think I ever could be happier,' she says, and her eyes are firm, wide, unyielding. She is perfectly serious. 'Thank you.'

I swallow hard. 'You know I love you.'

'Yes. I know.' She looks away, as if embarrassed.

'We were almost married, in a way.'

'In a way,' she says, and half smiles, catches my eye for a second. 'But you have someone else, now. Someone who's better for you than me.' She clicks the radio on, and I hear the same Ophélie Winter song they keep playing.

'Tanya? I like her,' I answer. 'But I don't love her.'

'Oh, I think you do. It's a different sort of love, I know, but . . .' She shrugs, smiles, as if to say *these things happen*, again. 'You'll get used to it.'

'I want to get used to *you* again.'

'Please . . . I have to go somewhere. Don't make this any harder.'

'Where do you have to go?' I ask her, puzzled. 'Let me come with you.'

'No,' she says. 'No . . . things . . . come to a natural end, you know? When you know it's time, you can't go back.'

'So that was our last time.' I lie back. I stare at the ceiling. I hate the colour and the smell and the echoing sound of this room. I hate the way she drains power from me, turns the situation round so that she is always in control.

'No,' she says. She leans over me. Her hair, cool and smooth, brushes my chest. She kisses me gently. Tenderly. '*This* is our last time.'

At some point in the afternoon, she slips out, soft and silent. I assume she has gone to the bathroom, but she doesn't come back. The bedclothes beside me are tangled and unoccupied.

I sit up, my eyes still rough with sleep. From my vantage point, the window above the bed, I can see the glittering green lawn of the house spread out in front of me, dropping to the white fence and then the slopes of the vineyards beyond, going down to the town. Jutting above the line of the slope, distant but visible, is the toffee-brown tower of the church, and I can make out some of the buildings of Gervizan shimmering in the heat. Cars flash secret messages up into the sky. Somewhere, beyond, there is the sea. I want to fly down and immerse myself in its coolness.

The shutters shelter me. I drink my tisane slowly, savouring the fruity aroma. I imagine the metal teapot from the kitchen, which is currently sitting beside my bed, must have been provided after numerous requests from bemused English guests. *'Mais, où est la théière?'*

Below, there are murmurs, clinks. I lean forward slightly. Nicole and Mike are sitting at the terrace table. Mike is pouring a beer and Nic is asking him something. He doesn't seem to hear her.

I look further out across the bright green lawns, down to where they drop towards the sea. Just then, a figure flits between two rose-bushes. So dark, it could be a shadow. I blink. Just what is that moving down there?

Then I see her, willowy and dark, turning for an instant towards the house, looking over her shoulder. As if she is checking she's not being followed.

And I must have lifted my hand to wave to her, for she briefly waves back, before hurrying on, over the rise and out of sight. No one else appears to have seen her. I roll back on to the bed and feel myself slipping back into drowsiness.

Faith stands at the window. She is a photographic negative. Her hair is neon-bright, her face greenish-black. She is looking down at me, her expression murderous. I try to move, but the duvet seems to have become too heavy to lift and is pinning me down.

She opens her eyes wide, and they burn with an alien, white fire. 'You know you can't escape me,' she says.

She begins to move towards me, her talons outstretched.

I awake with a gasp, sitting upright in the sticky, warm duvet. I'm breathing heavily, my heart thumping, and it takes me a few seconds to be sure that I am back in the real world.

Outside, the light is thickening.

I have been lying with my right arm twisted up above me, and now it feels positively rheumatic. I swing my legs across the bed, and massage my arm as I look for my flip-flops.

The house is strangely silent. Below, down towards the sea, I hear the odd cry, the occasional murmur of a vehicle. Otherwise, there is

264

nothing. Then, as if the silence had cleared the decks in readiness, there is a rumble of thunder, and I hear the first few drops of rain against the shutters. The weather is breaking at last.

I rub my eyes and splash them with water from the sink to revitalize myself. Then, trying to stretch the aches from my body, I open the squealing door to the landing.

The grey, rainwashed light filters through the landing shutters, uncovers a film of dust on the old oil-lamp, on the banister which I hold as I descend. That middle stair still creaks, louder than ever. The rain is hammering on the house now, battering the walls.

I stroll into the lounge. Nobody about. I see a note on the sideboard, under the camcorder. It's in Charlie's handwriting: *Gone for a walk and to buy some beers. Thought you wanted to sleep so we didn't wake you.*

Fair enough. I imagine them all leaving in bright sunlight and coming back soaked to the skin, and I can't help having a little smile to myself about that.

I'm still not sure where Faith was going before, but I'm sure they will run into her. After all, it's a small village, and there is only the sea beyond. I look out of the window and see gigantic clouds unfurling across the sea.

The raindrops bounce on the veranda, fizzing and sparkling. They are bright and huge like marbles as they clatter on to the stone, and I watch them pummelling the soft grass, forming runnels and ruts and puddles in a matter of minutes. The windows have begun to mist over.

I investigate the fridge, peering into its spectral light. There is one solitary bottle of Kronenbourg there. I lift it up, kiss its cold smoothness. 'Looks like you and me, mate,' I say.

I suddenly realize how hungry I am. I find the last remnant of today's *ficelles*, a stub of bread just a few centimetres long, fold it around a chunk of Camembert and munch determinedly as I make my way through into the cool lounge.

Just then, I hear the creak on the stairs.

It is one of those sounds which is unmistakable. I have come to know this house like a friend, almost a lover, in the past few days. I have reached the stage of being able to recognize her aromas and quirks and sounds. I know that creak.

The rain thrums like static, torrential now, splashing the windows and blurring the outside landscape. The thunder prowls across the bay and seems to gather itself for an onslaught on the house.

I take one, two, three steps forward so that I am standing beside the big wooden table with its globe-shaped bowl of marbles. The expanse of table stretches between me and the door to the hall. The door is slightly ajar, and I can hear –

I can hear someone breathing.

It has not occurred to me to arm myself with any of the wide selection of kitchen implements available. Right now, I would give anything to be holding the big laser-sharpened knife with which, yesterday, I was happily slicing up mushrooms. But the hallway is between me and the kitchen.

And then, I realize the breathing could be my own.

I step forward, edging round the table, so that I am no more than two feet away from the door. I stretch out my leg and hook the door with it, then yank backwards with my foot, so hard that the doorknob dents the wall and the wooden door vibrates.

The hallway is empty.

I look up and down, twice, just to make sure, and I stand at the bottom of the stairs and look up. There is nobody there. I breathe again.

Relieved but puzzled, I go back into the lounge and rub clean a portion of window, to see if I can make out any sign of the others returning. There is nothing. The path from the valley is empty, except for the incessant rain turning it into a dirt track. Beyond, the darkening trees have begun to bob their heads in the wind, and the sea is now steel-grey and turbulent.

I am right up against the window, smelling and almost tasting its dampness, and I wipe clean where my breath has misted it over. The rain is lashing hard against the window, blurring my view out across the land, but I can see the dark froth of clouds gathering above the sea, hurtling through the sky as if on a mission of destruction.

And then, there is a crash as the door to the hallway is thrown open.

I turn around from the window. I am in view. I can be seen, she cannot.

My face, captured forever in blurred pixels, is white and wide and terrible to behold.

★

266

She staggers forward and clutches at the table.

My heart is pounding and shaking, as if the rain is pummelling it too. With horrified fascination, I stare into her wild eyes, her chalk-white face, her sticky and unkempt hair. Her mouth is open and her eyes keep looking past me, through me. As if I am a ghost. As if she is a ghost.

There is a deep, horrible choking sound coming from the back of her throat.

The table tilts.

She reaches out her hand.

I see the table begin to move.

She slides into shot: a brief, blurred figure stretching out a hand.

There is something repellent, inhuman lurking within us all. There is a dark heart, which we know can be reached, but we do not know where or when or how. It comes unbidden. I know this to be true. I know this because of what happened. Because of the instincts that kicked in, the power that drove me then, in that moment, in this moment which I can *see* –

The blue vase slides, rolls, falls through the air. The table wobbles. It does not fall, but she does. She collapses to the floor with the glass exploding all around her.

She is five feet away. She is choking, spluttering. A glutinous, opaque dribble begins to dive from the corner of her mouth.

The sound of rain clatters in the room. Hundreds and hundreds of marbles cascade into all four corners of the lounge, rolling and rolling, spreading out from the epicentre, borne on a tidal wave of blue shards. She has fallen on her front, still breathing, but with her eyes wide and unseeing. Her face is pale and glistening among the marbles, like a fish.

Her hand reaches out to me. I am shaking uncontrollably. I step towards her.

Four feet.

My mind should not even be thinking about this. The automatics should kick in and you should be down there, helping, without even pausing for thought.

But I have paused. For a fatal moment, I think, and I remember.

Three feet.

★

I remember Mike Bradfield's sneering face, flickering in the light of a fire, telling me –

'You didn't know. You didn't *know*.'

I remember her mouth twitching in a knowing smile, in the pungent gardens outside Nic and Mike's wedding reception. Her cool, callous confidence that I would do exactly as she wished, exactly as she required.

I remember wanting to take control of her.

Two feet.

Unable to believe what I am doing, I back away from her, towards the glass doors. My hand is fumbling with the catch.

There has to be a way to end it all.

And I am running, I am running away through the torrents of rain. Running into the heart of the storm. My clothes, soaking, stick to me. The ground is pulped beneath my feet and all I can see is that beautiful face, that terrible face, that agony.

There is sand beneath my feet. I collapse on to the beach, gasping, choking. I can hear the sea roaring, just a few feet away from me, and it is like the noise in my own head.

I turn, trying to make out the lights of the *gîte* through the lashing whips of the tempest. All I can see are the dark shapes of the trees, malformed and angry in the dimming light, like demons ready to prowl across the dunes and take me with them into the heart of the storm.

I crouch there and let the rain hammer me, squash me, push me further and further into the soft, wet sand. I lie there. I do not know how much time passes. I can hear the sound of a hundred glass marbles clattering against the floor.

And I begin to stop shaking. I begin to acknowledge the enormity of what I have done. Of what I have not done.

But *what* have I done?

A strange, warm feeling of contentment begins to spread through me. I have nothing to worry about. I let the rain caress me. As long as the rain and the wind and the thunder know I am here, then no harm can come to me.

There is a noise, puncturing the tempest. It is a mechanical clattering, high in the sky. I can see lights moving across the blue–black sky, a gigantic thing from another world slicing the storm as it passes over. I am suddenly alert again. I crouch in the sand and stare at it as it goes overhead and then, just inland, hovers and begins to descend.

It is a helicopter. Salvation has come.

Around me, the wind and the rain tear through the sky like Armageddon. I close my eyes. Then I open them again, haul myself to my feet and slowly begin to walk back towards the house.

23 Vox Humana

Later, when it was all over and Angelica had gone for good, I went to the computer centre and got my PC equipped for sound.

The file contained her voice. Breathy, slightly drugged-sounding, and drenched in hiss and crackle.

My Faith. My love, my hate. The one I will never, ever forget, even if it all turns out to have been true and there is some better place than this. Somewhere to outsit eternity.

This was what I heard.

'I hope you'll forgive me for this. It's probably a bad idea. But if you've got this far, it means that you might understand.

'What happened? I don't think I can even explain it in terms anyone would recognize. Maybe it was the same as for everyone. Maybe reality was what happened.

'I just became aware that my life has been so concentrated, so full, so alive. It's almost as if the idea of having to go through another thirty, forty, fifty years of it is just too depressing to bear. I couldn't see myself as some dribbling, cantankerous old crone pissing herself and putting her teeth in a glass every night. Could you? Christ, so many people end up like that. Where's the human dignity?

'And in the end, I've just got bored. I just feel I've had enough. It's a frightening sensation when you can feel *yourself coming to the end of your life. Christ, the shit people talk about suicide. It isn't about running out in front of everyone with your wrists slashed and going* Look *what I've done, aren't I important? Nah. It's about being sick of it. About not wanting to* be *bothered any more. You realize the sun's going to come up again tomorrow and there's nothing we can do to change that, and you realize how little you actually mean. Like there's this all-pervading lethargy in you and you just want to switch off . . .*

'I never believed in God, not in that sense. Not Luke's God, the one you

270

knew and left behind. But slowly, carefully, something started to make itself known to me. That lethargy, perhaps. Like I was being called. As if there was another me on that side, ready to pull me right through the mirror of our death into . . . whatever lies beyond. I don't want death. I want a new experience. And she is there, willing to help me with it. To help me do it.

'When I still enjoyed life, it used to frustrate me how little I could do. You used to frustrate me. All of you. I know it sounds awful, but there was nobody I particularly connected with . . . nobody who was totally on my wavelength. I used to feel like I was the odd one out, wherever I went. I used to despair of you all. Mike with his new I'm-all-right-Jack philosophies, screwing everyone and everything and not giving a damn that he'd caused a man to kill himself. And Nic, so bloody wet that she couldn't even make up her mind if she wanted to divorce the bastard or not. Charlie, getting into all kinds of cloak-and-dagger bollocks with the dodgy taxman, over-complicating his life for the sake of an extra swimming pool, and all because that bloody wife of his needed something to take her mind off not getting pregnant.

'And then there was you. Yeah. You were always a fine specimen of humanity, weren't you? Yeah, we had a good laugh about Michael's insincerity and Luke's weirdness and Charlie being in the shadow of that awful cow, but what the hell did you ever do to justify your superiority? Standing there, watching, trying to pretend you weren't involved and it was all a bit beneath you. Anything to avoid making a decision about your life. God, the number of times I tried to provoke you, kick you, make you do something, anything. But no, you just wanted to sail through life, never meaning anything, never doing anything. Just living. You were quite happy to let someone else tell you what to do in the rest of your life, just like in bed. Get out of that fucking victim mentality. Do something. Do something useful!

'There were ways I could turn all this to my advantage, of course. I tried to be proactive. I tried, if you like, to cause trouble. To be a catalyst. Lots of people's lives will have been affected by me. One way or the other. Whether they like it or not, and whether they admit it or not. I was the messenger of the news no one wanted to hear. The bad penny. Yeah, well, I could live with that, because I at least made people think. Thanks to me, you weren't all just sitting around and stewing in your own apathy, were you? I kicked you. I prodded you. Like getting ants to fight.

'Yeah, I know. That sounds really supercilious. Like I was playing God or something. It really wasn't like that, honest. I just wanted you to explore your full humanity. People are so limited, so frustrated. They only use a small *part of what they're capable of. But you . . . I always knew you had something about you, but you didn't want to use it. Something dark and exciting.*

'But now, hey . . . you're getting used to life without me, aren't you? I had to leave you some time. You have to learn to stand on your own two feet.

'Maybe I'll see you again. Can't be sure, of course. Can't ever be sure.

'But then that always was the big question. Wasn't it?'

And that was all.

I played it back again and again, even tried adjusting the treble and the bass so as to see if I could get it to come clearer. But I could not tell if this message, this epitaph, this devastating final salvo was her own voice – or a seamless facsimile created by her sister, the consummate actress.

To this day, I still have no idea.

24 Bittersweet Symphony

It has been an extraordinary year: terrible, beautiful, exhausting.

I sit in my car, looking out at the river and the great bridge from the North. The sun is hanging low in the sky, swollen with vermilion light, looking soft and wet.

I close my eyes, and I can see the morning creeping in after that dreadful night. Ten days ago.

The flat is quiet and still. Outside, the murmurs of the waking city sound like messages beamed from an alien landscape. The clink of milk bottles, the chug of the suburban cars as they start their journeys to work, the whirr of the hydraulic lifts on the delivery vans. I can just hear the bells of St Mary Magdalen, about a mile away, chiming six.

I ache. My body feels punished, smashed apart and rebuilt by clumsy hands. My nerves are frazzled, exposed like old, bare wires. I am sitting on the edge of the sofa. My limbs hurt because I have not changed position for several hours.

A terracotta mug of coffee descends in front of me. The slender hand which holds it is slightly unsteady. I look up, through a haze of steam, and I see her sad, white face.

'Thank you,' Angelica says.

I take the coffee, uncertain, watching her eyes. I realize I am desperately hungry. 'Why are you thanking me?' I ask her.

'Because you helped me.' She shrugs. 'I feel I've done some good for once.'

I sip cautiously at the coffee. It's strong and milky. She has made it the way I like it. 'I see.' I am not sure what else to say. 'I didn't . . . realize.'

She gives me a sad smile. 'She used to call me Demonica, you know. The bad angel.'

I wince. 'She could hardly be said to be the virtuous one. And she certainly had enough demons.'

'Well, maybe . . . But I can start proving her wrong, now, can't I?'

'Perhaps. Yes.' I take another sip of coffee. It is revitalizing me. 'Maybe you're my guardian angel,' I suggest with a wry smile. 'Maybe I'm the bad one.'

'Well, you were certainly daring to the last, you know,' she murmurs. 'I can't believe how cool you played it. I mean, there must have been that thought in your head . . . That shattering guilt, as if you'd actually killed her with your own hands.' She squats down to face me. 'Staying calm enough to take that tape out of the camera. Now that was smart. I don't think even I would have thought of that.'

'I didn't plan it.' My voice is cold. I cannot look at her. 'It was just something . . . that happened. I still don't know how.'

'When you came back in?' she says softly.

'There was chaos in the house. Indescribable. I don't know why, but the camcorder had been overlooked. I . . . didn't plan anything. I just did it.'

She knows, anyway.

The very last shot on the videotape is of me, drenched and wild-eyed, striding towards the camera and reaching for the Off switch.

I remember that I took the tape out and put it, for then, into my pocket. When I went upstairs to get my things together, I put the tape at the bottom of my bag, where it remained throughout the ghostly, silent and surreal journey back to England. I must have put it in the post shortly afterwards.

I think I got the idea from *The Thirty-Nine Steps*. If you want something hidden for a few days, post it to yourself.

And then, the process began. I blocked. I forgot. The package gathered dust in the central post office. Until it was collected by Angelica.

She hoists her holdall on to her shoulder. 'I'll be seeing you,' she says.

'You're going?' I stand up, wobbling slightly, aware of the terrible state of my body. I push back a tangle of sticky hair from in front of my eyes. 'Now?'

She shrugs. 'I've fulfilled what I came to do, darling. You remember.' She sighs, and her eyes shift away from me, staring listlessly into space.

'Now you have to start doing the next thing. Not being afraid.' She reaches up, touches my cheek gently. Her hand is cold. 'You won't be afraid. Will you?'

'No . . . Where will you go?' I ask her in dismay.

'I've got places. Far away from here.' She turns, heading for the door. She looks over her shoulder and gives me a big, red smile. No teeth, just those lips, slightly sadder than before. 'After this, we might not be able to live,' she says, with a strange, contemplative tone in her voice, as if she has just recognized the possibility for the first time. 'But . . .' She shrugs. 'Then again, who does?'

The door closes, and she is gone.

Streams of cars and juggernauts and tankers hurtle across the bridge. Now, I drum my fingers on the steering-wheel and wonder what, if anything, she might tell.

Start doing the next thing. Not being afraid.

I wonder what she meant?

At some point, I took a decision.

First, I deleted the sound-file from my hard disk, then I found the relevant floppy and slipped it into my pocket. I then picked up the videotape. I also located a pair of sharp scissors, some old newspaper, some matches and a battered metal casserole dish.

I went down to the back yard which all the flats share. It was damp and putrid. The three huge steel bins sat in their usual place under the rubbish chute. I looked around, checked I was alone. Then I put the casserole dish down on the damp stone floor, took the videotape from my inside pocket and dropped it in. I then rummaged in my lower pocket, got out the computer disk and prised the metal clip off. I extracted the fragile wafer within and chopped it in half with the scissors, before throwing all the metal and plastic remains in with the video. Then I unfolded the newspaper from under my arm, screwed up four or five sheets and rammed them down inside the metal dish.

I lit a single match, dropped it in the dish and stood back. There was a curl of orange fire, which flared briefly, then a crack, like something snapping. Thick, greasy black smoke frothed from my homemade crucible and the stench of molten plastic and metal filled the yard.

It took a few minutes to burn itself out, during which I was carefully watching the back door to the flats. When the smoke seemed to die down, I peered into the container, coughed as the pungent tendrils took hold of my throat for a moment. I blinked. A shapeless, molten mass seemed to have welded itself to the bottom of the dish. I nodded in satisfaction.

Carefully, I pulled on a pair of gardening gloves. I dropped the dish and its molten contents deep inside the nearest of the large, metal bins, which I knew would be emptied tomorrow.

Then I turned and walked away.

Tanya Behler returned from Iceland three days after Angelica disappeared. She was quiet, contemplative, somehow resigned. I sensed that there was something she had to tell me, and I did not mind, because I thought I felt it too.

We sat down in the lounge, together in the same room but with a yawning chasm of carpet between us.

I told her about Hope Springs. She was shocked, but she made no move to come over and comfort me. I told her that Faith's sister had popped in for a visit, and that we'd had a drink together and that it had been very pleasant. She nodded, said that was nice, took her glasses off and cleaned them. Then she blinked a couple of times and put them back on.

We talked, calmly and with a sense of impending departure. We were adult, rational, calm; we discussed our differing expectations, our goals in life. We discussed what we provided for each other, the ways in which the relationship was supportive, the ways in which it was not. It was then that she leaned back, closed her eyes and told me, quietly and without emotion, that she was pregnant.

Out beyond the bridge, the sun is sinking, casting crimson fragments into the wide river.

I think back to three days ago. Just a week after Angelica's departure.

Once again, I found myself in the churning, stinking lift of the flats near Basildon. With my heart heavy, I ascended towards his home in the sky. I knew what had drawn me here before. It was clear now.

I was to be disappointed. I rang the bell twice, and I heard the door across the landing click briefly open again – no doubt the mystery occupant was sneaking a quick look at me. A woman, pale and chubby, came to the door, wiping her hands on a towel and looking at me with curious but not unfriendly eyes. When I asked about Luke, she wanted to know if I meant 'the young clergyman'. Now that the common ground of my visit had been established, we both seemed to drop our guard a little. She smiled in apology, told me that he had 'packed and gone' last week, saying something about his work being finished.

Feeling the disappointment thumping in my stomach, I asked tentatively if she had a forwarding address for him. She shrugged, smiled, said she was very sorry. I thanked her and said goodbye. When I was halfway to the lift, she called me back, brandishing what looked like a small green booklet. It was a parish magazine. He left this, she said. You must be able to find him there. And she pointed to the first line on the inside cover, which said: Priest-in-Charge: The Revd Luke Harrington, The Rectory, Longdale, Herts, followed by a telephone number.

Interesting. He had gone back. Maybe that was his way of going forward.

So I rang him.

'Oh. Hi,' he said, and it sounded very much as if I had interrupted something important.

'You're back where you were, then,' I ventured.

'You came to those flats,' he said. 'I wish you hadn't done that.'

'Sorry.'

'You haven't spoken to me for a long time.' (Was there a mild reproach in there, I wondered?) 'What have you been doing?'

'Look, I'm sorry . . . I have tried. I just . . . wanted to thank you for being there at the funeral. It was nice.'

'I always try to be nice,' he said. I wished I could read his expression. 'It doesn't always go appreciated. So . . . I'm glad.' A pause. 'I saw on the news about your education centre. Dreadful business. Have they caught the people yet?'

'The police are working on it.'

'And there were some problems with it not being properly insured? Is that right?'

'I think we're going to be able to rebuild it. Thanks largely to, ah, to a donation. From . . . an anonymous benefactor.'

'I see. How fortunate.'

Again, a pause. I expect he was wondering why I had bothered to ring.

'Luke, I, um . . . might need to talk to you about something in the next few days. I'm not sure. You know, in a . . . professional capacity, or whatever you call it.'

'Oh. Yes? All right then.' He sounded guarded. As if he didn't really want me to. Well, I supposed he probably didn't. Hearing confessions from friends must be one of the drawbacks of the job.

'If I ring you sometime next week . . . is that all right?'

'I'm sure it will be.'

'Okay. I'll speak to you then.'

As I put the receiver down, I smiled to myself. I knew what I was doing.

Luke may not feel that he is able to keep my secret. He may be faced with the most terrible moral dilemma of his career.

However, I know some things about him which may help the decision. Luke's not the most conventional of priests, I know that much. I'm not blind, and nor am I totally insensitive to the strange body language he has been exhibiting around me. Ever since he met me, in fact, there has been that strange tension between attraction and disapproval.

And I know the name of his bishop. A man who's often in the media for a rent-a-quote soundbite of moral condemnation, a church-man as old-school and by-the-book as they come, and who certainly would not sit back calmly if he knew the full truth of Luke's personal situation.

We may be able, then, to come to an arrangement.

Michael and Nicole Bradfield's marriage officially ended on 26 October, just over seven years after their wedding. The attempted reconciliation had failed. No other party was cited; Nicole filed for divorce and Mike did not contest. As no children were involved and the couple had been officially living apart for over two years, it was a simple and painless process. On the surface.

Nicole downshifted. She got a part-time job as a careers adviser and moved to somewhere near Birmingham. I have heard that she is happy.

Mike's property company continues to do well. I have no idea if he is happy. He never says.

The bridge, tall and proud and wide, is thronged with cars, their lights peeking out into the reddening evening.

And last. Five hours ago, this cold afternoon.

The trees wrote their spider-patterns against a steely sky, and a slight but chilling wind blew across me as I locked my car. I turned, and cautiously opened the creaking gate to the cemetery.

The flower I laid was a single white rose. There were no others on the grave today.

I suppose I must have crouched there, in front of that stone, for almost an hour. My legs ached, but I hardly noticed until the cold wind redoubled its force and made me shift my position slightly. There seemed to be no one else at all in the cemetery. Eventually, I allowed myself a sad smile, wobbled to my feet and rubbed my aching calf muscles. I was not sure why I had come here, and perhaps it was now time to go. I turned, stepped back on to the path, and saw Charlie.

He was standing on the rise, about twenty metres away, and I shivered as I realized that he must have been watching me for some time. He said nothing. He was wearing a long, dark coat which fluttered in the wind, and his hair and face were as grey as the surrounding stones. His eyes, though, were keen and bright. Staring right through me. I took a step further along the path, then another. His body did not move, but his eyes did. I knew he was watching me.

I stopped, biting my lip, wondering whether to climb the steps and join him, try to say something which might bring us together.

Of course, it was impossible for him to know. I told myself that. But something about him still frightened me. I had a sudden vision of him haunting this cemetery in his long coat and his grey skin, silent and spectral, day after day. Waiting. Wondering. To see if the truth would come to him, carried on the wind through this silent place, like the dust and the ash.

I turned, hurried back to my car. He watched me go. Unmoving.

★

The city throbs as it powers up, shifting into night-mode.

Angelica, I suppose, might tell someone what I did. Then again, she would do herself no favours through such an action. So I will wait, alone in the silence, for a telephone call that may never come. If it happens, then at least I know I am no longer chasing shadows. No longer stumbling through the alleyways in the city of half-light, hunting the ghost of a demented and fragmented love.

I am here without the aid of a God or gods: I may have no faith, but perhaps I have regained hope. As for the other, we'll have to wait and see.

I have come through. I may be wounded, confused, faithless, but I am me. I exist in this world, and I am ready to remain in this world.

I will live.

The light has almost faded now. It is time to go.